THE CLOGGER'S CHILD

'I couldn't go in one of them clubs,' she said slowly, never taking her eyes from his face.

Joe had always known when to play his trump card and he played it now. 'Who said owt about you singing in a club? No, love, it's a posh job I've got lined up for you tonight. It's a Masonic do in the Assembly Rooms, with men in bow ties and their wives in fancy frocks. They'll have paid two guineas for a slap-up meal and a dekko at a cabaret.'

Clara's eyes grew round. 'A cabaret? Like they have down in London?'

'Better'n London.'

'I'd have to wear me black.'

'You can wear your nightie for all I care.'

'Oh, Joe . . .'

The Clogger's Child

MARIE JOSEPH

ARROW BOOKS

Arrow Books Limited
62-65 Chandos Place, London WC2N 4NW

An imprint of Century Hutchinson Limited

London Melbourne Sydney Auckland
Johannesburg and agencies throughout
the world

First published by Hutchinson 1985
Arrow edition 1986

Printed and bound in Great Britain by
Anchor Brendon Limited, Tiptree, Essex

ISBN 0 09 942070 8

For Stuart, Sheila, Nichola and Antony

ACKNOWLEDGEMENTS

The author and publishers would like to thank the following for permission to reproduce copyright material: Stoll Moss Theatres; Chappell Music Limited; EMI Music Publishing Limited, London; Redwood Music Limited; MCA Music Limited and the Methodist Publishing House for allowing us to quote from the *Methodist School Hymnal*.

One

If you were wealthy and famous, then a good place to live was the London of Edwardian England. The King, come belatedly to his throne, was pining, but not too uncomfortably, for his mistress, the beautiful Lillie Langtry. She was touring the provinces with her own theatre company, enchanting every man who set eyes on her, even the very old, who saw in her the embodiment of their forgotten dreams.

On an early spring day in 1907, the trees in the London parks were turning slowly green, and in the West End theatres business was booming.

The suave and elegant Gerald du Maurier was striding the boards as Raffles, and at the Palace Vesta Tilley strutted the stage in trousers.

The streets of Mayfair were thronged with fashionably dressed women. The restaurants were crowded, and the parks filled with strollers out to enjoy the first warm sunshine that year. London was truly a good place to be.

There were slums of course, but then there was poverty everywhere. Not that one needed to think about it. And only in passing, if then.

Farther north, over two hundred and fifty miles away, the county of Lancashire was a windswept place, with cotton towns cross-threaded by narrow cobbled streets winding their identical ways down to the mills.

Up there, so it was said, life was sombre, grim and drab, a million light years away from the gaiety of London's West End.

And yet, in that same early spring, at Easter time, for four days and four nights the townsfolk of a certain cotton town in the northeast of the county had thronged the market square. As darkness fell, workworn Lancashire faces were illuminated by towering flares. Clog irons had struck sparks from the cobbles, and pennies and halfpennies, carefully hoarded, had been gleefully squandered on sideshows and roundabouts.

Collins's Dragons, the Flying Pigs and, most exciting of all, the Big Boats, swinging screaming occupants high into the air.

Flat-capped fathers, with wide-eyed children riding piggy-back on their shoulders, had skimmed rings at the hoopla stalls, trying with desperation to win a doll dressed as the Fairy Queen, or an orange-plushed teddy bear with crossed button eyes.

'Give us an 'apenny to go on the horses, our Dad!'

Young voices, hoarse with tiredness, red-rimmed eyes round with wonder at the music blaring out and the great roundabouts revolving merrily. Then, as the music increased to a terrifying tempo, a frantic clinging to the brass poles rising from the horses' backs, with the ring of watching faces blurring out of comforting recognition.

Mothers holding shawls round pinched faces, frightened almost out of their wits as their children ignored frantic warnings.

'Stop standing up in them swingboats! Tha'll end up like a squashed black pudding if tha doesn't sit down!'

Woollen mufflers flying as young legs bent to work the boats so high it seemed inevitable that the shouted warnings would become reality.

'Higher, our Albert! Higher, our Agnes! Tek no notice of our Mam!'

Noise and light, the smell of apples dipped in burned sugar; peanut brittle shattered into bite-sized pieces by tiny steel hammers. Coconut ice sticking to wobbly milk teeth, and brown saliva from treacle toffee trickling down small determined chins.

Overly excited families shoving through the milling crowds; wives pushing husbands past the booth with its bevy of 'London Ladies' on a raised platform, reluctantly forcing them to avert their eyes from the shivering girls showing strips of goose-pimped flesh between flimsy layers of vividly coloured gauze.

'Nowt there tha hasn't seen afore!'

'Aye, mebbe, but better spaced out, lass . . . or summat.'

Good-humoured clouts, a sixpenny plate of 'spud' pie from Sutcliffe's café across the square, then walking home through gas-lit streets, the Easter fair over for yet another year.

As the town hall clock struck midnight, with the crowds finally dispersed, the fairground folk began their all too familiar race against time.

At first light they would be on their way to Preston, leaving the square empty, its glories dimmed, as the stallholders moved in to erect their tarpaulin-covered stalls in readiness for the Wednesday market day.

In her caravan, drawn up in the dark shadows behind the flare-lit ground, Jessie Bead, the uncrowned queen of the fairground, lolled on her bunk bed, fully dressed, small black eyes closed in a twitching sleep. An unlovely woman, not much thinner than the Fat Lady in the Freak Show, Jessie's flesh flowed round her with an amoebalike fluidity, and because she had begun to lose her hair in her middle thirties, the receding hairline gave the impression that her face was at least twice its normal size.

Safely and comfortably out of the rain, now driving sideways across the market square, she dozed. That was all. It was said that Jessie Bead never allowed herself to do more than catnap. Every single detail of the organized hammering, banging, shouting informed Jessie that the heavy roundabouts were being a bugger to shift, but that the Flying Pigs had behaved themselves. Just for once.

Ugly, unfeminine, gross Jessie Bead, the doyen of the fair folk, with a mind as sharp as a newly stropped razor and a business acumen that would have put many a successful stockbroker on the Manchester Exchange to shame.

Round her middle, where once a waist had lingered, was

tied a massive canvas bag, its cavernous depths holding every single penny taken during the past four days. Four times she had wobbled on surprisingly small feet across the cobbles to the bank on the corner of Lord Street to change the day's takings into less wieldy notes and silver. But not until the caravans and the wagons were ready to roll would a penny be handed over in wages, each bleary-eyed recipient making his or her mark in Jessie's ledger. If anyone asked for more money, she could point to the appropriate page, blinding them by her calculations, proving that a rise was entirely out of the question.

Even as she lay napping, Jessie's plump hands rested on the bulge made by the bag, her fingers scrabbling like spiders over and around its lumpy contours. She patted it now and again to make sure it was still there.

By her side on the bunk bed, its muzzle resting on her pillow, was a loaded revolver that once, so it was rumoured, had blasted a man's head from his neck when he'd tried to wrest the canvas bag from its mooring. Jessie reckoned she could spot a phoney from a distance of no more than a good spit, and many a hopeful down-and-out looking for casual work had reeled backwards down the caravan steps with Jessie's raucous voice spiced with imaginative swearwords shattering his eardrums.

'This rotten world owes me nowt,' she was fond of saying. 'And I owe it nowt neither. I come from nowt and I'll end up as nowt, but in between there's nobody going to best Jessie Bead. Certainly not a man, with his brains in his trousers!'

Then she'd emit a roar of laughter that riffled her three chins and left her gasping for breath. 'Stupid pie-cans!' she'd end up, shouting gleefully. 'Fit for nowt but blowing the skin off their rice puddings, aye, and missing doing that proper most of the time.'

When, with a sudden rush of wind and rain, the caravan door flew open, Jessie reached for the revolver before her eyes opened. It was an unwritten law that until the dismantling of the fair was completed she was not to be disturbed. She'd seen them through the bustle of the four days' occupation of the market place – Sundays excluded; she'd taken on more casual workers than she was sure the lazy so-and-sos had needed, and there was nobody getting a penny piece till she said so.

Now she stared in disbelief at the man booting the door closed behind him, cradling in his arms a young girl as wet and sodden as if she'd been rescued from the sea.

With a rolling motion Jessie slid from her bunk, clumps of hair standing up from her head. Stretching out a hand, she turned up the wick of the lamp so that its light fell full on the face of the girl.

'What's going on, Neilly? What the 'ell's happened to her? She looks like a goner.'

Cornelius Brown, known as Neilly, lowered his burden onto Jessie's bunk bed. 'She were found behind the big tent. I reckon she's been lying there since it went dark. For hours, I'd say.' He snatched a red kerchief from his neck and mopped his face. 'One of the men trod on her belly, but he didn't see her an' it weren't his fault. I fetched her here, Jessie. I reckoned it were the only thing to do.'

Jessie sniffed. Neilly had been drinking. His face was wrenched out of shape with an emotion only partly gin-induced. He had a soft side to him, did Neilly. Jessie accepted that. He could drink all day, and generally did, but she had never once seen him incapable. He was her right-hand man and, rumour had it, once upon a time her lover. She accepted too that Cornelius Brown would lay down his life for her, if need be.

'I think the lass is dropping a baby,' he said now, his anxious expression belying the crudeness of his words.

Jessie bent quickly over the girl. 'Oh, may the saints preserve us, Neilly! You're right! Her big face hardened. 'How the 'ell did I miss it? How could I miss a thing like that?' She rolled up her sleeves, revealing arms like ham shanks. 'It's time I gave this lark up, Neilly. I knew the lass had run away from home, but then most of them have, we both know that.' She patted the girl's ashen face. 'It was the way she spoke that decided me to take her on. Top-drawer talk.' She began to unlace the girl's boots. 'You know I set a great deal on the way folk speak.'

Neilly kept nodding, agreeing with every word she said. It was policy, he decided, at a time like this.

'She's been on the stage, if you ask me.' Jessie started to unroll the long black stockings. 'Look how the crowds rolled in when she did her little dance. Aye, and she could sing as well, that's if she could've been heard over the row old Collins's Dragons made . . . She sniffed loudly and stood to face Neilly, hands on ample hips. 'Look sharp and put the kettle on. Get me scissors out of the box over there, and stop looking like you've lost a tanner and found a threepenny bit. It won't be the first time I've delivered a babbie.' Her voice was gruff. 'Remember I delivered me own a long time ago. Aye, and buried it in a shoebox the day after. Aye, *and* went back to work in the kitchens at the workhouse the day after that, and none the wiser.'

Taking a strip of towel, frayed but clean, she wiped the mud from the girl's face. 'She's got a fever. Likely pneumonia with lying out there.' Jessie laid a hand on the swollen stomach. 'No wonder this lass managed to deceive me. She's nobbut much fatter than a decent-sized football, but it's dropped, the little tiddler. I don't reckon it'll be long now.'

'I'd best be going, Jessie.' Behind her Neilly shuffled his feet. 'It's not a man's place. Not a man's place at all, at all.' As usual, when troubled, his Irish accent surfaced.

Jessie spoke without turning round. 'No. But the day will come. Cornelius Brown! You mark my words. The day will come when a man will be forced to watch his babbies being born, and then he'll be laughing on t'other side of his face when he sees what a woman has to go through.'

The girl moaned, a moan that rose to a scream.

'He should have been consecrated, the man who did this!'

Jessie heard the caravan door slam, then bent again to her task. Pulling up two layers of petticoats, she reached for a pillow and slipped it under the small of the girl's back. Bitten lips spotted with blood blisters were drawn back over sharp white teeth. But even in her agony, she was beautiful.

Jessie remembered clearly the day the girl had come to her caravan, begging for work. Something about the way she walked had suggested the trained dancer in her, and Jessie had immediately realized her potential. Although it had been a dark day, damp and misty, the girl's pale gold hair had glistened as if caught by a sunbeam, and when she spoke her accent and the clear cadence of her speech had told Jessie that she'd been brought up and schooled in a place far south of the cotton town where the fair was being held that week.

As usual, apart from demanding the promise of un-questioning loyalty, Jessie had asked no questions. 'It's hard work, lass,' she'd said. 'Even sitting outside the booth taking the money, where I'm thinking of starting you off till you can join the troupe. Cold winds and chapped hands. Smiling at the customers, giving 'em a taste of what's waiting for 'em inside. And you'll have to wear rouge and lipstick,' she'd added, gazing at the peach-soft skin with a silken fuzz of down by the ears, round which the Saxon fair hair clustered in babylike coiled curls.

'Run away from her family, I reckon. Give or take a few weeks and she'll have had enough,' Jessie had told Neilly later that day. 'She's nobbut a child when all's said and done. Running away with the gypsies, in her mind, or summat just as daft. Romantic, she reckons us to be, no doubt.'

Here, her cackling laugh had erupted, ending in a fit of coughing. 'Romantic? Sitting all day and most of the night in yon canvas booth, with the wind whistling round her ankles and her backside getting more numb by the minute. She'd'v'e been better off with the gyppos, I reckon. At least they light themselves a fire now and again.'

The girl's eyes flew wide with the shock of a pain that arched her back and brought the sweat streaming down her face. Transfixed by terror she stared up into Jessie's large face.

'You can't just go with the pain, lass.' Jessie leaned closer, suspecting that the huge green eyes were already glazed by blindness. 'When the next one comes you've got to work. To *push*. See, catch on to this bit of rag and bite on it next time. Hold on to me, love. Hold on to owt, but *work*! You *want* your babbie to be born, don't you?'

The eyes stayed open, showing no recognition, nothing.

When the next pain came her whole body went rigid as a plank.

'There's no strength left in her, poor lass. And it's a bloodless confinement as well.' Muttering to herself, Jessie rolled her sleeves farther up her arms, fired with a fierce resolution.

Nobody in their wildest dreams could have called Jessie Bead maternal.What softness there had once been in her had been subdued long, long ago. Fending for herself from the day she left the workhouse after the birth of her own baby, she had accepted the score. And the score was one she had written for herself.

'Expect nowt and you won't be sorry when nowt comes your way. Get nowt and learn not to be disappointed. Never call on God, because He won't be listening. All right, Jessie Bead?'

She knew the girl was dying. The long hours lying out there in the darkness and the rain had seeped away her strength as surely as if her life's blood had been drained away through a funnel. This beautiful girl didn't want to live. There was no fight in her. She had gone to a place from where there was no coming back. And if her babbie was going to be born alive, then it would have to do the work itself.

Dipping her hands in a tub of goose grease, Jessie's cure for all ills, she slid them round the tiny head, pulsating softly in the last throes of birth. Panting spasmodically, holding her breath at the crucial moment, Jessie did what she had to do. When at last the baby emerged, head first, mucus-coated limbs following, Jessie gave her own shout of triumph.

'A girl!' she yelled. 'A bonny, bloody perfect little girl! Thanks be to God!' she cried, forgetting that by her own code the Almighty would have had no hand in the miracle.

Tiny, wrinkled, the child was so beautiful that for a moment Jessie's coal-black eyes filled with tears. Outside the caravan the hammering and shouting rose to a crescendo. The rain beat down on the flimsy roof in a frantic drumming. Jessie blinked. It was as though a button had been pressed, bringing the sudden noise to her attention, shattering her concentrated calm of the past hour.

Slowly Jessie straightened up. *That* was the real world, outside in the rain and the tearing wind. And what she'd just witnessed hadn't been a miracle. Far from it. The girl, breathing her last, was just one more silly lass to have fallen for a bit of flattery from a man like the man who had once promised Jessie herself the moon if she'd let him do what he'd set his mind on doing.

Just for a second Jessie closed her eyes and saw a face. A strong face with a clear complexion and eyes as dark as her own, but tilting up at the corners. The prick of a moustache as he kissed her, the determined probing of a tongue, the whispered promises, and the weight of his body covering her own.

And nine months later, a baby with mauve-veined eyelids and skinned-rabbit limbs, lying in a cardboard shoebox, the whole thing weighing no more than a couple of two-pound sugar bags.

But this babbie wasn't going to die. Not if Jessie Bead could help it. Working as confidently and surely as a trained midwife, Jessie cut the cord and tied the stump with a piece of string from her pocket. Rubbing in a spot of goose grease for good measure, she wiped the baby with a frayed towel, then wrapped it in the same towel, before winding it tightly into a swaddling with a grey fringed shawl.

Only when this was done did she turn her attention to the mother. Putting her face close to the girl's ear, she whispered softly, 'You've got a gradely little lass, love. A right beauty.'

It seemed that the eyelids quivered. No more than the weak fluttering of a dying butterfly's wings. Jessie turned and, picking up the baby, laid it across the girl's breast. Taking up a limp hand, she gently stroked the tiny face with the lifeless fingers.

'I'll see to her, lass. I'll not have her fetched up with the fair folk, neither. I'll see she goes to a good home.'

The semblance of a smile lifted the corners of the girl's dry lips. Jessie narrowed her eyes. Maybe she was going to live, after all.

But when Jessie turned round from laying the baby on the dresser the shadow of death had already crept across the pale face, setting it into a waxen beauty. Already the nose had taken on a pinched look, even as the last faint sigh left the girl's body. Jessie felt her stomach contract. A birth and a death, in almost as many minutes. For a moment she stood irresolute, a long-forgotten phrase from an institutionalized childhood of enforced chapel-going seeping into her mind.

'The Lord giveth and the Lord taketh away . . . '

With a jerk of her head Jessie spat the words away. Fancy thoughts like that could safely be left to preachers with their mealy-mouthed rantings from pulpits. From the slackening sound of the hammering outside, she knew, without the need to consult any timepiece, that in less than an hour's time the fair would have to be off. The clank of harnesses told her that the horses were being brought from their stabling, and by first light the heavily loaded carts and wagons would be wending their way across the moors.

Opening the door of the caravan, she yelled at the top of her voice, 'Neilly!' The wind took her voice and tossed it away. The rain beat against her face and whipped her skirts back against her thick legs as she climbed down the steps onto the cobblestones. 'Neilly!' This time the power of her voice would have stopped an advancing army in its tracks. 'Neilly! Where the 'ell are you? *Neilly!*'

From somewhere out of the darkness, the bobbing lights, the frantically busy men, he came, running towards her. As he would always come running whenever she called his name.

'Is it finished, Jessie? Has the babbie come?' Like an ungainly lap dog he followed her up the steps and into the blessed shelter and comparative warmth of the caravan.

'She's gone.' Jessie pointed to the body, then jerked her head sideways. 'But the babbie's alive.'

'A boy?' The familiar sickly grin stole across Neilly's red face.

Jessie shot him a disgusted glance. He'd been drinking again. A bellyful by the look of him, but he was sober enough to do what she was about to ask him.

'Fetch Billy.' She stared at the puffy face of the big man. 'An' wipe that bloody stupid grin off your face. You'll be laughing t'other side of it before this night's done.'

Neilly stared back at her. If he was wondering why on earth she wanted to speak to Sillybilly, the town's idiot, who yearly hung round the fairground, tolerated by the fair folk on account of his shambling gentleness, he gave no sign. Jessie's word was his command. Always had been and always would be. Infuriating her, he sketched a wavy salute, stepped backwards, keeping his balance as always, and was gone.

Dismissing him from her mind immediately, Jessie moved into action. Checking first that the baby was breathing properly, she turned her attention to the dead girl.

For what she had in mind it was better to leave her dressed exactly as she was. If she were ever to be found, then robbery mustn't even be suspected. Jessie tightened her lips. But if Neilly did his job well, she would never be found. There'd be no wretched bobbies poking their long noses into Jessie Bead's affairs. Report the death and they'd be round, asking questions, holding up the exodus of the fair itself. Pulling down the girl's petticoats, noticing the fine embroidery on her camisole, Jessie began to button up the high-necked blouse.

This girl, this obviously high-born girl, had left her home and her own folk of her own free will. Jessie reckoned her age as about eighteen, though she'd said she was older when she'd come begging for work. More likely than not, they'd thrown her out. Toffs were like that. She glanced at the ringless left hand. Having a babbie out of wedlock would be a shame folks like that couldn't stomach.

'You poor little sod.' The crude word was spoken as reverently as a prayer.

The buttons on the sodden material were proving difficult for Jessie's podgy fingers to manage. She narrowed her eyes. Round the girl's neck, hidden by the blouse and the lace-trimmed camisole, was a thin gold chain. With a jerk Jessie pulled at it, feeling it snap. A long thin chain with some sort

17

of a medallion attached to it. Holding it close to her short-sighted eyes, Jessie took it over to the lamp.

Before she could make out the tiny engraved writing on it, the door opened with a rush of sound. With a sleight of hand that would have done a seasoned conjuror proud, she upped with her skirts and dropped the chain into the canvas bag slung round her waist. No point in giving them ferreting police anything to go on if they ever found the body. Finding it would be one thing; identifying it would be quite another. Turning round, she faced Neilly and the thirty-year-old boy who gawped at her with drooling mouth and the eyes of a child.

'She's just having a sleep, Billy,' she said, and he nodded. 'But don't tell the men outside. They'll think she's getting out of helping with the work.' Another swift dive into the canvas bag, two shilling pieces held out in her hand. 'Double your wages, Billy. One for helping, like you always get, and an extra one for saying nowt. You understand?'

The smooth face took on a cunning look. Jessie nodded. It would take wild horses to drag even a word from the thin, stoop-shouldered man, his cap dripping rain down his vacant face. She had known many Sillybillys in her childhood at the workhouse. Staunch, gentle and kind, they were worth a dozen of the others. Tell them a secret and it was a secret for ever. Give them even a pittance, and their gratitude knew no bounds.

Jessie screwed up her eyes, jerking her head towards the body, and speaking directly to Neilly. 'You know what to do?'

Again the twisted smile of complete understanding. Jessie shook her big head from side to side. Two men. One as drunk as a lord, and the other with the brain of a six-year-old, and yet she knew she could trust them to the end of the world, aye and farther than that if need be. It were a funny world, all right.

'*No trace,*' she emphasized.

Once again the irritating sketchy salute and the oafish grin on Neilly's pumped-up features. 'Aye, aye, mam!' he said.

Jessie took her long, voluminous black cloak down from a

18

peg behind the door. It was so full that the fair folk had often whispered amongst themselves that it would have gone four times round the Fat Woman in the Freak Show and still left enough stuff to go round Blackpool Tower. Pulling the hood over her head, she picked up the baby from the dresser and holding it close covered them both with the musty-smelling woollen cloth.

'You want to be careful you don't smother the poor little whippersnapper, Jessie.' Neilly had drunk too much to watch his tongue, but he knew when he'd overstepped the mark. 'It were only a joke,' he muttered.

'This babbie's not going in the workhouse.' Jessie's voice was a growl. She turned to Sillybilly. 'Now listen to me, lad. We've not got much time, but I want you to put your thinking cap on.'

'Yes, Mrs Bead.' The tall young man almost stood to attention. 'It's on, Mrs Bead.'

Beneath the black woollen hood Jessie's eyes shone like newly washed currants. 'Who is the kindest man in this town, Billy? Who loves childer?'

Sillybilly shuffled his big feet, hesitating only for a second. 'The clogger, Mrs Bead . . . I do his errands sometimes, and he never shouts at me, not even when I forget. He's the nicest man in the world, Mr Haydock is. He made these for me and he wouldn't take no money from me mam. He showed me how to clean them with banana skins.' Ruefully, Billy glanced down at his mud-caked footwear. 'A good rubbin'll bring the shine up again, Mrs Bead. They're not spoiled.'

'Can you show me where he lives?' Jessie moved towards the door. 'It's not far from here, is it, lad?'

'Just off Victoria Street, Mrs Bead.'

'Right then.' Without a backward glance, Jessie opened the door and stepped out into the dark night, her enormous bulk negotiating the three steps with a daintiness that wouldn't have disgraced a ballet dancer. Before she had taken more than a few steps the hem of her cloak, trailing along the muddy cobblestones, was soaking wet and she was forced to lower her head against the driving rain.

'This way, Mrs Bead.' Sillybilly pointed out a direction it was impossible to see. 'You all right, Mrs Bead?'

A grunt was the only answer he got. Jessie could feel the wetness through the cloak on her back. Holding the baby tightly against her chest left her without a hand to steady herself, and the cobbles beneath the thin soles of her boots were slippery with grease. The sounds of men working and hammering were fading now. Her breath came rasping in her throat, and only by concentrating on the metallic ring of Billy's clogs on the narrow pavements could she force herself to keep going. One more year with the fair, she told herself, then she could give up this way of life for ever. A bungalow at Lytham St Annes was what she had in mind. A life of respectability for her and Neilly, bought with the money she'd striven so hard to save. Bowing her head, she struggled on.

Years of overfeeding, of indulging herself in massive plates of potato pie washed down with gallons of milk stout, of taking little or no exercise, had made her short of breath and wheezy of chest. Her eyes bulged and the tops of her thick legs rubbed together in a smarting agony, but she kept on.

When Jessie Bead made up her mind to do something, she did it. When she had said this baby wasn't going into the workhouse, she had meant it with every fibre in her being. And not until she had handed her over to somebody decent would she be satisfied.

The street they were walking along was deserted. The shops were shuttered against the night, the gas lamps had been extinguished. A man, crazed with drink, caught them up as they passed the dim silhouette of St John's Church, but when he lurched towards them Jessie gave him a mouthful of invective that sent him reeling against a low wall. Jessie knew no fear. For a long time now she had lived and worked with the roughest of men, and their behaviour held no terrors for her.

'Nearly there, Mrs Bead.' The importance of being useful was making Billy light-headed, and he turned and smiled his queer, lopsided smile at her. 'The chapel's at the top of the next street, and the clogger's shop is just here at the bottom. You don't get corns nor chilblains if you wear clogs, Mrs Bead.'

'No, Billy. That's true enough.' Jessie stopped because he had stopped. She lifted her head and peered up at a door with an iron knocker set high. 'You can go now, Billy,' she wheezed. 'Get yourself back home and out of those wet things.' Her gruff voice gentled. 'You've been a good lad.'

Billy's grin was wide enough to split his face in two. 'An' I'll not tell nobody about the parcel, Mrs Bead.'

'The parcel?' Jessie held the baby close. God bless his simple mind; the shambling man-child hadn't even cottoned on to what it was all about. She smiled back at him. So much the better . . . so very much the better.

'I'll keep me gob shut, Mrs Bead.'

'I can trust you, Billy.'

When the sound of his clogs died away, Jessie lifted the knocker and let it fall three times against the door. She did the same again until a wavering light behind the yellow blind of an upstairs room told her the clogger was on his way down.

When the bolt was drawn back and the door thrown open, she saw a stocky man standing there, his strong features illuminated by candle flame. There was no fear sharpening his glance; nothing more than a gentle puzzlement as he raised the candlestick higher in his right hand.

Knowing instinctively and at once that she had found her man, Jessie thrust the swaddled bundle at him, watched him hold it awkwardly in his free arm, then saw his mouth drop open in amazement as the baby set up a wailing.

'Take it. Give it to your wife. Love it, and bring it up like your own.'

Jessie's voice was as deep as a man's, and before Seth could open his mouth to speak she had hurried away, the black cloak billowing out behind her like the sail of a ship.

Two

'Cheese and flippin' rice!'

Even in the direst of emergencies, and surely this was one, Seth Haydock never allowed a swearword to pass his lips. An ardent, godfearing Wesleyan Methodist, he believed that swearing was the work of the devil, and if a man couldn't express his feelings without cursing then he'd be better keeping his mouth shut.

That was Seth's code, and he stuck by it firmly.

Not that there hadn't been plenty of times in his forty years when a good old fruitful epithet wouldn't have come amiss, relieving the feelings he kept on a tight rein. But, as he was for ever reminding himself, the Lord Jesus had never cursed, and that was enough for Seth Haydock. No one could ever accuse him of being sanctimonious, but what his heavenly Father sent his way Seth accepted. Not passively, but with a quiet courage that had over the years made him many staunch friends.

He had accepted without rancour that he would for ever walk with a slight limp after a sniper's bullet had shattered his left knee on the hot plains of South Africa during the Boer War. He had accepted that his young wife's death from consumption had been the will of God, and he firmly believed that some day she would be up there waiting for him, blue eyes smiling and her hands outstretched to greet him.

'Cheese and flippin' rice!'

Heedless of the rain bouncing up from the cobbles, he ran out into the middle of the narrow street, the candlestick slipping from his grasp. The short street was shrouded in darkness, as silent as the grave. In four hours' time the knocker-up with his umbrella spokes tied to the end of his long pole would be making his way down from the chapel end, but now, in the small cold hours of a Wednesday morning, each and every window was shuttered blind.

The woman – if indeed she'd *been* a woman – had disappeared round the corner. The only recollection Seth had was of opening the door and instinctively holding out his arms for the bundle thrust into them. Whoever it was had skedaddled.

Seth's feet in the down-at-heel slippers were already soaking wet. The knocking had been so insistent he'd had time to do no more than drag his trousers on over his nightshirt, and that was clinging to his back like a wet poultice.

He stood there, a bewildered, stocky little man, frozen by indecision, even the primeval instinct for seeking a shelter deserting him.

The baby, shocked from its birth sleep, opened its mouth in a loud wail. The rain was falling on its tiny face, and the sight jerked Seth out of his stunned immobility.

He turned and went back into the house, kicking the door closed behind him. Without the candlelight to guide him, the way was hazardous, but Seth knew his little front shop down to the last wood shaving on the flag floor. Past the wooden counter with its brass foot gauge, skirting the long bench polished by his customers waiting their turn, he padded, groping his way through to the back room where, though the fire in the grate had sulked its way to a glimmer, there was still a comforting feeling of leftover warmth.

Laying the baby down carefully on the horsehair sofa set at right angles to the fireplace he reached up on the mantelpiece for a box of matches, struck one and lit the gas, hearing it plop into life, not surprised to find that his hand shook more than a little.

The soft light shone down on the baby's face, now purple with fury. Its eyelids quivered, then settled back into slits in the pallor of a round face no bigger than the perimeter of Seth's pint pot set on the table in readiness for his early morning tea. Mercifully the crying stopped.

23

Seth stood with his hand pressed over his mouth. 'Oh, dear God,' he whispered, and it was a prayer, not a blasphemy. 'Oh, dear God. What am I supposed to do now?'

The fire. That must be the first thing. Kneeling down on the pegged rug, Seth took the steel poker from its rest on the fender and carefully raked the dead ashes from the heart of the fire. The tiny red glow sprang to life and, oblivious of the pain shooting through his bad knee, Seth piled on sticks warming in the hearth, laid coal from the scuttle in a pyramid, then sat back on his heels with a satisfied look on his face as the fire took hold.

His wife, dead for almost a year now, had kept the black fireplace burnished to perfection. Once a week she had applied the blacklead with a small brush, polishing it up with a bigger brush, then finishing off with rags. The steel fender had been rubbed hard with emery paper until, as she had always said, it winked right back at you. As a tribute to her memory Seth had tried to keep it in the same condition. Apart from washing days, when Seth's combs and flannel shirts steamed gently on a clotheshorse drawn up to the fire, to be aired afterwards on the rack hoisted up to the ceiling, the little back room was a cosy place to be.

Calmer now, Seth looked round at the baby. It looked right somehow, sleeping away on the prickly sofa, tucked up like a parcel in the grey shawl. Tentatively Seth reached out and touched the fringe, drawing his hand back and tut-tutting when he realized it was damp.

Almost without volition he began to unwrap the baby, wincing when he saw the mark of blood on the towel from the recently severed umbilical cord. You didn't have to be a midwife or a doctor to know this baby was just new-born. Seth caught his breath as the tiny legs, mottled like a plucked chicken's, drew themselves up, then straightened out again. A little girl . . . And all of a piece. Nothing missing, not a finger, not a toe; all of a piece, and beautiful.

In spite of his less than average height, Seth Haydock had the hands of a man more than twice his size. Sitting on his low stool, worn into a comfortable hollow by generations of cloggers before him, hammering away at clogs mended dozens of times before, Seth's short broad fingers could handle his lengths of waxed gut thread as if they were strands of the finest silk. He could make a pair of red clogs for a baby – the only time a departure from the traditional black was permitted – and strike in the nails with less than a whisker between them. He could hammer in a tiny brass toeplate no bigger than his thumb and never falter, but now, as he carefully wrapped the baby up in the towel and grey shawl again, those same fingers shivered as if he was coming down with the Black Death.

When the baby began to cry again, his own face crumpled. 'Hush, little chuck,' he whispered. 'Don't take on. Seth'll get you back to your mam somehow.' Awkwardly, he lifted the baby, holding her against his shoulder, rocking his body to and fro, patting her back as he'd seen other women do.

Childless himself, Seth loved children. A great swelling rose in his chest as he felt the tiny body against his shoulder. Taking him by surprise, the tight feeling came up into his eyes, flowing as tears down his cheeks. Sobs tore at his throat as the fiercely held in grief since the death of his wife erupted. 'Oh, Clara! Clara!' Over and over he sobbed her name, crying with the new-born child in a paroxysm of despair over which he had no control.

This tiny creature should have been her baby. Clara's and his. For once Seth abandoned his calm acceptance of God's will. It should have been his wife sitting here in the middle of the night, holding her baby, with the firelight setting the brasses winking, and the red chenille cloth on the table glowing with the richness of ruby velvet. It wasn't right that his Clara was lying up there in the cemetery on its windswept hill, with the rain beating down on the jamjar of daffodils Seth had put there the Sunday before. She was only lying there till the day the trumpets sounded on the Day of Judgement, Seth believed that. He *had* to believe it. How else could he go on?

The baby had stopped crying, but he failed to notice. Fear held him rigid as doubts crept from the shadowed corners like evil living things. His eyes, a pale limpid blue at variance with the blackness of his hair, were wide with a terror he hadn't felt once in his days of soldiering. His hand cradled the baby's head, feeling the soft down whisper beneath his fingers.

Suppose it wasn't true? Suppose that when his Clara died her bright spirit had died with her? That even now the water was seeping into her coffin, as he'd heard it did, destroying all that was left of her? Seth lowered the baby onto his knee, hardly knowing what he was doing, touching the tiny pouting mouth with a finger. And immediately felt his finger taken in a sucking movement.

Afterwards, years afterwards, Seth knew that was the moment the fear went from him. The doubting, the terror, all gone. This baby was his. It had come to him out of the darkness that had been his life since Clara died. From where he couldn't even begin to guess, but it had been *his* door the stranger had knocked at.

'Take it. Love it,' the gruff voice had said.

Seth sighed. His prayers had been answered. 'Help me,' he'd prayed, over and over. And now the good Lord had replied.

Sentiment played no part in Seth's down-to-earth disposition. Mystical happenings he laughed to scorn, but as though an unseen hand had turned up the gas, it seemed to him that the little room was filled with light. In that moment he knew what he would do.

Leaving the baby safely tucked into a corner of the sofa, he took a taper from the cocoa tin in the hearth and lit the candle set at the end of the cornice. The stairs leading up from the little back room were narrow and steep, but he climbed them with the bouncing step of a young boy.

The bedroom on the left, at the front of the house, was furnished with a double bed and a flock mattress he pawed over each morning to smooth out the lumps, the way he'd seen his wife do. Over by the window with its yellow paper blind stood a wash-hand stand, with a water jug and basin on its marbled top. A row of pegs along the wall served as a wardrobe, and as Seth took down his jacket his glance rested on the high round table by his bed.

There they were, reassuring and familiar, his well-thumbed Bible and his copy of John Bunyan's *Pilgrim's Progress*. Their very presence gave him comfort. He took up the candle again. How could he have doubted? Bunyan's total certainty that there was a life after death had soothed and eased him into sleep many a night. What had he been thinking about, upsetting himself just now? His anguished tears had shocked him into a realization of his own unsuspected vulnerability, and yet he felt drained of emotion now, at peace, the way it was ordained that a true believer should always be.

The baby was sleeping peacefully, so Seth sat down in his rocking chair, folded his big hands over his chest and prepared himself for his long vigil.

Lily West across the street needed her sleep if anybody did, he told himself, bringing her to mind as if she'd suddenly appeared like an unlovely vision in the doorway leading from the shop. Lily West was so poor that, but for the Poor Law authorities stepping in, she and her family would have starved. Six sons Lily had borne, every one a scrounger and a scavenger from the day they could walk. Even the youngest one, Walter, a baby of five months old, had a shifty look in his crossed blue eyes, and Seth guessed it wouldn't be long before he was down on the market at closing time on Wednesdays and Saturdays begging for bruised apples, cut oranges, overripe bananas. The West boys, black-haired and blue-eyed, with more than a touch of the Blarney in their ancestry, known to every trader in the district for their cheeky grins and Lancashire humour.

'Go on, mister, gie us a toffee! Carry your bag up from the Co-op, missus?'

Clogged free by Seth from the day they could totter on bandy legs across the street to his shop, each pair of clogs passed down the line. And then, inevitably, the despair of their benefactor as they cracked their clogs on the stone flags to raise sparks, ending up with the iron dangling from its moorings.

Seth leaned forward to place a cob of coal dead centre on the brightly burning fire. Yes, he reckoned Lily West owed him possibly the biggest favour he was ever likely to ask from anybody. Taking his jacket off, he laid it gently over the sleeping baby, then went back to his chair.

Arnie West, Lily's shiftless husband, had dropped down dead in the street of a seizure the day his wife had told him she had fallen for the sixth time. But that wasn't what killed him, so rumour went.

'Found himself three sheets to the wind at old Mrs Lewis's Teetotal Mission,' the doorstep gossips had said. 'Signed the pledge against gambling, drinking and smoking. Promised God in front of witnesses to lead a life of cleanliness and constant sobriety. Found out what he'd done when he come to, and died of shock, the poor bugger!'

Seth half rose from his chair as the baby stirred, then settled back again, setting it rocking. Ah, yes. For a while it had seemed the workhouse would be the only solution, but folks in the street had rallied round and with the eldest two boys working and bringing in four shillings a week apiece, plus the free dinner tickets given to the lads still at school, the West family survived.

At almost five o'clock the baby woke and began to cry. Now was the time . . .

Outside the rain had stopped, but the cobbles were still wet and greasy, so treading carefully Seth carried his precious bundle across the street to the only house with an unmopped front step. Taking a deep breath he raised his hand and rapped smartly on the door.

Lily was a long time in answering, and when at last she stood there, peering out into the grey morning, Seth's heart sank. Never a sight for sore eyes when dressed in her best, Lily West in her night attire was enough to put even the hungriest man off his dinner.

At the age of thirty-four Lily West had the appearance of a woman well into her fifties. Her hair, already turning grey, was scraped back from her face and tied at the back with a piece of string. Years of undernourishment had rotted her teeth, which stuck out so much it was said she could eat an apple through a tennis racket. Although her legs were as thin as matchsticks, her body was top heavy with breasts as

28

billowed as a feather bolster tied in the middle.

'Can I come in, Mrs West?'

Seth followed Lily inside, wrinkling his nose against the musty smell coming from the once white flannelette nightdress and the woollen shawl round her shoulders. Only the determination fostered in him during the long waiting hours spurred him on.

'It's a terrible time to come calling.' He stood in the doorway of the back room as Lily lit the paraffin lamp set in the centre of the big square table taking up most of the space in the tiny room. No gas for Lily. Gas meant bills to be paid and, besides, the oilman wheeling his drums round the streets on his barrow was always a soft touch where Lily was concerned.

'My door's never shut to you, Mr Haydock.' Straightening up from lighting the lamp, Lily saw the baby for the first time. Her eyes bulged and her mouth dropped open in disbelief. 'God rest me soul, Mr Haydock! Where the 'ell have you got that from?'

Moving at speed round the table, she took the baby from Seth's arms. As she stared down into the little face a look of great sweetness crept over her features, a poignant reminder of the not unattractive girl she had once been.

'Who's a bonny little lad, then?' Her eyes over the baby's head were suddenly filled with suspicion. 'It's not our Jim's, is it?' She lifted her face upwards. 'He's nobbut fifteen, but he's a one for the lasses already.'

Seth looked Lily straight in the eye. 'It's a girl, Mrs West, not a boy.'

'Oh, I see.'

Lily did not see. She was far from seeing, but if nice Mr Haydock was for keeping his mouth shut then it was all right by her. To cover her confusion she tut-tutted at the baby. Who would've thought it of a chapel-going man like Seth Haydock? Her mind was going round in circles. Still, he *was* a man for all his hymn singing, and the Bible thumpers were often the worst. She jigged the baby up and down. Well, Seth Haydock wouldn't be the first man to have his sins come home to roost. Her imagination soared. Most likely the girl's mother, or her father, had fetched it round and just handed it over, and Mr Haydock being the upright kind of man he was had taken it in to do the decent thing.

She fingered the grey shawl. Not much of a clue there. Most of the women roundabouts wore shawls like this one, fastened beneath their chins to keep the worst of the weather out. Lily's head lifted. Her mind raced ahead. She could guess what Mr Haydock wanted, and the very thought of it was making her bosom twinge. She smiled.

'Looking for a wetnurse, Mr Haydock? Because if you are then you've come to the right shop. There's enough milk here for a dozen, *and* full cream. Just look at my lads. Not a runt in the whole of the litter.'

Seth stepped back a pace. He could feel a blush spreading up from his throat like a sudden scorch. He wouldn't put it past Lily West to undo the buttons down the front of her nightgown and feed the baby there, right before his very eyes. For hadn't he seen her doing the very same thing only last week on an unnaturally warm day, sitting out on her step feeding young Walter, as brazen as brass.

'Just for a start-off,' he said hoarsley. 'Till I get sorted out for bottles, and a tin of Cow and Gate.' Feeling in the pocket of his jacket he found and held out a ten-shilling note. 'For nappies and things,' he said wildly. 'And three shillings a week for you till the time she can go on the bottle.'

'Bottle?' Lily's brown eyes raised themselves ceilingwards. '*Bottle?* This little chuck's not going on no bottle, not while Lily West's titties keep filling up with the proper stuff.'

Seth felt he might faint. What on earth was he doing here, having such an unlikely conversation at five o'clock in the morning with Lily West? Why hadn't he waited till it got light, then taken the baby down to the doctor's? Or the town hall? Or the police station? Wasn't what he was doing, or thinking of doing, an unlawful, wicked act? A baby wasn't a *thing* you could take to yourself and keep. Somebody in this town had given birth to this beautiful child less than twelve hours ago. He stared at Lily with a hunted expression. But whoever had brought forth – the biblical expression came easily into his mind – this exquisite creature hadn't wanted it. He shook his head in disbelief. They'd wanted *him* to have it. *Him*. Seth Haydock. Knowing he was the man to cherish it and love it. Always . . .

'She can go in a drawer,' Lily was saying. 'But I'd be glad of a bit of blanket to line it with if you can spare it, Mr Haydock.' With the ease of long practice she sat down and began to unwrap the baby, her brown eyes soft as a doe's above her beaky nose. 'She's a proper little beauty all right, Mr Haydock. Just look at them tingy-wingy fingers. Oo's a lovely fairy, then?' She looked up suddenly. 'What are you going to call her, Mr Haydock?' A longing crept into her voice. 'If I'd had a girl I was going to call her Petal.'

'Clara,' Seth said quickly. 'After my wife. That's the only name I'd ever think of calling her. Clara.'

'Well, that's a bit off under the circumstances,' Lily muttered to herself. 'Foisting his dead wife's name on his little bastard.'

'Clara,' she said aloud. 'Well, there's plenty worse names than that, I suppose. Will you be having the minister up the top do her? You being a godfearing man.'

'Do her?' Seth hadn't bargained for this.

'Christen her. You know. Sprinkling her with 'oly water and that. I've never got round to having any of my lads done, but I can't see they're any the worse for it.'

A sudden noise on the low ceiling above their heads drew Lily's attention. 'That'll be our Joe. He's only seven but he's always first down. Goes helping the salt man saw his blocks for loading on his cart before school. Three foot long them blocks are, but you want to watch our Joe lift 'em.' She nodded to the boy rubbing the sleep out of his eyes as he stumbled into the room, tripping over what could only have been the pattern on the worn oilcloth. 'Say 'ello to Mr Haydock. Your porridge is in the pot, lad.'

It was obvious that the boy, big for his age, with rosy cheeks and minus his two front teeth, had got straight out of bed to climb into a pair of short trousers three times too big for him, and slide his bare feet into a pair of clogs, mended by Seth the week before. Already the toes were scuffed and dented. Seth's mouth actually opened to protest, but this

31

wasn't the time to deliver yet another lecture on the trouble he'd taken with this particular pair. The way he'd hand-cut the soles, getting them accurate to a fraction of an inch just by feeling the contours of Joe's sturdy foot.

With a last lingering look at the baby, Seth turned to go. 'I'll be back with the blanket, Mrs West. After the shop's shut tonight I'll start work on the cradle. A proper one with rockers. She'll be snugger in that than in a drawer.'

Backing away, unwilling to leave, he saw young Joe ladling porridge into a dish from the brown earthenware pot in the fire's side oven. Good thick oatmeal porridge, stiff and nutty from its slow all-night cooking. Just the thing to put a lining on a boy's stomach before he went out into the cold.

'Clara always used to have a pot like that on the go,' he said, and at once Lily jerked her head towards a rickety stand-chair.

'Get your feet under the table, Mr Haydock. Yon's a bottomless pot. There's more than enough to go round.'

'It's very kind of you, but no thank you.' Seth smiled at the sight of Joe hunched at the table, slurping the porridge down with a speed that made his blue eyes bulge. Halfway through scraping the dish clean, he stopped to knock a dewdrop from the end of his nose with the cuff of his felted jersey. There was a crackle of the brown paper that Seth knew was lining Joe's chest as he pushed the dish away. Twisting round in his chair, the young boy stared at the baby on his mother's knee.

'That's not our Walter, is it?' His eyes narrowed into suspicious slits. 'Have you 'ad it in the night, our Mam?'

Quietly Seth made his way through the never used front room, opened the outside door, only to have it wrenched from his hand as Joe shot off down the street like an arrow from a bow. Seth stood quite still for a while on the pavement. He looked up at the sky, paling into dawn, rubbing his chin thoughtfully. The drama of Easter was over. By now the fair, with its swingboats and hobby horses, would be well on its way to Preston, not to return for another year.

32

Seth walked across the street, limping slightly, shivering in the cold damp air, the urge to kneel down and offer up a prayer quickening his uneven steps. His Methodist faith was simple, based on his Bible. He had closed his shop on Good Friday to sit in his back room reading from the Scriptures. It was the first Easter since Clara had died, and it had seemed that the agony of Jesus in the garden, on the Mount of Olives, had merged into his own sadness.

On Easter Sunday the little chapel at the top of the street had been filled to overflowing, the men in their shiny best suits and the women showing off their Easter finery, even if for the majority it had been nothing more than a new feather on a well-brushed hat.

'Happy happy springtime,
Happy Easter Day.
Jesus Christ is risen.
And He lives for aye.'

Full-throated singing, faces uplifted. A swelling sound of promised joy. It was still there, resonant in his head, as if the music had never faded away.

Seth opened the shop door. A long time ago, before Clara took sick, he would sing as he worked, always hymns, from the Methodist School Hymnal passed on to him by his mother. And his customers, sliding up along the polished bench as their turn came nearer, would smile, borrowing for a while his good humour, envying his lightness of heart.

Back inside his own house Seth made his way through the shop to the back room where the fire still burned brightly in the shining grate. His own breakfast would be a couple of thick slices of bread smothered in margarine and jam, washed down with a pot of tea so strong a fly could walk across it without sinking. But this morning he wasn't hungry. Before he opened up his shop there was wood to sort out and plane, wood lovingly stroked by his big hands, his craftsman's hands, for the cradle for his own bonny lass.

Just for a moment his mind dwelled on the girl who had given up her baby into his keeping. Who was she? How old was she? Married, with so many mouths to feed another one was unacceptable? Fourteen or fifteen, taken against her will down some dark alley, with a mother desperate to hide her daughter's shame from the neighbours, knowing that Seth Haydock would never turn trouble away from his door?

Going over to the slopstone set beneath the window, Seth turned on the tap and splashed cold water over his face. Outside, across the back, lights were showing in upper windows. Already he could hear the clatter of clogs from the street as the mill workers made their way down to the mill. Soon the milkman would be here on his morning round, ladling the milk from the churns standing in his cart, his horse standing patiently waiting to be told to 'giddyup'.

How long would it be before his own child could be weaned onto milk from the farmer's best cow? Kept in a little skip, specially for her? Amos Platt would do that for him, Seth was sure. Without a trace of self-consciousness Seth went down on his knees to thank God for the miracle that was to transform his life.

He was busy at his bench when the shop door opened and a boy with the face of an angel stumbled in, holding up a clogged foot from which the iron dangled loosely. Alec West, five years old, stared at Seth unblinkingly.

'Me mam says can you feckle this afore I go to school? I've not been sparking. Honest, Mr Haydock. It just come loose on its own.' The dark eyes seemed out of focus as he sat down on the bench, holding a sturdy leg out in front of him. 'There's a baby in our house with a worm coming out of its belly. It were tied up with string. Me mam washed it all over in the washing-up bowl.' The small voice was hoarse and disgruntled. 'It's not as big as our Walter, but it cries bloody loud. Bleedin' loud,' he said, correcting himself automatically.

The next few minutes passed in companionable silence as, remembering the satisfaction of sliding up and down the slippery bench, Alec worked himself up to a good speed, almost falling off the edge in his exuberance.

'It's not got a cock, Mr Haydock,' he said at last, man to man.

'It's a girl,' Seth told him, trying hard to keep a straight face.

'Aw, flippin' heck,' said Alec, losing interest at once. 'Me mam says it's yours.'

Seth smiled then, somehow still managing to keep the row of tacks between his teeth. 'Aye, it's mine, Alec,' he said. 'Her name is Clara.'

'Clara,' Alec said, whizzing at speed along the bench. 'That's a rotten name. Me mam says that worm sticking out of her belly will rot off.'

'And your mam should know,' said Seth, mumbling through the hardware in his mouth.

In full agreement Alec nodded. He sat there, patiently waiting, bullet head on one side, while outside the street came to life and the clouds drifted, letting through a watery sun, lighting up briefly the shop, thick with the dust of years, pungent with the aroma of real leather.

Three

To a quiet godfearing man like Seth Haydock, being shown up in the street was an experience he didn't relish. He hated looking conspicuous. It ill became his recently acquired status as superintendent of the Methodist Sunday School. Especially when that nosy parker of a Mrs Davis from the top house sat back on her heels on the pavement and joined in.

'You want to take a strap to her backside, Mr Haydock.'

'Good morning, Mrs Davis.' Seth was all dignity.

The stout little woman leaned forward to finish off mopping the half-circle of flagstones in front of her step. 'By the gum, but your Clara's got a voice on her like the twelve o'clock hooter!'

Round the corner, outside the Co-op, Seth crouched down to wipe the tears running down his daughter's anguished face. When Clara cried she did it properly, with her mouth wide open and her eyes disappearing into cushions of reddened flesh. Seth knew that if he wasn't careful he was in danger of quite uncharacteristically losing his temper.

'Clara! Stop it! I'm taking you to school and that's the end of it.' He fought down an urge to clamp a big hand over her mouth and resorted instead to shaking her gently. 'Little girls always get taken to school on their first day. I won't do it again, I promise.' Standing up, he grasped her small hand firmly in his own and walked on. 'Why does it matter so much, anyroad?'

''Cos it makes me look like a soppy 'aporth, an' I'm not.' The wailing began again, but mercifully this time more as a continuous drone. 'I know the way, an' there's no big roads to cross.'

He pointed across the street to a little girl with a black ribbon bow on top of her carroty hair, walking sedately by her mother's side. 'See? There's Nellie Parkinson. Look what a good girl she's being.'

At exactly that moment the angelic Nellie shot out a red tongue, goading Clara into a maniacal frenzy. Snatching her hand away from Seth's grasp, she spat with such venom that a slimy globule landed halfway across the cobbles.

'Nellie Parkinson's a daft sausage!' she shouted. 'A flamin' smelly dirty sausage!'

'Spitting and swearing,' Seth said sadly, dragging his daughter firmly along the pavement. 'I know where you've learned that from.'

He sighed deeply. It had taken him a good hour to make sure that Clara was decent for her initiation into school life. She had clean clothes on from her vest outwards. He had fought and shoved with an unruly mob of women at the chapel jumble sale for the coat and dress, both of heavy navy blue serge, made originally for a child twice Clara's size. Her legs in long black woollen stockings ended in a pair of clogs so burnished and shining Seth felt a glow of pride each time he glanced down at them. And set straight on her barley pale hair was a hat wreathed in buttercups worn by his wife on a charabanc outing to the Lake District.

At the Sunday School Field Day her appearance might have passed unnoticed, but for the mixed infants in the Church of England School Clara was overdressed to say the least. Seth had chosen the school mainly because of the religious doctrine he knew would be part of the daily curriculum, and also because it was a mere five minutes' walk away from his shop.

'You can go by yourself after today,' he promised again, 'but you've got to be registered proper. I don't want the teachers thinking we don't know what's what.'

A clatter of clogs sounded behind them as the three youngest West boys whooped their way along the flagstones, stopping sparking their clogs as soon as they caught sight of Seth.

Joe, now twelve, long-legged in his short breeches, on his last term at school. Alec, now ten years old, as thickset as a wrestler, running pigeon-toed because his clogs were overdue to be passed down the line. And Walter, just five months older than Clara, but already a head taller.

The school gates were in sight now, and beyond the railings the tiny sloping square of asphalt called the playground. The school had a good reputation and Seth had been told the teachers were kind and dedicated, but the building itself was grim, of sooty, weathered stone, with narrow windows set high. Hordes of children rushed around, going nowhere, shouting and shrieking, pushing and jostling, jeering and fighting. Boys with ragged shirts hanging out of even raggier breeches, greasy flat caps pulled low over sullen faces. A group of girls, oblivious of the deafening noise, skipped solemnly with lengths of rope left over from their mothers' clotheslines, chanting in high clear voices:

'The wind, the wind, the wind blows high,
The rain comes scattering from the sky,
She is handsome, she is pretty,
She is a girl from the golden city.'

Seth's heart sank. How could he leave his one ewe lamb in the midst of such a noisy rabble? Clara's face was set in lines of stony indifference now, so he had no way of knowing what she was thinking, but her eyes, as green as grapes, moved warily in her flushed face as if she was carefully weighing up the opposition.

'You'll have to stop here while I see the teacher,' he told her, and she nodded.

Inside the school the walls were painted a shiny unsubtle green. Glancing into a classroom, Seth saw rows of long desks fitted with inkwells, and a blackboard and easel standing on a raised platform at the front. Although the school must have been cleaned during the Easter holidays there was still the overriding smell of chalk and stale urine. Following the neatly upright back of Nellie Parkinson's mother, Seth turned right into the room he remembered from his own childhood as the Teachers' Room.

It was little more than a storeroom with a row of pegs on the wall for the teachers' outdoor coats. A trio of folding chairs faced the headmistress's table. She was there behind it, handing out forms to the three women standing cowed and subdued before her. Miss Barlow, brown of hair, eyes and overall, the keeper of the cane which was conspicuously laid beside a pile of blue-backed registers.

Seth had wanted to speak to her privately; to explain that his child was motherless, that she was *different*, wilder and somehow desperate, as if she were trying to adjust to an alien environment. He wanted to explain that maybe he'd spoilt her more than a little, been too concerned for her, that she was his own little lass, used to nothing but kindness. His eye was caught by the cane. He imagined it wielded by this hard-eyed woman, swishing down on Clara's outstretched hand.

'Thank you, Miss Barlow,' he said, taking the form from her, promising to fill it in and send it back the very next day. And, intimidated by the women staring at him curiously, he turned and left the room.

In the playground he looked for Clara amongst the skipping girls, their long hair flying as they chanted their game. Nellie Parkinson was there, black ribbon bow bobbing as facing another bigger girl she skipped faster and faster.

'One pepper, two pepper, three pepper, four . . . '

Seth about-faced and saw Clara over by the far wall with the West boys. She was standing on her head, using the buttercup-sprigged hat as a mat, her legs braced triumphantly against the soot-blackened wall, the long navy serge skirts falling down to reveal her bloomers.

'Clara!' Seth's voice was a strangulated whisper, but his daughter heard him first time.

'Ta-ra Dadda,' she called out, her upside-down face rosy with effort and the pride of her achievement. 'See yer at dinnertime!'

As Seth reached the school gate, the going-in bell clanged in the two-handed grip of a young teacher. Immediately Clara

39

upended herself and hand in hand with Walter West ran to take her place in line. All without a backward glance at the thickset, desolate man walking away, his highly polished clogs making a ringing noise on the pavement.

Because it was the first day of a new term the minister was there to take the morning service. The Reverend David Maynard, a tall, upright man with fair hair brushed back from a noble forehead, a man who had been born and brought up in the green fields of Kent, and now followed his calling in the town of mills, massed houses, with the nearest tree or green grass in the Corporation park over a mile away.

Standing beside Walter, Clara eyed him speculatively. In his dog collar and dark suit he didn't look all that different from the minister at the chapel. Perhaps a bit thinner, that was all. Alec had pointed out a boy to her in the playground, telling her he was the minister's son. Swivelling her head round, Clara had a good look at the big boys on the back row. Yes, that would be the one standing next to Joe. His hair was the same colour as his father's, but his face wasn't as red.

'Pay attention, children!'

Miss Barlow was tapping with a ruler on the desk, smiling but looking cross. Staring straight at Clara. Walter was fidgeting uncomfortably. 'Stop turning round,' he hissed out of the side of his mouth. 'Else she'll 'ave you forrit.'

The Reverend Maynard was clearing his throat.

'Now, children. Before we say our prayer we're going to sing a hymn.' He beamed happily. 'Winter has gone at last.' Turning his head towards a high window he smiled at a watery sun setting the dust on the sill dancing. 'And what comes after winter? Does anyone know?'

A girl behind Clara shot up her hand. 'Spring, Mr Maynard.'

'Spring!' The vicar's beam widened. 'And so, to thank our God for all His many gifts to us as this most beautiful season begins, we are going to sing a hymn telling God that we appreciate His kindness.' He nodded and smiled at the teacher sitting at the upright piano. 'Ready, Miss Holroyd?'

With a nod of her head Miss Holroyd signified that she was, but before she began to play the vicar held up a hand. 'Now, children, Miss Holroyd will play the first verse, then I want you to put up your hands and tell me the name of the hymn.' He exchanged a conspiratorial wink with the pianist, then closed his eyes, waving his hand in time to the music.

Clara couldn't believe her ears. Her father had told her that the prayers and hymns might be a bit different from the ones she was used to at chapel and in Sunday School, and yet here they were starting off with her very favourite. Of their own volition her feet began to tap out the rhythm on the floorboards. The music sang in her ears. Six verses and six choruses that hymn had, and she knew them all! Her green eyes shone with the excitement of her discovery.

'Can anyone tell me the name of the hymn?' The vicar rubbed his hands together in anticipation, then looked up startled as Clara waved both hands about in the air.

'I know it, mister! I know every bleedin' word!'

The room grew very quiet. It was a biggish room with the slides separating the classes drawn back for the morning service, but a pin could have been heard dropping in the farthest corner.

Blinking his head as if he couldn't possibly have heard aright, the vicar inclined his head to catch the headmistress's whisper.

I see, his nod seemed to be saying. I see. He straightened up, clearing his throat. 'Clara Haydock. Would you like to come out here? To me?'

With a rush and a clatter of clogs on the hard floorboards, Clara came. He was so tall, this man in the round collar, she had to bend her head right back to look up into his face.

'All things bright and beautiful,' she said at once. 'I sing it for me dad, an' I sing it at Sunday School. I'm a good singer.'

The Reverend Maynard was somewhat at a loss. This child was no more than five years old. Miss Barlow, in a flurry of embarrassed whispering, had told him it was her first day at school, as if that accounted for the swearword that obviously came as naturally as breathing. The Reverend stroked the side of his nose, playing for time. This child with her corn-silk hair, her wide green eyes and her sun-kissed skin had the kind of beauty that caught at the throat. A child of the working class maybe; the rag-bag clothes told their own tale, but there was nothing of pinched meanness about the angel face; nothing of fear, or deprivation. This little girl had lived with love, was the product of it. Up to now. Up to this very day.

'Would you like to sing the first verse for us, Clara?' he heard himself saying. 'Would you?' Closing his mind to the disapproval emanating from the brown overall behind him, he nodded towards the piano. 'Ready, Miss Holroyd?'

Clara sang, standing quite still with her head raised and her hands clasped loosely in front of her. Her voice rose clear and pure. A child's voice, without depth, but distinctive and true. Singing for the joy of it, without a trace of shyness, mispronouncing some of the words, but getting the music right.

'The purple-headed mountain, the river running by,
The sunset and the morning that brightens up the sky . . . '

Miss Holroyd, instinctively playing with soft pedal down, the rows of children with mouths agape, trying to decide whether to watch the murderous expression on Miss Barlow's face, or try not to laugh at the new girl's showing off. Then when it was over, taking their cue from Joe West on the back row, clapping and stamping their feet in an orgy of delight at such an unexpected turn of events.

One single tap of a ruler on the teacher's desk was enough to still the clapping and stamping of feet. Miss Barlow's brown eyes betrayed no emotion, but the girls in their ragged pinafores, and the boys in their motheaten jerseys knew the reckoning would come. Not in front of the minister, never that. But later. As sure as eggs were eggs, later.

Clara decided she was going to like school. The bottom

class still wrote on slates with little grey slate pencils which squeaked in a satisfactory way when she copied the letters from the teacher's big board and easel. Singing, and slates. It was all far better than she could ever have imagined. Nudging Walter with a sharp poke of her elbow, she put him right when she saw he was drawing the belly of the letter b the wrong way round. Eager to help, she leaned sideways to spit on his slate, erasing the wrong outline with a determined rub of her sleeve.

'Clara Haydock!'

She whipped round to see Miss Holroyd, the teacher who had played the piano for morning assembly, standing behind her. Smiling, Clara held up her slate, anticipating the praise she felt was her due.

'Who taught you your letters, Clara?' Miss Holroyd's eyes behind the steel rims of her round spectacles were not quite true. Clara decided to look at the one on the right and let the other go its own wandering way.

'Me dadda, Miss.'

'Using your wrong hand?'

Clara blinked and glanced at the slate pencil held firmly in her left hand. Honest bewilderment clouded her green eyes. When the pencil was snatched from her and thrust into her right hand the bewilderment changed to dismay.

Miss Holroyd had been teaching for forty years. Her principles were deeply rooted in Victorianism, and as a strict disciplinarian she firmly believed that a child who wrote left-handed was as maimed as if it were mentally backward. It was a disobedience to the laws of her unforgiving God, and she would fail in her duty if the habit was not stamped out at once.

'From now on you write properly,' she said. 'With your right hand.' Her voice rose. 'And if I ever catch you with your pencil in the wrong hand again I'll send you to Miss Barlow. Do you heed what I say, Clara Haydock?'

In that moment the bright promise of the morning disappeared. As Clara struggled, the letters she knew by heart came out back to front, every single belly pointing the wrong way. She spat and erased, spat again and sighed. Her mind went blank, and during the following lesson in simple arithmetic her brain seemed to have atrophied.

Once, unable to believe what was happening, she surreptitiously transferred her slate pencil to her left hand, only to feel the weight of Miss Holroyd's ruler smash down on her knuckles, sending a shock of pain waves running up her arm.

When playtime came she was thoroughly demoralized. On that first day of term the ten minutes was extended to twenty to allow the four teachers to check the new pages in their registers with the headmistress's record. Clara made straight for the lavatories marked GIRLS, following a couple of bigger girls from the second class who walked with heads close together and arms around each other's waists. In spite of the feeling low down in her stomach that told her a visit was a dire necessity, she backed out in disgust, the smell of stale urine almost bouncing at her from the grimy stone wall.

The children were racing round the playground, chanting and skipping as if the two early lessons had merely interrupted their play. Clara saw Nellie Parkinson engrossed in a game of mothers and fathers, crouched down bandy-legged, holding a bigger girl's hand pretending to be a baby learning to walk. Contempt flared Clara's nostrils.

Over in the far corner of the playground the West boys squatted on their haunches in a serious contest of marbles. The familiar sight of Alec's ragged behind with the tail of a grimy shirt poking through a jagged hole lifted her spirits and sent her running towards them with the confidence of a homing pigeon.

At first Clara imagined the big girl with greasy black hair hanging in sausage ringlets was about to ask her to join in a game. Pulled up short by an outstretched skinny arm, she smiled, thinking she had found a friend.

'Show-off!' the girl said, pushing her face close. 'Bloody show-off!'

'Show-off yer bleedin' self,' said Clara at once.

When her arm was gripped and she was marched over to the far wall Clara twisted round, her small face set in a silent

44

scream for help. Not for nothing would she let them see how frightened she was, but she willed just one of the West boys to look up and see her plight. Even Walter, the crybaby of the family, would have done, but he had abandoned the game of marbles and was hanging upside down on the school gates, his eyes like Chinese slits in his thin face.

The wall was soot-ingrained, cold and hard to Clara's back. She was being held there, arms pinioned to her sides by a semicircle of grinning girls, laughing and yelling, finding her funny, as if there was something wrong with her face.

'Sing for us, Clara Cluck-cluck. Go on. Open your gob wide and sing for us!' A girl with sores round her mouth shot out a hand and took a piece of Clara's cheek in a ferocious nip. 'Miss Barlow would've 'ad yer forrit if the bleedin' minister 'adn't stuck up for yer. Soppy show-off!'

Clara looked down, chewing her lips. Her cheek stung, but she wasn't going to cry. Not for nothing was she going to cry. What was wrong with them? She sang at Sunday School and never got nipped for it. She fought back the tears pricking behind her eyes.

'Go on. Cry. Softy baby. Cry for your mam.' Another girl with dirt creases showing like a string of beads round her neck jumped up and down, taunting.

'She hasn't got a mam.' The girl who had frogmarched Clara to the wall leered triumphantly. 'Where's your mam, Clara Haydock? Go on. Tell us! Where's your mam?'

'She's dead.' Clara lifted her head to stare into the hateful eyes of the girl who had spoken. 'She died afore I was born.'

The shout of laughter startled her so much she lost control. With flailing fists and scratching fingernails, Clara went into the fray. She was trembling with fear and rage when suddenly her bladder emptied itself, running down her legs into a pool which spread into a shaming liquid island round her feet.

Her hair had come loose, her coat was hanging from her back; the elaborate bow at the front of her dress was torn half away, but none of this mattered. Clara stopped fighting to stare down at her shame.

'She's peed 'erself!'

'I've not!' Clara glared at the girl who had dared to suggest such a thing. Her fists were still balled, but the fight had gone out of her. Her one thought was to get home, back to the warmth and the love she had thought were hers by right.

With head down she pushed her way through the gawping ring of girls and ran straight for the school gates. The wind struck cold where her bloomers were damp, but the discomfort only added to her shame. Never, never could she live it down, and never would she try to because as far as Clara was concerned her first day at school was definitely going to be her last.

As she had bawled her way along the street on her way to school, now she bawled her way back. Women with kindly faces, swilling their flagstones, brushing the water off into the gutter, stopped to lean on their long brushes and shake their heads at her headlong flight.

'Isn't that Seth Haydock's little lass?' one asked her neighbour.

'Spoils her something shocking.' A bucket of soapy water was hurled fiercely from an open front door. 'They do say . . . ' For a few minutes the task was forgotten as two heads got together for a satisfactory gossip.

Clara ran on. A gypsy selling pegs and brightly coloured paper flowers froze with one hand half raised to a door knocker.

'That's a mighty big noise for a little girl to be making.'

Her voice was kind, but Clara wailed even louder. Gypsies put curses on people. Joe West had told her that. If you didn't put a silver threepenny bit in their hands they made terrible things happen. They stole children, and ate babies, boiling them up in black pans over their fires. Joe knew a lot about gypsies.

She had reached the top of her own street now, and there was the chapel, red-bricked and reassuring, where Jesus lived, with the entrance to the Sunday School not many doors away from the clogger's shop. Clara's loud sobs changed to hiccoughs as she came to the door, open to the spring morning.

Peering inside she saw three customers waiting patiently on the slippery bench. There were two old men smoking pipes, and a boy who should have been at school wiggling his stockinged feet as he waited for his clogs to be mended. Her beloved dadda was just out of her line of vision, but she could hear him hammering away and imagined him sitting on his stool, his mouth full of nails. For a full minute she held herself poised ready to rush inside, to climb on his knee and have him tell her that never again did she need to go to school.

'It'll be right, chuck,' he'd say, and it would be. Just because he'd said so.

But *they* would know. The old men smoking their pipes and the boy in his stockinged feet would listen how she'd written on her slate with the wrong hand, sung out in front of everyone, showing off like the girls in the playground had said. And worst of all, how she'd wet her bloomers, just as if she was a baby and not five years old.

Whimpering to herself, Clara ran round the back, unlatched the gate, walked quickly down the yard and let herself into the house. Here was safety. Here was the fire burning steadily behind the tall fireguard, and the pegged rug in its place in front of the steel fender. Clara knelt down on it, pressing her face against the wire mesh of the guard, closing her eyes against the comforting heat.

When she heard the voice behind her she jumped as if she'd suddenly been prodded in the back, turning her tear-stained face towards the boy standing in the doorway.

Joe West had been fighting. There was a blue swelling coming up just beneath his left eye, and as he jerked Clara to her feet the aggression was still with him. She could feel it coming from him as penetrating as the heat from the coal fire. His face, as he shook her none too gently, was unsmiling. At twelve years of age Joe was all legs and spindly arms, with an unruly mop of black hair which refused to lie flat at the back. He'd seen Clara run from the playground, and he'd guessed right that she was making for home, but before he fetched her back he had a score to settle with a boy who was laughing at what was going on. Thin and undernourished Joe might be, but what he lacked in stamina he made up in brute strength. Clara was only a kid, but she was as good as a sister to him, and when he'd left the playground it had resembled a battlefield, with Alec and Walter in the middle, fighting for fighting's sake, while the girls who had started it all squealed like stuck pigs on the sidelines.

'I'm taking you back,' he whispered, one eye on the door leading into the shop. 'Better me than your dad, because if he takes you it'll be worse for you. They'll think you're a soppy pie-can, an' you're not.'

Clara's bottom lip trembled. 'I'm not going back, Joe. I'm not going back, never. I *hate* school. I'm going to stop at home with my dadda.'

'Stop talking daft.' Joe began to pull her towards the door, but the hard look had gone from his eyes. His obvious kindness undermined her. Fresh tears spurted from Clara's eyes, running down her cheeks to drip from the end of her chin.

'They'll send the School Inspector for you,' he told her. 'An' he's a great big fella, with a konk on him as red as a beetroot. He could chew you up an' spit you out afore breakfast, Clara Haydock. So come on . . . we'll have to run like 'ell as it is.'

'I wet meself, Joe.' Clara looked up at him for a second, then hung her head. 'It run down the flags and everybody saw.'

Joe shrugged his shoulders then bent down to whisper in her ear. 'You got wet bloomers on?'

When Clara nodded, shame-faced, he startled her by giving a great leap upwards to the clothesrack suspended from the ceiling.

'Them yours?' he asked, pulling down a pair of navy blue knickers and thrusting them at her. 'Get changed into them quick. An' look sharp if we're goin' to get back afore the bell goes. An' stop yelling. It's nowt. I bet Miss Barlow's done it many a time.'

Joe could always make her laugh, and the ruder he was, the more she laughed.

'You're a comic, Joe,' Clara told him as they raced up the street hand in hand.

'Oh aye?' Joe yanked her along, their clogs clattering in staccato rhythm on the pavements. 'Well, there'll be nobody flamin' well laughing if they've all gone back in.'

But they hadn't. As they turned into the gate, the young teacher on playground duty was just coming out with the bell in her hand, holding the clapper steady until she got to the bottom of the steps.

The girl with sores round her mouth, the one who had nipped Clara, sidled up to her with an embarrassed look. 'You can play with us this afternoon if you wants to,' she whispered. 'When we gets back from us dinnertime.'

Clara nodded, too shy to speak. Alec West was grinning at her, and Walter actually took her by the hand to lead her into line.

Clara trotted more or less happily after the ferret-faced Walter, her self-assurance restored by the feel of the dry bloomers, and the fact that she had found a friend. The girl with the scabs on her chin leaned closer just as the bell began to clang. 'You've got nice 'air,' she said. 'An' I like your frock.' Almost overcome, Clara marched forward, but the best was yet to come.

As she followed Walter into the bottom classroom, a tall boy with hair almost as fair as her own caught up with her. His nose had been bloodied, and looked sore and tender, but he bent down and whispered in her ear.

'I liked your singing,' he told her. 'I bet anything if you were a boy and came to our church you would be in the choir.'

'You've bleeded on your shirt.' Clara blinked at the whiteness of the shirt revealed at the V-neck of a clean fawn jersey. She couldn't remember ever seeing both a shirt *and* a jersey worn together, not at the same time, and certainly not with a tie.

'It's nothing.' With a nonchalance that had Clara round-eyed with the surprise of it, John Maynard, only son of the

Reverend David, whipped out the end of his red and green striped tie and rubbed vigorously at the offending stain. 'I'll change when I go home at lunchtime.'

'Ark at 'im.' Walter shoved Clara back into line. 'Our Joe says they talk like that where he comes from.'

'Better than what you talk, anyroad,' said Clara disloyally, swinging briskly into the classroom, her confidence fully restored.

'No talking in line, Clara Haydock!' Miss Holroyd glared at Clara through her little round spectacles.

'Boss-eyed pie-can,' said Walter, without moving his mouth.

Four

Clara was almost out of her mind with excitement. It was all there, the drama, the glamour something inside her craved. Up there on the flickering screen a film star with luscious lips and long flowing hair hung by a sheet from a burning building. Tongues of flame licked dangerously close to her swaying body.

The background music, as loud and throbbing as the action called for, was being played on an upright piano by a stout lady wearing a hat. Clenching her hands together, Clara felt it jerk her every pulse spot into active response.

Suddenly, with a crashing of thumping chords, the stout lady stopped playing and closed the piano lid. The screen went blank, leaving Clara as stunned as if a bucket of cold water had been thrown over her.

The words 'The Perils of Pauline – To Be Continued Next Week' meant less than nothing to her. With Walter West on one side of her and Alec West the other, their cheeks bulging with the aniseed balls bought with Clara's Saturday penny, she had been transported out of her everyday existence into a world far beyond the confines of the little cinema at the end of a long, narrow cobbled street.

'I know Pauline gets down safe,' she told Seth. 'Joe told me.' Her face was pale, drained with emotion. 'He let us in for nothing through the side door when nobody was looking. He works there now on a Saturday afternoon,' she explained. 'He let us in without paying.'

Seth gazed on his nine-year-old daughter with something approaching despair. At almost seventeen, Joe West was already a hardened opportunist, working as a bookie's runner for most of the day, then wherever he could earn a dishonest penny for the rest. Twice he'd narrowly escaped being sent to prison as he lounged, hands in pockets, on street corners, taking his bets. The bookie he worked for had paid his fine and the very next week Joe had returned, cap pushed to the back of his head, black hair flopping over his forehead, on the lookout for potential customers.

Seth stroked his chin, wondering, not for the first time, how to say what he felt sure must be said. His religion was an intrinsic part of his life. Methodism ran in his veins. Right was right, and wrongdoing was evil; there were no shades of grey in between. The straight path of virtue was the only way to salvation, and Clara must learn that to sneak into the cinema without paying was definitely a sin.

'I'm going to be a film star when I grow up, Dadda.'

Clara jumped up onto the slippery bench, flung her arms wide, and began to sing:

> 'Joshua, Joshua,
> Nicer than lemon squash you are!
> You'll be pleased to know,
> You are my best beau!'

As she sang the last few words she pointed to the red ribbon bow on top of her head, innocently misinterpreting the meaning. When Seth's serious face widened into a reluctant smile, she took a handkerchief from the leg of her navy blue bloomers and waved it in circles above her head.

> 'Goodbye-ee, goodbye-ee.
> Wipe the tear, baby dear, from your eye-ee.
> It is hard to part I know,
> But I'll be tickled to death to go!'

The provocative innocence on her young face startled Seth. 'Joe,' he said at once. 'Joe taught you those words, didn't he?'

52

'He's going to be a soldier, Dadda.' Jumping down from the bench, Clara lifted her skirts and pushed the handkerchief back into the leg of her bloomers. 'He's going to tell them he's older than what he is, an' with him being so tall they'll never guess.' Her back, as she went through into the back living room, was stiff with pride. 'Joe says when the Germans see him coming they'll run like 'ell.'

Limping after her, Seth rubbed his chin slowly with a thumb and forefinger. In 1916 the war had been going on for two years, with no sign of it ending. Conscription had come in, and the looms in the mill at the bottom of the street were weaving cloth for bandages, or yards of cotton urgently needed for the munition factories.

Two of Lily West's big sons were in France, and to her pride their photographs had been in the local weekly newspaper. Jim, a private in the 1st Loyal North Regiment, had described in a letter to his mother how, when they were waiting to go over the top, the enemy guns had started up. The gas played on the enemy lines had been carried back on the wind, and as the eyeglass had come out of Jim's helmet the gas had got in and for a time he had been blinded. Bert West, in the machine-gun section of the 4th South Lancashires, was in hospital after being buried in a dugout for forty-eight hours. All Lily could do was count her blessings that they were still alive.

And now Joe was going to enlist . . .

Seth watched as Clara knelt down on the cut rug by the fire, the toasting fork in her hand and a pile of barmcakes on a plate in the hearth. What could you begin to tell a child of nine about the horrors of war? How could you show her the long list of casualties printed night after night in the evening paper? Overprotected his little girl might be, but she was sunshine in a dark room, joy on a cloudy day. After the initial shock of being disciplined at school, she had settled down, coming top in every subject except arithmetic, in which she was an inglorious bottom.

'If I could put me pencil in me proper hand I could do the sums,' she'd told her father. 'But they come out backwards way in me head when I'm using the wrong hand.'

'We're having a concert in our backyard next week,' she now told Seth, spearing a barmcake on the toasting fork. 'It'll cost an empty jamjar to get in, then me an' Walter will take the jars to the rag-and-bone man the next time he comes down the back an' he'll give us rubbing stones.'

Seth took a yellow slab of margarine from the dresser shelf and a knife from the drawer in the table. 'And what will you do with the rubbing stones?' he asked, trying not to smile at her obvious earnestness. 'Walter's mother never mops her step, and neither do I with folks traipsing in and out of the shop all the time. I can't see rubbing stones being much good to either you or Walter.'

Clara's sigh of exasperation lifted her shoulders almost to the lobes of her ears. 'Well, we'll *sell* them, won't we? To people like Mrs Davis at the top end of the street. She stones her front every morning.' A piece of bread had caught fire, and Clara blew on it fiercely, before adding it to the plate. 'We'll tell her the money's for the soldiers, then she'll likely give us double.'

'Clara!' Seth put down the knife and, sitting in his rocking chair, gently but firmly took the toasting fork from his daughter's hand. He was not angry. Anger was slow to run in his veins, but his face was troubled. When he spoke again his voice was deceptively quiet. 'And the money for the soldiers? What will you and Walter do with that?'

That was a hard one to answer. Clara had already spent and respent the expected pennies in her mind. For a penny you could get a whole quarter of toffees or, for a little more, a halfpennyworth of chips and a pennyworth of fish. Walter had seen a penknife in the window of a shop in Penny Street for fourpence, and for twopence she could treat Joe to a haircut, with a bay-rum squirt to follow. He'd have to look his best if they were going to let him into the war. Then there were *Comic Cuts* with stories of Weary Willie and Tired Tim. The possibilities were endless.

'I'm busy thinking about it,' she said innocently, tucking a wayward strand of hair behind an ear. 'But whatever we get, me and Walter, we'll split it between us. Walter might give it to his mam. She's always saying she hasn't got no money.'

'So you'd be lying when you told Mrs Davis the money was for the soldiers?'

'Only a little lie.' Clara wrinkled her nose. 'Everybody tells little lies.'

'And Joe was stealing from the cinema manager when he let you in free?'

'Not like taking it out of the manager's pocket! Not *pinching* it, Dadda. The manager's rich. He's got a *car*. An' a coat with a fur collar on.'

'Put that down!' Seth's voice rose to a hoarse whisper that seemed louder than if he'd shouted aloud. 'Leave the toast and look at me!'

Clara's eyes were very green in the firelight. 'You're not cross, are you, Dadda?'

'Exodus, Chapter Twenty?' Seth barked out the question. 'Verse fifteen?'

Clara chewed her lips. She hated it when her father talked to her like this. There was something in the way his lean face darkened that terrified her. Even the minister on his weekly visit to school didn't look like this when he talked about God.

'And God spake all these words, saying I *am* the Lord thy God. Thou shalt not . . .' Seth's pale blue eyes were burning into her own. 'Verse fifteen, child!'

Hurriedly, as if she was mentally reciting her ten times table, Clara went through the Commandments. 'Thou shalt not steal!' she said at last, on a rising note of triumph.

'And yet,' her father's voice was silken soft once more, 'you have stolen from the cinema manager and you are plotting to steal from our neighbours. You could see the thunderings and the lightnings, and the noise of the trumpet, and the mountain smoking, and yet you would not stand afar off. Not you, Clara Haydock. Do you *want* to burn in the everlasting Lake of Fire?'

Clara's head drooped low. Her dadda was acting like the lay preachers who preached in the chapel pulpit on Sundays. Pointing their fingers at her as she sat beside her father in their coffin-sided pew, their throats working against high stiff collars. For most of the sermon they would speak in quiet calm voices, then suddenly, just when she was far away in a daydream, they would pounce.

'Damnation awaits all sinners! You, and you, and you!'

She would jerk to attention, seeing herself surrounded by licking flames, with a sad and disappointed God watching from the shores of the burning lake.

Not a foot away from where she was kneeling on the rug, a piece of coal dropped from the grate sending a shower of sparks dancing across her line of vision. The heat was burning her left side and its flames seemed to be reflected in Seth's large pale eyes.

'Do you *want* to be a sinner?' he asked her softly, lifting her chin with a finger and smiling despairingly at her.

Clara felt her insides melt with love for this gentle man with his big hands and teeth all rotted at the front from his habit of holding the nails in his mouth. She knew now that she had done a wicked thing. She knew because her father had told her over and over again that the West boys would lead her into trouble if she let them.

There were tears welling in her eyes, but she made no move to dash them away. They added to the feeling of holiness creeping over her, a feeling she sometimes got when she sang hymns. Oh yes, for her beloved dadda's sake she wanted to be good. For his sake she wanted to be an angel when she died, singing away in heaven. Emotion swelled her chest, rising to her throat in a lump she found hard to swallow.

'I'll never be wicked again,' she promised fervently. 'Jesus won't know me, I'll be that flamin' good. I promise you, Dadda, God's honour, I promise.'

On the day Seth was busy in his shop checking a consignment of alder wood blocks newly delivered from a clogsole traveller, Clara and Walter gave their backyard concert.

It was a fine day and they had a good audience of children from the surrounding streets, each one clutching their entry fee of an empty jamjar. A few of the jars collected by Clara at the back gate looked familiar, and she guessed that they had been passed back over the wall to be presented again by jarless hopefuls, but she let it pass.

Only a week had gone by since her firelight confrontation with her father and she was still wearing an invisible halo. Her own share of any monies from the transaction with the rag-and-bone man was going into the war comforts box on the counter of the pork butcher's shop. Walter could tread his own path down the slippery road to hell, she had decided, his scorn washing over her and leaving her undismayed.

The first item was Walter doing a clog dance to the accompaniment of Alec, a cynical fourteen-year-old, beating a stick against one of Lily West's grimy pans, whistling at the same time a chorus from 'The British Grenadiers'.

Clara watched them impatiently. Walter was doing quite well. Joe, after one of his Saturday night visits to the Palace Theatre on the Boulevard, had given him lessons. Walter was wearing a bow tie made from one of Clara's ribbons, and the crispness of his rap would have done justice to a professional. He had what Clara considered to be a silly smirk on his face, and she couldn't wait for him to finish. Her heart was already beating fast and her eyes blazed. When her turn came at last she walked quickly to stand on the flagstone Walter had vacated, her hands clasped together beneath her nonexistent bosom.

'For my first item,' she announced, 'I am going to sing "Roses Are Bloomin' in Picardy".' A small boy sitting on an upturned bucket made a rude noise with his mouth, and she quelled him with a ferocious glance.

Her voice when she sang was as pure and true as a singing bird's. She had learned the words from a piece of sheet music 'found' by Joe during a closing-down sale at the piano shop in Farthing Street. The tune she had picked up by hearing it sung just once at a Sunday School concert a few weeks previously.

'But there's never a rose like yeoo,' she sang, clutching her chest and rolling her eyes to heaven. When her tiny audience fidgeted she sang a bit louder; when the boy on the bucket fell off his precarious perch she flung out her arms in a

57

dramatic gesture, holding on to her audience's attention by the sheer force of her personality.

A woman pegging out her washing in the next backyard came to look over the wall and listen as Clara started on her encore.

'I shall die,' sang Clara, 'I shall die. I shall die tiddly-i-ti . . .'

'Aye, an' you *will* die, young Clara, if your dad hears you,' the woman muttered, as Clara went on to sing the version brought back from France by soldiers on leave.

But the rudest verse was brought to an abrupt end as, with a flourish, the back gate was flung open to reveal Joe West in the rough khaki of a private in the East Lancashire Regiment, his cap set at a rakish angle over his grinning face.

'Joe!' Forgetting her final curtsey, Clara flew at him. 'Oh, Joe! Oh, they've let you in! Oh, I *do* hope you get there afore the war's over!'

Joe was in one of his comical moods. Clara could sense it even before he bowed low to the audience stolidly sitting or standing before him, determined not to go before they'd got their jamjar's worth.

'All together now!' Joe shouted, linking arms with Clara and marching up and down, singing at the top of his voice:

> 'Pack up your troubles in your old kit bag
> and smile, smile, smile.'

Excited at seeing his brother in uniform, Alec went berserk on the makeshift drums, throwing his sticks up in the air the way he'd seen the Boy Scouts do when they marched down the street on chapel parade.

'Smile, boys, that's the style,' sang Walter, his clogs striking the forbidden sparks on the flagstones.

'What's the use of worrying?' sang Joe, lifting Clara clean off her feet and whirling her round so that her full skirts flew up showing a good two inches of navy blue bloomers.

'It never was worthwhile!' Clara came to rest on her

tiptoes, her arms still clasped round Joe's neck, her rosy face an inch from his own as she smiled into his blue eyes, singing at him like an opera star at the height of her aria.

'Stop it! Stop this row! Now, this minute. Stop it!'

Like a gramophone winding down, the singing petered out. Only Walter, because his back was turned away, failed to see Seth standing at the back door, his face distorted by anger.

'Joe! Alec! Walter! Go home to your mother. This way, through the shop.' He touched Joe on a khaki sleeve as he walked past. 'There's a good lad.'

The small audience filed sheepishly out of the backyard gate. A few of them were regular, if unwilling, chapel-goers, and Mr Haydock, as well as being Clara's father, was the superintendent of their Sunday School. His was the power and the glory as they assembled in the big room on Sunday afternoons before going off to the vestries with their particular class. Mr Haydock led the prayers and the hymn singing, and it was sometimes hard to imagine him sitting on his stool in his little shop with his mouth full of nails when the Sabbath gave way to ordinary working days. No wonder he had looked as blazing as the hell he sometimes promised them from his platform on Sunday afternoons should they misbehave.

'I bet Clara cops it,' said a girl in a torn pinafore as they trudged down the cobbled back.

'Eee, I 'ope not,' said her friend, with a deep and mournful insincerity.

Inside the house Seth sat down in his chair, covering his face with his big hands.

Clara was ready to do battle. With her long pale-gold hair hanging down her back and her green eyes blazing she faced him, standing with arms folded on the cut rug in front of the fire.

'We wasn't doing nothing, Dadda. Just singing and dancing.' She stuck out her bottom lip. 'We was going to sing "Rule Britannia", with Walter doing the 'ornpipe, then we was going to finish with everybody singing "God Save the King". With me doing a descant,' she added, 'an' waving a flag.' Her head drooped. 'Till you came and spoiled it all.'

Seth lifted his head. The tears glistening soft in his eyes made Clara catch her breath in dismay. She moved to kneel down by the side of his chair.

'I'm sorry, Dadda.' Her own eyes filled. 'I didn't mean to be bad again.' She rubbed at her face. 'It's only a bit of flour out of the tin. Not proper powder like you told me only bad women wear. An' me lips are only red because I rubbed them with the colour from a scrap. It was me *stage* make-up, Dadda, that's all.'

Seth's voice was hoarse with sorrow. 'Jim West has been killed. His wife just came round with the telegram. They thought he was still in hospital after being gassed, but he must have gone back up the line.' Seth was swaying backwards and forwards in his distress. 'He was the best of the lot was Jim. Married, with two children and his wife expecting another.' In his distress Seth forgot that such matters were never mentioned. 'Poor Mrs West. How many of her sons will have to die before this war ends?'

Clara couldn't move or speak. This was her first brush with death. For her the war had been all flag waving, bands marching in the town and songs with rousing rhythms to sing. Jim had looked so handsome in his uniform on that last day when he'd come to say goodbye to his mother. Lily didn't like his small pale wife, but on that exciting day she'd been quite civil to her, wiping the dribble from her grandsons' chins before coating their dummies with condensed milk and shoving them back into their open mouths.

'Getting wed'll be the making of our Jim,' Lily had told Seth in Clara's hearing. 'She's nobbut a lass and as thin and pale as a stick of celery, but she'll make him get up in a morning and go off to work. Oh aye, a houseful of kids'll show our Jim what life's all about.'

And now Jim was dead. In France. There wouldn't even be a coffin to trundle through the streets on a cart to the cemetery with all his relations walking behind crying into handkerchiefs. He'd never tease Clara again, calling her 'butternob'. Never prop his old rusty bike against the window bottom, then bend down to snap off his trouser clips before he went into the shabby house to see his mam.

'Thy will be done . . . ' Getting up from his chair, Seth sighed the words almost underneath his breath. Then he went through into the shop and began his hammering, striking the nails in with twice his usual force.

'Where are you going, Clara?' His mouth was full of tacks. She heard what he said and took no notice. Like a pebble from a catapult she flew across the street and straight into the house opposite. What kind of a God was it who could *will* a lovely man like Jim West to die?

With her dirty apron held over her face, Mrs West was wailing and crying loud enough to wake the whole street. The little back room was crowded with four big sons standing helplessly round their mother's chair. Jim's little pale wife still clutched the telegram in front of her swollen stomach. Neighbours from either side were crying into the pot of tea they were making, and Lily's two grandsons, sitting side by side on the table in the middle of the remains of the dinner pots, were yelling fit to burst their lungs.

'It's Clara, Mam.' Joe spoke quietly into the top of the bowed head, and at once the apron was lowered, revealing Lily's face so blotched and swollen with weeping it made Clara's heart give a great lurch of pity.

'Me little angel! Me own little lamb . . . ' With a great cry Lily held out her arms, and not for the first time Clara found herself held against the musty-smelling breasts of the woman who had suckled her into life.

'Them bloody Germans!' Lily held Clara so tightly the breath went out of her body in a gusty sigh. 'That bloody Kaiser! I'd shoot him full of more 'oles than my sieve's got if I got near him. Who does the rotten old bastard think he is, taking my lad who wouldn't't've hurt a fly?'

'It's not God's fault, Mrs West.'

Clara surfaced from her whispered reassurance to stare straight into Lily's red watery eyes.

'God?' Lily's voice cracked with grief. 'What the 'ell has God to do with it? He can't do nowt, can He, sittin' up there on His backside?'

Reassured, bewildered, but somehow comforted, Clara

burrowed her head back into the acrid smell of Lily's bosom, adding her own noisy sobs to a mourning that at least made some kind of sense to her.

And that night, kneeling by her bed on the cold oilcloth saying the Lord's Prayer, she missed out the phrase 'Thy will be done'. On purpose. Like Mrs West had said: God couldn't do nowt, sitting up in heaven on His backside.

She climbed into bed, comforted.

Five

The concerts put on in the Methodist Hall at the top of the street were the highlights of the dark winter months. There was a raised stage at one end of the big room, with curtains that sometimes swished open and shut, but more often had to be dragged across by unseen hands. The upright piano had a tinny ring to it, but Mr Cronshawe, the organist, played it as if it were a Bechstein grand.

Every single seat had been filled for the Thursday and Friday evenings, and on the Saturday chairs had been brought in from the houses over the street and set in the aisles.

The newsagent's shop had sold out of coloured crepe paper. Anxious mothers had gathered it into frilly skirts, and fashioned poke bonnets out of a circle of cardboard plus a lot of imagination.

Miss Dobson from the potato-pie shop always filled the spot before the interval to sing the same song, with her tiny notebook of words clenched beneath her jutting one-piece bosom.

'Come into the garden, Maud!' she implored in her fruity contralto voice. 'I am here at the gate *alone*!'

'An' no bleedin' wonder with a mug like that!' Walter West, sitting between his mother and Clara's father, whispered so loudly that the two rows in front and two behind had to stifle their giggles.

Lily West had shrunk since the ending of the war two years before, in 1918. First Jim, then Bert lay buried over in France. When Joe had been reported missing the week before the Armistice, the flesh had fallen away from Lily's beaky nose and her once magnificent breasts hung like elongated sacks.

Though Joe had come back after the Armistice – turning up like a rotten penny, as he said himself – he had never lived in his mother's house again. Now and then he'd walk down the street with his slight swagger, impressing the neighbours with his camelhair coat, ordering his mother to hold out her hands so that he could fill them with pound notes. Before disappearing once again.

The interval had passed without Lily noticing. If she'd turned round in her seat just before the lights were dimmed for the second half of the performance she would have seen a tall young man standing at the back with his arms folded and his trilby hat pushed to the back of his head. But this was the moment they'd all been waiting for; this was the only reason Lily had deserted her own fireside to sit on a rock-hard chair with a lot of mealy-mouthed Methodists – Mr Haydock excepted, of course.

Lily fidgeted through a drawn-out dancing display, with five small girls attired in bright yellow crepe paper pretending to be sunbeams. But when Clara came on, walking slowly to centre stage, Lily glanced sideways and saw Mr Haydock's face light up with an expression of pride that brought tears to her own eyes.

The five small girls grouped themselves round Clara, looking up at her with wobbly smiles. Mr Cronshawe played a single opening chord and Clara began to sing.

At thirteen she was not quite a woman but definitely no longer a child. The young man at the back pursed his lips in a soundless whistle. By all that was holy, little Clara Haydock had grown into a raving, heart-stopping beauty! His mouth, beneath a recently acquired moustache, dropped open in astonishment. Why had he never seen it before? How could she have been living all those years right across the street from his mam without his seeing how she would be some day? Small high breasts were accentuated by the too-tight bodice of the long white dress, run up by a woman in the next street for last year's Anniversary Sunday services in chapel.

'Them tucks should have been let out,' Lily chuntered to herself through her protruding teeth.

'Lower the neckline of that ruddy awful frock and take that ribbon out of her hair, and she'd knock them for six at the Metropolitan down the Edgware Road,' the man at the back told himself. 'Marie Lloyd? She'd've been wasting her time!'

Clara's voice poured out from the rickety stage over her audience, every single word clear as a bell.

'Jesus wants me for a sunbeam,' she sang, her green eyes sparkling. 'To shine for Him each day. In every way to please Him. At home, at school, at play.'

Loving her audience, knowing most of them all her life, her warmth and natural affection seemed to draw them to her through the glorious sound of her voice, so that, closing their eyes, they could almost imagine she was reaching out to touch their faces with a gentle hand. Worried frowns smoothed out, tense shoulders relaxed; even Lily West's chin lifted and her eyes lost their lacklustre look.

'I will ask Jesus to help me. To keep my heart from sin,' Clara sang, and the centre-stage light shone down on her hair so that it glistened and glittered as if it had been powdered with gold dust.

When the clapping had died down, the yellow paper sunbeams, at a signal from Mr Cronshawe, ran from the stage. Left alone, Clara held her hands clasped together, waited for the softly played introduction and began her encore.

The war had been over for merely two years. Almost everyone in the audience had lost a husband, a father, a brother or a son. The world was slowly getting its breath back from the memory of the slaughter in the mud of Flanders' fields. Men coming back from the trenches were without jobs; some of them without homes. Lily West had taken in her widowed daughter-in-law and the three children, and the walls of the terraced house bulged with little boys and bigger ones, usually in a state of combat. Pushing, shoving, rolling on the floor when they could find a space, Lily trod the path from the fire oven to the table all

65

day long, growing scrawnier and more top heavy with every passing day.

Now, in the warm darkness with her hands folded on her lap and nothing to do but listen and watch, her face took on an expression of touching serenity. Clara was singing like an angel come down from the heaven Lily didn't believe in. Suddenly her bolster-shaped bosom gave an enormous heave and a tear rolled down Lily's beak of a nose to hang suspended there.

'There's a long, long trail a-winding . . . '

The silvery voice rose and fell. Clara was enjoying herself now. She could see the white blur of upturned faces and sense their rapt attention. She had been nervous just before she came on, but the minute she began to sing all trace of nervousness had gone. She could do anything she wished up there alone on the stage. She could sing so softly the people out there would lean forward in their seats. She could throw her voice and sing so loudly they would fidget with surprise.

'Where the nightingales are singing,
And a white moon beams . . . '

It was tempting to look up and point when she sang about the moon and, although Clara had followed the minister's wife's instructions at the rehearsals, she knew now that the moment had come to stand perfectly still without moving.

'Till the day when I'll be going
Down that long, long trail with you.'

Softly, softly she ended the plaintive song. Gently Mr Cronshawe let his hands slide from the piano keys. And the seconds of silence before the clapping began told their own tale. Flushed with the heady taste of success, Clara moved backwards to take her place in the closing tableau, standing apparently humbly in her place at the back, but hearing her own voice soaring above the others in a spirited rendering of 'God Save the King'.

Joe West tried the door of the shop twenty minutes later, walked through into the back room and gave Clara what she declared was the fright of her life. She was standing in front of the little round shaving mirror over the slopstone, still in her white dress, holding her long hair up on top of her head and smiling at herself.

'Joe!' As if she was still the child he remembered she ran into his arms, hugging him, covering his face with eager little kisses. 'Oh, I wish you'd seen me tonight!' She stepped back, throwing her arms wide in a gesture that was pure theatre. 'I'm going to go on the stage, Joe. Just as soon as I'm old enough.' She pouted. 'In about two years. Marie Lloyd was a star when she was sixteen. I've read all about her in a book.'

'That's nothing.' Joe grinned at her, stroking the embryo moustache with the tip of a finger. 'She's old now, at least fifty, and she's no beauty, but when she sings "My Old Man Said Follow the Van", you can hear her right to the back of the gallery.' He pretended to consider. 'You weren't bad tonight, Miss Haydock. Room for improvement, of course . . .'

'Joe! You heard me!' Clara flopped down in a chair, to sit with knees apart, looking up at Joe from beneath long dark eyelashes. 'You were there all the time!' She glanced towards the door. 'Sit down and tell me what you've been doing, Joe. Me dad'll be back soon. He's counting the concert money with the chapel treasurer.'

'So you won't be short of a bob or two for a few weeks?'

'Oh, Joe! You're still a comic, an' I do luv you.'

He smiled at her through narrowed eyes. Still the same young Clara. Saying straight out just what came into her head. Living with a man like Seth Haydock had left its mark, and yet when he'd watched her singing up there on that Methody stage there'd been a something smouldering in her eyes, some star quality, that Joe had recognized at once.

67

'I'll be back,' he said, meaning it. 'One of these fine days I'll come for you an' scoop you up in me arms, like the Red Shadow, and carry you off to me tent in the desert.' He shot out an arm and glanced at the silver watch strapped to his wrist, a present bought at Mappin and Webb's in Oxford Street, London, by the only girl in a quartet of novelty cyclists now playing at the Empire Theatre – the girl he now shared a room with in London's Bayswater.

Clara jumped up, staring at him in dismay, feverishly searching her mind for some way to detain him. The adrenaline was still flowing swiftly through her veins, and somehow Joe typified all the excitement she desperately craved. He was so handsome sitting there in his double-breasted coat, smoking a cigarette and flicking the ash in the vague direction of the hearth. He was a bit like Rudolph Valentino, except that Joe's eyes were blue and his hair was curly and not smarmed back with Brilliantine. Joe had got on in the world, just as she had known he would. Joe was clever. He lived in London, far away from this boring old town with the Sunday School concert the highlight of the year.

'Stop and have a drink,' she said suddenly. 'There's a bottle of rhubarb wine on the top shelf of the cupboard. It's been there for years and years.' She climbed on her chair and reached up into the cupboard set into the alcove at the side of the fireplace. 'A customer gave it to me dad instead of paying for his clogs to be mended.' She jumped down holding the dusty bottle triumphantly aloft. 'It's a bit cloudy, but it'll be all right. We'll have to drink it out of cups, but that won't matter.'

'He'll half kill you, Clara Haydock.' Sipping the sweet drink, Joe raised dark eyebrows at the unexpected strength in the cloying wine. 'Drink is the curse of the devil. Have you forgotten? One sip of that an' you're set on the road to hell.'

'It's only made out of rhubarb, you soppy a'porth.' Clara drank deeply from the cup then opened her eyes wide. 'Rhubarb's not liquor. Not like gin and rum and that kind of thing.' Reaching for the bottle she refilled both their cups.

'We'll have to drink it all, Joe. I can't put it back half full. Me dad'll never miss it. He's forgotten it's there, anyroad.'

'The bottle?' Joe nodded towards it. 'What you going to do with that, then?'

The drink was making Clara light-headed. Gulping it too quickly she ignored the feeling of nausea. Defiantly she took another long swig, feeling it run down her throat, making her gasp.

'Nice bit o' rhubarb gone into this, Joe,' she giggled. 'Come off Mr Pilkington's allotment, this did. You know Mr Pilkington? He sings in the choir. You remember him, Joe. Told the police on you that time you lit the bonfire on the spare land the night afore Guy Fawkes.'

'To Mr Pilkington!' Refilling his cup, Joe held it aloft. In spite of his head for drink, the well-matured wine was making his eyelids droop. He'd been on and off trains all day, in to Yorkshire and back across the Pennines. His ambition to be a music hall manager before he was twenty-one had been thwarted by the attitude of a jumped-up pompous theatre manager from Sheffield. 'Music halls are finished,' he'd said, pointing the stem of an evil-smelling pipe at Joe. 'Revues are the thing. That and picture palaces. Whoever sent you up here on spec wanted his head seeing to.'

Was the old devil right? Joe swirled the wine round in his cup before drinking deeply. Things were changing, that much was certain. And when the wind changed direction Joe West followed suit.

It was time he moved on. The girl he was living with was twenty-eight and well past her best. He stared at the bowed head of the young girl kneeling now on the rug in front of his chair.

The long white-gold hair had fallen forward hiding her face. Joe felt an ache in his fingers making him want to stretch out a hand to twist the silken strands in his grasp, pulling her head up so that she was forced to look into his eyes. It was three days since he'd lain with a woman, and at twenty years of age Joe's appetite for lovemaking was at its most voracious. She would be like clay in his hands, his little

Clara. Taking her innocence would be like taking sweets from a baby.

'Your dadda . . . ?' His voice was husky with the need in him.

'He told me to go to bed. Him and the treasurer were going to the minister's house to talk. They allus do after a concert.'

Her voice was slurred. She was halfway to being drunk, but not too drunk to know what she was doing. This was the way Joe liked his women to be. Pliant and yet in control. The heat rose in him as he looked down the sweetheart neckline of the white dress, seeing the tender hollow between her young developing breasts.

It was then the shame came over him. Jumping up so quickly that the chair rocked violently, he took his cup over to the slopstone and rinsed it under the tap.

'Give me that bottle.' He lifted it up and grimaced at its emptiness. How on earth had they managed to drink a full bottle between them? His legs trembled beneath him, but his gait was steady. 'Now give me that cup.' He tried to take Clara's cup away from her, but before she handed it over she drained it to the dregs. 'Now go to bed.'

She fell into giggles as he helped her to her feet, leaning against him, staring up into his eyes with her face all twisted, the features somehow undefined.

'I do luv you, Joe.'

'Stop saying that!' He had to hold her to stop her falling down. 'You're too big a girl to say that to a fella. For Christ's sake, Clara! Stop saying that!'

'An' you stop swearing. It's wicked to take the name of the Lord in vain.'

She was slurring her words, finding difficulty in getting her tongue round the syllables. He held her from him, looking down into her face with a hopeless expression. She was so beautiful, so young, so very, very young. Her skin had a warmth to it as if she spent hours sitting in the sun, and yet his mother had told him young Clara worked down in the basement of a jobbing printer's in Ainsworth Street, stapling sheets of paper, packing orders, coming home in the evenings with her fingers stained with printer's ink and her eyes smudged with exhaustion.

'An' that's because Seth Haydock wouldn't hear of her going in the mill,' Lily had said. 'At least she'd have had a trade in her fingers as a weaver. Aye, and had some young company. Fancy a bright lass like Clara working all day with two old men and a boy apprentice. I reckon it's a crying shame.'

Putting her from him, Joe buttoned the empty bottle inside his coat. 'I'm going now, but just you think on and grow up, our kid, because I'll be back.' He turned at the door. 'And get to bed. Go on! If your dad comes and catches you like that he'll murder you. An' the next time you have rhubarb make sure it's the kind you put custard on. Right?'

By the time her father came home from drinking his cocoa with the minister she would be in bed sleeping it off. And if Mr Haydock hadn't taken the bottle of wine down from the cupboard in all these years, then he'd more than likely forgotten its existence. Chuckling to himself, Joe patted the bulge in his overcoat. He supposed he ought to call in his mam's house, just to say hello and goodbye, but he'd left money for her in the usual place on the mantelpiece. And besides, the bed he had in mind would be a sight warmer than the slippery horsehair sofa in his mother's living room.

Rhubarb wine . . . Joe laughed to himself as he stepped off the kerb and missed his footing. Who would've thought it? He bet young Clara would have a right head on her the next morning. Whistling through his teeth, Joe turned the corner without a backward glance, narrowly missing bumping into a thickset man wearing a navy blue overcoat, a hard hat set squarely on his forehead.

'Goodnight, Joe.'

''Night, Mr Haydock.'

'Nasty night.'

'For them who have to be out in it.'

Seth walked on, shaking his head. Where Joe West was going at that time of night was none of his business, but if rumours were true then he was heading for a house a few streets away where a young war widow was said to always have a ready welcome for Lily West's wandering boy. Seth quickened his step. It took all sorts, and as far as he knew Joe was good to his mother. He opened the door of his shop and stepped inside. It was none of his business anyroad. Live and let live had always been the code he went by. Skirting the long bench and moving round the counter, Seth walked steadily towards the dividing door, pushing it open with one hand and taking off his hat with the other.

'Clara!' Coming from darkness into light he blinked rapidly. 'What are you doing up at this time?' He unbuttoned the heavy coat. 'You should've gone straight to bed, love. You'll be fit for nothing in the morning.'

Slowly, stretching her arms above her head, Clara stood up from the chair. Her hair was falling over her face and, as Seth stared at her in shocked surprise, she tossed her head to push it back. The sudden movement made her wince and from the vacant expression in her large green eyes he guessed she was trying to get him into focus.

'Oh, it's you, Dadda.' She smiled, and as she did so the upcurve of her lips turned into a grimace. She swayed where she stood, blinking at him as if the soft light from the gas lamp hurt her eyes.

'I feel sick.' She clutched her stomach. 'Oh, Dadda, I'm proper sick.'

Seth managed to lead her over to the slopstone just in time. Holding her head as she vomited, his glance was caught by the two cups on the draining board. Disbelieving, stunned and shaken, he sniffed at the dregs, his own stomach heaving in disbelief as he realized the truth.

Filthy, evil drink! And *two* cups! Seth closed his eyes for a moment, drawing a long breath. The shock was sending waves of prickly heat all down his body.

'Clara!' His voice was a shout. 'Look at me!'

Her small face when she lifted it was pitiful to behold. Eyes, nose and mouth all running moisture, a sour stench coming from her, and yellow stains marking the front of the white cotton dress.

'I will ask Jesus to help me. To keep my heart from sin.'

From somewhere inside his head Seth heard the words she'd sung just a few hours before, standing on the stage like an angel from heaven. A cold hard anger was growing inside him, but gently he wiped her face and led her to the foot of the stairs.

Upstairs in the tiny back bedroom he undressed her, fumbling with the buttons down the front of her high-necked flannelette nightgown, and tucked her into the narrow bed.

'Joe West's been here, hasn't he?' The question was asked in Seth's normal quiet voice, but his heart was hammering in his throat fit to choke him.

'I love Joe. He's going to get me on the stage.' Clara's green eyes were wide and trusting. 'Joe's my friend.' Even as she spoke she was asleep, childish mouth drooping open on a slight snore. The ends of her long hair were sticky with vomit, and with ice-cold control Seth dipped her flannel in the water jug on the marble-topped washstand and wiped the worst away. Then, taking the candlestick in his hand, he limped from the room, reaching the bottom stair before he realized he was still wearing his thick melton overcoat.

The fear was in him. The fear that had never really left him since the day he first heard Clara sing. Shaking now, he tore the coat from his shoulders and flung it to the farthest corner of the room.

His Clara was special – special and different. As different from the girls in the street as chalk from cheese. But she was growing up. He squeezed his eyes tight shut at the recollection of her rounded hips and the high firmness of her young breasts as he'd helped her into her nightdress.

Most Lancashire lasses were bonny. The cold damp climate gave them milk-and-roses complexions, hard work sturdied their limbs, and a down-to-earth humour brightened their eyes.

But his Clara was beautiful. Her distinctive colouring of white-blonde hair and that sun-kissed look to her skin set her apart.

And Joe West had seen all that. He had seen it, and he had

followed her home and given her drink. A lifetime of prejudice, of shunning the evils of the flesh, held Seth in a rigid grip of loathing for Lily West's favourite son.

He couldn't pray. For the first time in his life he could not take his worry and cast it at the feet of his Lord. Going over to the high mantelpiece, he gripped it with both hands and laid his head down on them.

Joe West had got mixed up with stage folk. Actresses, no better than whores. Painted Jezebels. Oh, Seth knew them for what they were . . . Never having set foot in a theatre, he still knew them for what they were.

There was a mill lass from Rochdale. Seth frowned as he tried to remember her name. Gracie Fields. Aye, that was it. There had been a piece in the paper about her not long back. On the stage since she was ten with her mother encouraging her, and singing now in a revue. With a voice as good as any opera star, but burlesquing her songs to get laughs. Living in lodgings no doubt, and mixing up with the kind of folks Joe West counted as his friends.

'Joe West!' Seth spat out the name as if it was an obscenity. If he could have got his hands on Lily West's fourth son at that moment he would have swung for him gladly. 'Cheating, lying,' he muttered. 'Walking into my house as bold as brass, giving Clara drink and putting wrong ideas in her head.' *Knowing* that Seth would see his child laid to rest beside his dead wife in the cemetery before he'd let her leave home and go on the stage.

Kicking out at the dying fire, Seth sent a shower of sparks up the chimney. The anger was seeping from him now, but he wasn't ready yet to go up to his bed. Sitting down in his chair, he lowered his head into his big hands and turned at last to prayer; God had given Clara into his keeping and with His help that trust would never be denied.

'I know she's going to grow up and meet a young man and marry some day,' he whispered, talking as naturally to his Lord as he did to his friends and neighbours. 'But let him be decent and hard-working; maybe with a trade in his fingers, and a good and kind heart to keep and protect her from the Joe Wests of this world. And if there's bad blood in her, may the influence of this house keep her from sin.'

The prayer was a long one, and the tiny red glimmer from the fire had faded into grey ashes before it was finished. But when Seth finally climbed the narrow stairs to his bed his mind was in its normal state of peaceful acceptance once again. Prayers *were* answered, he told himself as he folded his best trousers and laid them neatly beneath his mattress to nip in the crease for chapel the next morning.

Mebbe prayers weren't always answered in the way the supplicant wanted. Kneeling by his bed in his shirt, Seth acknowledged that the prayers for his wife to recover from her illness had gone unheeded. But wasn't it written that 'if we ask anything *according to His will*, He heareth us'? And wasn't it also written that no mischief shall happen to the righteous, but that the wicked shall be filled with evil? And wasn't it true that 'the way of the Lord is strength to the upright: but destruction shall be to the workers of iniquity'? Didn't the Good Book come up with the answer to everything?

Seth rose to his feet. And was comforted.

He was very weary. It had been a long day and tomorrow was the Sabbath. Closing his eyes for sleep, Seth suddenly opened them wide again.

Joe West would get his come-uppance. 'Vengeance is mine, saith the Lord.' Seth's normally soft voice was rough as he spoke the words aloud, hearing the echo of them in his ears as he drifted off into a troubled sleep.

The very next week, walking home from work, Clara was hurrying along the street, head bent against a driving wind, when she bumped into a tall young man walking just as swiftly in the opposite direction.

'Sorry!' They both spoke together, stepping backwards to move round each other.

'Clara! Little Clara Haydock! It *is* you, isn't it?'

She hesitated, but only for a second. There was no mistaking the thick fair hair, the twinkle in the amber eyes. But since she'd last seen him, John Maynard, the son of the

Church of England minister, had grown to well over six feet in height. Clara had to lean her head back to look up at him.

'It's me all right.'

Having been brought up with the West boys as her constant companions, she showed no sudden blush, not a trace of self-consciousness in her manner.

'Just look at you!' she laughed. 'Long mop and bucket, that's me and you. You're even taller than Joe.'

'Joe?'

'Joe West. You *remember*. He was in the same class as you before you took the scholarship and went on to the grammar school.' Clara's woollen tam-o'-shanter was dropping over her eyes so she pushed it back impatiently. 'He was a prisoner-of-war in Germany, but he's back now. Working in a job to do with the stage. He knows all the stars.'

She looked so bossily important that John laughed out loud. Of course, that was it. This was the kid with the unusual singing voice. The one his father still talked about. Suddenly he made up his mind. It was cold standing there on the windy street, but he wanted to go on talking to her. She was only a kid, but more lovely he reckoned than any of the stars she was so obviously struck on. What colour would you call her hair? Silver? Blond? And her eyes were as green as the sea with the sun shining on it.

'I live just round the corner. Up that street with the Toc H building on the corner. Why don't you come home with me and say hello to my pa? He was only wondering the other day what had become of you.' He grinned. 'What *has* become of you, Clara? What are you doing now?'

She looked down at her feet, frowning. She had told her father she would be late home, but the job they were working on had finished earlier than her boss had calculated, so she wouldn't be missed. Not just yet awhile.

'Might as well,' she said cockily. 'But I mustn't stop, else me dad'll come looking for me. With a big stick!'

As they walked along she glanced sideways at the tall figure in the light grey flannels and navy blue blazer. She'd always liked John Maynard, ever since he stuck up for her on that first awful day at school. He talked posh, too. His very *difference* intrigued her and always had, she reminded herself, recalling the way he'd stood out against the other boys in his shirt and tie, worn with and not instead of a pullover.

'I'm a dab hand with a stapler,' she told him. 'A thousand sheets an hour I can do, but my boss is too mean to pay me on piecework. When he takes his wallet out on a Friday, a moth flies out!' She was having to take little running steps to keep up with John's long strides, but still had enough breath to keep talking. 'You went to the university, didn't you? Were you the top of the class at the grammar school? I know you were at my school. Are you going to be a minister like your father?'

'No fear.' John grinned down at her. 'I'm not holy enough for that. Not by a long chalk. No, I went straight from college into the Royal Flying Corps, but I missed the best of the war. I'm in civil aviation now.'

'Flying planes?' Clara stopped to gaze up at the sky. 'Flamin' 'enery! Honest? You're not 'aving me on?'

John needed no further encouragement. 'Nothing to it, really.' Taking her by the arm he walked her across the street to a house set back from the road, and opened the door with a key from his jacket pocket. 'I was flying last week with my boss. A Major Watterson. A nice bloke. Got the DFC during the war.' He spoke with a studied nonchalance. 'We touched a hundred miles an hour, taking fourteen passengers to Paris. Two hours from taking off to landing. Quite a nice trip, actually.'

'Flippin' 'enery!'

Stuck for words for once, Clara followed him into the house, down a dark panelled hall, through to a large sitting room at the back, trying hard not to stare around her. A bowl of fresh flowers was reflected in an oval gilt mirror, and the overriding smell was one of wax polish and the sharp tang of some kind of disinfectant. There was actually a carpet on the stairs, she noted, crimson and blue, fastened down with gleaming brass stair rods.

'Mother?' John led her over to an auburn-haired woman sitting on a wide chesterfield. 'You've heard Pa talk about a girl who used to sing for him on his school visits? Clara Haydock? Well, here she is.'

Elaine Maynard put aside the pile of sheet music she'd been marking with a pencil and smiled. 'Hello, Clara.'

She lowered her eyes for a second in an instinctive attempt to hide her surprise. This beautiful young girl – Clara, the clogger's child? Rumours, whispers, memories of a scandal – or had it been a scandal? – surfaced for an unguarded moment. Then a lifetime of discretion, first as a vicar's daughter then as a vicar's wife, steadied her smile. She held out her hand.

'I've heard such a lot about you, my dear. My husband was so impressed by your voice. He was only wondering the other day what you've been doing since you left school. I think he misses you.' She patted the cushion by her side. 'I believe you sang a solo on Anniversary Sunday at your chapel? My cleaning lady told me she'll never forget it.' She picked up the sheet music again. 'I suppose John told you I take pupils for the piano and violin?'

Clara nodded, too overwhelmed to admit she hadn't known. John Maynard liked talking best about himself, she decided. He was standing there now, jiggling loose change in his trouser pockets, looking, she thought, like a wet weekend.

A totally uncharacteristic shyness was making her feel hot all over. She wanted to gaze round the room, but knew it would be bad manners. In the whole of her life, she told herself dramatically, she had never seen a room like this. There were long velvet curtains at the tall windows; nothing as sordid as a paper blind. There was a rose-patterned carpet beneath her feet instead of oilcloth and rag rugs. But best of all, over by the window stood a grand piano, with a vase of flowers on its polished surface, flanked by a marble bust of a man with bulging eyelids and a sad expression on his cold chiselled face.

She wasn't to know that by any standards the vicarage sitting room was sparsely furnished on a stipend that bordered on an insult. All she knew was that sitting on the wide sofa cushions was like sitting on a cloud after the horsehair prickliness of the sofa at home. And it went without saying that anyone owning a grand piano was bound to be rich.

Elaine Maynard was at a loss what to talk about next. The girl seemed dumb-struck by shyness. What a strange little creature she was, with the too large floppy tammy perched on the back of her head. And her hair was a most unusual shade – a cross between blond and silver. For a moment she felt angry with her son for producing the clogger's unusual child as some kind of trophy.

'Would you like me to play something for you?' The offer came from a kind heart, as if Elaine had known the one thing which would put the small girl in her rag-bag clothes at ease. She held out the music. 'I've been scoring this for the piano.'

'Oh, yes.' Clara nodded again, averting her profile from John's wink. How dare he try to make her laugh! Couldn't he see she *liked* his mother and wanted to hear her play? He really wasn't half as grown up or as nice as Joe, she decided. A bit immature. For his age, that was.

Elaine glanced at the marble bust on top of the piano. Chopin? Yes. One of his livelier pieces maybe. Her fingers skimmed over the keys.

Clara listened, her eyes half closed, her expression rapt. This was real music, the kind her untutored mind had been completely starved of. Chamber music, she supposed vaguely, the kind Joe and his brothers would have laughed to scorn. John had come to sit beside her; he was nudging her, but she refused to look at him. The music was saying things to her, transporting her to a realm of delight she'd never dreamed existed. Her fingers clasped and unclasped as the crashing chords filled the room with vibrant sound. When it was finished she sat quite still, not knowing what to say – knowing that whatever she said could never express the way she felt.

'Now!' Elaine swivelled round on the piano stool. 'Will you sing something for me, Clara?' She smiled. 'My son is a great disappointment to me. He hasn't a musical bone in his body.'

'Clara doesn't want to sing.' John pushed the flop of his thick fair hair back off his forehead with an impatient hand. He was wishing he hadn't brought Clara Haydock back with him now. He was wishing – why not admit it – that his week's leave of absence was over. There was nothing to do in this godforsaken town, anyway. How his parents had stuck it all these years he didn't know. They were developing northern mentalities, he supposed. He watched in disbelief as Clara got up and walked towards the piano. As if drawn there by a bloody magnet.

He stared down at his feet, sudden boredom settling on him like a descending cloud. The war had ended just too soon as far as he'd been concerned. Two reconnaissance flights, that was all he'd managed; and one of those a dead loss, as the Jerries had left nothing worth photographing. Sometimes he felt the blood was pounding in his veins so strongly it would blow his head off. 'Calm down, Maynard!' the Major would tell him. 'There's no call for daredevil tactics in this kind of flying. It's passengers and mail you'll be carrying, not bombs.'

'I'll just go upstairs . . . ' He left the room without them noticing he'd gone.

When Clara burst into the clogger's little front-room shop her green eyes shone as if a candle had been lit behind them. She was out of breath and clutched her side where a sharp pain stabbed behind her ribs.

'Dadda! I've been to the minister's house. You know, Mr Maynard who used to come to school on a Monday.' Taking off her tammy, she wrestled with the buttons down the front of her coat as if she couldn't get it off quickly enough. 'Mrs Maynard teaches the piano, an' she asked me to sing for her, an' I sang "Once Again 'Tis Joyous May", the hymn I sang on Anniversary Sunday.' She took a necessary breath. 'An' she said she would teach me to play.' Her eyes were filled with a desperate pleading as she came to lean against Seth's knee. 'I told her we'd get a piano, Dadda. We *will* get one, won't we?'

'Steady on, lass.' Seth put down the clog he was mending and rubbed his eyes. 'Now. Let's have a proper story. You say you went to the minister's house? To deliver some printing?'

Shaking her head so that the long fall of hair flew, Clara sighed a deep sigh of exasperation.

'I met John. You *know*. He was in the same class as Joe before he won the scholarship. Now he flies aeroplanes.' She dismissed all that with a wave of her hand. 'His mother says she'll give me two lessons a week for sixpence a time, but we have to have a piano. An' I told her we'd get one. Right away!' She patted her father's hand. 'Oh, not a new one. I know we can't afford a new one. Just a piano. Any old piano, as long as it plays.' Her eyes glowed with passion. 'I'll be able to accompany meself when I sing, Dadda. An' I'll be playing proper music. Chopin,' she said wildly. 'Mrs Maynard has him on the piano. Dadda! You're not listening to me!'

Slowly Seth got to his feet. 'Oh aye, I'm listening, lass, but what you're saying doesn't make much sense.' Limping over to the door, he shot the bolt. 'Now let's go through and have our tea. It's all ready. Then you can tell me again. I thought Chopin was dead, and yet you say he was sitting on the vicar's wife's piano?'

It wasn't much of a joke, and Clara refused to laugh. The praise Elaine Maynard had heaped on her head after she'd finished singing still echoed in her brain. 'Perfect pitch,' she'd said. 'A voice that cries out to be trained,' she'd told her husband, jumping up to greet him as he came in from outside, smiling at Clara and going over to warm his hands at the leaping fire.

'A piano,' Seth said, as if it was a word he'd never heard before. 'And sixpence twice a week for lessons. Does this Mrs Maynard think money grows on trees?'

For a long time now making ends meet had been a constant worry to Seth. Since the war had ended clogs were losing their popularity. Young mill workers were turning to shoes, saving up and paying over ten shillings for flimsy things that gave them corns and bunions and no proper spread for their toes. He stared across the table at Clara,

81

sensed the impatience boiling inside her, saw the desperate pleading in her eyes, and hesitating was lost.

'And there'll be no more silly talk about going on the stage?'

Clara's large eyes widened in amazement. 'I told you! I'll be playing proper music. Minuets and things,' she added vaguely. 'John told me his mother could have been a concert pianist if she hadn't got married.'

'That's the stage.'

'It'll be *years* before I'm good enough for that!' Clara laughed him to scorn. 'Ten years at least.' Spearing a forkful of tripe, she popped it into her mouth, chewing vigorously. 'Mrs Maynard says to be good enough for that you have to practise eight hours a day.' Putting the fork down she flexed her hands. 'Mrs Maynard says I've got piano fingers. I can span more'n an octave, Dad. Mrs Maynard says . . . '

Seth was doing sums in his mind. The small store of coins in the tin box beneath his bed had been sadly depleted during the past two years. The rent had gone up to eight shillings a week; the blockmaker he dealt with had put his prices up, and Seth would have nothing to do with the newfangled machine-made soles. They were made of beech and not alder for one thing, and for another a machine-made sole couldn't cater for any deformity in a foot. Alder was cut in the spring or summer when the sap was high in the tree, so that it absorbed damp. And who needed protection from the damp more than weavers standing at their looms on floors oozing water?

'Tha'll ruin theself, Seth,' a clogger from the other side of town had told him. 'Machines'll tek us all over in the end. Why not make friends with them instead of trying to fight 'em? An' forget about brass nails. Iron tacks do the job. Master craftsmen are a dying breed, Seth. Tha must know that.'

'It's not in me to cut corners,' Seth had said. 'My clogs'll stand up to the worst the weather can chuck at them, aye, and fit like gloves as well.'

'High principles don't fill empty bellies,' were his friend's parting words.

'I can start lessons straight away, Mrs Maynard says . . . '
Clara was still talking, waving her fork to give emphasis to
what she was saying, fixing Seth with the intensity of her
gaze. 'But I won't be able to practise . . . '

'Till we get a piano,' Seth interrupted, smiling. 'Cheese
and flippin' rice, how have we lived all this while without
one standing over there with the sofa pushed up against it,
except when a certain young lady does her practising?
Answer me that afore I die of amazement!'

Clara's arms round his neck and the hug she gave him
almost knocked him off his chair.

'Give over,' Seth protested. 'What are you trying to do,
Clara Haydock? Throttle the life out of your poor old
dad?'

It wasn't surprising that it was one of the West boys who
found out where an ancient upright piano was to be had for
the princely sum of £4. What Alec's rake-off would be for the
transaction Seth could only guess at, but he knew there'd be
something in it for the black-haired lad who had been out of
work for the past eighteen months.

'It's on the first floor of the YMCA, Mr Haydock,' Alec
told him. 'They've been given a better one, but this plays all
right.' He winked at Clara. 'Our Walter knows where he can
borrow a handcart to get it to your house. For fourpence an
hour,' he added. 'Dirt cheap at the price.'

'I'm glad you live across the street instead of next door to
us,' he told Clara as they walked through the streets the next
night. 'How much do you want to bet me that Mrs Bates
next to you does a flit afore long?'

They were a strange quartet hurrying with the handcart
along the darkened streets. Alec and Walter trundling the
cart, with Seth limping alongside on the pavement, and
Clara almost skipping in her excitement. A lone policeman
on his beat stepped out into the road and demanded to
know where the West boys thought they were going at that
time of night with an empty handcart. Seeing Seth, he
stepped back onto the pavement and, touching a finger to
his helmet, apologized.

'Begging your pardon, Mr Haydock. I didn't know you were with these two.'

'On official business,' said Alec cheekily. 'On behalf of Miss Haydock 'ere.'

'That larnt him,' said Walter, picking up his shaft again and doing little running steps along the cobbles. 'Frightening innocent folks like that.'

When Seth saw the piano, heavy dark mahogany, with ornate brass candlesticks on either side of the ivory keyboard, his first reaction was to wonder how on earth it had ever been manhandled up the single flight of stairs, along the corridor and into this large concert room.

'Well, it didn't *grow* here, Mr Haydock.' Alec knelt down on the floorboards and worked the pedals up and down with his hands. 'There's casters here all right, but they're rusted in. Reckon this bugger's been sitting here since Adam were a lad.' Getting to his feet, he grinned at Clara. 'Now why couldn't you have decided to learn the mouth organ? We could've carried that home in us pocket.'

'You two at that end.' Seth touched Clara lightly on her shoulder. 'We'll get it home, love.' He scratched his head. 'It's somehow bigger and heavier than I had visions of it being, but we'll manage.' He nodded at Walter. 'You help your brother at that end, and I'll back out with my end. Clara, you keep out of the way.'

Watching them straining to move the piano, Clara was struck all at once by the fragility of her father. During the past year or so he seemed to have shrunk, so that the nose on his strong face looked bigger, more bony. He was wearing the flat cap he'd worn for years to do his clogging, and beneath it his hair showed in thick greying tufts, giving him the appearance of an old man.

Alec and Walter were laughing as they pushed, but her father's forehead was already beaded with sweat, the veins sticking out as he struggled. All at once Clara wanted to tell him to leave the piano where it was, to forget the whole thing. Just to stop looking so ill and tortured, hurting his bad leg with every laboured step.

By now they were outside the big room, out on the wide

landing, the piano moving more easily.

'We haven't *lifted* it yet,' Clara heard Alec mutter. 'Want to bet we're all in the infirmary with a rupture apiece this time tomorrow?'

'The only way will be to turn it on its side.' At the top of the uncarpeted stairs Seth spat on his hands and rubbed them together. 'You two lads hold it back while I guide it down. Slow. Step by step.' He glanced over his shoulder at the long flight leading down to the tiled hall. 'Once down with it we'll be all right. Ready?'

'Careful! Oh, please. Do be careful!' Clara's plea was a whisper inside her head.

Seth peered round the end of the piano. 'Up with it, lads. Watch it! Cheese and flippin' rice, but it's a weight.'

'Got it, Mr Haydock.' Alec's gruff voice was subdued now, devoid of laughter. 'Sure you wouldn't like me to come down and take the weight with you? Clara and Walter could hang on to this end.'

Clara can keep out of it.' The piano was now on its side. They were edging it inch by inch towards the top stairs . . .

'The ruddy candlesticks are going to catch on the bannister. We should've levered it more towards the wall.' Alec's voice had a hint of panic in it.

'Up with it. Now!' Seth took a step backwards, found his bad leg wasn't strong enough to sustain him, and called out, 'Hold it! Hold it!'

Desperately the two boys tried to cling on, but the cumbersome piano, past the point of no return, toppled forwards. As though filmed in slow motion, it rolled over, sliding down the stairs, taking Seth with it.

'Dadda! Dadda!'

The jangling sound froze the blood in Clara's veins. The boys were there already, climbing over the piano, struggling to lift it while she stood looking down, her hands clasped over her mouth in a soundless scream.

'He's all right!' Walter's face, uplifted to her, was white with shock. 'It's not got him. It's only his arm and his hand.'

'We'll get you free, Mr Haydock.' Alec scrabbled at the piano as if he could forcibly lift it from where it rested, trapping Seth's right arm from the elbow against the wall.

'Dadda!' Squeezing herself past the piano, Clara knelt down and took her father's head on her lap. His face was as chalk-white as if the blood had been siphoned from it, but he was fully conscious as he looked up at her.

'I'm all right, chuck.' His pale eyes were glazed with pain. 'Get this thing off me, lads. Then get me home.'

The place had seemed to be deserted, but now the hallway was filled with people.

'It's wedged itself fast.'

'No room to turn it.'

'Call the Fire Brigade.'

'Loosen his collar.'

'Run and get a drop of brandy from the pub.'

'Oh, dear God. Just look at his hand!'

When they freed him at last, Seth's right hand hung limply from his wrist. Even as they stared it swelled, the blood pouring from a jagged tear in the palm where one of the candlesticks had pierced the skin, bursting the flesh to expose the fatty globules underneath.

Clara, held back by kindly arms, cried without making a sound. Seth's teeth were clenched hard together as he fought the agonizing pain. Yet when they brought the brandy he turned his head away.

'He's praying,' somebody said. 'A nip of the 'ard stuff'd do him more good than any prayer.'

Clara whirled round, but the sudden movement brought the floor up to hit her smack between the eyes.

'You want to keep your gob shut, missus.' Alec put both arms round the fainting girl. 'Here, gie us that brandy. Over 'ere.'

When the ambulance came and they lifted Seth onto a stretcher, a man stopped Alec on his way to the door.

'What about that piano, son? It can't stop there.'

Alec stared at him in disbelief. As the little crowd gasped in amazement he told the man exactly what he could do with the piano. In so many words.

'There's no call for language like that.' The man looked round him for moral support. 'It can't stop there. It's broken beyond repair as far as I can see.'

'Then chop it up first afore you do with it what me brother told you to do,' said Walter. 'Piece by piece, and I 'ope it 'urts. Like 'ell.'

'You go with Clara,' he told Alec. 'I'll take the cart back.'

'It's surprising what they can do these days.' The ambulance man was very kind on the way to the infirmary. 'They'll patch your father's hand up as good as new.'

But even as he said it, he knew it wasn't true. And the small girl with the big green eyes knew it too. By the way she just looked at him and said nothing, it was obvious she knew that every bone in her father's right hand was splintered and broken, the sinews torn beyond repair.

'He were the best clogger in town,' she whispered as if to herself. 'The best clogger in the whole world, my dad were.'

Six

Clara saw the man smoking a cigarette lounging against the wall the minute she stepped out of the little jobbing printer's front office into the street. She hurried past, head bent, sparing him no more than a cursory glance. If he – whoever he happened to be – was daft enough to stand there getting wet through, then that was his business. But when she heard his footsteps behind her, she quickened her own.

Fumbling in the crown of her felt hat, she pulled out a long hatpin, holding it in front of her like a dagger. When the footsteps slowed to match her own, she whirled round.

'Who do you think you are, following me?' She brandished the pin. 'I'll use it on you if you don't go away. Who *are* you, anyroad?'

They had come out of the rainswept darkness, into the light of a gas lamp. The man took off his trilby hat, sweeping it in front of him in an exaggerated bow.

'Clara! Little Clara Haydock! Don't say you've forgotten me already?'

At one time, he told himself, she would have hurled herself into his arms, covering his face with childish kisses. But now he stood there before her, dismayed when she didn't laugh, stunned by the thinness of her, shocked by the dull expression in her eyes. Holding her by the shoulders, he shook her none too gently.

'What's up with you, our kid? I told you I'd come back, didn't I?' Pulling her into his arms, he strained her against him. 'You know I always turn up sooner or later, don't you?'

Recognition brought no change in her manner. When he tried to kiss her, the push she gave him almost sent him reeling.

'That was *three* years ago, Joe West! Three flamin' years.' Anger choked her. She speared the hatpin into place again with a furious jab. 'Don't you care that your mother's been eating her heart out for a sight of you? Don't you even *know* that she's been ill with the pneumonia?' Clara's voice rose. 'An' what about your Alec, left with an iron on his leg after being buried alive in a pit fall out at Burnley? An' do you care a sausage that your Walter's got a girl into trouble and him not quite seventeen?' She pointed at the suitcase in his hand. 'You've not been home yet, have you? I bet you came here straight from the station.'

'To see you, sweetheart.' Joe turned her round and, walking jauntily, hurried her along the wet pavement. 'Don't be hard on me, love. I've never missed sending the money home. Once a month, regular, more money than me mam's seen in the whole of her natural.' He grinned. 'Joe's been doing all right for himself down in London.' They were into darkness again and he had to twist sideways to see the expression on her face. 'Didn't they tell you about the money?'

"'Course they told me!' Her voice dripped scorn. 'Pound notes in an envelope. No letter, no address, no nothing. You think money means everything, Joe West. Shove some notes in an envelope, then forget.' Her voice was shaking now. 'You know you've always been your mother's favourite. When you was reported missing in France she went out in the yard and banged her head against the wall. Till the blood came. Then you disappear again, making her think you don't care a tuppenny bun.'

This time when he pulled her into his arms she made no move to push him away. It was like holding a little bird, he thought, all small bones and softness. Her hair, escaping from the atrocious hat, tickled his chin.

'Was it *you* thinking I didn't care?' he whispered. 'Was it you really waiting for a letter?' Tilting her chin he looked into her eyes, surprised to see they were filled with tears.

'You know I can't spell. You know I was always bottom of the class. Writing letters isn't for me, love. You know me better 'n that.'

He'd forgotten how fierce she was, how loyal. If he'd thought about her at all it had been to remember her voice, that glorious singing voice, the like of which he'd never heard, not even on the London stage.

Keeping a protective arm around her, he guided her across the street, bending his head to whisper in her ear, 'Are you still rocking 'em in the aisles of the chapel with your singing, love?' He squeezed her closer to him. 'Want to know who came and sat in the stalls at the Palace Theatre down in London last week?'

'Who, then?'

'Charles B. Cochran, that's who!'

'An' who's he when he's at 'ome?'

Joe pretended to faint. He staggered along the pavement with a hand to his head then wheeled to face her, pointing an accusing finger.

'You mean to tell me you're going on the stage one day and you've never heard of Charles B. Cochran? My dear young lady, he's only the most famous impresario in the country, that's all! He's spotted more talent than you've had 'ot dinners.'

Clara was beginning to perk up a little. Half the things Joe told her she didn't believe, but he'd always been able to make her laugh. She could listen to Joe talking for ever.

'It was one of the great man's auditions. Savvy? He was just sitting there, leaning back in his seat, when a girl around your age danced for him with an umbrella almost as big as herself. She had a funny blob of a nose and a real cheeky face, and you should've seen C. B. sit up when she did her little piece. I can tell you now, that kid'll have her name in lights before long. Old C. B.'ll have her out of the chorus faster than your dad knocks nails in his clogs. She's not got much of a stage name, though.' Joe thought for a moment. 'Jessie Matthews. Bet he makes her change that.'

Suddenly, knocking his arm from her own, Clara turned to face him, squaring up to him like a boxer in the ring.

90

'I'm not coming any farther with you, Joe. I wasn't going home anyroad. I'm going to me Bible class.'

'Without your tea?'

She was very dignified as she glared at him. 'There's such a thing as food for the soul, Joe West.'

He grinned. 'D'you reckon Jesus'll have a chip butty waiting for you, then?'

She was walking away from him and he'd be damned if he'd run after her. Food for the soul, indeed . . . Picking up his case Joe turned on his heel, striding off in the opposite direction.

Only natural, he supposed, that Seth Haydock's daughter would go religious. Some of the Bible thumping was bound to have rubbed off on her. A loud burst of singing from a public house on the corner made him slow his steps, but he carried on. What a dump this town was. Half past six and hardly anybody about. Pubs and the odd theatre, that was all. A seat in the gods and a hot roasted spud from the cart on the Boulevard. Most folks would call that a good night out! It was like living in the Dark Ages up here.

There was no light streaming from the clogger's shop. Joe frowned. That was unusual. Mr Haydock always worked late, mending clogs for mill workers needing them the next morning. Seth's hunched figure, sitting on his stool, bathed in the dim light from the overhanging gas bracket, was part of the street.

Joe stopped, irresolute, shifting the weight of his case from one hand to the other. A peculiar sense of unease settled on him, as if someone had dropped a wet blanket over his shoulders. He was in no hurry to go home. After what Clara had told him he could anticipate the re-criminations, the tearful emotional welcome. Besides, there'd been something strange about Clara, some terrible change in her, quite apart from the religious thing. And if he'd been three years away, another ten minutes or so wasn't going to make no difference.

Opening the door of the shop, he stepped inside the darkened interior. From memory he skirted the long bench, moving sure-footed to the dividing door.

'Mr Haydock?' He was calling out as he entered the back room, and even before the words were out they died away in his throat.

The room was as bare as a prison cell. Gone were the rag rug and the red chenille cloth on the table. Joe had smelt poverty many times before, and it was there now, rancid and sickly sweet in his nostrils. The room was clean and tidy, but the black fireplace was dull, its grate empty, even though the man in the rocking chair crouched over it with hands extended as if warming them at a blaze.

'Oh, my God!'

It was the sight of Seth's right hand that brought the involuntary exclamation to Joe's lips. Red and stunted, shaped like the claw of some great bird, the big hand was curled in on itself, the once nimble fingers tucked grotesquely out of sight. Joe knew in that heart-stopping moment that Mr Haydock would never again hold his cutting block with one hand, operating a sharp knife with the other; never cut leather laces with a steady hand.

'It's me, Joe West,' he said, moving forward, candlelight catching the sheen of his black hair, showing up the healthy glow of his face, giving him in that street of white, pinched faces the appearance of a being from another planet.

Seth stared at him, the blood warming his thin cheeks. Three years of pain and frustration, when he'd been forced to realize the use of his right hand had gone and with it his living, had seared the sweetness from his soul. For a while, after he came home from the infirmary, he'd tried to work left-handed, holding his last between his knees. But even a child could have told him that clogging was a two-handed job. One day he'd thrown his hammer straight through the shop window, narrowly missing a small boy playing whip and top on the pavement.

'You . . . ' he whispered, getting up from his chair to stand not a foot away from Joe. 'How dare you come here!' The words came from the clenched brown teeth, sharp as the crack of a whip. 'Haven't you done enough? What are you here for? To gloat on your handiwork?'

Joe stepped back as the ugly claw of a hand was thrust into

his face. He moistened his lips. God knew he'd been blamed for more than a few things in his life, with good cause most of the time, but this?

'I'm sorry, Mr Haydock, but I don't know what you're talking about.' He tried a smile, then knew at once it was a mistake.

There was a cold black fury in Seth now. As if it had happened only yesterday, he saw Clara being sick over by the slopstone from the drink this man had given her. He heard her babbling about wanting to go on the stage, and he saw himself agreeing to buy the piano so she could learn to play proper music and forget the fancy notions put in her head by this man grinning at him as if he found the whole thing a joke.

He saw again the piano toppling over, felt its crushing weight on him, trapping his hand, bursting it open like a tomato thrown against a wall. He saw his Clara growing thinner by the week as she tried to manage on what she earned. He saw their bits and pieces going to the salerooms and his precious tools being sold for a pittance.

All this time the anger had been held tight inside him, veiled by the prayers he still mouthed, cloaked in a false sense of acceptance that it was God's will. Clara believed that. She was the one who had the faith now. Riddled with guilt, she blamed herself for the way he was. Because of the piano. The towering massive mahogany piano with its brass candlesticks and its jangling yellowed ivory keys.

'It's all your doing!' The shiny red claw was thrust into Joe's face again. 'You began it! Putting ideas into my child's head . . . '

The nearness of the hand was making Joe feel sick. The clogger had gone off his chump. Must have. In another minute he'd be starting a fight, and if he thought Joe West was going to spar with someone more than twice his age and half wick into the bargain, then he'd another think coming. Grasping Seth's arm, carefully avoiding the dreadful hand, Joe held him off easily.

'Now come on, Mr Haydock. Why don't you sit down and tell me what all this is about?'

As though the puny little man were a puppet on a string, Joe dangled him at arm's length. Seth's face was purple with fury; the veins in his neck bulged and his pale eyes protruded from their sockets. Once he had believed that the meek inherited the earth, but it wasn't true. It was folk like Joe West, who lied and schemed to get what he wanted, who did the inheriting.

'Go away!' he shouted, spittle forming at the corners of his mouth. 'Go back to where you came from. To doing God knows what. Break your mother's heart, but keep away from me and mine!'

Joe's lightly tanned face was a study in open-mouthed disbelief. With his total lack of understanding came the touch of fear, and when Joe was afraid his reaction was to grin.

'Steady on, Mr Haydock. There's no call for you to upset yourself. Just calm down and tell me what I'm supposed to have done. Man to man.'

The grin was the last straw. Seth heard the words spluttering from his own mouth, but the power to control them had gone. He knew that he was being held lightly and the knowledge drove him to even greater fury. At one time he would have been more than a match for this young man. Not all that long ago his arm muscles had bulged with animal strength. With a twist of his wrist he could have thrown Joe West away from him like so much driftwood. But the arm Joe was holding couldn't have knocked a fly off a rice pudding. Seth heard his heart pounding and blinked to clear the mist forming in front of his eyes. All his pent-up anger, the frustration of three long years, surfaced. At last he'd found someone to blame. Murder was in his heart, filling his soul with blood.

'You . . . ! You . . . !'

To Joe's astonished gaze it seemed as if the little man swelled like a toad, until his eyes rolled back and his mouth grew slack. When Joe let go of the wrist, Seth's body slumped, sliding down in slow motion to lie in a heap on the floor.

Before Joe knelt down to feel for a pulse he knew that the clogger was dead.

His first instinct was to run. As a boy he'd always run from trouble, and for most of the time without being caught. Putting his brown trilby on his head and picking up his case, he backed away from the inert figure sprawled with wide staring eyes on the floor.

He had done nothing. He'd never even considered striking a blow. But who would believe him? Certainly not a policeman, who would find out that Joe West had done time more than once. That would be the first thing they would turn up. Trust them. An inborn loathing of anything to do with the law surfaced, lending wings to his heels as he stumbled through the shop, jarring his knee against the counter, sending the clogger's stool clattering, with its three legs pointing ceilingwards. Pausing only to upend it, he opened the door and stepped out into the street, where the drifting rain was a blessing on his face. All he had to do was keep his mouth shut and he'd be in the clear.

The cobbles were greasy to the soles of his polished shoes. The doors of the little houses closed against the weather, the front parlours darkened, families crouched over fires in back living rooms. Nothing would happen. Not till Clara came home. With his hand to the iron knocker set high in the front door of his mother's house, Joe paused.

In his mind's eye he saw Clara groping her way through the clogger's shop, through to the bare candlelit room at the back, calling out to her father, maybe falling over the thing lying with its legs bent up and that terrible hand clenched in a last gesture of defiance.

Slowly Joe lowered his hand from the door knocker. Slowly he retraced his steps across the street, his agile mind working fast. There was a shop doorway just round the corner and he'd wait in there, then when Clara came along the street he would step out and pretend he'd called in the pub. She'd be ready to believe that of him. Shivering, Joe turned up his collar. That way he could see her home, crack on he'd like a word with her father; go inside with her and be there when . . .

Desperately he craved for a cigarette but controlled the longing. Suppose the match illuminated his face and somebody passing by recognized him? Suppose they checked and found he hadn't been in the pub after all? Suppose, suppose and bloody suppose! What a mess it all was. And what a homecoming! Shifting his weight from one foot to the other, Joe stared out from his shelter at the rain bouncing up from the cobbles, at the lamps shedding pools of light at regular intervals down the long street.

'Clara . . . ' he muttered to himself. 'Oh, little Clara. What'll happen to you now?'

From now on she'd be alone. Joe straightened his shoulders, a glow of something resembling righteousness flooding his heart. Not as long as he, Joe West, was around would she be alone. The resolution, coming unbidden, drove out the fear.

When Clara came at last, hurrying, head bent, on the other side of the street, Joe was his own man again.

'I'll see you home, love,' he told her. 'On this nasty neet.'

'I thought you'd've forgotten how to talk like that,' she giggled, making no protest when he took her by the arm, 'you living down south where they speak posh.'

'I'll just come inside with you and say hello to your dad,' Joe told her as they got to the little shop.

And his voice was as steady as a rock.

Seven

'He wasn't your real father, Clara. You knew that, didn't you?'

Joe was sitting on the edge of the table swinging his legs and smoking a cigarette. In the six months since Seth Haydock had died – of a pulmonary embolism, according to the death certificate – Joe had stayed in the north. He had offered Clara money which she'd refused, and food which she'd accepted, and now that the first terrible weeks of grief were over the colour had come back to her cheeks.

'I know he wasn't my real father.' She was down on her knees by the blazing fire, blackleading the grate, and the sight of her small bottom moving from side to side as she polished was giving Joe wrong ideas. 'He told me a long time ago that he'd adopted me, but it made no difference.' Clara sat back on her heels and pushed the hair back from her flushed face. 'I couldn't have loved him more.'

Joe lit another cigarette from the stub of the first. 'But don't you ever wonder who your real mam and dad are? You don't look like nobody round here, not with your skin that peachy shade.' He grinned. 'You look as if you've just come back from your holidays.'

'Holidays?'

'Yes, you know. The sea.' Joe made an undulating movement with his hand. 'You've never seen the sea, have you, our kid?'

'Have you?'

'Saw it a while ago, as a matter of fact, when I was working in Blackpool at the Queen's Theatre. The sea's big and wet. Nothing to it, really.'

'Then I've not missed owt, have I?'

It was a Saturday afternoon, Clara's cleaning-up day, and she wanted to get on. Methodically, just as Seth had showed her, she stowed away the two brushes, one for the blacklead and the other for polishing, in an old biscuit tin. 'Now, if you'll shift yourself I'll give that table a bit of a scrub. The water in the kettle should be hot enough now.'

Amused at her industry, Joe moved to the rocking chair. 'Want to earn a tidy bit of money tonight, love?'

Clara looked round from pouring hot water into the enamel bowl in the slopstone. 'Doing what?'

'Singing.' Joe leaned forward, bringing the chair with him. 'Seven shillings for two songs, and an extra one and sixpence if you get an encore.'

'You're 'aving me on.'

'God's truth, sweetheart.'

'On the stage?' Clara's green eyes were troubled. 'Me dad would never have let me go on the stage.' She took up a scrubbing brush and rubbed a bar of yellow soap along its length. 'He was set against that.'

'But he's dead, love!' At the expression on her face Joe waved his hand in a gesture of apology. 'Listen to me, Clara Haydock; you know what I do for a living?'

'You mean as well as playing cards for money?'

Again the wide grin. 'OK, OK. So I do make a bob or two on the side. No, I mean what I do as an entertainment secretary.' He raised his voice over the sound of heavy scrubbing. 'A sort of agent, that's what I am. Going round the clubs on the lookout for new acts. On commission, of course. The customers want more than to sit and drink these days, though they can knock back plenty of that. No, what they like is a bit of a laugh, and a bit of a singsong.' He set the chair rocking with his foot. 'You'd go down a treat.'

'Never!'

Joe nodded to himself. She was interested all right. He'd sensed that by the way she'd stopped that infernal scrubbing for a second. Now if she didn't go and bring God into it, he was halfway there.

'Wicked men go to those clubs, Joe. Me dad used to tell

me about them. He wouldn't have set foot in one, not for the town hall clock.'

'Wicked men!' Joe's tone expressed righteous indignation. 'Men who've done a hard week's grind in the mill or down the mine? Sitting there in their pit clothes, them that haven't had time to go home after their weekend shift to change?' He took a deep breath, weighing his words carefully. 'Your dad was a good man, love, and I liked him a lot, but he did put some damn fool ideas in your nut. There's more ways of praising God than getting down on your knees in chapel. I bet God likes a bit of a laugh on the quiet.'

'Oh, Joe . . . '

'Oh, Joe . . . ' he mimicked. 'D'you reckon Jesus is behind that door, listening to what we're saying?'

'Stop it!' Clara felt her mouth twitch. Joe really was terrible, but you couldn't help laughing at him. And he'd been so good to her, right from that night when he'd come in with her and they'd found . . . Her knuckles tightened on the wide scrubbing brush.

She was not quite seventeen. She tried so hard to be good. There were times when she hurt with the effort of thinking kind things about people all the time. She was young and lovely, and it was almost impossible to close her mind to all the things, the exciting things that must be going on outside the confines of the narrow street, the chapel at the top end, and the dark basement room where she counted, collated and stapled sheets of paper all day.

She had bad dreams too, and always about Joe. He was holding her like they did in pictures, with her hair all hanging loose over his arm, and he was kissing her, with his curly mouth moving over her lips.

She turned round, unaware that he could read every single expression on her face. Funny, she'd never thought of it before, but he did have a curly mouth. It never ever seemed to be set in a straight line. When he grinned there were two tiny dimples coming and going at the corners. She'd been so unhappy for a long time and yet now, with Joe teasing her, she could almost admit to being on the verge of happiness. Oh, yes, Joe West was a beautiful man!

'I couldn't go in one of them clubs,' she said slowly, never taking her eyes from his face.

Joe had always known when to play his trump card and he played it now. 'Who said owt about you singing in a club? No, love, it's a posh job I've got lined up for you tonight. It's a Masonic do in the Assembly Rooms, with men in bow ties and their wives in fancy frocks. They'll have paid two guineas for a slap-up meal and a dekko at a cabaret.'

Clara's eyes grew round. 'A cabaret? Like they have down in London?'

'Better'n London.'

'I'd have to wear me black.'

'You can wear your nightie for all I care.'

'Oh, Joe . . . '

It had been easy, but now the time had come Joe wasn't too sure. He'd promised the gaffer in charge that he'd find a fill-in for the baritone who would surely have sung 'The Road to Mandalay'. But when she was ready Clara didn't look much different than she'd done in her cleaning-up clothes.

The black dress she had on had come, he guessed correctly, from a chapel jumble sale. Made for a much older and stouter woman, it hung like a sack, doing less than nothing for her rounded curves. She was pale with nerves, and her hands looked red and sore from the caustic soda she'd used that afternoon.

'Seen the chap about your music?' he asked her, and she nodded, her eyes wide in the pallor of her face.

'You're on next,' he whispered. 'After the comic, and before the dancers.'

She nodded again, averting her eyes from the trio of girls dressed as scarlet soldiers. 'Showing too much leg,' he read into her shocked expression.

'Right!' he said. 'Knock 'em for six, love. OK?'

The audience sat at little round tables, replete and relaxed after a five-course meal and dancing to a four-piece band. They were businessmen in the main, mill and pit owners, doctors, solicitors, men from the Manchester Stock Exchange, and master builders of the new semidetached houses springing up round the outskirts of the town. Large cigars stuck in their flushed faces, glasses of brandy to hand, they felt a pleasing sense of indulgence at having brought the missus out for a good time. They were proud of the way she looked in her new frock after an afternoon spent at the hairdresser's having her newly cropped hair marcel-waved.

The women hadn't enjoyed the comic at all. He had delivered his patter in a broad Lancashire dialect they pretended not to understand, and most of his jokes had been on the risqué side. Corset bones dug into soft flesh as they clapped politely, then sat back waiting for the next turn.

When the MC announced that a Miss Clara Haydock would be taking the place of Mr Arnold Leadbetter, they tapped gloved hands together, then raised their eyebrows to their hairlines as Clara walked slowly to the centre of the ballroom. In the midst of all that colour and light she was like a small black rusty scarecrow. Hands clasped together, she announced her first item.

' "I'm For Ever Blowing Bubbles",' she said, nodding in the direction of the man seated at the piano.

Joe, watching from the open doorway, crossed his fingers behind his back, feeling the sweat break out on his forehead. 'Laugh at her at your bloody peril,' his grim expression said. 'Stop smiling at each other and *listen*, for God's sake!'

Halfway through the first chorus the fidgeting stopped. Clara's pure distinctive voice soared, every word clear, every note true.

'Just like my dreams they fade and die,' she sang, a hurt, plaintive, swaying note in her lovely voice. When she finished and the last notes died away, there was a telling moment of silence before the crack of applause.

Joe uncrossed his fingers, feeling a shiver run up and down his spine. 'I knew it,' he whispered, closing his eyes. 'I've always known it. Always, always, right from the beginning.'

'For my next item I am going to sing "Because God Made Thee Mine",' Clara was saying, giving the little nod to the pianist.

A professional to her fingertips, Joe told himself, giving himself the thumbs-up sign.

They wouldn't let her go. When she walked towards Joe, he pushed her back. 'An encore, love,' he whispered. 'You arranged with the pianist for an encore?'

She shook her head, laughing up into his face, cheeks flushed to a wild rose, eyes glittering with a feverish excitement. 'No piano for this one, Joe. I'm singing this one on me own.' Slowly she walked back to her place, holding up her hand to stem the clapping. 'This last one is for my father,' she said.

And for the first few moments her audience was as stunned and surprised as Joe himself. 'She's singing a bleedin' hymn,' he muttered to himself. 'Oh, Clara, love, you've done it now!'

The stillness in the room was profound. Not a cough, not a sigh, not a rustle of printed programmes. He saw a woman in a green taffeta dress reach for her husband's hand; he saw a florid-faced man wipe away a tear; and he felt a tingling in his fingertips. Real genuine star quality was a rare thing. Joe had seen enough of third-rate performances to realize that. His lips moved into their curvaceous smile. There was something in Clara's voice that reached out and touched even the hardest heart. It was a voice that played on the emotions, seductive without meaning to be, as sensual as a lingering caress.

'The day thou gavest, Lord, is ended,' she sang. 'The darkness falls at thy behest.'

A mother of a son lost on the Somme had tears running unchecked down her powdered cheeks; a businessman with a woman who wasn't his wife hung his head in momentary shame.

'Thy Kingdom stands and grows for-ever,
Till all Thy creatures own Thy sway . . . '

The last pure note died away. Clara stood with head bowed, the centre light turning her glorious hair to spun gold. The pianist, a classical musician fallen on hard times, played a surreptitious note as if to convince himself that Clara had ended the five verses as correctly true as he suspected. And the audience, after that drawnout momentary silence, went wild.

In the little anteroom the MC mopped his forehead with his handkerchief. 'One number,' he told the scarlet soldiers, 'that's all. We've overrun our time and they'll want to get on with the dancing.' He turned to Joe as the three girls pranced out into the ballroom. 'If I'd known what your girl was like I'd have put her on last.' He nodded towards Clara, quietly buttoning up her coat over the dowdy dress. 'Where did you find her, lad? She had that lot eating out of her hands.'

The loud music and the stamping of dancing feet as the girls went into their routine made him wince as if in pain. 'Sacrilege putting that lot on after hearing singing like that.' He peered round the doorway. 'See, they're talking amongst themselves, the audience. Not taking a blind bit of notice. Asking each other who she is.' He fingered a toothbrush moustache. 'I was over in Russia with the Royal Engineers when the Reds began their revolution in 1918. Slept in the tsar's palace I did, aye, and saw Pavlova dance. Heard the first guns firing in Petrograd, then ended up on a train to Siberia.' He straightened his bow tie. 'Pavlova had the same magic. She danced like that young lass sings, if you know what I mean. She's a proper singing angel, that's what she is.'

'My card,' Joe said, fishing in his pocket and handing one over. 'I'm her manager.' He tapped the card with a forefinger. 'I'm London-based, but any queries will reach me from there.' The Singing Angel, he pondered. Not bad. Not at all bad.

Already the three girls were back, the slight spattering of applause dying away to silence. The oldest girl, a bottle blonde with a made-up, haggard face, threw down the baton she'd been twirling round her head in the dance routine and marched straight up to Clara.

'You little bugger!' Her voice was tight with uncontrolled anger. 'You ran over your time on purpose. You knew you was practically cutting us down to nothing. There's a name for what you are!' Before Joe could move to stop her, she shot out a hand and gave Clara a stinging slap across the face. 'Who d'you think you are, singing a bleedin' hymn for an encore? What d'you think this is? A bleedin' church?'

'They wouldn't have you in a bleedin' church!' Tears of shock and outrage filled Clara's eyes. Joe could see that she was all for having a go. He stepped forward quickly.

'Naughty, naughty,' he told the panting girl, wagging a finger in her scarlet face. 'I was thinking of putting you on my books, but I've changed my mind. Sorry.'

'Professional jealousy, love,' he told Clara, leading her away, stopping only to accept an envelope from a bemused steward standing by the door. 'That was your first taste, and it won't be the last, you mark my words.'

'Were you really going to put her on your books?' Clara whispered as they went down the wide staircase leading to the main doors.

'Wouldn't have her handed to me on a shovel.' Joe put an arm round her, grinning down into her troubled face. 'Back end of a horse in a pantomime, that's all she's good for.' He kissed Clara's nose, pulling her round to face him for a moment. 'The rule in this game is never hit back. Dignity is what's called for. That girl's been working the clubs for years and she'll never get no farther – and she knows it. She's on her way down, and you're on your way up. Right to the top, my little sweetheart.'

'Was I all right, Joe?' Clara asked the question with no intention of fishing for a compliment. 'I was that scared I never even saw their faces, but they seemed to like me all right. Did *you* think I was good, Joe?'

'Not bad, love.'

For the first time in his life Joe West was drunk without having raised an elbow. Stuck in the doldrums for months now, he saw the future opening up like a shining road to wealth and success. He saw the money rolling in; he saw Clara's name in lights.

'Your clothes were all wrong, chuck, but we can remedy that.' He was walking so quickly Clara had to take little

104

running steps to keep up with him. 'And your name's all wrong. I can't see Clara Haydock raising much interest. Too ordinary.' He pretended to think. 'How d'you fancy being billed as the Singing Angel? Wearing white. With maybe an 'alo hovering over your nut?'

'Oh, Joe ... ' The indignity of the little scene in the anteroom forgotten, Clara's infectious laugh rang out. 'I'm not wearing no 'alo. I'd look a right pie-can in an 'alo.' Her voice faltered. 'I don't know what you're on about, Joe. You'll be gone soon, and I'll be back at work on Monday, same as ever.'

'Nothing's going to be the same as ever.' They were outside the clogger's shop by now, and Joe swung her round to face him. 'You're not going to work on Monday. You're never going to work in that basement dungeon again.' Tipping his trilby to the back of his head, he stared up at the navy blue sky. 'From now on you're working for me, Joe West, theatrical agent and talent scout. You'll have a fur coat, and diamond rings on your fingers. We'll stop in posh hotels and send down in the middle of the night for a potted-meat buttie. You'll never blacklead a fireplace nor scrub a table again. You'll have a maid to brush your hair and another one to paint your fingernails red.' Pushing open the door, he held it wide and bowed. 'An' your toenails, Miss Haydock, if you've a mind.'

Holding her hand, he led her through the shop, empty now apart from the scarred bench, the counter and Seth's three-legged stool, into the little back living room. 'What's wrong with the gas, love?' He came and took the box of matches from Clara's hand. 'Why are you messing about with candles?'

'Because candles are cheaper than gas.' Clara set the candlestick before him. 'You can go when you've lit that, Joe West. It's late, and people'll talk if they've seen you coming in with me when it's gone dark. Mrs Davis at the top end misses nowt.'

Joe put the candlestick down on the table. In its soft glow, lighting Clara's face from below, she seemed to him the most beautiful girl he had ever seen. Her eyes were big and yet uptilted at the corners, her mouth had a sensual droop to it, and her neck was so slender he felt he could have encircled it with one hand.

When he kissed her she clung to him. Because he was Joe, and because she loved him. As the kiss deepened, a fear took hold of her and she struggled, only to have his arms press her against him so that she felt the hardness of his body all down the softness of her own.

'You belong to me now,' he whispered into her hair. 'I'm going to look after you, and be with you, and love you.' He brought his face round to look into her eyes. 'An' the loving's going to start right now.'

This time when he kissed her she stayed quietly in his arms. There was no response, but no resistance either. At first, when he urged her towards the bottom of the stairs, she pulled back, but he held her face in his hands, trailed his lips round her eyes, down her cheeks, lingering before he covered her mouth again. The fear was still there as they climbed the stairs, but he was Joe, wasn't he? Nothing Joe did to her could do her harm. He had said he would make her into a star, but *he* was *her* star, the one bright star in her life. Where Joe was there was warmth and laughter, always had been, and always would be.

She trembled as he urged her over towards the bed. It had been a strange night, a mixture of terror and elation. Singing in front of an audience like that had made her feel happier than she'd felt for a long time. It was still there, that feeling, glowing inside her as he undressed her, tossing the atrocious black dress from him in a crumpled heap on the floor.

When he slid into bed beside her, she crept into his arms the way a child would creep into a loving father's arms after a bad dream. All she wanted was to be held, to have the fear and the loneliness of the past months soothed from her heart and mind. She was being a bad girl, but where had being good got her?

'Oh, Joe,' she whispered. 'I do luv you.'

He felt her tears on his own cheeks as he took her and when she cried out, what passed for his conscience made him draw back for a split second. But it was too late, and when her arms came round his back a fierce exultation took possession of him. She was his; little Clara Haydock had always been his, and he would make her happy if it was the last thing he did.

'You're crying, Joe,' she whispered when it was over. 'Don't be sorry. I'm not.' Lifting a finger, she wiped away a tear from his cheek. 'We'll get married now, won't we? An' you can come an' live here with me an' never go away again.'

'With me mam across the street, and you going out to work till I find myself a steady job?'

She missed the heavy sarcasm in his voice. 'Yes! Oh, Joe, we'll be so happy.'

Her long hair was across his face. He twined his fingers in its silky weight. 'We'll be happy, chuck. But not in that way.' He raised himself on an elbow. 'Weren't you listening when I told you things were going to be different? Starting on Monday, they're going to be so different you'll wonder how you ever lived like this.' He stared round the room, lit to vague shadows by a drifting moon seen through the square of window. 'We can't stop here, love. This house gives me the creeps.'

'Where will we go, Joe?' Her voice was thick, on the very edge of sleep. She was only a child, his troublesome conscience told him, and long after she slept in his arms he lay awake, hearing in his imagination the tap-tap of a hammer from the shop below as the ghost of Seth Haydock plied his trade. He saw in his fevered imagination the thickset man sitting on his stool, holding the nails in his mouth, and he saw himself as a small boy sliding up and down the long bench, waiting for his clogs to be mended before he could go to school.

He saw, too, his mother across the street, old before her time, worn out with worry and sorrows, still living in an overcrowded house with a future before her as bleak as the moors not all that far away.

'We're getting out of here,' he whispered to the sleeping girl, then, accepting that sleep for him was impossible, he gently moved himself to the edge of the bed, sat up and lit a cigarette, smoking the next hour away as he made his plans.

The man sitting in the second row of the stalls in the cold and empty theatre that Monday morning tipped his hat to the back of his head and flipped Joe's business card with the tip of a finger.

'So you say, dear boy, so you say. But what else can she do apart from sing?' He glanced at the card. 'Mr West?'

'She doesn't need to do nothing else.' Joe jerked his head in Clara's direction where she waited with head bowed in the aisle. 'Just give her a chance, Mr Boland. She's got a voice that could wring a tear from a spud's eye. You've heard nothing like it.' He spoke in a whisper. 'There's an opening for her in London, but she's a young girl and her family are set against her going.' He winked. 'She's a singing angel in every way, if you get me. Pure, like her voice.' The nervous grin lifted the high cheekbones. 'She's *different*, Mr Boland. Not a common bone in her body. You can see that just by looking at her . . . She's no Gertrude Lawrence and she's no Evelyn Laye.' He spoke as if he knew them personally. 'But she's one on her own, Mr Boland, an' that's just what the customer wants.'

As Clara waited, a feeling of panic attacking every nerve, for this important man to speak she studied him from beneath lowered eyelashes. It was a strong face, and yet fine-featured, with the width of the broad forehead made more pronounced by the fact that the brown hair had already begun to recede. The bushy moustache was to make him look older, she guessed, but the bright blue eyes were what scared her most. The vivid colour of bluebells, they were staring at her now, seeming to see right through her, as lazy and condescending as his cultured voice.

'Two minutes,' he said wearily. 'And she'd better be good.'

The stage was bigger and dirtier than Clara had imagined it would be. The rows of empty tip-up chairs seemed to stretch into infinity, and the pianist, a small man with a cigarette stuck to his bottom lip, was playing her music much too fast. Vamping with his left hand, he crouched over the keyboard like a tiger about to spring.

'Slowly. More slowly!' Had she shouted the words or were they just in her head? It was too late anyroad. Joe was glaring at her, nodding with his head to show her to get on with it, and Mr Boland had tipped his hat back over his eyes as though he deemed it a good time to have a quick kip. Clara hated him so much at that moment she could feel the emotion pricking under her skin like fine needles.

That man at the piano was *crucifying* her song. In a fever of anxiety Clara flapped her hand at him, but he was playing the introduction as if possessed. Jazzing it up so that it was hardly recognizable.

Joe had chosen the song for her. He'd told her that its plaintive melody and sliding rhythm suited her voice perfectly. It was by an American called Jerome Kern, Joe had told her, rehearsing her until she was word perfect.

'Look for the silver lining,' she sang, her liquid voice seeming to linger and caress each phrase, 'when e'er a cloud appears in the blue   '

She was actually gabbling in a vain attempt to keep up with the chain-smoking man at the piano thumping away crouched low over the keyboard, smoke wreathing him as if he sat in the middle of a cloud. He was enjoying himself immensely. He liked this tune and remembered playing it in pantomime at Birmingham the previous year for a chorus line of girls with grey clouds on their backs and yellow suns on their fronts, tap-dancing through their routine.

'A heart full of joys and gladness . . . ' he played, going tiddly-boom, tiddly-boom, tiddly-boom-boom-boom with his left hand, hearing in his memory the tap-tap of the steel tips on the girls' shoes as they shimmied towards the footlights.

Down in the stalls Joe turned angrily to Bart Boland slumped down in his tip seat, the hat pushed back now to reveal the blue blue eyes dancing with amusement. But before Joe could open his mouth to point out the obvious, Clara, almost beside herself with nerves and frustration, wheeled round on her heels, hands on hips, to face the pianist still belting away with eyes closed.

'Stop it! Stop it! Slow flamin' down and play it proper!'

She screamed so loud that the pianist's head jerked up, dislodging the stub of his cigarette, which fell on his knees. He knocked it away with a fierce slicing motion, then looked down into the stalls for further instructions.

Bart Boland's eyebrows ascended almost to his receding hairline. Sitting bolt upright in his seat, he let out a sudden shout of laughter.

'What's funny?' Walking quickly to the edge of the vast stage, Clara's green eyes blazed down into the auditorium. 'I'm a singer, not a bleedin' racehorse!'

She looked so comical standing up there all alone, the long golden hair tucked out of sight beneath a hat shaped like a chamber pot, Bart Boland was reminded for a second of a young Gracie Fields. Putting his arms on the seat in front of his own, he leaned forward.

'Can you kick, love?'

'Kick what?' Clara's paddy was up good and proper. Joe closed his eyes in despair. 'Him, for example?' She jerked her head towards the man at the piano busily lighting yet another cigarette. 'Oh, aye, I'll kick him 'ard if you ask me to. Stupid pie-can that he is!'

Bart was enjoying himself. Never before had he been cheeked by a young girl at an audition. 'Take your hat off, love.' His quiet voice had the ring of authority, and obeying automatically Clara snatched off the hat, dislodging hairpins so that her long white-gold hair fell shining almost to her waist.

Joe felt rather than heard the older man's indrawn breath of surprise. He relaxed, telling himself they were almost home and dry.

'Now lift up your skirt.' Bart made a movement with his right hand. 'There's a good girl.'

'What for?' Clara stared down at her skirt, worn longer than was fashionable and made for a much taller girl, Joe guessed. He closed his eyes again.

'So that I can see your legs, love.' Bart's tone was all sweet reason. 'I just want to see their shape.'

'I don't *sing* with 'em, do I?' All of Clara's strict Methodist upbringing was in the scorn of her reply. 'My father used to tell me about men like you.'

The moustache twitched a little. 'So she doesn't dance?' With studied insolence Bart Boland glanced at Joe's card again. 'Mr West?'

'No, I don't dance.' Clara answered for Joe. 'I sing to a proper accompaniment. *When* I get the chance. Covered up decent!'

'Take her away.' Bart waved a languid hand. 'And the next time you present her for an audition, make sure it's for the heavenly choir.' And with that he stood up and walked away up the long aisle to the exit doors at the back of the theatre, his hands in the pockets of his trenchcoat and the trilby hat pulled low over his forehead.

Joe watched him go. The pianist watched him go, before shrugging his shoulders and disappearing into the shadows of the wings, leaving a trail of smoke behind him. Clara stood alone on the vast stage, with Joe looking up at her, a thunderous expression on his face.

The row started the minute they were back inside the house. It would have begun before that but Joe was so blazing mad he marched ahead, striding out and kicking an empty cigarette packet so hard it landed on the opposite pavement.

Clara stood by the table in the back living room, arms folded as she glared at Joe. So he was mad. Then let him be. Clara reckoned *she*'d been the one badly done to that morning. She decided attack was her best defence.

'How dare that man with a hearthbrush under his nose ask to see my legs?' She tore at the buttons on her coat in such a fury it was a wonder they didn't pop off. 'What would've come next if he'd liked them? Me dad told me about wicked men like him. Men like him lead innocent girls into a life of vice, and sometimes they can end up with no nose!'

'God Almighty!' Joe clenched both hands and beat the air in front of him. 'Have you any idea just who that man with a hearthbrush under his nose is? Have you any idea who his *father* was?' He gripped the table edge hard as if he needed

111

the support. 'Bart Boland's father started his career by sweeping the stage at the Palace in Oldham. Some say he ended up the most powerful manager in all the country, not far behind Mr Cochran. And his son, his son *Bart*, mark you well, doesn't need to sit in some crumby theatre listening to nobodies like you, Clara Haydock. He's got far better things to do with his time.'

'Why did he then?' Clara was beginning to feel scared. She'd seen Joe angry many times before, but his anger had never been directed at her. She began to bluster. 'Him with his posh voice! He *insulted* me. What would've come next if he'd decided he liked me legs? Would he have asked me to take me blouse off so he could have a dekko at me bosoms?'

'You silly ignorant little sod!' Joe drew back his hand and hit Clara a resounding slap across her face. 'Don't you realize? Are you too stupid to understand what you did? Mr High and Mighty Boland doesn't come up here all that often. Not him. He's got a bloody great mansion in Cumberland, as well as a flat in London. He's *loaded*, our kid. Filthy rich. An' he won't be back to this godforsaken hole for a long time to come.' Joe actually beat his forehead with his clenched fists. 'Oh, my God! Chancing on him here this morning was the best stroke of luck I've had in years. Bart Boland has his pick of the best! He's turned down more singers than you've had hot dinners, and you just stood there ticking him off! You're finished, Clara Haydock. Finished before you've started.' He thrust his face close to hers. 'An' what about me? He'll class me with you, now. He never forgets, Bart Boland doesn't. Got a memory as long as a mill chimney, he has.'

The slap had shocked Clara into silence. Joe was staring at her as though he hated her, and when he suddenly let out a bark of a laugh with no mirth in it, she shuddered. When he took hold of her wrist and drew her to him, she didn't resist.

'God Almighty!' he shouted, and she could see a nerve jumping just beneath his right eye. 'You really take the biscuit! Bart Boland wasn't after your bloody virtue. He wouldn't touch the likes of you with a barge pole. Your head's filled with rubbish, put there by them mealy-mouthed Methodists singing their bloody heads off every Sunday at the top of the street.' He began to twist her wrist viciously. 'A girl doesn't have to be on the stage to be a wrong 'un. Like I said, Bart Boland wouldn't touch you if you came gift-wrapped in cellophane.'

'But *you* did!' Clara was weeping with pain and rage by now. 'You slept with me just so I'd go for that audition.' Her eyes swam with tears. 'An' now I could be having a baby. Sins have to be paid for, Joe West. An' I'll pay for what I did, that's for sure.'

Her nose was running as well as her eyes, and Joe looked at her with something approaching contempt. The bright perky little Clara he loved had disappeared, leaving this ignorant snivelling child, her head filled with religious nonsense.

'You won't have a baby,' he told her slowly, letting go of her wrist. 'I took care of that. I've never slipped up yet.'

'Oh!' Clara rubbed her wrist, glaring at him through tear-drenched eyes. 'An' did you love all them others as well? Did you promise them you'd marry them and take them away to a better life?'

'No!' Joe's temper was up again. 'No, no and no!'

'Why not, then?'

He was going to say because he didn't love them, but he knew she wouldn't believe him. She was like all the others, clinging, demanding, wanting to be the only one, to possess him body and soul.

'Look,' he said warily, feeling the anger seep from him, leaving in its place his usual devil-may-care acceptance of the way things were. 'We're not getting anywhere like this. You have a lot of growing up to do yet. Bart Boland was right when he said your place was in a heavenly choir. You're so steeped in religion you can't think straight.' He stared round the almost bare shabby room. 'If this is all you want, then there's nothing more I can do.' Reaching for his wallet he took out a wad of pound notes and flung them on the table. 'I've got a job to see to down south, but I'll be back, and

113

when I come back maybe, just maybe you'll have come to your senses.'

She couldn't believe it. He was going away again. He had said he loved her, had held her close and made love to her, but he was still the same Joe. No integrity, her father had said. For a moment she saw her father's face as he warned her about the West boys. 'Charm and nowt else,' Seth had said. 'Break your heart as soon as look at you.' Her body was shaking with the sobs she couldn't control, but with as much dignity as she could muster she picked up the pound notes and held them out to Joe.

'I won't be needing these,' she said. 'What is it for? Payment for what I let you do?'

'You little she-devil!' Now his anger was back. Knocking the notes from her hand he scattered them over the floor. 'Right, then! Get down on your knees, Clara, and see where prayers will get you. Go back to that job of yours, which about pays the rent if I guess right. Go up to the chapel at the top and see if any of them Bible-thumping Methodists will put a hand in their pocket to make sure you have enough to eat.' Suddenly he relented. 'I'll be back, Clara. When you've come to your senses and stopped acting like a baby, I'll be back.'

When the outer door had slammed behind him she gathered up the pound notes. It would have been a good feeling to throw them on the sluggish fire and watch the flames curl round their edges. For a whole minute she hesitated, then remembering the terrible three days she'd existed on stale bread and water from the tap, she reached up to the mantelpiece and tucked them safely behind the clock.

If she could have lied and said she'd been ill it would have perhaps been all right. But a lifetime of being conditioned to tell the truth no matter what forced her to explain to her boss that she had taken the day off to attend an audition.

'All day?' he asked. 'It took all day?'

Clara shook her head. 'I didn't think it worth coming in the afternoon,' she confessed, biting her lips as she thought about the long afternoon spent sitting in her father's rocking chair, half listening for the sound of Joe opening the front door and coming through into the little back room, holding out his arms and asking for her forgiveness.

She knew that her boss, a dry stick of a man with hair the colour of dead ashes, had a granddaughter just left school. The girl had been down in the basement room once or twice lately, hindering rather than helping, marvelling at the speed at which Clara worked, trying to emulate her, then pushing her fringe back and laughing when she failed miserably.

'I'm afraid we had to fill your position, Miss Haydock.' The grey eyebrows were as domed as a church archway. 'Work can't be held up while you fancy yourself as Nellie Wallace.'

'But for all you knew I might have been ill!' Clara stuttered over the injustice. 'You wouldn't have known where I'd been if I hadn't told you!'

'The position is filled.'

He had the grace to turn away and, as Clara opened her mouth to speak, the young girl with the fringe came up from the basement, carrying a pile of circulars which slipped from her grasp as she negotiated the curve of the stone steps. Spreading like a fan, the thin sheets of paper spattered, sliding down the basement steps to lie disordered in untidy heaps.

Why, Clara thought with a quick return of pride, I could've carried a pile three times that high and never dropped one. The natural good manners, so carefully taught by Seth, dictated that she should at least offer to help pick them up, but remembering the years she had slaved down in that basement room, stopping on without a penny overtime, acting as errand boy, manning the little front office while her bosses had their dinner, brought a flush to her cheeks and the sparkle back to her eyes.

'I'll have me cards, if you don't mind,' she said haughtily, making for the front office. Treading on one of the flimsy sheets of headed paper. On purpose.

Eight

Bart Boland came from a wealthy Cumberland family. His father, Amos Boland, had been bitterly disappointed when, after a promising career in the Household Cavalry, his son had gone determinedly into theatre management.

'It's in the blood, after all,' Bart had said. 'Look what you did when Grandfather left you all his money. You went and invested the lot in the running of the Empire Music Hall. Wasn't it at Northampton? There were so many I've lost count.' He punched his father on the shoulder. 'Come on, Dad. You know I can't go on playing soldiers all my life.'

Now, at the age of thirty-seven, accepting no favours, Bart had worked his way up to become managing director of no less than four theatrical companies.

On the day when Clara sang for him he was trying his best to fight off a crippling depression. His wife had refused yet again to travel down to London with him, saying she must stay with their two children. And that on no consideration would she bring them to London to live away from the wide acres of farmland in which their red-brick house was set.

'Go back to your chorus girls,' she'd told him after a blistering row. 'They mean more to you than I do, even though I believe you when you say you've kept faithful to me. But it's only a matter of time,' she added. 'I'm nobody's fool.'

As well as the slow but sure deterioration of his marriage, Bart saw the slow but sure demise of the music hall. One by one theatres were being turned into picture palaces. The new and popular revues he saw as merely mindless stopgaps in the decline of variety.

But in spite of his depression, Bart could still spot genuine and rare talent. It was said that his long nose quivered when his interest was aroused.

And no one could have guessed the extent of his interest on that Monday morning when the young Clara Haydock, in the guise of the Singing Angel, had lost her temper on the stage and shouted her disgust.

The trouble was in finding her. Bart regretted tearing up Joe West's business card, even though it wasn't Joe he wanted to see. He'd known more Joe Wests in his time than was good for his incipient ulcer. In his opinion the Joe Wests of the world came like cardboard cutouts, identical in their greed and grasping ambition.

He hadn't got where he was without using what they called in the north his 'loaf', however, so when his Bentley drew up outside the clogger's shop he tapped his driver on the shoulder.

'Be a good chap and see those kids across the street don't climb on the bonnet. I don't expect to be long.'

He stood on the flagstones, bare-headed in the rain, waiting none too patiently for his knock to be answered, only to step back in surprise when the door was flung open to reveal a girl with sparkling green eyes, obviously all set to hurl herself into his arms.

'I thought you was Joe!' Clara stared at Bart in dismay. 'He said he'd come back, so I thought it was him.'

Recovering herself quickly, she held the door wide and invited him in, staring in amazement at the shiny black car standing at the kerb. 'I'm sorry I was rude to you yesterday,' she told him as she led the way through the almost empty shop. 'But that man playing the piano did ask forrit, you know.'

Bart was enchanted. She was talking to him as an equal again, and they were, God dammit, they were. Snobbishness Bart had never been able to tolerate. She was even more stunningly beautiful than he remembered. She'd been crying, that much was obvious, but there was a proud tilt to her head and a glint in her eyes that showed she wasn't out for the count, not by a long way.

'May I sit down?' His voice was low and courteous, with no trace of the wide vowels of his northern upbringing.

Education, Clara thought, indicating her father's old rocking chair. That was what education did for a person. Monkey-quick, she picked up the rhythm of his speech.

'Make yourself comfortable, Mr Boland,' she said. There was a tiny seed of hope inside her, but she wasn't going to count no chickens, not yet awhile. Not before he'd said what he'd a mind to.

'Your manager?' Bart's eyes twinkled. 'I hope he won't mind my dealing with you direct?'

'He won't know, sir.' Clara's green eyes twinkled right back at him. 'I give him the sack yesterday.'

'Did you, indeed?' Bart had seen a lot of poverty in his travels round the country, but never anything approaching the desolation and bareness of this small back room. Real poverty had a special smell to it, a kind of lingering sweetness in the air, as if a corpse had been left to rot beneath the floorboards. He rubbed his chin thoughtfully. She was so young, this child, so painfully thin, with her waist no bigger than a hand's span and her great green eyes shadowed as if she hadn't slept for weeks. And wasn't that surely a bruise on her cheek with a tiny cut on the cheekbone as if from a signet ring? The blue eyes hardened.

'I'll come straight to the point, Miss Haydock. I didn't feel you had a fair hearing yesterday.'

'Steve Donoghue on the piano?'

'Precisely.' Bart hid a smile, stroking his moustache. 'In spite of the galloping major at the piano, I did get a decided impression that you have a voice.'

Clara nodded eagerly. No point in false modesty if the little seed of hope inside her was going to germinate.

'I'm the best singer round hereabouts. An' the loudest if I want to be.' She twitched at the neck of the outdoor coat she wore to keep out the cold. 'I'll sing for you now, sir, if you want.'

Startled, Bart inclined his head. 'I'd like that very much, my dear.'

So, clasping her hands in front of her, standing perfectly

118

still on the threadbare oilcloth, Clara lifted her head and sang.

'Moonlight and roses . . . ' The lovely melody rose and fell as Clara sang with no trace of embarrassment, each sighing note pure and true. 'Bring memories of you,' she ended, drooping her head as if anticipating a thunder of applause.

'Thank you, my dear.'

The tingle down his spine that Bart never ignored was there strongly now. For a moment he was stuck for words. This girl was a *natural*. Not a Gertrude Lawrence; not a Gracie Fields; not even a young Jessie Matthews, for whom he predicted great things. This girl was *unique*. His quick glance took in the terrible room. She was like a flower on a muck midden, he thought, shaking his head.

But 'The Singing Angel'! Never! The vivid blue eyes flickered up and down for a moment, taking in the swell of Clara's full breasts beneath the hideous coat. He could swear her legs were all right too, in spite of the fact that she had refused to reveal them. With decent clothes and that appalling accent changed, this girl could reach the top. It was there in the way she stood, in the tilt of that proud head, in the purity of her diction. And that hair! It was almost impossible to believe she'd been brought up in this little back street, in this house which reeked of mice droppings.

He leaned forward. 'Can you spare the time to tell me something about yourself, my dear? I caught you on the point of going out, didn't I?'

'Oh, no.' Clara glanced down at the coat buttoned up to her neck. 'I always wear me coat till the fire gets going properly.' Lifting the lid of a beaten copper scuttle in the hearth, she recklessly threw on a precious cob of coal. 'Would you like a cup of tea, sir? It'll only take the kettle a minute to boil once the fire gets agate.'

Bart shook his head. 'Not for me, thank you. Now tell me. Are your parents out working? I've come to talk to them, actually.'

Clara hesitated. Joe had said this man was important, and he certainly looked it in his tweed overcoat, with his neat collar and tie fastened with a small round gold pin. He

119

wasn't as old as she'd first thought either, and handsome, especially when he smiled. There was a kindness about him, and hadn't her father always said that if a person was kind then all else fell into place? Suddenly she knew she could trust this Mr Boland.

'Me father's dead,' she told him with a catch in her voice, 'and me mother gave me away when I was new-born. Me father was a clogger. That was his shop through there, but he wasn't me real father.' She sighed. 'I'm a bit of a mix-up sir, but it didn't matter when he was alive. Now,' her head drooped, 'I'm on me own, sir. There's just me.'

Accustomed to hearing sentimental sob stories from actresses who swore they'd risen from the gutter itself, Bart fixed Clara with his penetrating gaze.

'What if I said I believed you'd just made all that up?' he asked.

'I'd say you was a flamin' liar, sir!'

Bart Boland hadn't had what he called a good old belly laugh for as long as he could remember. Throwing back his head he laughed as if he were coming apart at the seams.

'That wasn't meant to be funny, sir.' Clara was all indignation now. 'I don't tell lies. Me father would've had me over his knee for lying.' She sighed. 'I was a bit of a job for him at times.'

'Your father, the clogger.' Bart nodded, in full control of himself again. 'The Clogger's Child! That's it! Look here, my dear. I can offer you a ten-week engagement with one of my smaller companies touring the northwest, with an option of, let's say, five years at £5 a week to begin with. But you'd have to pay your lodgings out of that, so it's not exactly a fortune.' He began to button up his coat. 'It will be hard work, and some of the digs won't be up to much, but there's a good friend of mine in the company who will look after you if I ask her. Miss Dora Vane. She used to be one of a trio, singing and dancing. My father thought the world of her.' He stood up, setting the chair rocking of its own volition. 'Dora Vane was on the bill at the Palace Theatre here when it reopened. On the same bill as Charlie Tempest, I'm almost sure.' The blue eyes twinkled. 'But that was a bit before your time.' Holding out his hand, he took Clara's cold fingers in his warm grasp. 'I'm going now to tell the producer exactly what I have in mind for you.' He jiggled her hand up and down. 'And don't worry. I promise you'll be covered up decent.'

Still smiling, he walked through the shop and out to the front door, a tall man who still walked as if he were on parade. 'Go down to the theatre at ten in the morning for rehearsal. They'll be expecting you.'

Clara watched in awe as the uniformed chauffeur came round the car to hold the door wide.

'I'll be keeping an eye on you.' Bart turned his head to talk over his shoulder. 'No need to worry.'

He was still smiling as the large black car drew away from the kerb. Clara waited until it had turned the corner, then she went inside the house and burst into tears.

She cried for joy; she cried for the miracle which a tall man with the brightest blue eyes she had ever seen had made happen for her. Then she cried for Joe, who should have been with her to share that joy.

He would come back; Joe always turned up sooner or later, but this time it would be too late. Clara's face hardened as she reminded herself that Joe had gone away, after making love to her, after *spoiling* her for any other man. Because that was true. One man, one woman, like the Bible said. Clara stared into the flames leaping round the coal she'd hurled on to warm Mr Boland. She had given Joe West her absolute, unquestioning love; nothing held back, not even her purity. She was quite serious, rocking herself to and fro before the fire. Joe had *spoiled* her, then, to add to her shame, he'd gone away.

There would be no more tears for Joe, Clara told herself firmly. She had cried for him as a child, without reason, with the pain a child feels. But no more. She might send him a complimentary ticket some day for one of her shows, then maybe allow him in her dressing room, just for old time's sake. And she'd extend her hand graciously to allow him to kiss her fingertips . . . If she was in a good mood, that is.

'Do you know where Joe is?'

Clara faced Lily West in the untidy shambles of the back room in the house across the street. Alec slouched in a chair by the fire, his leg in its clumsy iron caliper stretched across the hearth, while beneath the big square table two small black-haired boys played with a paper of margarine, blissfully tasting and smearing it greasily over each other, their dirty faces rapt.

'Do I ever know where Joe is?' Lily's laugh wheezed through her protruding teeth. 'I've never known where to find our Joe, not since he was big enough to climb over the front step.'

She was rocking a third child on her knee, a baby curled round her cushiony breasts. Fred's latest, Clara guessed, and yet another boy by the look of the bullet-shaped West head. For a little while Clara watched her with affection. It was an obsession Lily had for babies, it had to be, how else could she have lived out her life in a house teeming with children for all the years Clara had known her.

'What do you want our Joe for?' Alec stared at her suspiciously. 'He's gone back to his fancy woman in London if he's any sense. There's nowt for him up here.'

'What fancy woman in London?' Indignation flared Clara's nostrils. 'Who said Joe's got . . . what you just said?'

The loss of his job and the ugly contraption to help him walk had turned Alec into an embittered young man. 'London, Manchester, Sheffield, Newcastle.' His mouth curved into a sneer. 'Our Joe's got women everywhere. There's no woman goes short while our Joe's anywhere about.'

'That's enough, our Alec!' Lily's brown eyes shot daggers at her son. So that was the way the land lay. Poor little Clara. Lily rocked the baby fiercely, holding him so tightly he let out a squeal of protest. She'd always known that Joe and young Clara were as thick as thieves, but she'd thought it was a childish thing, even – God forgive her ignorance – a brother and sister feeling they had for each other. She smiled at Clara.

'He'll be back, love. We never know how long he's going to stop away, but he always comes back. And sends the money,' she added, unable to keep the pride she felt for her favourite son out of her voice.

Clara wasn't listening. She couldn't take her eyes off Alec, because what he had just said was true. It was a vindictive truth showing in his eyes. Since losing the use of his leg and his job at the pit, Alec told hurtful truths to everyone. She swallowed the lump in her throat. Blindly she reached out for a chair and sat down. Hadn't she always known Joe wasn't to be trusted? Could she really have been such a fool believing he had chosen her out of all the others to love? If Joe hadn't been sure Mr Boland had dismissed her as a nobody, then he might have stayed. And she'd let him . . . oh, dear God, she'd even believed he would marry her!

From somewhere deep inside her she dragged up the tattered remnants of her pride. 'I've got a job. A good job that means I have to go away.' The colour was coming back into her cheeks. 'I'm giving the house up, Mrs West, but there's a few things you can have if you want them. A bed, the big table and a couple of chairs. The rest went to the salerooms a while ago.'

'A bed? Did you say a bed, lovey?' The chance of getting something for nothing made Lily sit up. Clara could almost see her mind working overtime. 'There's never no money to replace things.' In her imagination Lily was seeing the bed upstairs, the one eaten away with woodworm. The one which only last week had collapsed beneath the weight of three warring small boys.

'And the bedding to go with it.' Clara stood up. 'You can come across and have a look, Mrs West. There may be other bits and pieces as well.'

In spite of her distress she couldn't hide a smile at the look of gloating eagerness on Lily's plain face, a look compounded of greed and necessity.

'How much do you want for them, love?' Lily fingered the blankets on Clara's bed. 'Our Joe left me some money before he went, and I could . . . '

'Nothing,' Clara said quickly. 'I'll leave you the key and the rent book paid up, and you can hand it in for me when the rent man comes on Friday. The things you can take just when you like.'

Tenderly Lily stroked the big jug standing in its basin on the wash-hand stand. Not a chip in it and, dear Mary Mother of God, that pillow on the bed was feather, she'd stake her life on it. The strip of rug would go a treat in front of the slopstone, and as far as she could remember there was a zinc bath hanging on a nail outside on the backyard wall.

In her elation she failed to notice that what was left were the bare essentials. That to keep alive Clara must have sold even the pictures from the walls. A lifetime of doing without, grabbing what was rarely given, had turned Lily into the sort of woman God never intended her to be.

'I'll get our Fred to give Alec a hand with moving them across the street. When it's gone dark,' she added. 'We don't want that Mrs Davis from the top end asking if you're doing a moonlight flit.'

Something in Clara's face softened her plain features into sudden compassion.

'You've always been such an independent little lass,' she said, sitting down on the edge of the bed, touching the pillow where her son's head had lain not all that long ago. 'Our Joe . . . he's not . . . he's never tried anything wrong with you, has he?' Yes, the pillow *was* feather. She'd been right in that. 'But no. He wouldn't. Not with you. You're more like brother and sister.'

Clara nodded, keeping her face averted. 'All your boys have been like brothers to me, Mrs West.'

'An' this job? You're such a little whipper-snapper to be going away on your own.' Tearing her glance reluctantly away from the bed, Lily stood up. 'I hope there's going to be somebody looking out for you, love. Your father would turn in his grave if you got into any kind of trouble. Haunt you, he would, from the other side.'

With a last lingering glance, Lily padded towards the door. 'At least leave me your address, then when our Joe comes home next I can give it to him. He won't like you going away and him not knowing where.'

'No!' Clara's voice rose almost to a shout. 'For one thing I don't know no address, Mrs West. I'll be moving about. An' for another, this is something I've got to do on me own.' At the foot of the stairs she turned and laid a hand on Lily's arm. 'I'm not a child now. Me father's dead, and that leaves me to fend for meself.'

'You've allus got me.' Lily's long nose quivered. 'I know I'm not much cop, but I've allus been there, Clara. Across the street, an' whatever trouble you're in, well, God knows, I'm used to trouble. You could say me and trouble has been bedfellows all me life.'

There was such genuine anxiety on the familiar troubled face that Clara relented. 'It's the stage, Mrs West. I've been offered a good job singing on the stage. An' I'm burning me bridges because bridges are supposed to support and my support went when my father died. It's what I've always wanted to do, and when I'm famous I'll come back and bring you . . . ' The green eyes twinkled. 'I'll bring you a fur coat, and that's a promise.'

Lily's laugh was a rusty wheeze, as if it hadn't been used for a long time. 'Me in a fur coat! Oh, my sainted aunt! That'd make her up at the top sit up, wouldn't it? Lily West in a fur coat! She'd have kittens, old Ma Davis would. Her eyes'd stand out like chapel 'at pegs if she saw me coming down the street in a fur coat. Oh, Mother of God, that'd be the day!'

When she'd gone, padding her way across the street in her down-at-heel slippers, Clara sat hunched in an uneasy and unnatural calm round the tiny fire. Suppose Joe came back in the few days left to her before she left the street for ever? Suppose they'd made a baby that night they made love? Joe had said it would be all right, but how did he *know*? Her ignorance and innocence would have surprised most girls of her age, but Clara only knew what she read in books from the library, and not one of them had told her exactly how a baby was made. And besides, Joe had said . . .

Oh, to hell with Joe! Clara said the words aloud, then opened her eyes wide at her own daring. If she'd been a Catholic she'd have crossed herself. If her father had been there to hear he would have made her wash her mouth out with soap and water. Bringing her father to mind brought a rush of tears to her eyes. If he'd still been alive, Bart Boland and his offer would have been turned down flat.

'No child of mine will ever set foot on the stage.'

Clara could hear him saying just that to Mr Boland, politely but firmly. She could actually see him walking over to the door with his slight limp and holding it wide for Mr Boland to pass through. Clara got up from her chair and wiped her tears away with the back of a hand. As Joe had said, the clogger was dead.

And with her father gone there was nothing to keep her here. The sloping narrow streets, the tall mill chimneys, the morning sound of the knocker-up tapping on the windows with his long pole, followed by the clatter of clogs on the cobblestones; all these were a part of her life, and yet already they seemed like shadows in a dream.

She was never coming back to live in the street. Never. Never. Never! Going over to the slopstone, Clara ran water into a cup and stood there drinking, looking out down the sloping backyard where once she'd given a concert with the entry fee an empty jamjar. That was the day when her father had come out to tell them that the first of Lily West's sons had been killed in the war.

Clara shrugged. Looking back and memories were for old people, not for her. Tomorrow she would be starting a new life, and all this – turning she surveyed the bare, almost empty, room – this part had been the dream. The reality was about to begin.

Nine

'You mean you've cut yourself adrift? Left yourself without a roof over your head? With nowhere to go if this show folds?' Dora Vane shifted the stub of a cigarette from one side of her mouth to the other. 'You've a lot to learn, chuck. I've seen more shows fold than you've had hot dinners. And by the look of you, you've not had many of them lately.'

Clara had never seen anyone who looked like Miss Dora Vane, not in the flesh at least. Billed as the 'Northern Star' at the turn of the century, Dora's hair was a bright fierce red shade, a colour at shouting variance with the purplish rouge dotted high on her sunken cheekbones. She wore a blouse with an old-fashioned high-boned collar over which her treble chin flowed when her head was in any other position than tilted back.

'Look, chuck.' She took Clara's arm as they made their way over the tramlines to the wide sweep of Blackpool's promenade. 'I've stood in the wings at every blinkin' rehearsal. I *know* you've got a voice, but I have to be honest with you, I can't for the life of me imagine what Mr Boland's thinking about.'

The wind took her round hat and whipped it from her head. Anchored to her hair by two long hatpins, it flapped like a sailor's collar in the breeze. Undeterred, she stopped and, opening a faded carpet bag, took out a third pin and rammed it home so fiercely that Clara shuddered for the safety of her brains.

'Breathe in, love,' she ordered. 'Get this good ozone right down in your lungs; you're going to need all your strength when we open tonight.'

'You mean you don't think I'm really good enough?'

As they stood by the railing, staring down at the wide expanse of golden sand and the sea glinting in the far distance, Clara felt the beat of her heart change for a terrifying moment to an uneven rhythm. *Remember Me* was a bits-and-pieces kind of show. Jack Tremain, the man who had written it, was the producer and the pianist. He'd made it quite clear that as far as Clara went he was doing what young Mr Boland had said he must do. Left to himself Clara had guessed he would throw her out of the show.

In *Remember Me* there were short sketches, one of them a clever satire on the 'Land fit for heroes' supposed to have been inherited by the men returning from France. It was Dora's job to drill the chorus girls, and drill them she did, her smoke-ruined voice yelling at them from the stalls. The star of the show was a coming-up-to-middle-age soubrette, who could be Marie Lloyd or Nellie Wallace in less time than it took for Clara to catch her breath in admiration. And there was Matty Shaw, a comedian in a straw hat and baggy suit, who sang 'Twenty-One Today' with a verve that belied the fact that he'd been singing it for the last twenty years in halls up and down the country.

'If there isn't a real birthday girl or boy in the audience, we plant one,' he'd told Clara. 'And nobody's ever cottoned on to the fact that the cake's made of cardboard.'

Miserably, Clara gloomed out to sea. 'Matty says I should be in opera.'

'He could be right at that, chuck.'

Dora wasn't being deliberately unkind. It wasn't in her nature, but for the first time in her long career she was doubting the wisdom of her beloved Mr Boland. This small girl, in spite of her startling beauty and unusual singing voice, didn't fit.

'I saw Archie Pitt's show, last summer.' Dora's boot-button eyes regarded Clara steadily. '*Mr Tower of London*, it's called. I don't suppose you've seen it, chuck? No, well, never mind. Anyway, there's an actress in it called Gracie Fields,' Dora continued mercilessly. '*She* has a fine voice, too, but as well as singing she takes part in the sketches, and *clowns* and

128

ad-libs. She's *versatile*, chuck, in other words.'

'And I'm not?'

'Well, hardly, chuck.'

'An' you think they'll boo me off the stage when we open tonight?'

Oblivious of the panic in Clara's voice, Dora nodded. 'They might at that. Maybe if you moved around the stage a bit? Put some actions in?'

The professional side of Dora's nature had taken her over completely. Constructive criticism was food and drink to a real pro anyway. Why, she'd had her own act changed many a time, with only an hour to curtain call. Suddenly, to Clara's horror, there on the promenade, with holidaymakers walking up and down, she whipped a scarf from round her throat, lowered it to her hips and proceeded to wiggle.

All that was puritanical in Clara's nature came out in her voice. 'Dora! People are staring!'

Holding the scarf at arm's length, Dora pirouetted round it, blowing kisses at a startled man in tweed plus-fours. 'It's not a bit of good standing there like a stick of celery looking for the salt. Folks on their holidays come for a laugh, for a good night out, with a pretty girl's figure to ogle at.' Throwing back her head so that the three chins did their disappearing act, she proclaimed in a ringing voice, 'The Folly Theatre of Varieties, Peter Street, Manchester. Eighteen eighty-three. Miss Dora Vane, appearing with Dan Leno, Lottie Collins and Marie Lloyd! That was me, folks!'

Clara felt as if her whole body was one big blush. She tried to catch hold of Dora's arm. '*Please*, Dora! People are laughing at you!'

'I've got it!' Swinging round, Dora faced the sea, holding out her short arms as if to embrace the waves. 'This is what you should be singing tonight. A song with a bit of oomph in it.' Her voice, the rattle of cockleshells in a tin can, wheezed across the sand dunes:

> 'Yes, sir, that's my baby,
> No, sir, don't mean maybe,
> Yes, sir, that's my baby nee-ow . . . '

A small semicircle of fascinated onlookers had gathered, and suddenly Clara could stand no more. By the time she had reached the foot of the stone steps leading down to the sands, Dora had turned to face her audience.

> 'By the way, by the way,
> When we reach the preacher I'll say . . . '

Her raucous voice followed Clara, who ran as if pursued by devils across the stretch of clean golden sand riffled up into hard ridges by the receding tide. It was painful to her feet; she felt every undulation through the thin soles of her boots, but undaunted she ran on.

Dora might be a professional through and through, but Clara was not. What fragile confidence she had possessed in her own talent had gone, squeezed out of her like air from a pricked balloon. Whatever had made her think she was good enough to face an audience of hard-headed northerners? The audience tonight would be a far cry from the kindly neighbours sitting in their pews at the chapel, sending out waves of sympathy and encouragement to a local girl they'd known since she was big enough to play hopscotch on the flags outside her father's shop. The audience tonight couldn't be compared, either, to the Masonic ladies and gentlemen soothed into responsiveness by a five-course meal and top-price brandy.

A stick of celery? Singing 'The Old Rugged Cross'? Wearing a dress like a nightie, and without a single wiggle to raise a laugh?

Oh God, dear God, the Father of the Jesus she had once imagined lived in the chapel at the top of the street. Clara's cry was a prayer. Was He there, this God of her childhood, somewhere out across the wide stretch of shimmering sea? If she asked Him nicely, would they like her tonight? Was a voice without a wiggle no good at all? What would she do if they booed her off the stage? Where could she go?

And where was Joe, who had started it all? Was Mr Boland wrong and Joe right? Was she a fraud, a nowt? And if Joe came back now, this minute, running towards her across the sands with his cheeky grin, would this terrible fear leave her as he took her in his arms? Joe had said the sea was big and wet, and he'd been right about that!

Clara cried her terror aloud. 'Oh, stop thinking about a man you know is no good! Stop pretending you love him! You're not Joe's girl, an' you never have been. You're on your own, Clara Haydock, an' you've just got to make them like you tonight, because if they don't then you're finished!'

The water was lapping round her feet; the far horizon gleamed like a silver ribbon. A seagull swooped and wheeled, but she felt and heard nothing.

Turning round she walked slowly back; even raised a hand in greeting when Dora called her name in a voice that would have put a foghorn to shame.

'What's *wrong* with her?'

Standing in the wings that night, Matty Shaw faced Dora Vane, his face beneath its layer of greasepaint tight with disbelief.

'Why isn't she singing the song she was supposed to sing? What the 'ell's got into her? She's murdering it! Oh, God, they'll murder *her*!'

Already the audience, faces burned brick red by the sun and wind, were fidgeting in their seats, nudging each other, actually laughing out loud.

'Oh, my God!' Matty covered his eyes with his hands. 'What *is* she trying to do with that awful red feather boa? They think she's a stripper!'

'Baby, won't you please come home?' sang Clara, tripping first to one side of the stage, with the spotlight desperately trying to keep up with her. And missing.

''Cause your mamma's all alone . . . ' She beckoned coyly as if to an unseen lover, and the rowdier element in the audience began the slow handclap.

The glorious voice, pitched far too high, rose in a wail of despair. An orange, neatly fielded by the violinist in the orchestra pit, convulsed the, by now, almost hysterical audience.

'The curtain!' Matty, making frantic signs, wheeled on

131

Dora in fury. 'This is your doing, you dimwitted has-been! I wondered what you were doing coming down so early.' Almost purple with rage, he waved both arms at the prompt side. 'The curtain, for God's sake! Get her off!'

'Now you just stop that and listen to me!'

Five minutes later he was down on his knees by Clara's side in the bleak dressing room with its row of empty firebuckets lined up against the wall. His voice was so gentle and tender that Clara's noisy tears flowed afresh.

'Do you know what young Mr Boland would have done if he'd come into the theatre in time to hear you killing a song that was all wrong for you in the first place?'

'He'd've sent me packing. After he'd admitted he'd made a terrible mistake in giving me a chance.' Clara's head drooped so that her hair fell forward, hiding her face completely.

The old comedian's fish-flat eyes filled with pity. 'He made no mistake, love. Mr Boland's too canny and hard-headed to make that kind of mistake. He wanted you to sing your own kind of song, in the way you sing, without embellishments ... ' Matty snatched the red feather boa from the back of Clara's chair and hurled it to the far corner. 'He knows you are *different*, so different that folks sit up and take notice.'

He talked to the top of Clara's head, knowing she was listening, praying she was taking heed.

'Pretty girls who sing and dance are two-a-penny in this business. Mimics are two-a-penny. Bum wigglers are two-a-penny.' He said the word deliberately, knowing it would shock and, sure enough, Clara lifted her head. 'But *beautiful* girls with special singing voices don't exactly grow on trees. There's a freshness about you that catches the throat. A *goodness*.'

Turning to Dora hovering guiltily behind him, Matty's voice hardened. 'And you ought to be down on those rheumaticky knees of yours begging this lass's forgiveness. Aye, and Mr Boland's as well, because if he ever hears of your flamin' interference you'll be the one sent packing.'

'He's right, chuck.' Dora's chins wobbled with the force of her emotion. 'I was trying to turn you into another Dora Vane. You don't realize that, but Matty does.' She clasped Clara's shoulder with a heavy hand. 'It's the nineteen twenties now; they want a straight delivery, no playing to the gallery.' She exchanged a nod with Matty. 'And that's what you're going to do. You're going on in the second house and you're going to put your own song over the way Mr Boland told you to. No moving, no nothing.' The fingers pressed hard into Clara's shoulder. 'For my sake, love. For old Dora's sake, chuck.'

'Never!' The green eyes were wide and staring with sheer terror. 'I'd rather die! I don't belong. Mr Boland was wrong.' She stared wildly round the dingy room. 'Even *he* can be wrong sometimes, I bet. I'm going to go back to me digs, then in the morning I'm going to catch the first train home. I'm *engaged*,' she improvised. 'I'll be getting married soon.'

The sympathy on Matty's broad face disappeared as quickly as if someone had taken an india rubber to it. Reaching out, he hauled Clara to her feet.

'You've heard of Charlie Chaplin? 'Course you have. Well, you listen to me, me girl! He didn't walk straight into a solo spot like you. Not him. Dancing in the street to a barrel organ was the way he got started. Took a part in a pantomime playing a dog, Charlie did. No spotlight for Mr Chaplin.' Matty shook Clara none too gently. 'You listening? Played your home town in 1903, and what as? A page in a two-bit play, and a *wolf* in *Peter Pan* two years later. Years and years of taking any part before he made it big in America. And you imagine he's got where he is without getting the bird?'

Wrenching her hands from Matty's horny grasp, Clara made for the door, only to bump into seven girls of the chorus shedding feathers as they went, screaming for Dora to help them change into their costumes for the next routine.

This time Matty made sure. Holding Clara by both arms pinioned to her sides, he thrust his sweating face into hers.

'You give up and Mr Boland'll want to know why. He's a

good man till he's crossed, and when he finds out, Dora'll have to go.' He twisted Clara round so she could see Dora feverishly buttoning a redhaired dancer into a sequinned catsuit. 'And where will she go? To the workhouse? The country's littered with old timers like Dora, *starving* on account of dedicating their lives to the theatre. Bloody *starving*, Clara. Is that what you'd do to her?'

'Mr Boland wouldn't do that.' But even as she protested Clara remembered Bart Boland's penetrating blue gaze and suspected that Matty was speaking the truth. From somewhere inside her bruised heart she dredged up the remnants of her courage.

'All right, then,' she said slowly. 'I'll try again. Just this once. For Dora.'

Clara's solo spot was just before the interval. The act preceding hers was a trio of girl contortionists, scantily dressed, who twisted their lithe bodies into unlikely positions. They weren't meant to be funny, but the second-house audience, determined to enjoy themselves or bust, laughed uproariously. When one girl actually managed to sit on her own head, a man from the circle shouted, 'Oo's got a filleted backside!', provoking the audience into delighted laughter.

Standing in the wings, Dora turned to a whey-faced Matty. 'God help the poor little lass,' she whispered. 'They're out for blood tonight.'

Tripping off, the girls made straight for the dressing rooms. 'It's a bullfight that lot should be watching. Ignorant devils.'

Delaying her entrance to the last possible minute, Clara walked slowly out of the shadows of the wings, her eyes fixed, as if she stared at some distant horizon.

Silently Dora and Matty watched her move into the centre spotlight. In the pit the conductor took up his baton. The pianist played the opening chords, stopped, played them again, then swivelled round on his stool with a questioning expression on his face.

'She's dried.' Matty's whisper was a moan. 'Oh, dear God, she can't find her voice.'

Sheer blinding terror held Clara in its grip. Her heart was pounding so loudly and unevenly she felt she must surely die. Frantically she turned towards the wings and saw the easel by the footlights with 'The Clogger's Child' printed on the board in large letters.

She clenched her hands so tightly the nails dug into her palms. 'The Clogger's Child'. That's who she was. Little Clara Haydock who had been able to sing almost before she could talk. Clara with the godgiven voice. Hadn't her father once told her that?

Suddenly her vision cleared. She saw the dim shapes of heads, the white blur of faces upturned. Waiting to diminish her. Just biding their time to show their contempt.

Her head lifted, the green eyes blazed, and pure and clear her glorious voice poured out.

For the first few bars the audience were obviously startled into submission. Was this what they'd paid good money to see and hear? A slip of a girl in a white frock singing a flamin' sacred song? The joker in the circle leaped to his feet, only to be dragged back by his companion.

'Give 'er a chance, mate. Just pipe bloody down, will you?'

'So I'll cling to the old rugged cross . . . ' Every word distinct, every note as pure as rainwater. The quiet after the storm. Still serenity after the noise and colour that had gone before. Not a rustle, not a movement. From the front stalls right up to the gods where the audience sat on wooden seats. The music soaring, dying, caressing, then rising again. Memories of mothers humming the same words as they rocked in their chairs by the fire. Gramophones wound up, the needle lowered onto the record. Sunday afternoon tea of bread and jam and fatty-cake spiced with currants.

'And exchange it one day for a crown . . . '

In the wings Dora and Matty leaned on each other, overcome by emotion.

'Mr Boland was right.'

'He's always right. I deserve to be shot.'

Clara came off, bemused by the thunderous applause, to be pressed to Dora's scented bosom.

'Go back, chuck. Hold out your arms to them, then curtsey low.'

'But like Mr Boland said, no encore.' Matty wagged a finger in Clara's flushed face. 'Keep 'em shouting for more.'

'Oh, my God!' Dora's face was as purple as the chiffon pussy-cat bow at her throat. 'They're giving her a standing ovation!'

Blackpool, Burnley, Bolton, Warrington, Wigan and Manchester. Six towns in as many weeks, with *Remember Me* often showing the 'House Full' sign.

The small company travelled by train each Sunday afternoon, each member carrying his own props and costumes as well as personal belongings. Wherever they went Dora took Clara with her to share a room, and more often than not a bed.

'This sweetheart of yours? The one you said you was engaged to. Funny he's never once turned up to see the show.' Dora, searching the bed in the Bell Vue lodgings at Manchester for bugs, straightened up to rub her aching back. Her tiny eyes were shrewd. 'You made him up, didn't you, chuck?'

Clara didn't want to talk about Joe. For over a month now, ever since what should have come hadn't, she had tried to put Joe West to the back of her troubled mind. God was kind and all-forgiving. He wouldn't punish her for what she'd done with Joe. Not now when things were getting better and better. Hadn't God said that none of man's sins would be remembered against him? God *never* sent *affliction* as a punishment for sin. Not if you repented and prayed for forgiveness. As she'd been doing, night after night, lying beside a snoring Dora in some lumpy bed.

Dora was rubbing this particular mattress with a bar of yellow soap. 'Always fetches 'em. Little red blighters aren't blessed with brains.' She stared hard at Clara. 'Aw, don't look like that, chuck. Better than rats anyroad. I remember one digs I was stopping in . . . ' Her expression deepened

136

into anxiety. 'You've gone as white as a piece of bleached fent, love. Here, come and sit down for a minute.'

Living so closely together, in enforced intimacy, hadn't left room for secrets, not even feminine secrets. Dora stared down into Clara's pinched face, feeling the scalp beneath her thatch of red hair tighten as she allowed a suspicion to take hold of her. For almost seven weeks now she'd been closer to Clara than if she'd been her own mother, and not once had Clara had an 'off' day, or mentioned a backache, or moaned about what the other girls called the 'curse'.

'Oh, love,' she said helplessly. 'If you've anything to tell me, then tell me now. Look at me! Come on. Old Dora's heard it all before, you know.'

'What are you on about?' Clara stood up abruptly, turning her back. 'It's time we were unpacked. I've got to go and rehearse my song for this week.' Her smile was as strained as if it had been painted on her face and left in that position to dry. 'It's a new one called "The Bells of St Mary's". They're going to try and get a bell effect into the orchestration.'

Dora levered herself up off the bed and told herself she could do no more. Time would tell. Oh, dear, dear God, time would surely tell.

Dora was wearing an accordion-pleated chiffon dress that day, a dress more in keeping with a state banquet. It billowed out beneath her velvet cloak, and when they went out into the little grey street Clara saw a woman across the way nearly fall off her doorstep in astonishment.

'Hope she got 'er eye full.'

Dora's sense of humour had completely deserted her. The tearing anxiety was pricking away in her stomach with the force of a whole paper of pins. She was responsible for this small girl, dammit. Mr Boland had put Clara in her care, and, besides, she was fond of her. Well, all right then, she *loved* her, and if her suspicions were right then she'd find the man who'd done it and make him squeal for mercy.

Head jutting forward, bottom sticking out well behind, Dora walked beside Clara through one little grey street after another, her thoughts as grim as the expression on her face.

137

In the middle of the week the *Manchester Evening News* ran a full column on the girl singer billed as 'The Clogger's Child'.

Who said that music hall has waned in popularity since the war? *Remember Me* purports to be a revue, but it hasn't strayed far in concept from variety. If you want to hear an angel sing, go and see 'The Clogger's Child' hold her audience in her hands. Hear her wring a tear from even the hardest heart with the glory of her unique voice. We predict that one day she'll be a household word.

'Like Cherry Blossom Boot Polish,' said Clara. 'Fancy that!'

She stayed in bed later than usual one morning. There was no fireplace in the tiny room she shared with Dora and she was shivering with cold. She wanted to sleep, but when she closed her eyes the bed dropped away beneath her.

'I feel a bit sick,' she admitted. 'My back hurts, but I'll be all right.' A winter fly buzzed round her head and she swiped at it with a languid hand. 'If it lands on my face, I'll scream,' she said in a coldly despairing voice.

The pain in her lower back was so bad that evening that she allowed Dora to dress her as if she were a child. Dora's fingers, fumbling with the row of tiny buttons at the high neck of the long white dress, smelt of strong cheese, and Clara turned her head away, swallowing the bile in her throat. Dora's face was so close that Clara could see the way her lips looked, as if they'd been gathered with needle and thread. Her lipstick ran into the vertical wrinkles, and orange-tinted powder was pressed heavily into the purse-shaped bags beneath her eyes.

'Let's have a bit more rouge tonight, chuck,' she was saying. 'You're that pale they'll think it's a corpse coming on.'

'I'm all right, Dora.' Clara bit her lips hard as a vicious cramplike pain moved round her back to stab her abdomen. She had to force herself to stand upright, and when she saw herself in the mirror she recoiled from the sight of the rouge standing out against the deathly pallor of her skin.

138

There was a question begging to be asked in Dora's eyes, but Clara turned on her before she'd even opened her mouth.

'I've *told* you. I'm all right.'

But waiting in the wings for the familiar music and the bronchial wheeze of sound as the dusty green and gold curtain rose, a fresh wave of pain brought beads of sweat out on her forehead.

'You're on, chuck.' Suddenly Dora wanted to cry. With her long golden hair hanging loose Clara looked like a child on her way to bed. But she wasn't a child, was she? Dora wiped her eyes with the end of her pussy-cat chiffon bow. Young Clara was having a miscarriage. Dora had lived too long and seen too much not to recognize the signs.

'Just let her get through her song,' she prayed, clasping her hands together. 'She believes in You, so help her now. Just let her sing her song . . . '

On centre stage, in the dazzling spotlight, Clara sang as if she'd been wound up then ordered to sing. There was a mist in front of her eyes, and though she knew the pain was still there she found she could sing through it.

In the short time since joining the company she had changed from amateur status to professional, and so she sang the way her audience had paid to hear her sing. Not an untrue note, each word with the ecstasy of a bird in flight, the lower notes so deep and rich they sent a shiver down the spine.

When it was over and she stood in the small telling silence before the applause, it seemed the dusty boards came up to hit her hard between the eyes. When she fell the audience rose to their feet as one man.

'Are you her mother?'

The young doctor at the big teaching hospital down the road from the theatre was finding it hard to look away from Dora's brightly hennaed hair. He had worked thirty-six hours without a break and it showed in his eyes.

'I'm her friend,' Dora told him. 'You can tell me what's wrong.'

The doctor was sticking to the rules. He was too tired to do otherwise. 'So you're not her next of kin?'

'She hasn't got no bleedin' next of kin!' Dora had sat up all night on a hard bench. Her feet had swelled and her corsets were killing her. 'I'm all she's got! I'm *responsible* for her. I *love* her! If anything happens to that child, it'll break my heart.' The pancake make-up had not survived the long night well and Dora's anguished face was not a pretty sight.

Sitting down by her side on the bench, the doctor threw protocol out of the window.

'I'll try to explain it as simply as I can,' he said.

'I *know*, Dora. The doctor told me.'

Two days later Clara was sitting up in bed, her fingers pleating and repleating the turned-down sheet.

'I've been a wicked girl. I did a wicked thing and this is my punishment. If I can never have a baby, then that is God's will.'

'Rubbish!' Dora lowered her voice to what she considered a whisper. 'If that God of yours punished girls for doing what comes naturally, then the human race would die out. If that's religion, then I'm glad I'm a heathen.' She leaned forward. 'Why didn't you tell me? That's what I can't forgive. All that worry stiff inside you.' She sniffed. 'Quinine the girls try first, then a whip-round for the forty quid or so it costs for some foreign woman to help them. Help them? My God, I've seen girls . . . '

'Please, Dora.' Clara looked pained. 'I'm not like that. You know I'm not.'

'Like what?' Dora's voice rose again. 'You don't have to be wicked to get caught. Most of them were like you, let down by a man who promised them the earth, then cleared off.' She took a handkerchief from her large straw bag and touched it to her nose. 'Clara. It's got to be said now and never mentioned again. The baby you were having was growing in the wrong place – in a tube – and they had to operate to remove it. So having another baby when you get married some day won't be all that easy.'

'I don't care.' Clara wouldn't meet her eyes. 'Dora. Please?

140

I have to pay for what I did. Don't you see?'

'No! I do *not* see!' As Dora's corncrake voice rang out in the stillness of the long ward faces raised themselves from pillows. 'I don't like your God, Clara Haydock!' So great was her anger she almost spat. 'You're a human being, child. Not a bleedin' saint!'

Suddenly aware of the staring eyes from the rows of beds, she turned round, the flowers on her hat bobbing as if in a high wind. 'Want a bit of a singsong to cheer you ladies up?' she asked, standing up just in time to see a tall pale sister coming through the swing doors.

'Well, never mind.' She kissed Clara goodbye. 'I've forgotten the best bit of news.' The button eyes shone. 'The company's got a London booking – well – on the outskirts anyroad. And Mr Boland's sent word you're to get your strength up before you follow on.'

'Does Mr Boland know what's been the matter with me?' Remembering those vivid blue eyes, Clara's heart sank. 'Will he find out, do you think?'

'Mr Boland?' Dora whirled round in indignation. 'And what if he does? He won't be looking for ways to punish you. Not like that God of yours.'

Nodding to the sister, she walked away down the ward in her floating dress with a none too clean pair of white pumps showing beneath. Wisps of red hair escaped from the bun at the back of her head onto the black velvet collar of her cloak, and before she disappeared through the swing doors she turned round.

'London, think on!' she bellowed. 'Piccadilly Circus, Leicester Square, London, chuck! Think on . . . '

When she'd gone the ward seemed very quiet. The sister's eyebrows raised themselves almost to her scraped-back hairline, but before she could say a word Clara spoke quickly.

'That was my mother,' she lied with pride.

Ten

At first Clara wrote regularly to Lily West. She always included a forwarding address, but now, after more than two years without a reply, she gave up.

'Maybe she's kicked the bucket, chuck?'

Dora Vane stopped sewing lace into the neck of a pale green crepe-de-Chine nightdress to peer at Clara over the top of the spectacles she swore were only worn for show.

'Or maybe she can't write? A lot of people will never admit to that, you know.'

'But Alec could write. Or someone could write. Even if Walter's married or living somewhere else – he could write.'

Clara was stretched out on her bed, taking her rest before the evening's performance – a rest Dora insisted she took, especially on the days Clara played cabaret after the show.

The Boland revue, with new acts added over the years, was playing a winter's season at the Holborn Empire, and after the last performance Clara was whisked by taxi cab to a Soho nightclub to sing as lead-in to the star. By her side on the bed was a copy of the *Daily Express*, with her first mention in Hannen Swaffer's widely read column:

'The Clogger's Child,' he proclaimed, in the way every utterance of his turned into a proclamation, 'has real star quality. She moves little during her act, but when she does, watch out for your blood pressure. Her voice, had it been trained for opera, could rise easily above the strings of a full orchestra. Her low notes are dark and rich, and her high notes fill the theatre with no sign of the irritating tremor which seems to afflict most of the West End's leading ladies

142

warbling up the nostrils of their leading men. The haunting quality of her voice goes on in your head, long after the curtain has come down and you've wended your way home. She sings with her heart, this beautiful young girl from some northern slum.'

Impatiently, Clara pushed the folded newspaper away from her so violently it slid from the shiny eiderdown onto the floor.

'You know, Dora, I never thought, not once, that I came from a slum. I suppose it's only folks who have never lived that way who consider themselves qualified to label those narrow little streets as slums.' She linked both arms behind her head, smiling. 'Our street was so quiet and respectable, you wouldn't credit it, Dora. Flags mopped first thing, window bottoms stoned, washing hanging out in the backs full of smuts from the mill chimneys. And the coal carts and the rag-and-bone men trundling down the backs.' She smiled. 'I've come a long way since then. I have'n all.' She waved a hand round the bedroom, a part of the flat at the top of a Georgian house in Conduit Street. 'Remember the awful lodgings we stayed in on tour, Dora?'

'I'd still be staying in them but for you, chuck.' Dora's pudgy face gentled into open affection. 'You've taken me up with you, and I can't forget that.'

'But you *work* for your living.' Swinging her legs over the side of the bed, Clara stood up, the front of her lace-trimmed housecoat opening to reveal a pair of jade green satin camiknickers. 'Housekeeper, seamstress, chaperone. I couldn't manage without you, and you know it.'

'Chaperone? Huh!' Dora's rough voice was laced with disgust. 'What do you need a chaperone for, may I ask?' She stabbed her needle into the delicate material. 'Ever since you had that trouble all that time ago you've never let a man come near you. And you don't need to look at me like that. It's not natural coming straight back here every night, sleeping all morning then walking the streets in the afternoons when you haven't got a matinée. Where do you go, for heaven's sake?'

Clara sat down again on the bed, her green eyes dreamy.

'Piccadilly Circus sometimes.' She turned to smile at Dora. 'It's so beautiful at midday with all the flower girls sitting round their osier baskets, busily wiring buttonholes to sell in the evening. All those taxis, cars and red buses going round and round. And then Shaftesbury Avenue, Dora. Do you know, all the theatres along there have long queues even at that time, with people wanting gallery seats? And Lyon's Corner House. Oh, I wish you could walk well enough to come with me. I sit there eating poached egg on toast and drinking a cup of tea, *hugging* myself, Dora, because I'm here . . . And then Wardour Street. Dora, it's so *short*, but there's so much crammed into it. Old bookshops, a window full of wigs. And a framed letter from Sarah Bernhardt.' Her gaze shifted as she lowered her voice to a whisper. 'And prostitutes, Dora. Fallen women, standing as still as waxworks. It's *fascinating*, can't you see? If we were to live here for ever I'd only see a part of it. It's *London*, Dora! The most marvellous city in the world.'

'Spoken like a true Lancastrian.' Dora pushed herself heavily out of her chair and came over to help Clara into her street dress. Her powdered face was clownlike in its thick coating of make-up. 'Is that all you ask from life? The company of an old woman like me, and walking the streets on your afternoons off, with a poached egg in Lyon's eaten on your own? What's happened to your insides? Have they dried and shrivelled like mine?' The lines down her cheeks deepened. 'It'll show in your voice. A woman has to love to sing the sort of songs you're singing now. And I don't mean loved by that God of yours either! Because that's not enough.'

'That's a terrible thing to say!'

'So I'll burn in hellfire?' Dora took up a tortoiseshell brush from the dressing table and motioned Clara to sit down on the padded stool. 'You know what's wrong with you?' She tugged hard at a knot in the silky fall of white-blonde hair. 'You're frightened of men. Your head's so full of puritanical religious claptrap, if a man laid a finger on you you'd faint dead away. You've got God and Satan, and that man who let you down, all fighting a losing battle in your head. And one day you're going to fall in love. Then what will you do?'

She looked so genuinely worried that Clara turned round. Taking the brush, she held the liver-spotted hand to her cheek.

'No more sewing tonight, Dora. To bed with your malted milk. All right?' Snatching up her wrap from the bed, she smiled. 'I'll fall in love just to please you one of these fine days and when I do you'll be the first to know.'

Outside the house the taxi was waiting. It was always there, at exactly the same time, standing by the kerb, the driver hunched over the wheel. Clara would have preferred to go to the theatre by bus, sitting on the open top deck with the small cover of waterproof sheeting over her knees, feeling the rain on her face, but she knew that would never do, not now she was almost famous.

Almost, she reminded herself, sitting back on the leather seat, pulling the fur collar of her white coat up round her face, hugging herself once again with the delight of seeing the theatres they were driving past coming alive for the night's performance.

'Here we are, Blondie.' That was the taxi driver's name for her. 'And there they are,' he grinned, giving her the thumb's-up sign. 'Not as many tonight with this rain.'

As usual the pavement outside the theatre was lined with a small crowd, young women in the main at that early time. Typists and shopgirls, mouths agape as they stared at Clara in her white woollen coat with its huge silver-fox collar, slim legs in white silk stockings, white kid shoes with pointed toes on her slender feet.

'Coo! Isn't she lovely?'

'It was in the paper yesterday that the Prince of Wales came to hear her sing.'

'They say she gets fifty pounds a week.'

'No wonder she can wear white on a mucky night like this.'

The last speaker, a girl with bold dark eyes and hair cut in a piquant fringe, a style which she hoped made her look like Jessie Matthews, turned round as a man in a brown trilby hat tried to push his way to the front.

"'Ere! Who d'you think you're shoving, mate? Didn't your mum teach you no manners?"

Joe West stared into the vivacious face with the blank gaze of a blind man. Shrugging his shoulders, he elbowed his way back through the crowd to mingle with the people thronging the pavement on their way to the theatres and restaurants lining each side of the busy street.

Clara was achingly tired when her taxi dropped her outside the tall house in Conduit Street at two o'clock the next morning.

The cabaret and show had gone well. It was making a lot of money now, and even the chorus girls and the lead dancer, a girl who had grown too tall for the ballet, swallowed their jealousy to admit that it was Clara's two solo spots which filled the theatre. Coming in out of the cold that bitter January, her voice seemed to warm them.

'Listen!' it seemed to be saying. 'There is so much beauty in this world of ours. I am here to remind you of it. Just listen to me. Singing to you is what I was born for. Singing to you is all I want or need to do.'

'Carolina moon, keep shining . . . ' Each note silver clear, each cadence heart-stopping in its purity.

Sometimes the more sensitive souls would sense a loneliness in her as she stood with pale golden head bowed to acknowledge the applause. Women in the stalls would unpin the flowers from their dresses and throw them at her feet.

Tonight she had brought an armful of flowers home for Dora, and as she held them awkwardly in one arm, scrabbling in her purse for her key, a man stepped out from the shadows.

'Hello, Clara.'

There was no mistaking that voice, nor the sinuous smile beneath the wide brim of the rain-soaked trilby hat. Clara stared at him for a long moment without speaking, then opened the door and motioned for Joe to follow her in, surprised at her calmness, reminding herself that it was

146

because she had always known he would turn up one day. Up the narrow oak stairs they went to the top landing, the flowers spilling from her arms as she unlocked the door.

And only then, with the door closed behind them, did she turn and look properly at him, and what she saw narrowed her eyes and made her heartbeats quicken.

This man, this boy she knew from her childhood, looked ten years older than his twenty-six years. The dark hair still curled over his forehead, the grin was still there, but the handsome features had coarsened, grown bloated, the dark blue eyes sunk deep in their sockets.

As she stood there staring at him, it seemed as though everything in her was stilled. Her brain, her breathing, her heartbeats, all held as in a vice. Before she could move he was beside her, pulling her into his arms, straining her against him, his mouth searching for her own.

'Clara. Oh, my little Clara. If you knew the times I've longed to do this. Kiss me. Hold me. Oh, love, there'll be no more going away from now on. This time it's you and me, the way it's always been. But for ever.'

At last she came to life. With heart pounding, with limbs trembling, she fought and struggled until he stood away from her, still sure of himself, only faintly puzzled by her reaction.

'What's wrong, love? I *told* you I'd come back. I was the one who said you'd be a success. With your name outside the theatre. I told you that when you were a nothing. Remember?' For an instant she saw the creeping fear in his eyes, then at the blink of an eyelid it was gone. 'You're not angry with me, are you, our kid?'

The sheer nerve of him, the blatant hypocrisy, the taken-for-granted acceptance of her welcome, made her sway and widen her eyes in disbelief.

'Angry with you? Did you say *angry*?' The huge fur collar on the white coat was suddenly choking the life out of her. With shaking fingers she unclasped the heavy fastening and threw the coat over the back of a chintzed settee. 'Do you think the world stands still when you go away, Joe West?' Clasping her hands together she was surprised to find they were sweating. 'You left me in my father's house without a job, with *nothing*, and you didn't care! Because you thought I'd failed the audition at the Palace Theatre you wrote me off! You thought I would never have another chance. So you went away.' Glancing towards the door leading into Dora's bedroom she frowned. 'Whatever you have to say to me, say it quietly, please.' She walked to the settee and sat down. 'My . . . my housekeeper is asleep through there.'

'Your housekeeper? Bloody hell!' Joe glanced round the room with its velvet curtains and comfortable chairs. 'You've come a long way, our kid.' A half-smile still played around his lips. 'Remember when you chopped three stand-chairs up for the fire because you hadn't got the money for coal?'

'I don't forget anything.' Clara spoke quietly. 'How is your mother, Joe? And Alec? Do you *care* how they are?'

Joe sat down in a wing chair opposite to the settee. He could hardly believe the difference in her, even though he had expected to find her changed. He frowned and bit his lips. There was no man in her life, that much he'd found out, and yet this was no longer his little Clara with adoration in her green eyes ready to follow where he beckoned. Telling him off first, then being ready to forgive. He wished he didn't feel so ill. It was an hour at least since he'd had a drink. He'd upended a bottle into the gutter outside the house, cursing, but knowing he'd have to stop where he was if he wanted to catch her coming home.

'You haven't got a drink, have you, love?' It was no good, he had to ask, but when her mouth set hard he knew he'd made a mistake. Once a Methodist, always a Methodist. His dry lips twisted into an ugly grimace.

'No, you don't care.' She was speaking again, this stranger with the calm face and the changed accent. 'I've had a long time to think about you, Joe, and I've realized you've never really given much thought to anyone apart from yourself. And no, I haven't got a drink. By the look of you you've had far too much already.'

It was too much. Anger rose in him like a lick of flame. The sanctimonious little devil! Religion did that to some

148

people. Set them above others who didn't read their Bible every day. It was there, sure enough, on the mahogany wine table by the fireplace, with a leather marker in, showing her the place. Almost without knowing it, he was by her side on the wide-cushioned settee, gripping her by the arms, forcing her to look him in the eyes.

'Has't forgeet 'ow tha used to talk?' Deliberately he lapsed into broad dialect. 'Tha's still little Clara Haydock from t'clogger's shop. Still her what wet her britches on her fost day at schoo'.'

Before she could twist away, he cupped her chin to bring her mouth round to his own. There was a wild desperation in the way he kissed her, forcing her lips apart, trying to push her backwards to lie beneath him. 'Clara,' he muttered thickly. 'Remember how we were that time? You're still my girl. Always have been and always will be.'

Her mouth felt bruised and hot, but she knew instinctively that to fight back would only inflame him further. Tangling her fingers in his thick curly hair she forced his head back. Her green eyes blazed into his.

He began to bluster. 'Aw, come on now, Clara. Don't pretend. You've not got where you are without going with other men. But I understand. None of that counts with me. I've been in this game too long not to know what goes on.'

Still she held him away from her with a strength she hadn't known she possessed.

'I was going to have your baby, Joe, but I lost it, and nearly died. You *shamed* me!' For a second she loosened her hold on him as the memory of those terrible weeks of fear and uncertainty rose to remind her of the way it had been. Her voice rose and sharpened. '*No* other man has touched me since then. I can do without men, Joe West. So you see how wrong you are!'

He was not all bad. His mother had always maintained that, and the shock of what she had just told him unnerved him, so that he slid from the settee to kneel on the carpet, burying his head in her lap.

'Aw, Clara,' he whispered brokenly. 'I didn't know. If I had known . . . '

149

To her horror he began to cry, rough unmanly tears, with his shoulders shaking and the sobs rasping in his throat. For a moment she was tempted to stroke his hair, but her hand refused to move. As she sat there her heart felt as hard and cold as stone.

'Where did you go, Joe? After you left me alone? Where did you go?'

She had to bend her head low to catch what he said, and as she listened her heart grew colder still.

'I went to South Africa. To Cape Town.' The Irish lilt that always came into his voice when he was troubled was there now. 'I was living with this girl, well, this woman, really, and she was offered a two-year contract for a tour in a variety show. She wangled me in somehow as an assistant stage manager. Honest to God, Clara, if I'd known about the baby I'd never have gone.'

'And what *would* you have done, Joe?'

'I'd've stuck by you. You know that.'

'Married me? Lived with me in my father's house? Gone out and got a decent job?'

'You know I would. I love you, Clara. I always have.'

His words came muffled, choked by sobs, and suddenly she knew she didn't believe him. With a cold hand still squeezing her heart she pulled his head back, forcing him to meet her eyes. With a finger she made the gesture of wiping away the tears from beneath his eyes, knowing there were none, that there never had been any tears. And the expression on his face told her that he knew she had found him out.

Pushing him away roughly, she stood up. 'Get up off your knees, Joe. Stop pretending to cry.' Her voice was weary. 'What kind of a fool do you take me for?' Walking on unsteady legs she went towards the door and opened it wide. 'She's thrown you out, this girl . . . this woman . . . hasn't she? You came back to London and you saw what had been happening to me. You thought you would cash in, Joe, just as you've always cashed in on an easy option. Just go. Now, – this minute. I'm waiting, Joe.'

He got to his feet, feeling his stomach muscles contract.

This wasn't the small Clara he'd left behind in Mill Street, tearful, vulnerable, hanging on his every word. But she wasn't as calm as she appeared to be. He could feel the tenseness in her. As he made to pass her, he caught her to him.

'You don't mean it really. This is what you want. Your head may be filled with righteous claptrap, but it's me your body needs.'

As his mouth covered hers and she smelt the stale drink on him, she managed to free one hand to claw at his face. When he clutched her breast and her mouth was free she screamed.

'Dora! Oh, Dora! Help me, help me!'

For the rest of his days Joe would never forget the apparition which appeared in a doorway leading off the sitting room. Dora in her voluminous nightgown with her red hair in rags, holding aloft a heavy cut-glass vase, was a sight to make the blood run cold.

Relinquishing his hold on Clara, he managed to duck as the vase crashed into the wall behind his head. Before he could gather his senses the old woman came towards him, picking up a long paperknife from a coffee table as she advanced.

'Oh, my God!' Muttering curses, Joe turned and ran, clattering down the narrow stairway, pausing for breath only when he reached the pavement, turning to shake a fist at the upstairs window before making off into the darkness with the rain pelting down on his uncovered head.

Back in the upstairs room Dora lowered herself into a chair, and when Clara dropped on her knees and put her arms about her, she held out her hands and looked down at them. The knife fell from her fingers.

'I wanted to kill him,' she muttered brokenly. 'It *was* him, wasn't it? The one who made a baby with you and went away?'

When she saw the answer in Clara's eyes, she shuddered and put her face in her hands, swaying backwards and forwards with the rags in her hair standing out like porcupine quills.

'I know now I could have killed a man,' she whispered. 'Aye, and swung for him gladly. I would have stuck that knife in his ribs and enjoyed hearing him squeal. For you,' she added. 'For you, little chuck, just for you.'

'Oh, Dora . . . Dora . . . ' Reaching up Clara pressed the fiercely red head against her breast. Then they sat there, without speaking, bound in love, with the rain beating against the window, and the long night slipping by outside.

Eleven

'If Mr Boland's taking you to the Café Royal for lunch, then it means he thinks you've arrived.'

Dora insisted on climbing stiff-legged down the stairway to see Clara off. 'He's never taken you anywhere as posh as that before, has he? You ought not to be *walking*,' she scolded, panting for breath in the doorway. 'You should arrive decently in a taxi. And at least ten minutes late. Men know where they stand with a girl if she keeps them waiting.'

With a satisfied nod she looked Clara up and down. That lynx collar in the neck of the short black coat was just right, and with her hair tucked away inside a scarlet cloche hat Clara was a real bobby-dazzler. A bit too plain an outfit for Dora's own taste, but then the young could get away with anything. Clara's shoes were all right though, even though hardly suitable for winter pavements covered in a light coating of snow from a recent fall, high-heeled and flimsy and costing the earth from Jack Jacobus's shop in Shaftesbury Avenue. Dora admitted to herself that her own days for wearing shoes like that had long gone.

'Stop running!' she called after Clara's flying figure. 'You'll get there before he does if you're not careful!'

And there, sure enough, outside the Café Royal, was Mr Boland, getting out of a taxi, bare-headed in the cold January air.

'Dora told me I ought to keep you waiting.' Clara smiled up into his eyes as he kissed her briefly on her left cheek. 'Shall I go away and come back in ten minutes to make you appreciate me more?'

153

Bart laughed and gave her hands a little squeeze. How lovely she was, with her enormous green eyes crinkling as she teased him. In this mood she was enchanting, sensual in body and gesture, carrying her head as a stalk does a flower, as though she'd danced all her life. In that split second he saw her as she would have looked skimming across the stage in a ballerina's frothy tutu, light as air, with that proud head held high. Not for the first time he wondered. Billed as a clogger's child she might be, but surely somewhere in her background someone had danced? She even walked like a dancer, he thought, as he followed her into the restaurant, and yet he knew what her answer would be if he questioned her again.

'I am the clogger's child,' she would say firmly. 'He was my father, the only father I ever wanted or needed. Don't try to open Pandora's box for me, please, Mr Boland.'

The head waiter came forward to show them to a corner table with sofa seats. 'Good to see you again, Mr Boland,' he said, eyeing Clara with obvious approval before discreetly summoning a waiter to take their coats.

Bart couldn't take his eyes off her. 'Don't you think it's time you called me Bart? We've known each other for a long time now, Clara.' Without thinking what he was doing he covered her hand with his own, only to draw it back as her eyes flew wide and a faint blush stained her cheeks.

At that moment the menus arrived, covering an awkward silence. To Clara's relief he handed them back to the waiter with a smile.

'Will you mind if I order? I know my way round this menu pretty well.'

'Oh, yes, please. I can eat *anything*,' Clara assured him solemnly, giving an audible sigh of relief.

'Ah, well, in that case . . . ' Bart's blue eyes were twinkling. 'I think fresh salmon to begin with, and maybe a bottle of chablis, followed by fillet steak with baby carrots and peas, and a bottle of Pommard.'

Clara waited until the waiter had moved away before leaning forward to whisper urgently, 'Mr Boland. Bart . . . ' A deep blush stained her cheeks. 'You know I don't drink.

154

Have you forgotten? I signed the pledge!'

Bart sighed, drumming with impatient fingers on the starched white tablecloth. 'What will happen to you, Clara, should you relax those principles of yours for long enough to drink a glass of wine?'

As her eyes widened in surprise he felt momentarily ashamed. He studied her intently from beneath well-defined eyebrows. When he spoke it was so quietly she had almost to lipread to catch what he was saying.

'This fear you have, Clara, of a personal damnation. Methodism is surely more than that? Do you honestly still believe in the punishment of hell?' He waved a hand. 'All those perfectly respectable women drinking wine with their lunch – are they condemned to burn in the Lake of Fire?' His voice rose a little. '*Jesus* turned the water into wine, didn't He? Doesn't that salve that puritanical conscience of yours?'

Immediately all the hurting memories came back to her. Joe smelling of the terrible demon drink; the taste of it in her own mouth as he kissed her. Her father's beloved face, dark with fury the night she drank the rhubarb wine. Sermons from the pulpit in the chapel at the top of the street, with the minister waving his arms about as he pontificated on the evils of alcohol. Joe's father dying of it, dropping like a stone in the street, smashing his skull on the cobblestones.

Clara bit her lips hard. Her throat felt parched and dry as she looked round the beautiful scarlet and gilt room, at the women lifting their glasses and sipping elegantly. Not one of them behaving badly or rolling in a drunken stupor on the floor.

'My father . . . ' Clara's voice faltered as she fought with her conscience.

'Your father is dead, Clara.'

Joe had said that, sitting on the edge of the table in that far off little living room, swinging his legs and grinning. He had said those exact words, but in a totally different way. The man saying them now had a strong face gentled by compassion. His eyes were blue also, but they were wide and candid, the blue of a summer sky.

'I do not wish to make you drunk, my dear.' Bart nodded for the wine waiter to fill her glass. 'I would hate to be seen dining with an overebullient girl, however pretty she may be. But you must learn to enjoy a drink in moderation. You can't be part of the world you live in at present without acquiring a slight sophistication.' He raised his glass. 'So much unworldliness scares me, Clara. There are men far more ruthless than I who would take advantage of your attitude.' Leaning forward he curled her fingers round the stem of the glass. 'To you, my dear, and to what I have to tell you.' The blue eyes brimmed with laughter as Clara, with obvious reluctance, raised the glass to her lips and took a tentative sip.

Long before her glass was empty Clara began to feel happier than she had felt for a long time. The delicate taste of the fresh salmon and the smooth taste of the wine on her tongue brightened her eyes. The ruby red Pommard, drunk with steak as tender as butter, warmed her through and through, so that as the wine waiter moved forward to fill up her glass she stared at Bart in astonishment when he shook his head and motioned the man away.

'That's enough,' Bart said in a tone so stern, so paternal, Clara felt a giggle bubble in her throat. 'Now, before we have coffee I have something to ask you.'

'You have?'

Clara was so happy she was actually humming to herself. Oh, Dora had been right. She had been stupid shutting herself away from *life*. And this was certainly living. The brandy Bart was drinking with his coffee glowed like liquid fire. He was such a gentleman. Married too, so quite safe. Maybe her father's ideas had been a bit, well, just a little *narrow*? Clara noticed a man across the room staring at her, and turned her profile swiftly away, still very conscious of him. A small smile played around her mouth. Oh, the lovely things money could buy. She'd never thought of it like that before.

'How would you like to go to America, Clara?'

Bart was enjoying her reaction. Green eyes opened wide as Clara gave him her full attention.

'What did you say?'

'America, my dear. New York. Broadway. You've heard of a man called André Charlot?'

'With Anton Dolin and Jessie Matthews,' Clara said at once. 'In rehearsal for the opening at the Prince of Wales Theatre later on this year.'

Bart nodded. 'He took a revue to New York with Jack Buchanan, Beatrice Lillie and Gertrude Lawrence, so he's done the spadework.' Bart chose a Havana cigar from the box held out to him by the waiter, and didn't speak again until the small ceremony of trimming and lighting it was over. 'The Americans are used to spectacle. Loud, glittering spectacle. Girls walking down wide white staircases. But Charlot's revue opened their eyes to something more subtle, a rapport between the audience and the cast. The rapport you have with them the moment you begin to sing.'

'But I . . . ?' Clara couldn't quite take in what he was saying. 'Can you honestly see me with a big ostrich feather pinned on my head?'

Bart smiled. 'Let me explain. I won't be taking all the cast from *Remember Me*. Most of the acts wouldn't make the transition anyway, and I'm hoping for a continued run here.' He finished his cup of coffee. 'But you're different. The Americans haven't seen or heard anyone quite like you. They're a simple folk, Clara, in the main. Religious too, most of them.' He gave her a shrewd glance. 'I predict your name will be up in lights on Broadway before the end of the year.'

'I've never been abroad.' Clara was trying hard to adjust to the idea. 'And I don't know any Americans. Dora will love it. I can just imagine her face when I tell her.'

'Dora won't be going.'

'Then I'm not going, either.'

Bart's face changed. 'Do you know how old Dora is, for Pete's sake?'

'Seventy something. She doesn't like to talk about her age.'

'*Eighty* something! She was an old trouper before you were even born.'

Beckoning over the waiter, Bart requested the bill. The head waiter moved forward and presented Clara with two dark red carnations and a pin.

'I'm not going anywhere without Dora,' she said softly, fastening the flowers at the neck of her dress. 'If she's as old as you say she is, then she needs me all the more, doesn't she?'

'If you want to powder your nose, I'll see you in the lounge.' Bart's voice was tight with anger. 'I have another appointment at three, so don't be too long.'

'I don't want to,' Clara said quickly, following him miserably out of the restaurant. 'Powder my nose I mean.' She allowed herself to be helped into her coat by the same waiter who had taken it from her. 'Surely you can understand?'

'We open in Boston.' Bart's voice was tinged with impatience. 'I wan you. I'm not an easy man to cross, Clara.'

'And I'm not an easy one to be dissuaded once I've made up my mind.'

'Rehearsals begin in July.' Ignoring her, Bart strode furiously ahead, the set of his shoulders showing his anger.

'But where would she go?' Clara was still seething as she walked with Bart through the foyer and into the bustle of Regent Street. 'I'm paying the rent of the flat we're in now.' She stood still on the pavement, almost in tears. 'Her arthritis is so bad there are lots of things I have to do for her. She can't look after herself.'

'Then you must see she can't go.'

All the happiness of the lingering lunch in the palace of velvet sofas had evaporated. It was beginning to rain and Bart knew that if he didn't get a taxi straight away he would be late for his next appointment. A newsboy ran along the pavement, shouting at the top of his voice, 'One thirty winner! Paper! Paper!' A taxi drew in to the kerb and, to Clara's dismay, Bart climbed in.

'I'm not going!'

Beside herself with rage at the high-handed way he was

treating her, Clara actually shook her fist at the back of the taxi moving off into the afternoon traffic. Leaving with her the furiously annoying picture of Bart Boland's smooth head framed in the window, with the smoke from his not quite finished cigar curling up and round his ears.

All the way back to Conduit Street Clara justified her reaction. People, *feelings* came before ambition. 'Love not the world, neither the things that are in the world.' Jesus had said that. Her inherent ability to fit a Bible quotation to any given situation had never deserted her. Dora needed her now, just as she had needed Dora in those first hard months of joining the company.

Who would button Dora into her flowing gowns now that the misshapen arthritic hands could no longer manipulate the tiny buttons and loops? Who would help her in and out of the bath, and who would apply the henna to her still luxurious hair now she could no longer lift her arms? For years Dora had dressed others; now it was only right that someone who loved and understood her fierce sense of independence would do the same for her.

The high heels of Clara's flimsy shoes did a sharp staccato rap on the pavement as she hurried back to the flat. No wonder Mr Bart Boland was no longer living with his wife, if the rumours were true. Him with his blue eyes and a moustache like a hearthbrush stuck beneath his long nose. Important he might be, not too important for Clara Haydock to stick up to him. He'd come to the wrong shop for that kind of subservience.

Dora was waiting for her when she ran up the stairs and opened the door of the flat. Through Bart's eyes, despising herself for doing so, Clara noticed the way she had to bend almost double before she could rise from her chair. When Dora picked up an envelope from the low table, Clara saw how she had to slide the paper over the edge before she could grasp it between finger and thumb, leaving the other fingers sliding away useless like so many limp sausages.

'This came by hand, chuck,' she told Clara. 'Not long after you'd gone. I tried to get to the door in time to see who it was going back down the stairs, but I wasn't quick enough.' Her smile was apologetic. 'I've lost my stick again, love, or I'd have spotted whoever it was.' She wrinkled her thickly powdered nose. 'You'd better wash your hands after you've read what's inside, that envelope looks as if it's been somewhere nasty.'

'It's about Joe.' Clara looked up from the sheet of cheap lined notepaper. 'He's ill.' She pointed to the address, holding it out, until she remembered that without her glasses Dora was almost blind. 'Stacey Street, off Cambridge Circus.' With a swift pull the carnations at her throat came adrift from their pin. 'Don't bother to put them in water. I never liked carnations, anyway,' she told Dora. She glanced at the Westminster-chime clock on the mantelshelf. 'I can be back in an hour. Plenty of time to get to the theatre.'

With a speed that surprised Clara, Dora shuffled herself towards the door to stand dramatically with her arms spread as wide as they would go.

'Over my dead body!' Her chins, loose and hanging now from lack of flesh to support them, wobbled furiously. 'For one thing, you've to have your rest. You've got cabaret on top of the theatre tonight, and you didn't sleep well last night.' She glared at Clara. 'I heard you moving about after you came in. And for another thing, that letter's a trick to get you there. He won't come here because he knows I'll kill him, so he's trying it on.' There were tears in her raucous voice. 'He's no good for you, chuck. I got his measure the minute I clapped eyes on him. He's a scrounger, a liar, and he made you more unhappy than any girl has a right to be.'

'I know, Dora.' Clara walked to the door, standing so close to the old woman she could see the rouged cheeks drawn down into creases, each crease filled with orange-shaded powder. 'You are right. Joe is no good. I knew that a long time ago, but if he's ill and if he needs me, I have to go to him.'

'Why? For God's sake, why?'

Clara nodded. 'Yes. For God's sake. That's why.'

Knowing when she was beaten, Dora moved aside. She couldn't fight God, not Clara's God anyway. 'Don't blame

160

me if you're dead on your feet. And don't blame me if it's all a trap. I wish I'd never given you the letter,' she shouted, her rough voice spiralling after Clara as she ran down the stairway.

When she went back in and closed the door she found that her heart was beating wildly in an uneven rhythm. When she knocked her glasses case off the table and onto the floor she tried to bend over, forgetting that her spine was as rigid as a poker.

'Bugger that Joe!' she yelled. 'And bugger this arthritis! What's happening to me? Me, Dora Vane, who once could stand on her head!'

Stacey Street, off Cambridge Circus, was a cul-de-sac shadowed by tall early-Victorian houses. Clara paid off the taxi and, checking the number on the letter still clutched in her hand, made her way to the far end.

At that time of day there were no bookies with their bowler-hatted lackeys carrying Gladstone bags, no punters sidling towards them; but the door at the end house was ajar and, hesitating momentarily, Clara pushed it open and went inside.

For a second or two she blinked, trying to adjust her eyes to the harsh light from a naked lightbulb swinging from its cord above a table covered with betting slips. A man wearing a brown overcoat with the collar turned up was studying the small print on the back page of the racing edition of the *Evening News* and picking his teeth with a silver-plated toothpick. He stared at Clara with a decided lack of interest.

'You come abaht Joe?'

She nodded, holding out the letter. 'This was delivered to my flat.' She glanced round the almost bare room, wrinkling her nose at the stale smell of cigarette smoke so pungent she felt if she put out a hand she could touch it. She shook her head. 'But there must be a mistake. Joe can't be here.'

The man picking his teeth put the paper aside and leaned across the wide desk. His neck was thick, his face as florid as a bruised tomato, and the teeth he'd been working on were as yellow as clotted cream. Until his sixtieth birthday his broad body had taken and absorbed every excess that life could give, but lately his overindulgence was beginning to take its toll. At one time the beautiful girl standing before him would have brought a glint to his eyes and an even more hectic flush to his cheeks, but today he felt his age.

'You've made no mistake, gel. He's here all right. And if he's not out of this place before I lock up for the night I won't be responsible.'

'But the letter says he's ill!' Clara handed over the scrap of paper. 'How can he be here if he's ill?'

With an enormous sigh the bookie got to his feet, catching his head on the low-hanging lightbulb, setting it swinging, throwing shadows on the walls like dancers in some evil rite.

'In here,' he called over his shoulder. 'An' you 'eard what I said. Take him home wiv you. Do what you like wiv 'im, as long as you get him *out*.'

When the door closed behind her Clara's heart jumped. The winter afternoon was dying now and the only light came from a narrow window set high in the wall. If the bookie had made his fortune, Clara thought wryly, he hadn't spent any of it on this place. It was as cold as a tomb, with the walls running damp and mud oozing through the cracks in the concrete floor.

'Joe?' Moving forward, stepping gingerly over a heap of rotting cardboard, Clara went towards a mattress set at right angles to the window, to stand looking down on what at first glance appeared to be a pile of rags. 'Joe? Oh, Joe ... ' Heedless of the fine silk stockings, the expensive coat, she knelt down on the uneven filthy floor. 'You really *are* ill. Oh, Joe, is this where you *live*?'

He was running a fever. Through the dim light coming from the filthy little window she could see the way his eyes sparkled and glittered. His mouth was swollen, his lips dry and caked with a white scum, and his dark curly hair looked as if it hadn't been combed since she'd seen him the previous week.

Reaching for her hand he gripped it fiercely. 'I had to get

drunk,' he told her in a strange rambling high voice. 'After you sent me away I began to drink.' His head moved restlessly from side to side. 'I thought I'd never do it again, not once I'd found you, but when I need to drink I can't stop. Five, six days I was at it, then somehow, don't ask me how, I found my way here.' He looked away from her. 'I used to spend a lot of time hereabouts before I went to South Africa. You know?'

'I know, Joe.'

All at once she was a little girl again, seeing Joe standing on windy corners with his flat cap perched on the back of his dark curly head, waiting for bets, taking the rap when the police caught him at it, knowing the bookie would pay his fine so he could begin all over again.

'I don't blame you for sending me away.' His voice was maudlin now, slurring on the edge of the fever which burned inside him. 'I'm no good for you, Clara. I'd only drag you down.' He coughed weakly. 'You were always a cut above me. Even as a snotty-nosed kid running around in your father's clogs. You've always been a cut above.'

'Stop it, Joe!' Getting to her feet, Clara walked as quickly as she could round the rubble to the door.

'May I use your telephone, please?'

The man in the brown overcoat was picking his teeth again, staring morosely at the newspaper through a magnifying glass. Wearily he indicated the telephone surrounded by piles of paper at the corner of his desk.

'Help yourself, gel. Ring Timbuctoo as far as I care, as long as you get him off my back.' He narrowed eyes set in valleys of mottled flesh. 'What in Gawd's name is a gel like you doing with the likes of him? I don't wish him no harm, but he's trouble, gel. Big trouble. From the day he was born, I reckon.'

Clara made her entrance on the stage that evening with only seconds to spare. Settling Joe into hospital hadn't been as easy as she'd thought it would be. When she'd told the sister she couldn't wait even another minute to see the doctor after he'd examined Joe, the expression in the nurse's eyes had withered Clara's ebbing confidence.

What was she going to do with Joe when he came out of hospital? This time the issue wasn't cut and dried, black or white, a straight choice. All Clara's religious convictions warred one against the other in her head.

'If you were the only boy in the world . . . ' she sang, causing every man in the audience to smile as if she meant it just for him. She didn't love Joe. Her love for him had died a long time ago, but that didn't mean she could desert him.

'There would be such wonderful things to do . . . ' A man in the front row sighed audibly. Clara could actually see his eyes glistening.

Joe and Dora. Both of them needing her. She stood with bowed head as the applause rose to a deafening crescendo.

'How can I go to America?' she asked Matty, sitting in her dressing room surrounded by flowers.

'How can you not go, love?' Matty was having to work harder than ever for his laughs these days. His square face oozed sweat through his clown's make-up. 'The graveyards are full of indispensable people. Have you never heard that saying?'

When he left her, she bowed her head in prayer: 'Oh, God. Show me what to do. Give me a sign. Help me to decide.' But when she opened her eyes the indecision was still there, hurting hard inside her, and not for the first time in her life she realized that the values instilled in her by her father didn't always translate to the life she had chosen for herself.

As she stood in the darkened wings waiting for her entrance in the second-house performance, her mind was still in turmoil. 'In all thy ways acknowledge Him, and He will make plain thy paths . . . ' As for her father before her, the comforting words came easily to her mind, but this time without meaning. Slowly she walked into the spotlight, as lovely as a dream in her white dress.

The song she sang was a wistful number, a new song being whistled by every errandboy in London. To Bart Boland, standing alone at the back of the stalls, it seemed to typify all

164

he was beginning to feel for his young protégée. His anger had evaporated by now and as far as he was concerned the American trip was on. Not an hour before Dora had told him . . . He half closed his eyes, seeing Clara walking down Broadway clinging to his arm, or more likely riding with him in a big black limousine down 42nd Street.

> 'Won't you tell him, please,
> To put on some speed,
> Follow my lead?
> Oh, how I need
> Someone to watch over me . . . '

Bart was so engrossed in the audience's mesmerized reaction to Clara's interpretation of the song he failed to notice a tall fair man rise from his seat and make his way quickly out of the exit doors at the back of the theatre. And if he had seen, it would have signified nothing. Bart was a man with a purpose, and after his talk with Dora in the upstairs flat of the house in Conduit Street, that purpose looked like being brought to a satisfactory fruition. He frowned as a chorus girl moved her lips in a silent exchange with the girl on her right. The audience, he knew, would notice nothing but, making a mental note of her name, he narrowed his eyes, already in his mind giving the befeathered girl the ticking off he felt was her due.

'You look more like your father every day, God rest his soul.'

After letting Bart in, Dora had groped her way back to her high-seated chair, holding on to the furniture to steady herself. Bart was shocked at the deterioration in her and wondered how on earth Clara could have imagined Dora would have coped with the rolling deck of a transatlantic liner.

Dora, settled now, gave a dry chuckle. 'Clara told me to go to bed, but I like to please myself.' Putting her red head on one side she simpered at him from beneath eyelashes stiff with mascara. 'Why don't you marry her, Bart? She's crying out for a man to look after her, and your marriage is finished from what I've heard tell.'

Now it was Bart's turn to laugh. 'You're a wicked old woman, Dora Vane. You don't improve with keeping and that's a fact. I can't marry anyone till the divorce comes through, and besides, what makes you think Clara would have me?'

'She'd have you if I put her up to it. That lass is like a ship without a rudder. You put her in this game without a thought as to how she would cope. She's still sticking to the rules ingrained in her by her religious fanatic of a father.' Dora sniffed. 'Religion is all right as long as it doesn't stop folks from getting on with living.'

'I put her in your charge Dora.' Bart's vivid blue eyes narrowed. 'It strikes me you're the one in need of looking after, old girl.'

'Cheeky!' Dora sounded like her old self again, then suddenly her face sobered and her eyes filled with a bleak despair. 'I'm living too long, Bart, lad.' She held up a misshapen hand. 'No, don't contradict me. They'd put me down if I was a dog. It's only this stubborn old heart of mine keeping me going, and that's not behaving as it should. The doctor told me last week he could find me a place in a nursing home where I could have proper care.' The loose chins quivered. 'And I'd like to go, but it's twenty-five guineas a week and where would I get that kind of money?' She fixed him with a beady stare. 'And I haven't told Clara because she wouldn't let me go. And if I insisted she'd offer to pay. She knows I get lonely sitting here for hours at a time while she's working. So she'd pay, and she'd go and live in some awful little room and visit me every day.' Her rough voice rose. 'That's how good she is! She'd ruin her life for me because I won't die easy. Not if I was being looked after proper and having the kind of company I need.' She leaned forward showing a wrinkled cleavage down the front of the long frilled teagown. 'There's a lot of the old timers in that home. Top of the bill most of them were at one time. Singsongs they have, so I've heard.' Her feet tapped out a rhythm as she rambled on, talking too quickly as the lonely do.

Bart looked round the room, at the bric-à-brac of a lifetime in the theatre cluttering the low tables, at the Spanish shawl draping the back of Dora's chair.

'My father used to tell me how you stopped the show when you sang about the Spaniard who blighted your life.' He smiled. 'He said a man once threw himself over the balcony and broke his neck trying to get to you.'

'Poor mad fool,' Dora said, her face alight with the joy of remembering. 'I went to his funeral with a wreath made in the shape of a Spanish guitar.'

Bart sat back in his chair and crossed his legs. This was where he had to tread carefully, very carefully indeed. 'I think I know of a way in which we could all be happy,' he said slowly. 'I don't suppose Clara's told you that I want to take her to America with part of the company?'

Dora gave an unladylike whistle. 'She rushed out . . . ' she began, then clamped her mouth tight shut. 'Go on.'

'She refused, of course.'

'Because of me?'

He nodded. 'But it would be the making of her, Dora. You see, the Americans are slowly weaning themselves away from variety. They've already had a taste of a more intimate kind of show. Gertrude Lawrence and Beatrice Lillie and Jack Buchanan have shown the way.' His eyes were ablaze with enthusiasm. 'The way I see it is this: for Clara's first song she wears a drab skirt and blouse and a hat covering her hair.' He waved a hand to illustrate. 'A backcloth of greys and browns, with maybe a clogger's bench in the foreground. Just the one spotlight on her as she sings. Then, when they're stunned by the beauty of her voice there's a moment or two of complete darkness. A pale green curtain comes down and she steps in front of it with the shabby clothes whipped away, leaving her in a long white dress.' His voice quickened. 'Just as the spotlight picks her out again she takes off her hat, throws it into the wings, shakes her head and lets down that wonderful hair. *Then* she sings a modern song. There's a beauty called "Bye, Bye, Blues". She has a natural

167

rhythm and when she closes her eyes and sways . . . '
Suddenly he seemed to remember where he was. 'There's
nobody like her, Dora.'

'And you're in love with her?' Dora's question was merely
a continuance of his thoughts.

'I'm in love with her, Dora. I think I've loved her since the
first time I set eyes on her.'

'So, if I can convince her . . . '

'That she must go to America. That the nursing home is
where you most want to be. That the fees will be paid from
some benevolent society.'

'That I'll be shocking the matron with my rendition of the
Spaniard who blighted his bleedin' life . . . '

'Then we're home and dry.'

'Have a fag and give me one,' said Dora. 'You're wicked,
Bart Boland.'

'That makes two of us,' said Bart, taking out his cigarette
case.

Clara's face was coated with cold cream when the knock
came on the door of her dressing room. She asked whoever
it was to come in and didn't bother to turn round, so sure it
would be Matty come to reason with her again.

She saw him first reflected in the mirror, an exceptionally
tall man with a flop of thick fair hair falling over his
forehead; with amber eyes that laughed into her own.

'John! John Maynard! Oh, it *is* good to see you! Oh, what
a wonderful surprise!'

Without quite knowing how it happened, she was lifted
out of her seat and turned into his arms, sticky face pressed
against his.

'Little Clara Haydock.'

Grinning from ear to ear he held her from him.

'What do I see when I come back to London but a face I
know well looking at me from a dirty great photograph
outside the theatre! So what do I do but join the queue for
the three and nines, and *voilà!* There you are warbling away
on the jolly old stage.' His eyes crinkled into laughter.

'Remember when you stood at the front of the whole school to sing "All things bright and beautiful"?'

There and then he sang the first line, and there and then Clara joined in, gazing up into the tanned face, like a musical comedy star singing to her handsome leading man.

It was a miracle. Maybe it was the miracle she had prayed for. This man was a part of her childhood, a joyous part, with no dark shadows clouding her memories of him. John Maynard, whose father had listened to her recite the Catechism every Monday morning. John, who had worn a shirt *and* a pullover to school, and got his nose bloodied for her. Whose mother had played a piano on which rested a plaster bust of Beethoven, or was it Chopin?

'I'm taking you out to supper.' He looked down at the glowing face upturned to his own. What marvellous luck finding her like this, just when his job was turning out to be far duller than he had anticipated. Surprising himself, he bent his head and kissed Clara full on the mouth, a lingering sweet caress.

And that was the scene Bart saw as, without knocking, he opened the door.

'Forgive me,' he said, walking quickly away down the musty corridor, a dignified man in a brown suit with a calm expression on his face belying the aching disappointment in his heart.

Twelve

The next afternoon, because there was no matinée, Clara rode on the top of a bus with John Maynard to Regent's Park Zoo. They were alone on the top deck and beneath the stiff tarpaulin over their knees John held her hand.

Most of the girls he'd known – and he'd known plenty – had cropped their hair in a style called the bingle, a club cut part way between a bob and a shingle, but all Clara had to do was to pin her hair high on her head, so that beneath the small cloche hat her vivacious little face was like a flower. He burned with desire for her, and as the red bus swung into Park Lane he turned her gently towards him and kissed her full on the mouth.

Although she didn't pull away, her green eyes darkened.

'It's all right,' he said. 'I love you. We're going to get married. You'd like that, wouldn't you?' Shaken by her nearness, he heard the words say themselves. Then knew that he meant it. 'Now that I've found you, it has to be.' Slowly he trailed a finger down her cheek. 'I won't stand in your way. In the way of your career, I mean.'

When they climbed down from the bus and went through the turnstile into the zoo, Clara shivered and pulled her fur collar closer round her throat. Since John had walked into her dressing room the night before, her life seemed to have taken on a dazed intensity, so that, as Dora would undoubtedly have said, she didn't know whether she was coming or going.

Dora had been asleep in her room when, after the cabaret, Clara had crept into the flat. They'd had another row this morning when Dora had said she was going into a nursing home, paid for by some benevolent society Clara had never heard of.

'Over my dead body!' Clara had shouted dramatically, wan through lack of sleep, spreading her arms wide the way Dora had spread hers the night before.

'And you're going to America,' Dora had told her. 'I'm doing what I want to do, and you're going to do what's right for you.' Then she'd blushed, remembering too late that Bart had asked her to keep his visit a secret. 'Matty told me,' she'd lied. 'He phoned me after you'd gone on from the theatre. That's how I know.'

Standing by the railings, staring at a stork huddled deep into its feathers, Clara leaned against the man by her side, glad that his arm was round her, glad that he loved her, reminding herself that he had come in answer to her fervent prayer for a sign. Tall, very English-looking, with his fair hair and complexion, John Maynard had grown into a handsome man. Clara sighed and leaned a bit closer.

'Cold, love?'

Clara nodded. It was good, too, to hear the familiar Lancashire endearment, although like herself John had lost most of his northern accent.

'I like being somebody's love,' she told him childishly, and he swung her round and gazed deep into her eyes.

'Then marry me,' he said softly. 'Next month, next week. Tomorrow?'

'John,' she said suddenly. 'Let's go somewhere we can talk. Somewhere warm.' She wrinkled her nose. 'This place smells.' Pinching her nose between a finger and thumb, she grinned. 'I'm not an animal person, John.'

'So you don't want to see the monkeys with red bottoms?'

'Not particularly.'

Laughing, hand in hand, they made their way out of the zoo. Hailing a taxi, they rode to Trafalgar Square, crowded with people buying pigeon food and standing to be photographed with the birds perching on their shoulders and outstretched arms. The taxi was stuck in a traffic jam, so John paid the driver off and held out a hand to help her out.

'There's a teashop over there,' he told her. 'Just in time to escape the rain.'

'Toasted teacakes and a pot of tea for two,' he told the waitress bustling to serve them before they'd begun to remove their gloves and unbutton their coats. 'Now. When shall it be? You don't want to wait until June to be a bride, do you?'

Clara looked directly at him. Behind her, through the huge window, John could see a pair of ex-service men, medals in place on their breasts, one of them playing a trumpet and the other beating a drum. Nine years or more since they'd stood ankle-deep in mud in the trenches, and still they begged for coppers.

'Tell me again about the man you work for,' Clara said.

She'd been going to say something else, John was sure of that, but he obliged. She'd tell him whatever it was in her own good time. Bottling things up had never been one of the young Clara's habits. He had a sudden vision of her chasing round the school playground with the West boys, yelling her head off and swearing like a trooper because one of them had pinched her hair ribbon.

'Well, as I told you, he's got a title. Lord Broughton.' The two men had walked past the window now, so he could forget them. 'He has two private planes, and I fly one of them for him. Mostly round Europe. He's a newspaper proprietor and I fly copies of his papers to Paris, Berlin, Brussels, Amsterdam. I've been doing it for a year now and the pay's tremendous. The old man talks about pounds like we talk about shillings.'

John shifted comfortably in his chair. The warmth of the restaurant was getting to him and he felt relaxed and happy, flattered by the way Clara seemed to be drinking in his every word. There was nothing like being seen in public with a pretty woman to give the old ego a boost. He raised his voice deliberately as the waitress came to place a heavy plated teapot and hot-water jug on the table.

'I think the most disappointing job I had was after I stopped doing commercial flying. I joined a circus putting on shows with the old Avro trainers up and down the country. Risking your neck when there isn't a war on isn't

172

much fun.' By the way the waitress put down the milk jug John guessed she was listening. He leaned back in his chair. 'One of these days I'm going to fly over the Alps, but I'll need a better plane. One to reach a sufficient altitude.'

'Oh, my goodness . . . ' Clara's reaction was all he could have hoped for.

'There are problems with frozen fuel lines over fifteen thousand feet, but give or take a few years and I reckon passengers will be flown on the Munich–Milan–Rome route as a matter of course.'

When the buttered toast came he ate his with gusto, licking his fingers and accepting a piece from Clara's plate. His total absorption in whatever he did, his *exuberance*, amused and disconcerted Clara at one and the same time. She found herself watching his movements, almost willing him to be still. Wondering if he was nervous, and knowing he was not.

He drained his cup and held it out for a refill. 'I'm ready for a change,' he told her, screwing up his paper napkin and dabbing his mouth with it. 'Yes,' he said, as if continuing a sentence begun in his head, 'the new aircraft are more luxurious than the most up-to-date express train. Prince George enjoys flying, princes and film stars catch the headlines when they fly, but it's the well-to-do businessman who keeps the European routes going. Fifty per cent more expensive than travelling by train and boat, but why should they care?'

'I have to go now.' Clara began to pull on her gloves. It was no good. John wasn't in a listening mood. And besides, for what she had to tell him the place, the time, *everything* had to be right. She was sure the waitress was trying to hear their conversation, standing there with her order pad hanging from a black ribbon tied to her belt, her eyes behind the whirlpool lenses of her spectacles blank with apparent boredom.

'I have to be at the theatre in just over an hour's time, and before then I have a hospital visit to make,' she said. 'It's only across the road.' She hesitated. 'It's someone you used to know well.'

She looked very young, very vulnerable in her chamber-

173

pot hat, with little tendrils of hair escaping at the sides to fall softly onto her cheeks. So serious. He couldn't help smiling at her, couldn't stop reminding himself of his luck in meeting up with her like this. Paying only scant attention to what she was saying, he immediately got up to settle the bill, joked with the cashier in her glass-walled booth, then bounced back to leave a far too lavish tip beneath a butter-smeared plate.

'Joe West.'

Clara said the name as they ran across the street, dodging the traffic, John's hand firmly beneath her elbow.

'He was with you in the top class, but he stayed on after you passed for the grammar school.'

'Not one of the snotty West boys?' John stood quite still on the opposite pavement, the fine lines at the corners of his eyes crinkling into laughter. 'There were *dozens* of them, weren't there?'

'There were two less when the war ended.' Clara moved slightly away from him. 'Two of the West boys never came back, John.'

'Good Lord, I've offended you!' He looked astounded. 'I'd no idea you were that thick with them. Which one did you say is in there?' He jerked his chin towards the big teaching hospital with its wide frontage, standing back from the road.

'Joe.'

'Ah, Joe.' He looked up at the sky. 'Of course I remember him. Weasel-faced bloke, always in and out of the nick.' At last she had his attention. 'What's he doing down here? Running a betting shop in the Mile End Road?'

Clara drew herself up to her full height. 'He's *ill*. Ill and alone.' A gust of wind ruffled the lynx collar, seeming to add to her anger. 'He never had your advantages. He was working when he was seven years old!' Her green eyes dared him to speak. 'My father told me he used to leave the house long before the mills started. To chop up blocks of salt, John. And his moth . . . ' Her face flamed as she recalled the inescapable fact that Lily West had wetnursed her. 'His mother cared for me when I was a baby, so Joe is like . . . '

174

'Your brother?'

'Yes!'

Stunned by what she could only see as her own hypocrisy, Clara turned swiftly and walked in front of the taxi rank to the entrance of the hospital, but before she could go inside John was beside her.

'I'm not coming in with you,' he said.

For a moment he thought with amazement that she would hit out at him.

'I never asked you to,' she said coldly.

'We're quarrelling,' he said, astounded. 'What about, in heaven's sake, love? What about?'

She walked quickly away from him, small heels clicking, her back ramrod straight.

'I wouldn't if I was you, mate.' A cab driver, hunched over his wheel, shook his head in mock dismay. 'Let her cool off, mate. It's always the best way.'

Nonplussed and furious, John stood for a moment looking down at his shoes as if trying to make up his mind. He winked at the cab driver, turned up the collar of his coat and strode long-legged towards Trafalgar Square. A bus trundled by, caught in a mesh of traffic, and he swung himself aboard.

Joe was much better. Clara could see that cleaned up, shaved and with his dark wavy hair neatly combed he was halfway to being human again.

'You're out of breath,' he accused, gazing at her from beneath hooded eyelids. 'And that's a daft hat. It's like a po.'

'Joe,' she said, coming straight to the point, 'where did you go that night you left my flat?'

'You mean after that old woman charged at me?' A faint suspicion of the grin she remembered so well lifted the corners of his dry lips. 'It's not long since I could've lifted her *and* a bucket o' coal up in one hand.' He tried to raise himself up on his elbows, only to flop back on his pillows, his head spinning.

'I want to know where you were *living*, Joe. Because,

before the ambulance came, that man in Stacey Street told me he'd found you down on the Embankment.'

'That's it, then.' Joe lifted an eyebrow. 'That's where I was living.' His cracked lips twisted in a wry smile and his dark blue eyes mocked her. 'Cardboard's the next best thing to a blanket. That's if you can find the right size.' He closed his eyes, waving a hand in front of his face as if dismissing her. 'Thank you for coming to see me, Clara Haydock. Isn't this where you say a prayer over me?' The afternoon had died quickly and the harsh ward lights were suddenly snapped on. 'The visitors went ages ago,' Joe told her, looking at her steadily. 'You'll cop it if the ward sister catches you. You have to be pegging out before they have even next-of-kins in here out of visiting hours.'

'But you're not dying.' Clara heard the rattle of the food trolley at the other end of the ward. 'What's wrong with you, Joe?'

To her horror he began to laugh. A strange staccato jerking sound, and all the time he was laughing his bloodshot eyes mocked her. 'Don't you know? Oh, God, that's funny.' He put up an arm as if to shade his eyes from the too bright light. 'No, I'm not dying, our kid. That would be too easy.' He raised his head, and his fingers scrabbled at the turned-down sheet. 'They'll have me out of here as soon as I can stand on me own two feet. Beds are for sick folk, Clara, not for drunks.'

'But you're not drunk now.' Clara reached for his hand, surprised to find it horny, hard and hot to her touch. 'You've still got a fever, Joe.' She started to get up from her chair. 'I'm going to find the sister and have a word with her. She'll tell me, if you won't.'

The burning hand tightened on her wrist. He spoke very clearly. 'I'm a drunk, our kid. An alcoholic, if you want the proper term. A sodden, pissed-out, no-good meths drinker, if you want the gospel truth.' His swollen eyes were suddenly and disconcertingly merry. 'An' you always did want the gospel truth, didn't you, little Clara?' He ran his tongue over his dry lips. 'Money, an' I'll drink whisky; no money, and I'll sup owt. There's no hope for me, Clara. I knew there wasn't no hope when I came to find you, and I knew there was even less when I saw what had happened to you.'

'Nothing's happened to me!' Forgetting where she was, Clara raised her voice. 'I haven't changed, Joe! I'm still the same person!' Her face was as solemn as a child's, as dedicated as the Sunday School teacher she had been not all that long ago. 'I can help you, Joe. The Lord will help you, if you let Him.'

'Him?' Joe turned his face away. 'You still beating the drum? Don't you *ever* give up?' He turned back again. 'I went up home when I returned from South Africa. The bad penny turning up again, you know?'

The supper trolley clattered nearer, but Clara heard nothing. She was sitting quite still, steeling herself for what was coming, knowing it was bad.

'Your father's shop isn't a shop any more, Clara. There's a net curtain in the window and an aspidistra plant. There was a fat woman wearing a mob cap standing on the doorstep. Her arms folded over a cross-over pinny, an' she had eyes like a pair of glass alleys missing nowt.'

'And *your* house, Joe?'

The young nurse with the food trolley stopped at the foot of his bed.

'Bugger off,' Joe told her pleasantly. 'Report me to sister, but for now do what I said.'

The ward orderly handing round the plates of mashed potato and pale steamed fish advanced on Joe with a 'stop that nonsense' look on her pointed face.

'Want that muck slap in your kisser, luv?' Joe's voice was a whisper of silk.

'You're a naughty boy, Mr West.' Backing away, the orderly moved on to the next bed.

'An' you're a pissed-out old faggot,' Joe said, smiling with his teeth.

Clara's eyes never left Joe's face. 'And *your* house?' she said again, rocking herself backwards and forwards on the edge of her chair. 'Your mother, Joe?'

'Dead.' Lifting a hand, he studied it intently. 'Alec went for our Fred's wife with a knife. She'd been taunting him about his leg, telling him he could find some kind of a job if he tried hard enough.'

'Yes?' Clara was a child again, rocked against Lily West's cushiony breasts, peering up through her hair at the beaky nose, the mouth that never quite closed over the decayed, protruding teeth.

'Mam went to stop them and got the knife.' Joe pointed to the black hairs on his chest. 'Here. So Alec hanged himself in the backyard. The hook she used for her washing line wasn't high enough, so he prised it out and drove it in higher up the coal-shed wall.'

Clara's hand fluttered up to her mouth. The tea she had drunk and the buttered teacake were there, sour-tasting, making her retch. She rose from the hard chair. She didn't know where the toilets were, they could be anywhere in those echoing corridors, but she knew she had to escape before she disgraced herself.

'So you see,' Joe was saying in that light, controlled voice, 'that Jesus you used to say lived in the chapel at the top of the street must've gone on his 'olidays that day. Are you ready for the prayer now?' Grief for the only woman who had never seen any wrong in him choked his voice. 'Will a Catholic prayer do, Clara? Or don't they count?' Closing his eyes Joe chanted the words he'd heard his mother recite when things were going wrong, her own incantation to fend off the inevitable: 'Holy Mary, Mother of God . . . '

Outside in the corridor Clara bumped into the ward sister coming back on duty, an expression of outrage on her face at the unbelievable spectacle of someone actually *running* from her ward.

'She wouldn't let me back in,' Clara told Dora. 'Joe's bed was at the far end of the ward, and she practically held me back with her bare beefy arms. She kept on quoting the visiting times to me, reciting them in a singsong voice.'

Snatching off her hat, Clara shook her head to free the long fall of hair. 'I told her I couldn't come back at seven o'clock, that I *worked* every evening, and she looked me up and down as if she was thinking that there was only one job, apart from nursing of course, that a girl could do at night. And you know what that is!' She pushed at her hair, lifting it away from her forehead. 'I'm going back to the hospital in the morning, visiting time or no visiting time, and I'm going to give Joe some money.' She tore at the buttons down the front of her green woollen dress. 'A hundred pounds,' she said wildly.

'Then you'll be pots for crackers.' Using the curved handle of her walking stick, Dora scooped up the dress from the floor. 'An' if I'm not here to chip in with my bit of pension towards the rent of this place, and if you're still set on refusing to go to America, then I reckon you *might* end up on the streets. Especially if Mr Boland refuses to renew your contract.'

'He wouldn't do that!' Clara made for the bathroom, shedding bits of clothing as she went. 'He's not that sort of a man.'

'You do like him, then?' Dora's voice was a shade too eager.

Clara turned round. 'For someone of his age I suppose he's all right. Why?'

Before Dora could think what to say, she disappeared into the bathroom. Over the sound of running water her voice came muffled. 'Joe's in a terrible state, Dora. He's been drinking. Meths, he said, but you can't tell when Joe's making things up. If this water isn't hot enough, I'll die!'

Dora's twisted fingers itched with the longing to help Clara out of the rest of her clothes and into the bath. But there was always that damned modesty to take into account, as well as the fact that Dora accepted she would be more of a hindrance than a help. So she sat still in her high-backed chair, her once busy hands idle in her lap.

'Joe's been sleeping on the Embankment. With cardboard to cover him.'

Dora closed her eyes, imagining Clara scattering bath salts lavishly into the warm water. 'So you've persuaded yourself you still love him?'

'No!' Clara's voice rose. 'I *needed* him once, but I don't

179

think I ever loved him. But he's a part of my life, and just to cross him off now wouldn't be . . . '

'Christian?' With difficulty Dora prised herself up from the chair and limped across the room to lean against the half-open bathroom door. 'And a hundred pounds would set him up for life?' She gave an unladylike snort. 'He'd sup every penny of it, you soft 'aporth, just as fast as he could pour it down his throat.' Her harsh voice softened. 'When I knew you wasn't coming back for lunch today – and I'm not asking where you've been all day because I know you're not in no mood to tell me – when I knew I had the day to myself, I went to see the place where I'm going to live.'

'I'm not listening!' There was the sound of water gushing from a tap, but the voice that had once made itself heard right to the back seats in the stalls was more than a match for running water.

'It's out Twickenham way. A fine old mansion, with at least five acres of land to it. Every penny raised by our profession, and only forty residents living in.'

Dora shifted her weight from one swollen ankle to the other. It was no good. Standing was even worse than walking. Muttering to herself, she made her way slowly back to the haven of her high upholstered chair, her bosom beneath the scarlet silk organza of her teagown rising and falling with the effort. But she could still shout if she'd a need to. Arthritis hadn't seized up her tonsils, thank the Lord.

'There's a long waiting list,' she bellowed. 'I've been lucky. Lucky! D'you hear me?' She closed her eyes.

'I hear you, Dora.' All at once Clara was there before her, a large white bath towel hiding her nakedness, her hair skewered on top of her head. 'Lucky? Is that the right word?'

The question was asked so harshly, Dora flinched. Painted blue eyelids lowered themselves over the suddenly unguarded expression in her eyes.

'Mr Boland was here, wasn't he?' There was a sad note of resignation in Clara's voice. She sat down on the chair Bart had occupied the night before, tucking the towel carefully round her bare legs. 'I smelled his cigar smoke when I came in.'

'Mr Boland?' Dora heard herself trail off miserably.

'He wangled you a place in the home so I'd go with him to America, didn't he? Gave them a huge donation to ensure just that. Didn't he?'

There was a moment's silence before Dora began to bluster. 'You think I'm such a bleedin' martyr I'd have myself put away just so you could go to America with a clear conscience? Without the millstone of an old ailing woman round your neck?' The helpless hands on Dora's lap lifted to rest on the padded arms of her chair. 'I've *told* you. I *want* to go into the home. It was all right when I could be with all the gang at the theatre every night. I'd got company then. Harry at the stage door, Matty, and the girls.' She sniffed. 'What company have I had from *you* today, come to that?'

Immediately the telltale blush rose to stain Clara's cheeks with bright colour. 'I've been wanting to tell you,' she said quickly. 'An old friend came backstage to see me. I've been seeing him today.' She put a hand to her throat. 'His name is John. John Maynard. His father was the minister of the church belonging to my school.'

'So that makes him all right?' Dora was being peevish and didn't care. 'I'll be able to have a bit of a singsong when I move,' she said, as if Clara hadn't spoken. 'Some of the girls are old friends. Arda Arlene, Phyllis Nelson.' Her eyes were all at once sharp with spite. 'Neither of them have worn as well as me.' Complacently she patted her jacked-up bosoms. 'Dropped. Right down to her kneecaps in poor Phyllis's case.'

Getting up from her chair, Clara walked towards the bedroom, trailing the white towel behind her.

'So you don't want to meet my friend John?'

Dora closed her eyes against a recollection of young Bart Boland sitting in the chair Clara had just left. She remembered the way his eyes had softened when he'd admitted his love for Clara, and the way Dora had known at that very moment in her heart how right they were for each other.

'Friend John?' she asked in a voice choked with disappointment. 'Then he must be a pansy. There's only two sorts where women are concerned. Pansies or lovers. One or the other. *Friends*, never!' Stiffly Dora twisted round in her chair, her powdered face creased into lines of vindictiveness. 'Mr Boland went with me this afternoon to look over where I'm going. He cares about people, Mr Boland does.' She was very tired and more than muddled in her thinking. She had thought it was all going to work out right. The home for her, and Bart Boland marrying Clara. The two of them walking off into the sunset together. She could have died easy then, the two people she loved most in the world married to each other. 'More than your friend John does . . . '

Dora's eyes were suddenly quite blank. Confused with the effort of thinking, remembering her life in detail from years back, and yet nothing of what happened the day before, the anxiety in her was almost too terrible to bear. Who *was* this John? And if she knew him, why couldn't she remember a single thing about him?

'I'm living too long,' she barked in the voice that seemed to have grown more rough-edged in the last few minutes. 'It was Mr Boland who took me to see over the home,' she said again, wanting for some inexplicable reason to be nasty. Stiffly she twisted round in her chair. 'I can see your bare bum!' she shouted. Getting her own back. For what, she wasn't quite sure.

That night, bathed in the shimmering spotlight, Clara sang a song from an old Broadway musical. It was Jerome Kern at his best, and as she sang the man in the front row of the stalls lifted his fair head, his expression one of total pride and possessiveness.

'And when I told them how wonderful you are,
They didn't believe me,
They didn't believe me . . . '

Her voice was as smooth as slipper satin. She sang the beautiful song straight, as a ballad, the way Kern had written it, and before she reached her final chorus the audience was singing along with her. When it was over John absorbed the applause as if it had been meant for him. In that telling moment he made up his mind that before he left for Amsterdam the following morning he would have made Clara promise to marry him.

He took her to dine at Gennaro's in Soho where, true to the current fashion, at least half the women were wearing fringed shawls draped decoratively over their long evening dresses. He saw the way they glanced quickly at Clara, then away; but not before he had seen the naked envy in their eyes. In her simple dress of pale green georgette, with its high round neck and long tight sleeves, and her hair caught back from her forehead with a twist of the same material, she was as beautiful as a dream. John raised his glass to her.

'I'm sorry about this afternoon.' His smile was rueful. 'I didn't know I had it in me to be so jealous.'

'Of Joe?' Clara's glance was direct. 'Of weasel-faced Joe West, with his dirty nose?'

'Steady on, love. I said I was sorry.' Leaning forward and patting her hand, John's smile broadened. 'Men can be bitches as well as women, you know.'

Clara looked around her. The restaurant was crowded, and she guessed it would be quite a while before the waiter reappeared with their order. All of London seemed to be dining late that evening. Some of the men in white tie and tails, and the women with cropped shining hair, smoking between courses, with cigarettes in long holders held in slim white hands.

'They don't grow women like these where we come from,' she said. 'It's a different world.' The wide set green eyes were suddenly bleak. 'I wonder what Lily West would have made of all this?'

Her head was still aching from the aftermath of her visit to the hospital, and from Dora's petulance and childish behaviour before she'd left for the theatre. It had been a long day, and she still hadn't been honest with John. He was going away in the morning and it had to be said.

'I loved Joe once,' she whispered in her husky voice. 'I'd loved him when I was a child and that same loving spilled

183

over, so that when he came home three years ago I slept with him, and I got pregnant.'

She saw John take a deep breath as he struggled to achieve some sort of expression, but before he could speak Clara held up a hand.

'No, don't say anything, not yet.' She pressed her lips together and gazed up at the ornate ceiling. 'I lost the baby. They took me to hospital, and the doctors scraped what was left of it away. There were other complications, so I may never be able to have children . . . ' She finished on a sigh, staring at him mutely, the blood drained from her cheeks.

'Oh, my God!' John had found his voice at last. 'But he stood by you? He offered to marry you when you found you were . . . ? Oh, my God!'

'He never knew.' Clara wanted to weep, but this was not the place for such self-indulgence. 'He went away even before *I* knew.' Her eyes pleaded for understanding. 'He was like that . . . is like that. No one can keep Joe tied down.'

'But he knows now?'

'He knows now.'

John stared down at a plate of thinly sliced smoked salmon being placed before him by a waiter who had been told so often he looked like Rudolph Valentino he felt he must act the part.

'You can see the bloody pattern on the plate through this,' John grumbled as the waiter minced away. Picking up his wedge of lemon he squeezed it fiercely between thumb and forefinger. As he wiped his fingers on the starched damask napkin, anger flashed like a swift moving shadow across his face.

'Why did you have to tell me? To ease that damned puritanical conscience of yours?'

In the semi-darkness of the restaurant the faces at the tables had taken on a kind of luminosity. John's anger was that of a child deprived of its favourite toy. Never a deep-thinking man, his emotions, his actions were all superficial, and he was struggling now to understand. He was a man of the world, wasn't he? And he hadn't exactly been celibate over the years. Forking up a piece of smoked salmon, he stared at it morosely. In his job only a monk could have turned his back on temptation. Girls threw themselves at men who flew planes. Especially the years he'd spent with the circus. And there was that time on the Paris run when, due to an engine problem, he'd been grounded for almost a week. The long-lashed amber eyes narrowed. But for God's sake, he was a *man*! And that was different!

And yet . . . and yet . . . Suddenly in that crowded place he wanted her. Just thinking, imagining what she had done with that roughneck Joe West flamed his senses. He felt the heat rise in his body.

'Are you going to go on seeing him?' he asked gruffly, taking a bread roll and breaking it into crumbs. 'I couldn't stand that.'

Her eyes were downcast. 'I'm going to see him at the hospital tomorrow morning.' Clara hesitated, some instinct warning her not to mention the money. When she lifted her eyes he saw the pain in them. 'Terrible things have happened to Joe's family. If your parents hadn't moved away from the north they would have known. It would have been in the papers.'

'I don't want to know.' Aversion to hearing what she might tell him sharpened John's voice. 'But knowing the Wests I can imagine.'

'No you can't!' Clara was instantly furious. 'How can you possibly imagine what it was like for them? A mother left with six boys to bring up. With no money coming in but what she got from charity, and what little they earned. *I* was poor, John. I know what it was like, so don't look at me without remembering how I used to be.'

'Charity . . . ah, charity.' The anger and the desire in him suddenly dissolved. Stretching a hand, he ran a finger lightly down Clara's cheek. 'Though I speak with the tongues of men and of angels, and have not charity, I am become as sounding brass or a tinkling cymbal.' His smile was very sweet. 'See? I haven't forgotten all my father taught me.'

The tall man settling his companion into her chair at the next table saw the tender gesture. He was very elegant that evening in his white waistcoat and tails, suave in a subtle way, the furrow in his forehead etched deeply, the eyes bleak.

Raising her eyes, Clara met Bart Boland's cold blue gaze and as she acknowledged his slight nod her face flamed. Flustered, she inclined her own head.

'Someone you know?' John waited until Bart was seated with his back to them before he whispered the question.

'Yes, I know him.' Clara spoke in a low voice. 'He's Bart Boland.' She shielded her face with her left hand. '*Remember Me* is his show. And the girl with him is Adele Astaire. She's in *Lady Be Good* at the Empire Theatre, a dancer with her brother Fred. She's very pretty, isn't she?'

Already they were talking animatedly. Clara could see the way Miss Astaire was listening intently, her chin cupped in her hand and a smile playing round her lips. Although she couldn't hear a single word Clara could imagine Bart's voice, soft, almost soporific. She could see his long fingers curved round the stem of his glass. Was he asking the dancer to join him on Broadway? Was he promising her the moon and the stars if she and her brother would choreograph the Broadway version of *Remember Me*? And did any of that matter? Did she give a tuppenny damn about Mr Bart Boland's plans?

'When we're married I won't expect you to give up the stage,' John was saying. 'I wouldn't want you to stop singing.'

'You still want to marry me? After what I've told you, do you still feel the same?'

'It's gone,' John said quickly. 'If you never mention it again, then neither will I.'

He means it, Clara thought, feeling the tears prick behind her eyelids. He is a good man, just as his father was a good man. Believing in forgiveness and putting that belief into practice.

'You came into my dressing room that night in answer to a prayer.' Her expression was serious. 'I'll be a good wife to you, John. I give you my promise.'

John smiled at her. It had always been his way to blank his mind against any unpleasantness, as thoroughly as if it had never been. It was the only way he could cope. And, oh, dear

God, she was so lovely. And innocent too. He felt sure of it, in spite of what she'd just told him. Suddenly he felt about ten feet tall.

'My own career isn't decided yet.' The smile on his lips seemed to be spreading right through his body. It was a long time since a girl had looked at him the way Clara was looking at him now. It was the feeling he got when he was soaring high above the clouds, as if there was nothing he couldn't do. It was the feeling he'd had flying with the circus, when he'd looped the loop, his plane merely an extension of his own well-controlled body. The smile seemed a part of him.

'I won't be working for Lord Broughton for ever,' he told her. 'I'd rather be flying passengers than bundles of newspapers any old day.' The flop of fair hair had fallen over his forehead and he pushed it back with an impatient hand. 'The advances in passenger flying are unbelievable. They have heated cabins, and sponge-rubber seating. One bench for three passengers and easy chairs for two more. And a speed up to a hundred and twenty miles an hour!' At that moment he looked about eighteen years old. 'If only I hadn't to leave you tonight to pick up that damned plane in Amsterdam . . . Give me your hand, love.'

Clara held out her hand, then felt his thumb moving in tiny caressing circles round and round her palm, up and onto the pulse at her wrist.

'I want you so much,' he whispered.

Experienced in lovemaking, knowing exactly how to arouse with the slightest of movements, he was gratified to see the blush staining the fresh colour in her cheeks to an even deeper hue.

When the waiter with the Rudolph Valentino hairstyle brought the note to Clara, she thanked him with a bemused expression on her face. When she'd read it she pushed it quickly into her purse.

'Just a request to be at rehearsal earlier than usual in the morning.' She glanced briefly at Bart's back. 'A *summons* really,' she added, a hint of defiance in her voice. 'Nothing to worry about at all.'

With no regard at all for visiting hours, Clara walked into the big teaching hospital the next morning straight from a hurried visit to her bank.

'Stars lie abed in the mornings!' Dora had shouted from her room. 'All this gallivanting will ruin your looks, you mark my words.' Sinking back on her pillows, she'd remembered how it had been when she was young, when sleep was merely a waste of time, to be taken in snatches, when after appearing on the stage she had sometimes talked all night. And loved all night . . . 'Old age is a *bore*,' she muttered, turning over and going back to sleep again.

Fate was on her side, Clara decided, hurrying past sister's little room, seeing her bent over her desk engrossed in paperwork. Thanking God for small mercies, she made her way into Joe's ward.

At the foot of his bed she came to a sudden halt, eyes wide, the carefully worded speech she'd prepared in her head dying on her lips. There was a man in the bed, a bearded man with a gaunt face and staring dark eyes, a man who raised his head to stare at her with obvious pleasure.

'I seen you,' he grinned. 'I seen your picture. Pull up a chair, doll. Just what the doctor ordered, you are. Come to cheer us all up with a bit of a song, dearie?' Winking at the patient in the next bed, he levered himself up on his elbows, baring his lips in a toothless smile.

With his laughter following her down the long ward, Clara walked away with as much dignity as she could muster, the small cuban heels on her patent leather shoes making little tapping noises on the well-scrubbed floor.

'Joe? Joe West?' She stood in the doorway of sister's little office. 'He's not . . . ?' She faltered, knowing he was dead, but waiting to be told. She could feel her heart beating so strongly it whirred in her ears. In that moment she forgot she had come to say goodbye to him; all she knew was that he had died, alone with no one to hold his hand.

The sister looked up from her desk. Taking off her spectacles, she pinched the bridge of her nose between thumb and forefinger. And stared at Clara with something akin to distaste.

It wasn't fair that anyone could look like the young woman staring at her with large green eyes wide with anxiety. Not at that time on a cold winter's morning, with the rain lashing down outside. The pale green of Clara's princess-line coat accentuated the colour of those incredible eyes. Tendrils of pale gold hair escaped from the close-fitting matching hat, and her lips were rouged to match the wild rose in her cheeks.

Sister put up a hand to her own face in an involuntary gesture. Without needing to look in a mirror she knew exactly what she looked like. Drawn, exhausted after a night spent at the bedside of a dying man, hearing his rasping breath, waiting for the exhalation that never came; she was so tired her mouth felt stretched as she spoke.

'Visiting hours are from seven thirty to eight o'clock in the evenings, and three o'clock to four Wednesday and Sunday afternoons.' She turned back to her desk. 'And if you've come to see Mr West then you're wasting your time. He discharged himself during the night when the staff were busy with other things.'

'But he's not got nowhere to go!' In her distress Clara used the double negative of her Lancashire childhood. 'It was raining all night. Where would he go?'

'He'll be back, no doubt.' As she saw the colour drain from Clara's face, the sister's nursing training took precedence over her emotions. Moving forward to take Clara firmly by an elbow, she pushed her down into a chair. 'Did you eat breakfast?' Her voice softened as Clara stared up at her without understanding. 'Mr West is beyond help, my dear. You must surely know that?'

'So he *is* ill? *Really* ill?' Clara stared down at the purse on her lap. 'He hasn't got any money. Nothing at all.'

'He has now.' Sister pointed to a space at the corner of her desk. 'Pennies for the blind. Only coppers, but enough to buy him that first drink or two.' The telephone rang and after she unhooked it from its stand she covered the mouthpiece with her hand. 'You'll want to talk to the almoner. It's the ground floor, the door on the right at the foot of the staircase . . . Hello? Hello? Yes?'

When she turned round again Clara had gone.

On the way to the theatre, sitting in the back of a taxi, Clara found herself making wild and dramatic plans for finding Joe and weaning him off the drink herself. She saw herself wandering along the Embankment in the middle of the night, bending over sheets of soggy cardboard to see if Joe was lying underneath. She would make it quite clear to John that together they must find Joe and restore him to health. They were after all fellow Lancastrians, *Christians*, dedicated to helping each other. In spite of what John had said, he wasn't a hard man. Oh yes, John would help her to find Joe when she asked him to.

She was not yet twenty. Her thinking was still an unsophisticated jumble of belief in what was right and intolerance of what was wrong. Joe was weak, she acknowledged that, but he was a victim of circumstance, the result of his mother's total lack of discipline. Lily West had loved her sons in spite of their thieving ways, *because* of them, Clara suspected. Joe had never known the comfort of an ever loving God holding him fast in love. Joe had sneered at God.

The cab driver, turning round as he drew up outside the theatre, saw his passenger sitting with eyes tight closed and gloved hands clasped together on the back seat. Praying she'd get a part in the show, he concluded, not recognizing her.

'Good luck, miss,' he shouted as Clara crossed the rainswept pavement. 'I'll say one for you, if you like.'

Clara didn't hear. She was late for rehearsal, and if there was one thing Bart couldn't tolerate it was unpunctuality. If he could find the time to sit in the earliest rehearsal, then he expected his girls to be there before him. It would be a waste of time explaining that for the past hour she'd been all alone in the hospital almoner's tiny office waiting for her to finish her round of the wards. For Mr Boland, the show was all.

He was there in the stalls, sitting in a swirl of cigar smoke, with his heavy greatcoat round his shoulders. Waiting, Clara knew, for a note out of place, ready to tear down the aisle, overriding the producer whose job it was to correct and advise.

The entire company was on stage, singing the opening chorus, and Clara, whose appearance was confined to her own solo at the end of the first half of the performance, breathed a sigh of relief. With any luck her absence would have gone unnoticed.

'Here!' Bart's voice was curt and clipped. 'Sit by me, Miss Haydock. I suppose we should be grateful that you've turned up at all.'

He had eyes in the back of his head, Clara told herself, doing as she was told, muttering apologies that were waved away with an impatient sweep of the hand holding the cigar.

As the chorus came to an end a hush descended over the auditorium. The rehearsal pianist, a wizened old man who had once played with the Vienna Symphony Orchestra, ran his fingers up and down the keys in a final flourish. The company waited for a soft-shoe shuffler to take his place in the tableau.

Bart, wearing his coat like a medieval cloak, walked down to the footlights.

'So that's the new song?' Holding out a hand, he addressed the pianist. 'I'll have that sheet, if you don't mind. Is the composer here?'

No one moved. If the luckless one was there, Clara surmised, he was having the sense to keep quiet.

'The lyrics are fine.' Bart held the music at arm's length. 'But the music is lamentable.' He ran a finger down the sheet. 'Who told the orchestra they didn't need to come in this morning?'

Again no one moved or spoke. Bart put a hand to his forehead. 'Well, has anyone passed on the message to eliminate the violin for this number? Or told the violas they've to serve the rhythm as well as the melody?'

He knew it all, Clara thought, sitting quietly in her seat. If he had the time he could write the score, improve on the lyrics, produce, find the backing, choose the dancers, even choreograph the dancing numbers. *And* make the costumes, she wouldn't mind betting. No wonder he was so intolerant of weakness in others.

'Either this tune is rewritten or I find a different composer,' Bart was saying. 'I don't expect perfection from your voices. If folks want that they can go to the opera, but I've heard many a chapel choir sing with more feeling than you lot put into this number. What are you trying to do? Turn the customers away?'

All at once his shoulders slumped; the heavy coat slid from them and dropped to the floor. He was very aware of the small girl waiting as still as a mouse behind him. Without turning round he could see the bruised look around her eyes telling of an almost sleepless night, and in his imagination he saw the fair-haired man lean across the table in the restaurant and run a finger down her cheek.

'That's all for today.' He nodded at the pianist. 'But you stay. I want to go through Miss Haydock's song.'

On stage Clara took off her coat and laid it across the back of a chair by the prompt corner. In her pale green woollen dress with its draped cowl collar she walked centre stage and waited quietly for the pianist to play her introduction.

'Take off your hat!'

She did as she was told, shaking her head to release the long shining fall of her glorious hair. Bart closed his eyes, knowing that the sensuous movement was entirely without provocation, despising himself for his gut reaction to it. There was a depth to his blue eyes Clara hadn't noticed before as he jerked his chin downwards telling the pianist to play the opening chords.

It was the song beginning to be associated with Clara's name, the lyrics by Herbert Reynolds, the music unmistakably by a Jewish boy born of German stock in New York to a father with a gift for making large sums of money. Jerome Kern.

The plaintive melody might have been written for the girl who had never had a singing lesson in her life, but who sang straight from her heart. Bart had to remind himself that he was there to listen critically, not to stand like some stage-door Johnnie openmouthed in silent adoration. By the final chorus there was the suspicion of tears in his eyes, a moisture he blinked angrily away.

'And when I told them how wonderful you are,
They didn't believe me,
They didn't believe me . . . '

Bart's bones seemed to liquefy with tenderness.

'And when I tell them,
And I'm certainly going to tell them,
That you're the boy whose wife one day I'll be,
They'll never believe me,
They'll never believe me,
That in this great big world you've chosen me . . . '

The tired old man at the piano slid his fingers from the keys and bowed his head. If he wouldn't be laughed at for a sentimental old fool he would say that the voice he'd just accompanied was that of an angel down from heaven, each note silvered with heartfelt sweetness.

'This young girl,' he said to himself, 'will one day be the greatest name on the British stage. Given the right teachers she might have sung the leading operatic roles anywhere in the world – Florence, Naples, Paris, London . . . '

His head jerked upwards as he heard Mr Boland say in his quiet voice, 'Half an hour's break, Mr Bach, and thank you. You play well.'

The bent old man shuffled his way into the darkness of the wings. Of course he played well! Hadn't he once conducted his own orchestra before the war, before they took everything and everyone belonging to him, branding him as a spy? He'd thought he'd come to the end of the road before he met Mr Boland. Bart Boland, the English gentleman, the famous West End impresario, who had the courtesy to remember and to call a very old and very tired man by his name.

'That song,' Bart was saying, joining Clara on the stage, 'is one of the songs I want you to sing when we open in Boston.'

Clara wheeled round to face him, one arm inside the sleeve of the pale green coat. 'But I'm not going to America! I *told* you.' Her eyes were bright with anger. 'You thought that when you'd . . . ' she struggled to find the right word, 'when you'd *manipulated* Dora into the home everything would be settled.' Furiously she fought her way into the tight armholes of the single-breasted coat. 'I meant what I said, Bart. I'm not going.'

'Because you want to be on hand to visit Dora every day.' Bart's tone was weary. 'Because you refuse to realize that Dora will be happier with her own kind. That you can't see she's come to the end of the road anyway, that her mind is slipping into senility, that in three months' time, if she lives that long, she won't even recognize you.'

'And because I'm getting married,' Clara said.

For a moment his head jerked back as though she had hit out at him. Bart had to swallow hard before he could bring himself to speak.

'To the boy from home?' he asked quietly.

Clara nodded. 'Yes, to the boy from home. I've known him since I was a child.'

'And you're no longer a child?'

Bart stared at her for a long time without speaking. He had known, as indeed he suspected that everyone had known, about the baby Clara had lost, and about the boy who had deserted her when she needed him most. Dora had sworn him to secrecy, and being a man of his word Bart had not only kept silent but managed to push the whole sad story out of his mind.

'So he finally came back?' he said at last. 'And you find you still love him?'

Clara moved her head slightly. 'You're talking about Joe,' she whispered. 'How long have you known about Joe?'

It was very quiet there on the big stage, with the empty seats in the auditorium stretching in tiered rows. Bart picked up her hat from the piano and handed it to her. 'Does it matter?'

'You mean it doesn't matter?' They were whispering as if they were in church, the shame that Clara still felt and would feel for the rest of her life flooding over her. It was a moment of such intensity that the air seemed to shimmer between them.

'I knew you were more sinned against than sinning.' Bart stretched out a hand as if he would draw her to him. 'I know you, Clara, and I know that once having given yourself to any man you would be bound to feel committed to him.' The intense blue of his eyes deepened. 'Do you understand what I'm trying to tell you, my dear?'

'But I'm not like that!' The words seemed torn from her. 'Joe *did* come back, but it's not him I'm marrying. What kind of a person do you think I am?' She spread her hands wide. 'I stopped loving Joe the day I realized he had gone away not caring what happened to me. My father taught me respect and, respecting myself, how could I hold fast to a love that was a waste of time?'

'Then who . . . ?' The sadness in Bart's face was livened now by bewilderment. 'Is there another boy you left behind? The fair one I saw you with at Gennaro's last night?'

'Two of them,' Clara told him. 'Two boys in the same class at school. Joe, who had nothing, and John, the son of the Church of England minister.'

'Ah . . .' Enlightenment flickered across Bart's expression. 'And he's followed his father into the Church?'

'No. He's a pilot. He flies planes in Europe. For a newspaper magnate.'

'And you want to be there, waiting for him when he comes home?'

Clara bridled. 'I intend to be a good wife to him, if that's what you mean.'

Bart turned away, walking with his long stride out to the wings and back again, hearing his wife's voice shouting after him the last time he left her to travel down to London, 'Is that all you need me for? To be here, like a good little wife, waiting for you when you decide to come home for a while? Do you blame me that I've made a life for myself, and do you wonder that the children hardly know you?' Her voice had risen to a scream. 'Stay away this time, Bart! Don't feel you have to put in an appearance now and again for the sake of your conscience!'

'But it's my *job*!' He had turned at the door, wasting his

time he knew but trying just once again. 'Come down to London. We'll take a house there. You can keep this one up here for the children's summer holidays. Give it a *try*. You'll make friends down there. You can even ride as much as you want to. London is greener than you think.' He had picked up his case. 'You knew what I was when you married me. You knew my work meant I'd be London-based.'

'But I didn't know you'd want to be there nine tenths of the year, did I? I even kidded myself you could work from home when the telephone was installed.'

'*My* job? Worked from home?' He was shouting at her now, giving back as good as he got. 'What about *your* job? Isn't marriage a partnership?'

'With the man the bloody managing director!' she'd yelled after him, slamming the door in his face.

That was two years ago. The gentleman farmer she'd been friendly with for years had almost moved in with her, according to rumour. Bart saw his children once a year, but had never seen his wife since that day.

'Unless this John of yours understands show business,' he said, coming back to Clara and speaking as if he had never left her side, 'it won't be easy.' He hesitated. 'Couldn't you wait until you're of age? Couldn't you change your mind about America? The show needs you, Clara.' He drew a long breath. 'And *I* need you, too.'

'To help the show to be a success?'

'That, yes, and to give you time to be sure you're doing the right thing.'

'In marrying John?'

'In marrying someone who turned up at a time when you are emotionally vulnerable. When Dora, whether you like to admit it or not, has come to a stage where she needs far more care than you're able to give her. And because someone from home has turned up at just the right moment, giving you the security you crave, reminding you of that little street you've never really left behind.'

She had always talked to him as an equal, and she wasn't going to change now. 'You know what they'd've called you in our street, Bart?' The green of her eyes had darkened to

196

emerald. 'Clever-clogs Boland. That's what they'd've said. An' you're right. I am still part of that street, an' I always will be. I can talk posh, an' I can wear a coat that cost ten pounds, but I'm still me inside. An' me is little Clara Haydock, playing hopscotch on the clags in me clogs, an' running to school with a rag pinned to the front of me dress to wipe me nose on when the teacher says "blow".'

'An' me is accepting that you were right and I was wrong about Dora. She needs more care than I can give her.' Her chin lifted. 'But you were wrong about thinking you could persuade me to sail to America. Where I come from a girl stays with her man when she marries. He is the breadwinner and his job is more important than hers. What kind of a start to a marriage would it be with me three thousand miles across the sea and John coming home from his flights to an empty flat? I'm going to be a good wife, Bart, an' I couldn't be that on your terms. No so-called *success* is going to make me swell-headed and throw me off balance. I've got my priorities right.'

An apologetic cough heralded the return of the pianist. Silently he slid onto the piano stool and placed his hands on the keys. He would stay like that, head bowed, for as long as was necessary. The £8 a week he was being paid had to be earned, and if part of that time entailed being merely an extension of the rehearsal piano, then he was more than willing to oblige.

Privately he considered Clara's next song to be wrong for her. Gershwin had written it for a deeper contralto voice, an *older* voice with power. When Clara turned her flushed, angry face towards him and nodded, he began to play. His opinion had counted for less than nothing for a long time now.

> 'Some day he'll come along,
> The mn I love.
> And he'll be big and strong,
> The man I love.

The emotion and, yes, the *power* in Clara's voice brought the old man's head up sharply from his shoulders. She was belting the song out with such passion, if an audience had been there it would have brought them to their feet. Startled, he nearly played a wrong note.

> 'And when he comes my way,
> I'll do my best to *make him stay* . . . '

Was there nothing this slightly built girl couldn't do with her voice? The old man shifted his foot to the soft pedal. It wasn't an accompanist she needed, merely a soft breathing as a muted background to her singing. She was letting the words speak for themselves, giving them such feeling that the old man felt the hairs on the back of his neck rise. The song might have been written for her, and she was singing it in a smoky tone, technically not quite permissible, but with none of the metallic quality of a run-of-the-mill dramatic soprano. Her lower tones were so rich, they filled his heart with pain.

Suddenly Bart could take no more. Clara was taking the song, *using* it to convey her feelings to him. This was no young girl eaten by ambition, putting her career first and hoping her life fitted in around it. She was the kind of girl every man hoped to meet one day.

Knowing he could bear no more, Bart swung round, clattered his way down the aisle, letting the doors at the back of the auditorium swing back with a noise that reverberated right through the empty theatre.

And more quietly now, as though the emotion had been drained from her, Clara finished her song.

Thirteen

On the day of her wedding to John Maynard Clara woke early. Pulling a white satin dressing gown round her and tying the long sash at the side, she went through into the tiny kitchen of the flat in Conduit Street to make herself a cup of cocoa.

'Cocoa?' John had teased her about her liking for it. Surely your cocoa-drinking days should have been left behind by now? Coffee's the thing you should be drinking.' His amber eyes had teased with their slightly mocking expression. 'Cocoa's a sign of your working-class origins, love. It should be drunk wearing a mob cap on your head and a cross-over pinny tied round your middle.'

But Clara clung to the small comforting routine. Putting a spoonful of the cocoa powder into a cup from its yellow and orange rectangular tin, she added sugar and a little cold milk before mixing it into a smooth paste. The boiling water from the kettle gave the drink a good froth, which she drank first with pleasure, closing her eyes as she savoured the fragrant brew.

It was going to be a beautiful day. She could see powder-puff clouds sailing serenely across a bright blue sky. All at once her sleepiness vanished and she knew she was looking forward to all the day would bring.

At a party the night before John had convulsed the entire company with his out-of-tune rendition of a song he'd told them he only sang when he was tiddly:

'I fly in the sky,
Ever so high.

Surely you've heard,
I soar like a bird.
When I fly, when I fly,
When I fly, when I fly.'

He'd landed at Croydon Airport only the day before, coming straight to the theatre and sweeping Clara into his arms. 'I was in Copenhagen last week,' he told her. 'Passenger routes are being opened up all over Europe. Soon you'll be able to sing in London one night and Rome or Venice the next.'

He'd walked up and down, talking with his hands, totally unable to keep still. 'I saw rednecked farmers from Germany with catalogues of the big cattle sales sticking out of their pockets. You should have heard them praising the virtues of flying, as opposed to sitting for hours in a luxury express train. It won't be long before practically every businessman in Europe will refuse to travel by any other means but along the air routes.' He'd stuck both thumbs up in the air in a gesture of triumph. 'And yours truly is in at the beginning!'

The sheer force of his enthusiasm had been so infectious that Clara, sipping her cocoa, could almost imagine he was there with her, tramping up and down the kitchen, talking with his hands, his eyes shining and his fair hair falling forward over his forehead.

'It won't just be passengers, either. Already we're using planes for transporting breakable electric light bulbs, sensitive chemicals and furs. D'you know, love, the Prince of Wales flew from Paris to London recently on a special plane! But it's his brother George who enjoys flying. I've been told he never asks stupid questions like, "Is the plane safe?" or "What happens if the engine fails?" '

How *young* he was. Clara finished her cocoa and went to run her bath. The seven years' difference in their ages seemed to disappear entirely at times. He was the fun and laughter she'd denied herself, coming straight back to Dora after work each evening. He was a light in a dark room, and what did it matter that they'd been able to spend so little time together? He was part of her childhood, and he saw her

200

not as she was now, successful and coming up to being rich, but as she used to be. John had known her when she really *was* the clogger's child, sparking her clogs when her father wasn't looking and spitting on her slate to rub her sums out when she'd added up wrong.

And besides all that, how proud her father would have been to see her marry the minister's son. Even a Church of England minister's son. Clara stepped into the warm water. Methodists worshipped the same God, even if they did sing His praises more loudly and in more tuneful rhythms.

Carefully she soaped herself all over. John had said that a true Methodist couldn't really ever enjoy what life offered because they were always looking over their shoulder to see if the devil was clapping his hands, knowing they'd suffer for it later. Was that true of her?

'You're guilt-ridden, Clara Haydock,' he'd told her, and she'd shouted back, amazed at her fury.

'I was *born* into guilt! Can't you understand? Not knowing either a mother or a father, how can I feel otherwise? It's all right for you, coming from a normal straightforward family with parents who passed on to you their good points, and a few of the bad. But me? How do I know what lies hidden in my ancestry? My father might have been a drunk, or a murderer even, and my mother? What kind of woman was she to give her new-born baby away? She didn't want me, that's certain!'

Another thing was certain and that was that John didn't cleave to his own parents. He never spoke about them, and when she had wondered if they could come to the wedding he'd mumbled something about them being too old, too ill to make the long journey from the North Yorkshire village to which they'd retired.

'That's another working-class thing, wanting to live in your parents' pockets when you're grown up,' he'd said, but Clara knew that if her father had been alive he'd have been there at the wedding to give her away if he'd had to come all the way in an ambulance.

'Oh, my lovely father, who was never my father,' she whispered as she dried herself. 'Would you ever have forgiven me for singing on the stage? And would my marrying the minister's son have made up for it?'

There it was, just as John had said. The guilt, the worriting if she was doing the right thing. And the burning in hell that would surely follow if she wasn't.

There was nothing unnatural in her thinking about her mother and real father on her wedding day, surely? A happy childhood with the clogger didn't preclude her from wondering about them, did it?

When two hours later she stepped out of her taxi in front of St George's, Hanover Square, her face was serene, her expression unclouded with any of the disturbing thoughts which had made her eyes fill with tears as she dressed. A small crowd waiting in the sunshine surged forward to catch a glimpse of the bride.

'She's not wearing white!' A girl in a bright yellow dress turned in obvious disappointment to her friend. 'I was sure she'd be wearing a wreath and veil.'

'But she looks lovely, doesn't she?'

'Just like a mannequin out of *Vogue* magazine. You can't tell she's got stockings on, they're that fine.'

Clara was wearing a pale pink dress with a flounced skirt, each flounce bound with satin cut on the bias. A long pearl necklace dangled over her fashionably flattened bosom, and her hat, pulled low over her brow, was trimmed with wild roses handmade from silk in a slightly deeper shade than her dress.

When John turned round from his position in front of the altar steps and saw her, his eyes filled with sentimental tears.

In that moment he vowed to himself that he would love and cherish her for ever.

In that emotion-filled moment, he meant it with all his heart and soul.

When Clara made her first appearance at the matinée that afternoon, the audience rose to their feet.

'Congratulations!' someone in the gods shouted out loud, and the entire audience took up his cry. 'Congratulations!

Congratulations!'

From the wings where he waited John was pushed, with a mock show of reluctance, onto the stage. Hand in hand with her new husband, Clara bowed her head in acknowledgement of the thunderous applause. She could feel the excitement emanating from John, and she knew he was loving every minute of the adulation.

'What's *he* bowing for? He's not done anything to be proud of,' a chorus girl whispered in the wings.

'Not yet.' The girl standing next to her giggled. 'Wonder if he'll find the time before tonight's performance?'

At last, to quieten the excited audience, the conductor tapped smartly on his stand with his baton. Reluctantly John walked off stage.

'I might give them a bit of a dance if they do the same this evening,' he told the giggling dancers, slapping one hard on a behind embellished with a curling feather. 'Then that lad who dances with his sister at the new show at the Empire had better watch out.'

'Who? Fred Astaire?' The feathered bottom gave a cheeky twitch. 'Oh, my God, have you seen him dance?'

'*Seen* him?' Surrounded by girls showing strips of bare flesh, John was experiencing the same sensation he got at the controls of his plane flying high above the clouds. 'Seen Fred Astaire dance?' he asked. 'I *taught* him! He'd be nowt a penny without his sister, anyroad,' he added, knowing that an exaggerated Lancashire accent was always good for a laugh.

It was a pity that John Maynard hadn't inherited his mother's musical talents, or even his father's presence in the pulpit before a congregation. Given the ability to play any instrument, he would have turned his back on any tutor at university trying without much success to guide him into a love of the Classics. Given a voice, he would have been another Al Jolson, belting out his songs to an enraptured audience, absorbing the applause like a sponge. Given even a mediocre talent for dancing and rhythm, he would have worked his way out of the chorus by the sheer force of his exuberance.

But up in the cotton town where he'd spent most of his childhood men who danced were pansies, and so he'd gone none too willingly to his father's old university, escaping from there into a war that for him had ended all too soon with the Armistice.

Flying gave him the glamour his extroverted nature craved. With his white silk scarf knotted nonchalantly round his neck, wearing his flying togs, he came, as they said in Lancashire, 'into his own'. Not knowing the meaning of fear, he thrived on it as some men thrived on hard work. What was irking him now was the dull routine of flying newspapers from one European capital to another. If he could have come to the theatre dressed in his flying helmet he would have basked in the attention from the girls. When he'd read an article that said flying aeroplanes was the most dangerous occupation there was for a man, his chest had actually swelled. Some day he'd decided, in the not too distant future, he would show the world his mastery of his flying machine by night-flying passengers distances unheard of in the commercial field. He would personally shrink distances, so that his name made headlines in all the papers. He would be a legend, recognized everywhere he went by adoring crowds hanging on to his every utterance. And if some flyer with the money to back him didn't get there first, he'd fly the Atlantic solo from east to west. It was being talked of already, and he knew it could be done.

In the meantime, he had long since discovered how attractive he was to women. Mannequins, show girls, all of them a sop to his ego, but not one of them as beautiful and famous as his new bride. Listening to her singing now, almost sensing the audience catching their breaths, he blessed the day he'd found her. Marrying her that morning had given him the chance to live vicariously in the charmed aura of her success. Marrying her had been the stroke of luck he could never have envisaged.

He hadn't been able to understand the firm stand Clara had made during their brief engagement against any form of lovemaking apart from kisses and cuddling. He couldn't understand how that scruff Joe West had succeeded where he had undoubtedly failed. But if she wanted to behave like the virgin she wasn't, so be it. His patience would be rewarded.

Clara sensed the difference in him when she came off stage after her last song at the end of the evening's performance. His hand on her back burned through her dress, and in her dressing room he kicked the door to behind him and pulled her close up against him. She felt the hardness of him and when he kissed her it was in a different way. So different she struggled for a moment, revulsion sweeping through her.

Forcing her lips apart he thrust his tongue into her mouth. Holding her fiercely to him he ground his body into hers. Still bemused by the rapturous applause of the audience, drained by the emotion she always put into her singing, she wasn't ready for the immediate switch to passion, and her whole being cried out against it.

Surfacing from the kiss which seemed to go on for ever, she began to talk nervously. 'Have you ever seen so many flowers? Look, John, they've been arriving all day.' Ignoring the mulish expression on his handsome face, she picked up a card attached to an enormous display of dark red roses. 'These,' she told him, 'are from Bart. He must have cabled the order from America.' Taking a single rose, she held it for a moment against a flushed cheek. 'He's forgiven me for not going with him. I really let him down, you know. Sometimes I wonder how I managed to make a stand. He isn't an easy man to cross.'

'It's time we went home, Clara.' Almost snatching the rose from her, John pushed it roughly back into the vase. 'Come on, love. Let's escape now before they all come in expecting another party.' He glanced at the bottles of champagne cooling in the row of fire buckets. 'We'll slip away. It's been a long day, and they'll understand.'

His eyes had darkened again. In another minute he was going to kiss her. Clara's heartbeats quickened. But not like that. Oh, please not like that . . . She stared at him, at the hectic flush staining his cheeks, and in that moment he seemed like a stranger. There was no familiar laughter in his eyes, no teasing; his grip on her arm as he urged her towards the door made her wince with pain.

'I can't go like this.' Wrenching her arm away, she stood rubbing the place where his nails had dug into her soft skin. 'Not without my cloak, and without ... some of the flowers.'

In one single movement it seemed John snatched her cloak from a chair, draped it round her shoulders, and thrust the nearest bouquet of flowers into her arms – the roses.

In the back of the taxi they dripped water from their long stems onto his trousers. When he tried to take them from her she shook her head, holding them to her like a shield. In the flat the first thing she did was to put them in water again, conscious of the fact that John was behind her in the high-ceilinged sitting room, taking off his jacket, unbuttoning his waistcoat before sitting down in Dora's chair to unlace his shoes.

'I took your case through into the bedroom when it came round this morning,' she whispered, reluctant to move away from the heady scent of the roses. 'Would you like a drink of something? Or are you hungry? It's a long time since you've eaten. They'd sent in sandwiches to go with the champagne.' Her voice faltered at the expression on his face. 'I could have brought some with us, that is if you're ... '

'Come here, Clara.'

She walked towards him slowly, every step a conscious effort. What was wrong with her? This man was her husband. She had promised, in the sight of God that very day, to love and obey him for as long as they both lived. It was just that – it had come to her in the taxi ride from the theatre – that, because of Joe, he imagined she knew what to expect. Even knew what to do.

And she could never tell him that when Joe had taken her she had been hardly more than a child. That she had hardly known what she was doing. That she had never gone through the adolescent yearnings of wanting to understand her own feelings, her own body, the way she now knew other girls did. Those dreaming searching years had been stolen

206

from her by a father who rocked himself by the fire, nursing a crippled hand. When other girls had been out 'ladding' on the wide road leading to the Corporation Park, she had been working both at home and in that basement room, keeping her father from starvation.

And Joe . . . He'd been *comfort*, not what this man holding out his arms to her imagined. John was cupping her face in his hands now, amber eyes glittering as he looked down at her. It was too late to say all the things Clara knew she should have said, too late to try to make him understand that really, for her, it was the first time.

After the kiss, holding nothing of tenderness in its searching passion, John spoke to her in a voice rough and alien with the force of his longing. 'You go through and get into bed. I'll smoke a cigarette before I join you.'

She had no idea what it cost him to say that. But in her long white dress, with her pale gold hair hanging loose, with her green eyes filled with what a man would have to have been a fool not to recognize as fear, John's better nature asserted itself. If she wanted to be wooed on her wedding night like some tremulous virgin, then so be it. If she wanted a Prince Charming, he could play that game too.

'But hurry up, darling,' he whispered, striking a match for his cigarette with a hand that trembled. 'I've waited a long time for this moment.'

When he walked swiftly into the bedroom she was kneeling by the bed, wearing a high-necked nightdress, hands folded as she said her prayers. For a second the shutters opened wide on an almost forgotten childhood. He remembered his mother standing by his side to hear him say his nightly prayer: 'God bless Mummy and Daddy and all my friends at school. And make me into a good boy. For Jesus Christ's sake, Amen.'

The memory held him still, then, as Clara turned her head, he went to her, lifting her onto the bed. Tearing at his clothes in his haste to be rid of them, he got in beside her, drawing her to him, the desire kept in check for so long flooding through him, so that all control vanished.

It was over so quickly that Clara couldn't believe it. His

weight on her had been suffocating, his feverish words of love lost in the tangle of her long hair. She sensed his hurt manly vanity as he held her, promising it would be better next time. And when it happened again, and it wasn't, she lay awake with him sleeping soundly beside her, wondering why men seemed to like so much what they did.

He woke at five in the morning, and though she closed her eyes and willed herself to cooperate and be a part of him, she felt more alone than she had ever felt in the whole of her nineteen years.

'Oh, darling,' he whispered later, and the light seeping through the drawn curtains showed her his handsome face with a golden stubble of beard on his chin. He was watching her with an expression compounded of love and triumph, tinged with gratitude.

'You're so wonderful,' he whispered. 'One day everyone in London will know your name. The lights of Piccadilly will seem to dim beside it. When you sing I'll be there watching them watching you, knowing you are singing for me.' He placed a hand on her thigh. 'And knowing you belong to me.'

'I'm cold without my nightie,' she told him, feeling peevish and mean, yet immediately regretting her words as he pulled her tightly up against him, massaging her all over with hard rubbing movements.

When they walked into the Home much later than planned, with Clara carrying the roses for Dora, it was obvious that in that first telling moment Dora was struggling to remember just who they could be.

Clara smiled at the old woman, a soft warm smile. 'It's me. Clara,' she whispered. 'How are you, Dora?'

Bart had been right. Gradually over the past few weeks Dora had slipped further into senility. Her face was still made up as if for the stage, her dress as befrilled and colourful as ever, but as she lowered her head Clara was saddened to see the wide white parting in the brightly hennaed hair. In the large, sunny lounge chairs were arranged round the walls, as if their occupants were at a ball waiting for the band to strike up and partners to glide towards them to ask if they could have the first dance. Half the women were asleep, white heads nodding over spade-flat chests, walking sticks looped over the backs of their chairs.

'Who's that man?' Dora's voice had lost none of its power as she glared at John squatting on his heels by a wheelchair, charming an old lady into a fit of giggles.

Clara knelt down and took Dora's hand. 'You know who that is, you old fraud. It's John. We got married yesterday, and I wished more than anything that you could have been there.'

'To see you married to *him*?' Dora had changed suddenly into a frail birdlike creature with a plaintive wobble in her voice. 'He's not young Mr Boland, is he?' Her faded eyes filled with a bleak watery despair. 'He's the one you should have married, little chuck. He would've known how to make you happy.'

'I *am* happy.' Clara patted the twisted hand lying so passively in her own, then made the mistake of talking to Dora as if she were a child, soothing her with comforting words. 'Mr Boland has a wife already, dear.'

'Not any more, he's not!' Dora's indignation flared in her eyes, the woman she had been not so long ago taking over from the quavering one of a few seconds earlier. 'Divorced, that's what Mr Boland is, with his wife getting custody of his two children. Poor man.'

'Mr Boland is in America.' Clara glanced across the room at John, still holding his captive audience of one spellbound. '*That's* the man I'm married to, Dora. You're getting a bit mixed up today, dear.'

'I'm *never* mixed up!' Dora's voice deepened to a growl. 'And don't call me "dear". You never used to. It makes me feel *old*.'

As John came over she was asleep with the suddenness of a stone dropping down a well, hands twitching at the rug over her knees. Before he could speak she was awake once again, glaring at him from beneath heavily pencilled-in eyebrows, one at least a quarter of an inch longer than the other.

'Is this your son?' she shouted to the old woman in the wheelchair. 'I thought you said he never came to see you? Does he peroxide his hair?'

'That's the last time we're coming here.' Holding Clara firmly by an elbow, John almost marched her to the door. He shuddered. 'If that's what growing old is like, then, please God, let me die young.'

Twisting away from him, Clara turned round to see Dora crying silently, her mouth wide open in a wail of incomprehension. Drawing her arm from her husband's grip, she spoke quickly, the expression in her green eyes daring him to interfere.

'I can't leave her like this. She's all confused, and it's the knowing she's confused that's killing her. Wait for me outside. I have to talk to her again.'

His footsteps sounded very loud on the beef-tea-coloured oilcloth of the passage leading to the heavy front doors. Clara's lips tightened for a moment; then in a few swift steps she was back at Dora's side, kneeling down to look into the ravaged face with the tears running down past the corners of the gaping mouth. The lace-edged handkerchief she used to mop up Dora's tears came away stained with yellow ochre face powder and coral rouge.

'Don't cry, Dora.' Clara dabbed at the trembling chin. 'See, you're making me cry too.' She watched as Dora moved her head sideways, like a child refusing to be comforted. 'I love you, Dora.' Clara willed understanding back into the vague expression. 'If I do it quietly, would you like me to sing for you?'

It was a strange thing to say. Clara acknowledged that, but in that moment it was all she had to offer, that and the love she felt for this old woman with approaching death written plain on her grotesquely made-up face.

But suddenly Dora was asleep again, the organdie frills on her purple blouse rising and falling with the hoarse rattle of her breathing. Getting to her feet, Clara kissed the crown of the bowed head with its ring of undyed hair showing like a bald patch. She walked quickly out into the passageway, unable to bear any more.

John was outside waiting for her, smoking with fierce impatient puffs. When he saw her he threw the cigarette away, flicking it over a rhododendron bush before pulling her into his arms.

'I'm sorry, love.' He was all contrition as he stared down into her troubled face. 'I'm not very good with old sick people. Maybe I saw too much of it when I was a small boy and my mother used to take me with her on some of her sick-visiting.' His finger traced the contours of Clara's mouth, and she knew he was trying to apologize. 'Old age will come to me and to you,' he said. 'But not yet. Not for a long, long time yet, my darling.' He glanced back at the red-brick building. 'Being reminded of it, of the way we'll be some day, makes me feel physically ill. Old age isn't dignified. It's pathetic, it's cruel, it's a lingering on this earth with one foot already deep in the grave.'

Clara shook her head. 'No, you're wrong, quite wrong. There is a dignity there if you look for it, if you listen for it. Very old people have a lot of wisdom.'

To her amazement John's face flushed a deep angry red. 'Just for once, love, just once look straight on at things the way they are. Not through a veil of sentimentality. Wake up, Clara! That religion of yours has blanked your mind to reality. Your thinking is archaic!' He lifted her feet clear of the ground, swinging her round so that she gave a small scream of protest. 'They were all potty in there! If they were dogs they'd have been put down long ago.' As he set her down his eyes blazed into hers. 'When it's my turn to go, give me a good clean death, spiralling down out of a bright blue sky. One big slam, then nothing. That's the way to go.'

Walking down the long winding path his mood changed with a speed that left Clara in a state of bewilderment. He actually whistled softly to the rhythm of their steps. She glanced sideways at the handsome face, the wide forehead, the straight nose exactly the right shape for the perfect balance of the classical features. In spite of his recent outburst John walked at ease with himself, obviously assuming that her mood matched his own.

'You feeling all right?' At the kerb he stopped, searching the length of the tree-lined road for a cruising taxi cab. 'You look quite pale, love.'

'I'm wondering if I'm really as sanctimonious as you say.' For the first time in years Clara used a swearword. 'And it's a fine time to go talking about bloody dying on the day after our wedding. That's wrong thinking if anything is.'

There on the pavement John hugged her close, throwing his head back and laughing as if he were coming apart at the seams. 'You don't know how funny that sounded, coming from you. I didn't know you knew words like that.'

'And plenty more.' Clara joined in his laughter. 'When I was little me and Walter West were the best swearers in our class.'

A gleaming taxi came bowling along towards them and John stepped out into the road waving his arms as if he were doing semaphore.

In the back seat of the cab he put his arm round her, pulling her close and dislodging her hat. 'We've got all afternoon to ourselves,' he whispered softly into her hair.

Closing her eyes, Clara leaned into his shoulder. It was going to be so easy to make him happy. She'd noticed before how he shied away from any form of unpleasantness. Next time she visited Dora she would go by herself. John was so *young* really, and maybe *she*'d lived too long with sadness. First with her father's depression after his hand got smashed, then with Dora, who for the past two years had lived wholly in the past. It was time she relaxed and just let herself be loved. And the other thing . . . well, she'd get used to it, maybe even get to like it in time. Opening her eyes, she saw a young woman pushing a pram with a baby sitting bolt upright at either end and a toddler clinging to her skirt as she waited to cross the road.

Other women obviously put up with it and didn't seem to mind. And it certainly wasn't a thing you could ask anyone about, or seek advice. Perhaps the discomfort and the disappointment at the speed with which it was over were natural and would right themselves in time?

When John made love to her that afternoon, with the

212

curtains drawn against the sunshine, she moved against him and told herself that this was what love was like.

And in giving of herself she experienced a kind of pleasure that dissolved all fear and hurt. If that wasn't love, then she knew no other name for it.

Fourteen

Arlene Silver, fashion editor of one of London's glossiest magazines, was enjoying her month's working assignment in New York. Nature had intended her to be plain but, knowing every trick in the book, she had turned herself into a striking beauty.

She was used to being stared at and accepted men's attentions as her right. A party where she wasn't the centre of attraction would have been a wasted evening for Arlene. It took her the best part of an hour to apply her make-up and burnish her chin-length auburn hair, but the result, she would have been the first to admit, was worth every minute.

She was dining late that evening, after the heat of the long summer's day, in a new bootleg club down on West 45th Street, and after the meal was finished and a cup of fragrant coffee put before her, she rested her elbows on the table, cupping her face in her hands. She sighed with such deliberation that the marabou trimming round the neck of her jade green gown fluttered as if it had suddenly come to life.

What was the point, she wondered, in a man possessing eyes as blue as the sea if those eyes were not adoring her over the width of the pale pink linen tablecloth? Not bothering to smother a yawn, she stared around the room, taking in the famous and glittering personalities there for the club's opening.

She could see Grace Moore, Marilyn Miller and the William K Vanderbilts, all enjoying themselves with the same abandon as if they'd been in a private house party. At another table a pretty blond girl leaned on Harpo Marx's shoulder, laughing uproariously at something he'd just said. Already Arlene's trained mind had filed away the details of the women's dresses, noting the cut, recognizing in most cases the designer. Her enjoyment of the cabaret, with Jack Buchanan, Gertrude Lawrence and Bea Lillie making their debut as night-club entertainers, had made her wish she had a Union Jack to wave. It should have been a night to rememeber, but for Arlene there was one vital ingredient missing. And that was the besotted admiration of the man sitting opposite her.

Closing her eyes, she shut herself off from the noise and laughter and began to compose in her mind the week's fashion article for her magazine in London. As she formulated words and sentences in her head, she could almost hear the clack-clack of her portable typewriter. 'Hold everything, dear reader. This you will find almost impossible to believe, but our own Gertie Lawrence has been seen around New York bare-legged! Yes, that's right. Bare-legged! Without stockings!'

Here, Arlene decided, she would maybe put in a quote from Carmel Snow, fashion editor of *Harper's Bazaar*: 'The idea is disgusting. It will *never* be done by nice people.

'Bare legs at Ascot! That'll be the day,' Arlene said aloud, gratified to see at long last a spark of interest in the amazingly blue eyes of her escort.

'I'm sorry.' He smiled, giving her his full attention. 'You were saying?'

Arlene put her glossy head on one side to study him from beneath eyelashes stiff with three coats of spit mascara.

'Bart Boland,' she whispered softly in her husky voice, 'what's eating you up, darling? I've known you for a long time, man and boy, and, well, let's be honest about it, you could have been eating a chip butty on the end of Morecambe Pier for the attention you've paid to your food tonight.' Stretching out a hand tipped with scarlet fingernails, she trailed a finger down the craggy lines at the side of his mouth. 'Come on. Tell Arlene your little problem. I promise I won't use it as copy, even though my editor does fancy the odd spot of human drama mixed in with the fashion. You're all burned up, aren't you, sweetheart?'

Bart gave her a long level look. Arlene Silver was a crazy woman. Her age was anyone's guess. Twenty-five? Thirty-five? Forty? She'd given up the stage long ago, realizing she wasn't star quality.

'Can you see me, darlings, hoofing it in the back line of the chorus with drooping bosoms separated by a wrinkled cleavage?'

So, with a small legacy from her parents she'd gone round the world. Just for the hell of it. Arlene was smart; as smart as the paint on her vivacious face, and yet, Bart knew, underlying it all there was a softness, a sweetness she would have denied with her dying breath. 'But then I'm a sod,' was her favourite remark.

'I got a letter this morning.' Bart coughed as if in apology. 'Telling me that someone I've known for a very long time has died.'

'A woman?' Arlene leaned forward, prepared to drag it from him, word by perishin' word if necessary.

'An actress.' Bart bit his lip. 'Well, more of an entertainer really. A jewel of a woman with a voice calculated to drown a ship's siren. And that was when she was whispering.'

Arlene waved away the offer of more coffee. 'How old was she, love?'

'Eighty-five? Ninety?' Bart fiddled with the bowl of coloured sugar, stirring its contents with the small engraved spoon. 'She stopped counting when she got to sixty. She died in a nursing home, bewildered and unhappy. I put her there,' he said in a low voice. 'As I saw it, there was no choice.'

A sudden burst of laughter from a table in the corner brought his eyebrows together in a frown. 'The letter I got today was from a girl who liked, well, *loved* this friend of mine. She'd never known her own mother, you see, and I suppose she needed a substitute, and Dora had never had children, so . . . '

'I *hated* my mother,' Arlene said gently. 'But go on, darling. I'm a sod, as well you know.'

'The letter said that the end was pretty terrible. No details, but I can see it all.' His voice broke. 'Dying, you know, not being sure who she was, or where she was, come to that.'

Arlene's razor-sharp brain was working hard enough to earn double time. To die at eighty-five, ninety, well, surely that was doing what came naturally? Around her late fifties was the age Arlene had decided she was prepared to go. When she needed spectacles to cross the street or when her pubic hair turned grey would be about right. She narrowed her eyes. No, it wasn't the old woman Bart was grieving for, and, goddammit, he *was* grieving for someone, so . . . ?

'This girl? The one who wrote the letter?'

'Clara,' Bart said at once, as a shadow passed across his face. 'A singer in the London-based revue of *Remember Me*.'

'A good voice?'

The expression on his face made her want to cry. Arlene didn't go much on souls, but Bart Boland's soul was mirrored in his eyes. Even a sod could see that.

'There's an indescribable quality in her voice,' he was saying quietly. 'I found her, in a two-up, two-down little house in a back street in Lancashire. She was wearing her outdoor coat because she couldn't afford to build the fire up.' He looked away. 'She'd cheeked me at an audition, and I suppose that made me curious about her.' He looked up again and Arlene almost flinched at the depth of blue in his eyes. 'She sang for me, there and then, standing in that awful long coat in a room almost bare of furniture. The rest you can guess.'

'You became her lover?'

'No!' Bart's voice rose. 'She was a child!' He seemed to falter. 'At least, I *thought* she was a child. But her voice . . . It's the purest thing this side of heaven. It has a quality in it I've never heard before.'

'Why don't you marry her?' Arlene always said what she thought. 'Your divorce is through, isn't it?'

Into her mind flashed the recollection of a cocktail party in London. Was it eight or nine years ago? Bart there with a woman he introduced as his wife. A hard-faced woman standing by his side, chin raised as if she was trying to avoid a bad smell. A bitch on two legs, putting her husband down every time he opened his mouth. Emasculating him, but in a well-bred way.

'So why don't you marry your little singer?' she asked again. 'You're not meant to live your life on your own, Bart.' She glanced round the crowded room. 'You're in this business, I know, but there's something sets you apart. You're a different breed, darling. Given the chance, I'd've seduced you myself long before this.'

'She's married.' Bart swirled the brandy round in his glass before drinking it down. 'To a parson's son from her home town.' He grinned. 'Better looking than me. And younger than me.'

'But not right for her?'

Bart's laugh startled her, but after a moment she joined in, realizing that at last this lovely man's attention had switched to her. And he *was* lovely, even if his ears did stick out a bit and his hair receded more than a little from that wide lined forehead. Placing a cigarette in a long ebony holder, she accepted a light, then blew a perfect smoke ring up to the high ceiling.

'Now I know why you write the way you do.' Bart looked up from busying himself with an enormous cigar.

'And how *does* Arlene write? Go on. Do tell.'

'You remind me a little of Dorothy Parker,' he said at once. 'You say things other people only think, and though your words are wrapped in velvet they can sting.'

'I know.' Arlene's eyes sparkled now that they were talking shop. 'I only wish I *could* write like Dorothy Parker. She has such a gorgeously acerbic wit. You laugh, then you think, Oh Lordy, she's done it again.'

'She'd have made mincemeat of *Remember Me* if she'd reviewed it.'

'I think not.' Arlene's eyes twinkled. '*I* gave it a good mention, even though I knew they'd panned it in Boston. And now, look where you are. The Broadway vultures call you the English Gent. Goddammit, Bart, give them credit, the sods. What they said about your show made it into an overnight cult with the New Yorkers. The girls shimmying

218

down white staircases balancing harvest festivals on their heads have had their day. And you, smarty pants, you knew it, didn't you?'

For a long moment their glances held, locked in affection, liking and trust. It was a good feeling, and suddenly Bart held out his hand.

'Let's get out of here, shall we?' he said softly.

Walking down 42nd Street in the heat of the afternoon, with the third shirt of the day sticking to his back, Bart Boland looked like a man at peace with the world.

The feeling had come on him as he'd left Arlene Silver at five o'clock that morning when, clad only in a peignoir, she'd kissed him lightly, whispering her goodbyes. She was sailing for home in a few days, but they wouldn't meet again. Loving friends, that's what they were. Bart's smile widened as he remembered. Making love to Arlene had been a joyous thing, a wonderful, purely physical thing, with no promises to be kept afterwards, no protestations of undying faithfulness.

'You needed that, didn't you, darling?' she'd said as they lay side by side afterwards in her rumpled bed. 'Forget her, Bart. The world isn't well lost for love, believe you me.'

With his loping stride, Bart walked on. Arlene could be right. He wasn't the kind of man to spend the rest of his life pining for the unattainable. That was for the romantics, not for a man with a divorce behind him and two children growing up hardly knowing him. And last night Arlene had showed him that he wasn't cut out to be a monk! Laughing at the very thought, Bart stood waiting to cross the street.

And there, three thousand miles from home, waiting to join the milling crowds on the other side of the street, with the skyscrapers holding in the overpowering heat of the day, Bart said her name.

'Clara . . . oh, little Clara . . . '

As swiftly as it had come the moment passed and he was moving with the crowd, walking a little less quickly now, not holding his head quite so high.

'But you slept with her, John!'

Clara faced her husband in the bedroom of the flat in Conduit Street, hands clenched at her sides, green eyes blazing in the pallor of her face. The late summer day in London had been unbearably hot, and as she spoke there came the first low rumble of thunder.

'How can you dismiss it as just a flirtation when she's boasting to the other girls that you slept with her?'

'Slept with her. Slept with her.' John repeated the words in a singsong voice, wagging his head from side to side so that the fair flop of hair fell forward over his unwrinkled forehead. 'Why do you say that when it isn't true?' The champagne he'd drunk that night wobbled his features into a lopsided grin. 'A couple of hours on a couple of afternoons, that's all it was. You're the one I sleep with. You should know that.' A giggle bubbled inside him. 'I don't keep you short, do I?' Not wanting to look at her, he busied himself with the difficult task of tying his pyjama cord in a knot. 'Used to be a bloody Scout,' he muttered. 'Passed tying knots in the Cubs, but they were with string, not with this slippery . . . this slippery shilk shtuff.'

How on earth had she found out? Sitting down heavily on the side of the bed, he pressed his fingers against the throbbing pain in his temples. Trust that stupid dancer not to keep her gob shut. Gob? He hadn't used that word in years. 'Shut yer gob. Shut yer gob.' Nice word 'gob' . . . He turned round and shot Clara a venomous look. By all that was holy, she was a dark horse. Known all day, she had, since the morning's rehearsal. Kept it to herself through two performances, singing with never a falter in her voice, standing like she was standing now, as still as a flamin' statue. He groaned aloud. Why wasn't she like other women? Why didn't she throw something at him, or curse, or even land him one? From where did she get that . . . that stillness? She should have been a flamin' nun.

He heard himself begin to bluster. 'So we're quits now, aren't we? You with your precious Joe, and me with a girl whose name I'll have forgotten by next week.' He wondered if he was going to be sick. 'It's tit for tat now, so for heaven's

220

sake take that wounded look off your face and get into bed.'

'You can't *compare*!' There were no tears, but Clara's voice was hoarse with humiliation. Coming round the bed, she stood before him, green eyes blazing. 'I thought Joe was going to *marry* me! We were both *free*, can't you see? He was a part of my life, not some casual pick-up to while away an afternoon!'

'Hah!' John raised his head too quickly and winced as a pain shot through his eyes. The drink was making him canny, and now she'd given him the key to put her in the wrong. Now he could be the one hard done to. His smile wobbled his features out of recognition. 'What am I supposed to do when there's a matinée? Sit twiddling my thumbs in your dressing room? Take up bloody knitting? Have you once stopped to think what it's like for me?'

Clara lifted a hand as if to strike him, then drew it back. 'You could find another job. Flying was your life till you married me. It isn't right for a man to hang around doing nothing. You're bored, now the fascination of being backstage has worn off. It isn't like you expected it would be. Is it?'

He flushed a dark red with selfrighteous anger. If there was one thing he couldn't tolerate it was adverse criticism. Admiration he accepted as his due, but Clara was putting him in the wrong, and by God he wasn't going to stand for that. Feeling at a disadvantage sitting down, he stood up and, though the room swayed around him, he felt better.

Since packing in his job with Lord Broughton immediately after the wedding he had discovered he was losing the admiration of young girls who had looked upon fliers as equal to God. Now he milked that same adoration from the girls in the chorus, fooling around in the wings, tickling and nipping as they waited to go on. He clenched his fists. If only Clara would *weep*. That he could do something about. He walked to the dressing table and sat down on the stool, averting his gaze from his tripled reflection in the swinging mirrors.

God! He looked as bad as he felt. Disgruntled and sorry for himself, he began to bite his nails, chewing morosely

221

round each finger end. Marriage to Clara hadn't worked out the way he'd thought it would. A clap of thunder was echoed by the pounding in his head. Moaning with pity for himself, he buried his face in his hands, and when he looked up again Clara had gone into the bathroom, closing the door firmly behind her.

God, but she was a cold fish!

He got up and walked over to the wardrobe to pat the pockets of his jacket in search of his cigarettes. Why did drink sharpen his intelligence so that he saw himself straight on? If it wasn't so damned late, and if it wasn't raining like the clappers outside, he'd go out. If he'd anywhere to go, that was.

Lighting a cigarette, he drew smoke deep into his lungs, exhaling it through his nostrils. He had to face up to the fact that he wasn't as popular as he used to be. Some of the crazy antics he got up to seemed plain daft even to himself, if he admitted it. He was losing his audience, while his wife, blast her, was daily adding to hers.

The cigarette was making him feel dizzy, but he persevered.

Only the week before, on his way with three of the girls to a teashop, he'd climbed the scaffolding trimming the front of a bank, hanging from it with one arm, making monkey noises. Just for a laugh. The girls had laughed all right, but they'd walked on, leaving him dangling there like a silly fool, till at last he'd had to climb down and follow them along the street.

Never once, before they married, had he suspected that Clara worked so hard. That had been because he was away most of the time, of course. Rehearsals, matinées, evening shows, cabaret. With him sitting at a table on his own like a lemon, hearing the same songs over and over again, and drinking till his head spun . . . as it was spinning now.

Clara had undressed in the bathroom and when she came back she was ready for bed. He could hardly bear to look at her small set face. So this was the glamour of show business, was it? With his wife rocking on her feet from exhaustion, and them rowing like a married couple from the street where she used to live. His voice loud and protesting, and hers rough-edged with humiliation. Sitting down again on his side of the double bed, he drooped his head into his hands and trickled a sentimental tear through his fingers, hoping she would notice. So the honeymoon was over? So what, he wondered, as selfpity engulfed him, came next?

His face cleared a little when Clara came to sit beside him. He guessed she was going to forgive him, because her religion was based on forgiveness. But blast her, he wasn't going to *allow* himself to be forgiven!

'And when ye stand praying, forgive, if ye have aught against any; that your Father also which is in heaven may forgive you your trespasses.' Mark, Chapter 11. Verse 25.

John felt his whole body tense. He knew the way it went, and if she quoted it he felt he really would be sick, right then and there.

How often he'd been forced to sit in a high-backed pew, listening to his father preaching a sermon based on his favourite passage from the New Testament. So that the son he was now rejected such sentiments, preferring to interpret them as patronage.

When he raised his head Clara saw the tears on his cheeks and a small tic beating away in his lower eyelid. Locked in the bathroom, she too had been facing up to the truth. Perching uncomfortably on the edge of the high bath, the thought had come into her head that already her love for her husband had died. The music that had gladdened her heart from the day he had walked into her dressing room, as if in answer to her prayer, had somehow drifted away.

She had no idea that her very stillness was scaring John silly. No idea that he would have known how to deal with her screaming at him. Used to women who threw tantrums, he *didn't* know what to do, so he got into bed, burying his head in his pillow.

When she got in beside him he sank almost at once into sleep, with the comforting thought that she'd have got over it by the next day; but, lying awake by his side, Clara stared up into the darkness, hearing the thunder dying away over the rooftops.

223

It was surprising her now that what was hurting most was the knowledge that everyone in the show must have known what was going on. There was still deep within her the legacy of her strict working-class upbringing; the importance of keeping up appearances, the belief that a marriage was truly made in heaven. In her well-remembered childhood, she had known women with husbands who cheated on them, drank their wages away, even beat their wives into cowed submission. But the cry was always the same: 'He's my husband. How could I even think of leaving him?' Then, with typical Lancashire commonsense: 'And anyroad, where would I go?'

She wasn't surprised the next morning to face a husband who now saw himself as the deeply injured party.

'I thought that giving up my flying for a while would please you. We hardly saw each other when I was working for old Broughton, so I thought that having me around was what you wanted. Now I know different.'

As usual he had wakened before Clara, as bright as a brass button the moment he opened his eyes.

'I'll apply to Imperial Airways this time. They're passenger flying from Croydon.' He sprang out of bed, as refreshed as if he'd gone to bed at ten the night before, with a glass of Horlick's malted milk to help him sleep. 'I know they're looking for experienced pilots for their Silver Wing Service on the London to Paris route. I could be just what they're after.'

As he shaved in the bathroom Clara heard him whistling a tune from the show.

'After all, we are *desperate* for money,' he said sarcastically when he was back, his face as smooth as his mood. 'I won't be a drag on you any longer.' Standing with his back to her, he knotted his Flying Corps tie neatly at the neck of his white shirt. 'I'll have to get a room somewhere near Croydon, but that can't be helped. I'll come back here on my days off. That's if you can bear the sight of me.'

Still whistling, he emerged from the kitchen ten minutes later with the daily help's apron tied round his middle and a teatowel looped over his arm. On a tray he was carrying two cups of tea and a plate of slightly charred toast.

'Grub up!' he announced, looking for all the world like the naughty little boy he would always be. 'Rise and shine, me beauty!'

In October, with the days growing shorter and the London streets made magical by gaslight, Clara was offered a month's engagement singing at the Savoy Hotel. When the letter of congratulation came from Bart, John was there, at the Conduit Street flat, on one of his days off.

By now he was, as he had predicted he would be, flying with Silver Wing, staying in Croydon while on duty call and enjoying every minute of his double life. He was the proud owner of a car, an Austin coupé, and the night before had beaten his own record for burning up the miles between London and Croydon.

To make the daily help laugh he was sitting at the table wearing his linen napkin tied beneath his chin like a mill girl's shawl. When she brought in the toast rack he jumped up from his chair and took it from her with a bow.

'By gum, but tha's a sight for sore eyes this morning, Mrs Williams.' He pretended to peer closely into her wrinkled face. 'Wasn't it you I saw at Romano's last night? Dancing the Black Bottom with the Prince of Wales?' When she gave a shriek of laughter, the sound was like manna to his soul. He knew she repeated all his sayings to her friends because he'd caught her on the telephone one day, bellowing into the mouthpiece with tears of mirth running down her cheeks. 'Back to the saltmine, Mrs W,' he shouted, reaching out to slap her behind with his still-folded morning paper, before sitting down again and staring hard at his wife.

Engrossed in her letter, Clara was ignoring him, and he couldn't bear that. It frightened him more and more. The blokes he worked with at Croydon had laughed at his antics at first, then made it plain that enough was enough. Because they were mostly southerners, he told himself, lacking a proper northern sense of humour.

'Trouble at t'mill?' He clasped his hands together as if in supplication. 'Don't give me me cards, Mr Boss Boland.

Don't send me back to a life of jam butties and three looms in t'mill.' Lifting his head, he began to sing in his tuneless voice, 'She was poor, but she was honest . . . '

'You can read it if you like.' Clara passed the letter over to him. 'Bart's really pleased about the Savoy booking. Says it's the top spot for cabaret, but he doesn't want me to change my act . . . Anyway, read it for yourself.'

Taking the letter, John mimed placing an eyeglass in his left eye, screwing his face up and even groping around on the floor by his chair to find it when it dropped from his grasp. Using an accent so clipped it would have made the young Noel Coward sound as if he was drawling, he began to read, skipping the first few paragraphs.

'Leave the risqué songs to others, my dear.' Remembering he was still wearing the linen napkin on his head, John tore it off and adjusted the imaginary monocle. 'Let them wear their revealing gowns and flashy jewellery. *Remember*, my dear, always remember, you are unique.' Wagging a finger, John continued. 'There's no one quite like you on the West End stage at the moment, and in that very difference lies your well-deserved success.'

'Fancy that!' said John in a mincing tone, turning a page.

'But at the Savoy you will be singing to a sophisticated audience, many of them celebrities in their own right. At first they may not understand your act, but don't be afraid. Stand quite still and sing. Simply sing, my dear. I'll be back in England for Christmas, I hope, and by then even your sternest critics will be praising you.' For the last few lines John put his hand on his heart, adopting a Shakespearian ringing tone in his voice. 'They'll listen, little Clara. Reach out to them as only you can do. Sing them into that stillness. Don't try to emulate Gertrude Lawrence, Gracie Fields, Evelyn Laye or any of the current revue stars, however much you're tempted to. Promise me?'

'What a load of old codswallop!' John threw the letter back across the table. 'I thought you said *Mister* Boland had one of the shrewdest minds in show business? I reckon he's off his chump. If you do your normal act at the Savoy, they'll puke into their smoked salmon. It's oomph they go there for; a bit of the old ooh-la-la.' He held out his hands as if he were weighing a couple of melons. 'You've got a nice little figure, so why not give the boys an eyeful? Otherwise they'll crucify you.'

Clara watched as John knocked the top off his boiled egg, then cut a slice of toast into 'soldiers', a childish habit he still kept to.

'Dora once tried to change me into what I could never be,' she said quietly, folding the letter back into its envelope. 'And it didn't work.' She hesitated, trying to make him see the reason of it. 'I didn't come up the way most of the other girls did.' She bit her lip. 'I was never seen dancing round a barrel organ, or singing to a queue outside the theatre. The way I was brought up, the stage was a rude word and girls who went on it finished up gone to the bad. When *they* were singing in clubs and entering competitions I was singing in the chapel choir, or twice a year at Sunday School concerts. Or in front of the class at school.' Her eyes willed John to remember and to smile with her, but he was busy dipping a 'soldier' into his egg and sprinkling salt on it. Because she wasn't saying what he wanted her to say, he'd stopped listening, she realized. 'Bart once told me my voice is really an *operatic* voice, an untrained operatic voice, and so . . . '

John leaped to his feet, opening his arms wide. 'On with the motley, the paint and the powder . . . ' His flat voice slid up and down the notes, then with his hand on his heart he proclaimed in a ringing voice, 'We are bringing you this broadcast straight from La Scala, with Miss Claramino Haydocktorino singing the role of Nedda. In Italian! As she is spoke!'

Clara had to laugh. He looked so funny in his brown woollen dressing gown, waving a finger of toast like a baton. But when he sat down again his expression changed swiftly to one of contempt.

'Don't listen to me, of course. Listen to anyone but me. Listen to your bloody hero over there in New York.' Throwing down his napkin, he pushed his chair back and stood up. 'What's his second name? Svengali? I don't know why you didn't go with him in the first place since you think he's so bloody marvellous!'

When Clara pushed her own chair back and stood up, gripping the edge of the table, he flinched. Now she was going to give him a piece of her mind, and rows made his head ache. Why didn't she behave like a normal woman and *cry*, for God's sake?

'You know well why I didn't go to America.' Her voice was low with restrained anger. 'I couldn't go when Dora needed me.' Her chin lifted. 'Oh, all right, then, I was trying to be Florence Nightingale, instead of being practical. But I'm not practically minded, am I? I put people first, *other* people, because that's the way I was brought up. Then you came along, and I wanted to stay with you, and marry you, because that's another thing I was brought up to believe. That a good marriage was worth more than anything else.' Her eyes filled at last with tears. 'But you're either playing the fool or being sarcastic, nothing in between. I've tried and tried to see you as I first saw you, a boy I used to know, a boy who once had his nose bursted for fighting for me. An' I can't.' Angrily she dashed the tears from her cheeks with the back of her hands. 'Our life together is a mess, John, and you know something? I've stopped blaming myself. I'm not the kind of girl you should have married. You should have married someone like yourself, who doesn't give a . . . a monkey's arse for anybody!'

The crudity, coming from Clara's lips, startled him more than all her impassioned speech had done. In that moment he could have gone to her, pulled her into his arms, promised her he'd be different, pleaded with her to start again. But it was too late, and he knew it. She'd taken the ball out of his court and he wasn't going to stand for that.

'All right then,' he sneered. 'Go and make a fool of yourself, if that's what you're determined to do. But don't say I didn't warn you. I know the kind of audience you'll have to face at the Savoy, and they'll laugh their socks off at you. Just wait and see!'

He marched into the bedroom banging the door violently behind him, leaving Clara to sit staring at the toast 'soldiers' lined up by his plate. As if on parade.

Fifteen

On the afternoon of her debut at the Savoy, with no matinée to take her mind off the evening ahead, Clara closed the flat door behind her and went for one of her walks through the London streets.

There was a cold wind blowing up from the river, and as she turned in the direction of Covent Garden she could smell the sickly sweet odour of rotting cabbages mixed with the sharp tang of apples. Making her way down Shaftesbury Avenue, she saw that there were already long queues snaking along the sides of the theatres, with people waiting patiently for a chance of the cheaper seats. On her way back to the flat she walked through Golden Square and into Regent Street, where she stopped outside a window dressed out in furs. Pastel mink jackets, ermine stoles and squirrel coats.

'When I'm famous I'll buy you a fur coat,' Clara had promised Lily West a long time ago, and Lily had clutched her sides, laughing fit to bust.

'Nay, love,' Clara remembered her saying. 'An' what would Mrs Nosey Parker up at the top end of the street have to say about that? Her eyes would stand out like chapel 'at pegs if she saw me traipsing down the street in a fur coat. Oh, Mother of God! That'd be the day!'

Now that Clara could afford to walk into the big store and buy any coat she set her mind on, it was too late. Because Lily West was dead.

Shivering suddenly as if a goose had walked over her grave, Clara walked on, an eye-catching figure in her beige coat trimmed with beaver, her hair pushed up inside a small round beaver hat.

Four of her friends were going with her to the Savoy after

the theatre. Matty, two of the girls and Tony, the male lead dancer. Clara was glad of that. John had rung to say he was sorry he couldn't get back to town because of an early flight, and she'd told him it didn't matter. It *should* have mattered, but it didn't.

'It's a pity John can't be here tonight, love.' In the back of a taxi pulling away from the theatre Matty twined Clara's ice-cold fingers in his own. 'But then, I expect it's hard for him to get away. Planes don't fly on their own.'

Matty didn't like John Maynard. The old man reckoned the handsome flyer had come into young Clara's life at the wrong time. On the wrong cue. With all that business of Dora going a bit potty, the young lass had been at her most vulnerable. Matty's nostrils jerked sideways with the force of his sniff. And craftily the handsome flier had taken advantage. Matty squeezed Clara's hand. Old Dora had been like a mother to her, and if Matty was any judge, a mother was what she needed right now. Not hard as nails, this bonny lass, like most of them. Stand on their grandmother's belly most of them would to reach what they called stardom. Aye, and lift their skirts for any man who would help them on their way.

Matty's small mouth chewed on nothing as he angered himself with his thoughts. He'd known what was going on between John Maynard and that girl from the chorus line. The one with a face like a yard of tripe. Aye, an' as well as that, Matty knew what was going on in Croydon. A married woman by all accounts. The blighter even had the nerve to bring her to town now and again, picking her up on the way back. An' him a vicar's son at that. He glanced at Clara's face, his soft heart aching for her. Singing to a lot of toffs was a sight different from what she'd been used to, but she'd show them. Matty patted her hand, his rubbery features gentled by affection.

As the taxi turned out of the Strand, wheeling sharply into Savoy Court, he saw that Clara's eyes were closed as if in prayer.

John Maynard had been in one of his self-sacrificial moods all day. The unwritten law was that before an early flight the pilot must have his full quota of sleep, but rules had never bothered John overmuch.

The most marvellous idea had occurred to him that very afternoon. If he drove fast and hard the minute he came off duty he could be at the Savoy in time to surprise Clara. If he drove even faster than that, there would be time to stop off at the flat and change into his penguin trappings. Then, after the cabaret finished in the early hours, he could drive back to Croydon and, with his usual luck, none would be the wiser.

It was a cold night, a night without stars, and when he got to the flat, frozen to the marrow, the first thing he did was to pour himself a treble whisky.

There was actually time for him to pick Clara up from the theatre. He debated this point, pinching his lower lip between finger and thumb, shaking his head as he thought of a better idea. Mightily pleased with himself, he swirled what was left of the whisky round in his glass and drank it down.

The way he saw his little drama was this: Clara was to be stunned and grateful, absolutely bowled over by his unexpected appearance. Preferably spotting him sitting there as she was in mid-song. The management was bound to give him a table; bound to once they knew who he was. He closed his eyes, raising the empty glass. He would raise his glass to her, like this, and people would stare, and wonder . . .

So, in the meantime, before he changed, there was time for another drink.

The glass was halfway to his lips when the doorbell rang, but before he went to see who was there, he got up from his chair to study his reflection in the mirror. Standing well back, he admired the expensive cut of his new grey flannels and the way he'd tied his yellow cravat into a Prince of Wales knot. A pity he'd have to change – he always felt that sporty clothes were more him.

When the bell rang for the second time he walked over

231

and opened the door.

'Forgive me for calling so late, sir, but does a Miss Haydock live here? A Miss Clara Haydock?'

The man on the landing was dressed in a uniform known the world over. John gave him a gracious smile. He had a lot of time for the Sally Army. Always had. Decent chaps doing a worthwhile job. Taking his wallet from the inside pocket of his jacket, he extracted a ten-shilling note.

'Keep the change,' he smiled, wondering where the fellow was hiding his collection box. 'A good cause. You chaps do a magnificent job.'

The man with the strong face, grizzled hair showing at the sides of his peaked cap, shook his head. 'I'm not collecting, sir.' His manner was quietly respectful. 'You are, sir?'

'Maynard. John Maynard.' John was being very patient, very helpful. God's Army, his father had called these chaps. Smiling, he waited for the officer to explain.

'Joe West. Does the name mean anything to you, sir?'

So that was it. John hesitated, forcing the officer to explain further.

'Joe West,' he said again. 'A man we picked up earlier today, suffering from pneumonia and malnutrition, I'm sorry to say. A man who doesn't appear to have eaten a decent meal in months. With only hours to live, I'm afraid.'

'Sodden with drink, I expect,' John said quickly. 'You chaps deserve a medal.'

'Yes. Pickled in the stuff, sir.' The officer's eyes were the kindest John had ever seen in a man's face. 'He'd been sleeping rough for a long time, but you know, sir, a craving for drink is as clearly a disease as diphtheria.' He tried not to look at the glass in John's hand, and instead consulted a piece of paper torn from a notebook. 'So Miss Haydock doesn't live here now? The man mumbled this address, but in his state he could be remembering someone he knew from his childhood, or have it all wrong.'

'Probably.' John held out the ten-shilling note. 'Have this anyway, officer. Every little counts, I expect.'

'God bless you, sir. Sorry to have troubled you.'

The officer turned and made his way down the stairs. Propped against the kerb, his rusty bicycle was parked a yard away from John's car. Mounting the lopsided saddle, he pedalled away down the street. If ever a man was in need of God's salvation, it was that man with the cold light brown eyes. Muttering to himself, he rode on. He was bitterly cold and very hungry, but there were two more calls to make that night. Bending his head against the freezing wind, he reminded himself that it was not his mission to play God, no matter what his own private thoughts might be.

'Judge not,' he told himself, rounding the corner, working his legs like pistons to get up a bit more speed.

Back in the warmth of the sitting room John glanced at the clock, checking the time on his wristwatch. If he hurried he could be at the theatre in time to catch Clara *before* she left for the Savoy Hotel.

'Joe West is dying. He is asking for you,' he'd tell her. He hadn't asked the officer exactly where Joe was, but a quick telephone call to the tall headquarters building in Queen Victoria Street would soon sort that out.

Pouring himself another drink, wasting valuable time, John sat down in a chair, imagining Clara's face when he told her. Her green eyes would open wide, the fresh colour would drain from her cheeks and she'd go to see Joe West. She would *bloody well go!*

Clara wasn't the main attraction in the cabaret. They were trying her out, he knew that. But a lot of important people would be there, come especially to hear her sing. The papers would be represented, and Clara had told him herself that James Agate was almost sure to be there. A word from the famous critic in the right direction could set Clara onto even bigger things. Now that revues were slowly dying the death, it was cabaret where she would make her name. Radio, records, they were all beckoning. And dance bands were already broadcasting. Ambrose at the Mayfair Ballroom, Geraldo, Harry Roy at the Cavour Restaurant, Leicester Square, and of course the Savoy Hotel Orpheans with Caroll Gibbons. Clara's voice would be wonderful with a big band to back it.

Tonight could set her on a great wide golden road stretching ahead. He was sure of it. Even though he'd told her that her act wasn't sophisticated enough for the glittering clientele of the Savoy Hotel, he had to admit that he had seen her with his own eyes reaching out with her voice to confound even the most hard-bitten critic.

The Savoy. In his mind's eye John saw the doorman in his green frock coat with its polished brass buttons. He saw the marbled entrance and the spacious reception area with the crystal chandeliers shining down on hothouse flowers arranged on low tables. He could almost smell the fragrance of expensive luxury pervading the place. Closing his eyes, he could imagine the subdued clink of cutlery and glass in the restaurant on the other side of the high white archway. It was a world John craved for, where money brought slavish attendance from a staff who pandered to one's slightest wish. Oh, yes. He'd done his homework on the place a long time ago.

'For excellence we strive.' That was the famous hotel's motto, and if Clara went down well that night she held the key to all that luxury. Dear God, she held it all even now in the persuasive beauty of her singing voice, in the sincerity and honesty which shone from her wide green eyes.

There was another motto, too: 'The show must go on.'

John turned his glass between his fingers. But he knew his wife all right. He could read her like her precious Bible. Because a finger from her past beckoned, because a rotten no-good son of an Irish navvy reverted to his upbringing and wanted to be given absolution before he died, Clara would run like some po-faced nun to hold his hand.

Clara wasn't the only one to have been forced as a child to learn the chapter of St John off by heart. He frowned, trying to remember. 'But whoso hath the world's goods and beholdeth his brother in need, and shutteth his compassion from him, how doth the love of God abide in him?'

John got up and began to pace the room. Passages to be memorized, usually as a punishment for some boyish prank. And yet it was strange how the appropriate words surfaced at times. Once a vicar's son, always a vicar's son, he supposed. But that didn't mean he had to *listen* to the words. That didn't mean they always signified. That was where Clara made her mistake. It was being said in some quarters that the New Testament was partly fiction, anyway.

John was seeing himself now in his own best light. Clara needed saving from herself, and who better than her husband to do it? No, to tell her about Joe West would be madness.

Much later he was whistling as he ran down the stairs, anticipating the look on her face when she saw him in her audience. He would raise his glass to her, and she would maybe walk towards him as she sang.

Joe West drew his last tortured breath in the very same moment that Clara bowed her head to an applause that had the waiters scurrying from the kitchens. Clapping with hands held high above their heads, the normally laconic diners at the Savoy Hotel were going wild.

Clara was smiling, holding out her hands to them, excited by the tumult of approval, accepting the flowers, smiling across the room at John.

Exactly as he'd planned.

Sixteen

'I don't believe you!'

Standing with her hands on her hips, yelling at the top of her voice, Clara reminded her husband of the young girl he'd known as the clogger's child, running wild in the street with the West boys.

'You're not working every single day over Christmas week and on into the New Year! You're lying, John Maynard!'

His smile was neat and sarcastic. 'Revert to your origins then, and throw me out. Open the window and hurl my clothes after me into the street below! That's what the women in your street used to do, isn't it?'

The fury fermenting inside Clara's chest had paled the fresh colour from her cheeks. Her apple green satin peignoir fell apart at the front showing her shapely legs in silk stockings, held up by beribboned suspenders. In that moment John wanted her so much he could feel his heartbeats quicken. If he hadn't been half afraid of her when she had her temper up he would have lifted her into his arms and carried her through into the bedroom.

'Yes! That's *just* what the women from my street used to do.' Her voice dripped scorn. 'But they were martyrs! Doormats! Putting up with anything because they knew there was no escape.' She held up a hand as if to fend him off. 'It must be a defect in my character, but I can't live with it, John. Either you stay faithful to me, or you stay out of my bed!' She tilted her head to one side. 'An' if I did throw you out and your clothes after you, I'd pray a car would come along and splash them all with mud. That would give me a good feeling.' She stabbed a finger into her chest. 'Right here!'

'She means nothing to me.' John heard himself being truculent. 'What do you expect me to do all on my own in that poky flat in Croydon between flights? Play bloody patience?' He began to feel sorry for himself. 'I just like women's company. There's no sin in that, is there?'

'She's been *living* with you!' Clara's voice was ragged with shame. 'She's answered the telephone twice when I've tried to ring you. Who is she, John? Why is it necessary for you to have more than one woman?' Her temper flared so that her green eyes blazed like emeralds. 'Marriage is all important to me, just as it is to the women in the street where I lived.' The shame and humiliation was sapping the last of her control. 'But you wouldn't want me with you, would you? There'd be no way you could go on leading your double life with me there all the time.'

When he slapped her hard across her face, her head jerked back with such violence she felt her neck would surely snap in two.

Turning and running away from the full horror of what he'd just done, John jerked the door open, almost knocking over the tall man on the landing. A man in a dark grey suit with a Christmas-wrapped parcel in his hands.

'John!' Clara heard the slam of the big front door downstairs, then found herself staring up into well-remembered blue eyes.

Bart had come round to the flat almost straight from the boat train at Victoria. Hearing angry voices, he'd been on the point of going away, and now he looked with dismay at the hollows in Clara's cheeks and the distinct mark of the slap spreading across her face, sparkling her eyes with unshed tears.

'I've come at the wrong moment,' he said inadequately. 'Shall I go away, my dear?'

Clara's distressed eyes met his. 'Bart,' she whispered, shame enveloping her. 'I didn't know you were coming back so soon.' Pulling her robe closer round her, she stepped back. 'Please come in.'

Dropping hat, coat, gloves and the present on the nearest

chair, Bart came to her, taking both her hands in his own. He spoke to her carefully, measuring every word, touched to the heart by the way she was looking at him, her green eyes so very big, one cheek deathly pale and the other . . . Gently he lifted a finger to touch a tear glistening on the tips of her long eyelashes.

'You're not the first couple to have a lovers' quarrel, my dear. If you want to cry it out alone, then I'll go away.' His voice was so gentle and yet so strong Clara felt the tears spill over. 'But we *are* friends, and friends have shoulders for crying on, you know.' He wiped the tears away with his fingers. 'The Clara I know never used to cry.' He smiled at her. 'Now, aren't you going to cheer up and open your present? I searched the whole of New York to find just the right shade. Then make me a real English cup of tea. I think we'd both like that.'

Putting her from him reluctantly, he picked up the parcel and handed it to her. 'Peeled grape green. That was the colour I had in mind and, yes, I was right,' he added as Clara held the exquisite crepe-de-Chine blouse up to her eyes.

Oh, Bart,' she said shakily. 'It's so good to see you again. Do you really want a cup of tea, or are you just being kind?'

Sitting down in the chair that had once been Dora's, Bart stretched out his long grasshopper legs to the fire. 'Tea and toast,' he affirmed. 'With the rain against the window.' He smiled at her, his blue eyes crinkling round the corners. 'Then I'll know I'm home.'

When the tea was drunk and the toast all gone, they sat opposite to each other in the warm room and talked the next two hours away.

He told her about Broadway, with its cops, its fight promoters, bookies and song pluggers. He told how people he thought were strangers would come up to him in the street, punch him in the shoulder and say 'Hiya, Mr Boland!' or 'Hi, Bart!' or sometimes even 'How ya doing, pal?' He described the huge neon signs, the honky-tonk gift shops, and the shooting galleries, and he said that on Broadway a show was either swell or it stank. No in between.

'And yours was swell.' She was calmer now. 'Thank you

for your letter, Bart.' She pushed a wayward strand of hair behind an ear. 'You were right about Dora. I couldn't have managed her the way she was towards the end. Not and worked as well. That's why I wrote to you in the way I did. It was my way of saying I was sorry.'

'You should have come with me to America.' His eyes were very steady. 'If you'd done that, things might have turned out very differently.'

'I know.' She leaned forward, trying to make him understand. 'I'm going to tell you something, Bart, that will make you despair of me.'

He lifted a hand to shade his face from the fire. 'Try me.'

It was long past the time when the tall standard lamp should have been switched on, but as she began to speak Bart knew that the darkness was her ally. Quietly he waited to hear what she had to tell him.

'I'm not terribly ambitious, Bart.'

'You're not?' Bart prayed the smile he couldn't control was unseen. 'Go on, love.'

'Well, of course, the success I've had means a lot. The *money* it's brought with it has given me a room like this, and beautiful clothes.' She sighed and curled her feet beneath her on the big armchair. 'I wouldn't like to go back to being poor. I'm not that daft. It's just that I've found out that the acquisition of money and possessions doesn't necessarily make a person happy. *Ambition* is all right in its place, but I've seen girls lie and cheat, and even break their own hearts, just to get to the top. To be a star.'

He could see that her eyes were very tired, and knew it was time for him to go, but she needed to talk, and so he stayed.

'I suppose what I really want is to be a happily married woman, with children, if that were possible; with a husband who is a breadwinner, and with me singing now and again at local concerts.' She looked very young and earnest as she tried to explain. 'The stage has given me everything, and yet in a strange way it's given me nothing. I told you you'd despair of me.'

Bart was shaking his head. 'You're wrong, my dear. There are women the world over who would give up all they had to feel and think like you. You're the wise one, my dear, and your John is a lucky man. Is that what you were quarrelling about? Because he couldn't see things your way?'

She refused to answer that, and for a while they sat in silence. No one, she thought, had ever treated her so gently. In the firelight she could see the lines round his blue eyes that had deepened since he went to America. He wasn't half as handsome as John, and somehow Clara suspected that John's face would always look the same, even as he grew older. There was nothing written there. It was an unfinished face.

But her thoughts and the conversation were getting out of hand. She got up and walked over to a small mahogany writing desk.

'This came the other day,' she told him, holding out a letter. 'Enclosing this.' From her finger dangled a gold medallion on a thin gold chain. 'It was sent to the theatre, addressed to the Clogger's Child. The stage-door keeper handed it over to me.'

'From a fan?' Bart was smiling as he reached up to switch on the lamp by his chair. 'You'll have to expect this kind of thing, you know.'

'Not from a fan.' She came to perch beside him on the chair's padded arm. 'Read it, please.'

Sensing the urgency in her voice, he unfolded the sheet of lined paper.

'Dear Miss . . . ' The writing was printed in capitals, the words badly spelt and running over the lines.

'You don't know me, but I saw about you in the paper. It was telling of your life before you went on the stage, and when it said you wos born in 1907 at Easter, I knowed it wos you. It said as ow you wos given to the clogger by person unknown, wrapt in a grey shawl which you still have. Well. I was there when you wos born. Yor mother was with my dancing troop in the fair. She wos not wering a wedding ring, but she had the enclosed round her neck when she dyed. I have kep it all this time, and now I have seen the wicked of my ways, and want you to have it afore I go to join my

240

Maker. I have been living a respectful life ever since leaving the fair the year after you wos born, so hope you will not persecute me. I am glad you have got on so well.

Yours truly,
Jessie Bead

When Bart looked up, Clara dropped the medallion into his hand. 'There's a name and also the name of a regiment if you look closely.'

Holding it up to the light Bart peered at the tiny engraved lettering. 'Captain Charles Foley. The Boer War,' he said at once. 'This is a privately made thing. The sort of thing men had designed for their wives, or their sweethearts.' He examined it again. 'What does John say about all this?'

'He would dismiss it.' Clara blushed. 'He knows I was probably illegitimate, but he doesn't like to dwell on my background. You see, coming from a straightforward family, he thinks my beginnings are a bit, well, *News of the World* or *Peg's Paperish*. This new thing . . . about the fairground . . . no, he wouldn't like that.'

Bart took a long, slow, deep breath, holding back his own feelings. 'So now you know your mother didn't *give* you away. That must help a little?'

'Dora told you I thought that?' Clara nodded. 'Dora would have advised me to throw the letter away. She didn't believe in raking up the past.'

'But you're not Dora.'

'I'm not Dora.' Her face was so sad, so lost. 'And you're not John.' She frowned, realizing she had at least to try to explain. 'John is sometimes rather selfish. He isn't always able to understand a person's feelings. He doesn't want to know anything about the way it was for me. If he doesn't want to listen he switches off in his mind. Dora saw him as cold and unfeeling, but he's just *unthinking*. He certainly wouldn't want to hear about this.'

Leaving the letter and the medallion with Bart, she went back to her own chair.

'You see, if you've been part of a normal family, if you've known from the beginning who your parents were, even if

241

you haven't lived with them, there's an invisible mark on your forehead which spells "security". If you have red hair, it's because your mother had red hair. If you like to paint, it's likely that your father did too. Even if they died when you were very young, there are those who can tell you things. That your mother was clever and kind – or selfish and stupid. *They existed.* And because of them, *you* exist. They're your heritage, I suppose.'

'And you feel this . . . ' Bart held up the medallion again ' . . . this Captain Foley could be your father?'

'My *real* father, you mean?' Clara smiled. 'I had a father, Bart. No one can ever take his place, but, oh, I don't know . . . I have to believe that it was meant for me to receive this letter and the medallion. And sometimes –' her head drooped a little –'there is a need in me to know my own.'

'Because your husband has failed to wipe out that need,' Bart added silently to himself, turning away so that she could not read the expression on his face. 'Do you want me to follow this up, my dear?'

His eyes were so concerned when he turned back to her, Clara felt the tears prick behind her own eyelids. She had told him so much, given away her unhappiness, she felt, and he had listened for hours, just as if there weren't a thousand and one things he had to do now he was back in town. She knew his divorce was through, but there was sure to be someone else. Maybe he'd met someone in America? Bart wasn't the kind of man to be too much alone. And yet he was a man's man.

She knew all these things, and yet there was so much more she didn't know. And so much she *wanted* to know, she realized suddenly.

When the telephone rang she started violently. Immediately Bart got up, collected his things and walked to the door, his coat over his arm.

'Hallo? Yes, John.' Clara held her hand over the earpiece. Bart held up the medallion, an unspoken question in his eyes.

When she nodded, he dropped the slender chain into his pocket then went out, closing the door quietly behind him.

242

Seventeen

By the time spring came Clara had worked out, quietly and without bitterness, her own philosophy. This was an acceptance that all life was a compromise in some way or other. Her father had said that true happiness only came with a positive acceptance of the will of God, but there were days when her spirit rebelled and she wanted to cry out against what seemed to her to be impossible odds.

John now came and went as he pleased, sleeping in Dora's old room. Clara had stuck to her guns about that. He had to be sexually faithful to her or she would not have him in her bed. At first he'd refused to believe she meant it, but after fierce and angry scenes he now bowed ungraciously to the inevitable.

Sex, Clara persuaded herself, meant little to her. It was, she decided, a disappointing pastime, and for the life of her she couldn't imagine why such a fuss was made of it. It never once occurred to her that for all his promiscuity her husband was an inadequate and selfish lover.

In the meantime she had her career; she had money; she had friends, Bart in particular. She was a free spirit, in charge of her own destiny, and how many married women in the twenties could say that?

Bart was planning a new revue to open as a tryout in Birmingham in September. It was to be called *Lovin' You*, and the title song, a catchy number, had been written specially for Clara by an unknown young man from Wales. Waltz time – a plaintive little melody, it suited her voice to perfection:

'The meaning of life is clear to me,
Lovin' you, lovin' you . . . '

Clara hummed the song over to herself that spring-lit day
as she walked down Bond Street on her way to the theatre
from a dress fitting. She was taking dancing lessons, and
already was able to move gracefully through the opening
number, although the lead dancer would be the real star of
the show.

'Lovin' you, just lovin' you . . . '

Maybe the Prince of Wales would come to the show when
they moved back to London; maybe the brilliant Noel
Coward would look in, be so impressed that he'd offer to
write the book, lyrics and music for Bart's next show. Maybe
. . . maybe . . . Clara walked on, her little Cuban heels
tapping on the pavement, so filled with youthful optimism
that more than one man stopped in his tracks, wheeling
round just to watch her walk by.

When she got to the theatre, she went straight to her
dressing room, took off her outdoor clothes and put on the
silk wrap-over robe hanging behind the door. She was very
early for the matinée that afternoon. Her fitting in Bond
Street had been over and done with quickly, and it was a
strange feeling sitting alone in her dressing room with no
footsteps echoing down the long narrow corridor outside,
no sense of anticipation which grew stronger as the time for
curtain-up drew closer.

Switching on the lights round the oblong stretch of
mirror, she sat staring at her illuminated reflection; at the
conglomeration of pots of cream, different sized brushes,
sticks of greasepaint, all juggling for position with a battered
electric kettle. The brick walls were painted in a bilious
shade of yellow, and the lead dancer's dressing table was
jammed against the far wall. Clara smiled to herself. Even
Lily West would have tut-tutted through her protruding
teeth at the shabby untidiness of the little room.

Joe . . . Clara thought. Where was he now? She unscrewed

244

the top of a massive jar of cold cream. Like the proverbial bad penny, Joe always turned up again. She applied a blob of the cream to the end of her nose. One day the door behind her would open and he'd walk in, grinning, bursting to tell her of some wild scheme or other, laughing off the days when he'd been down and out. Living not for yesterday, or even today, but always for tomorrow. Clara wiped the cream off again with a wad of cotton wool. Time meant nothing to Joe. He'd knock and walk in, then be surprised because *she* was surprised.

When the knock came at the door, she spun round, flustered, clutching the silk robe closer round her throat.

'Yes, she's here. Mind if we come in, Clara?'

Before she could speak Bart walked in, followed by a man in late middle age, a man of average height wearing heavy horn-rimmed spectacles and carrying a leather briefcase. Almost immediately he took off the glasses, blinking owlishly, and as he did so Clara was struck by his handsomeness. He didn't have John's looks with regular features and a smooth fair skin; in fact the stranger's nose was a little crooked, and there were deep clefts running down cheeks showing the aftermath of a youthful acne. His hair was thick and greying, speckled, like the ashes of a dead fire. A gentleman, Clara decided in that first startled moment. A country squire sort of gentleman.

'Clara.' Before she could rise from her chair, Bart came and laid a hand gently on her arm. 'It's better that you sit down.' He turned. 'Captain Foley. This is Clara.' His grip tightened. 'My dear. It's taken a long time to trace him, and I never thought he would just turn up like this . . . but I believe this is your father.'

The immediate shock was so great that Clara stared at the stranger through dazed eyes. She could actually feel the blood draining from her cheeks, and swayed where she sat.

'I had no choice but to do this my way.' The stranger's voice was baritone, alien, as he spoke to Bart, ignoring her. 'To *announce* my arrival would have meant . . . ' He shrugged his shoulders without finishing the sentence.

When Clara's vision cleared, she saw the acute embarrassment on his face and felt the anger emanating from Bart.

The captain's glance slid away. 'I've made some trumped-up excuse to come down for the day. It hasn't been easy. I'm due back this evening. Back home,' he added.

'There's a chair there. You'd better sit down.' Bart kept his hold on Clara, making no attempt to be polite. 'You could have written. Or telephoned. Anything rather than this.'

'No!' The captain looked no more at ease sitting down than he had standing up. 'No more letters. Do you realize the damage you could have done, writing openly to my house like that?' He glared at Bart. 'It was just fortunate I happened to be alone when the post came. Letters are shared in my family.'

'Do you mind leaving us alone, Bart?' Clara heard her voice, high with a kind of hysteria, but her heartbeats were steadying now.

'If that's what you want.' With a squeeze of her hand, Bart nodded curtly to the man perching on the very edge of the hard chair, then left the room, closing the door sharply behind him.

'I'm sorry.' The man put on his glasses again. 'It hasn't been easy for me to get away, not at this time of the year. I've had to lie.' He frowned. 'Mr Boland's letter was a terrible shock. Terrible. I'd no idea . . . '

'That I even existed?'

Clara marvelled at her calmness. Her reaction was confusing her. Now the initial shock was over it was as though all her emotions had gone cold on her, leaving her stranded in an empty void of unnatural serenity. Turning, she switched on the kettle, keeping her face averted as she busied herself with the tea things. 'We'll have a cup of tea,' she said in a tight little voice.

How often in her dreams had she imagined this moment? Meeting her real father, being clasped in his arms, seeing her own features reflected in his face . . . The milk looked a bit off, but it would have to do . . . And now it had happened. She shuddered. If this man touched her she would scream. He was just a man who had walked in from the street, nothing more.

He was really discomposed, she could sense that. Scared. Running scared. It was funny really, she supposed. Not a bit like a similar situation in a book or a play.

'The kettle won't be long,' she said, sitting down again.

'You're very like your mother,' he said suddenly, and for a horrified moment she thought he was going to lean forward and kiss her. 'Seeing you like this is upsetting me greatly.' He took off the glasses again and she saw the panic in his eyes. He stared at her unhappily. 'I stayed on in the Army for a while after the war. The Boer War.'

She felt acutely sorry for him. He was like a strung wire, she thought. Forcing himself to say what must be said.

The kettle came noisily to the boil and Clara got up to attend to it. As she passed the captain his tea her hand was quite steady, but when he took it from her the cup jittered and rattled in its saucer.

'Sugar?' Clara held out a bowl with a spoon embedded in its contents.

'No, thank you.' He stared down at the cup for a second or two, then, as if it had defeated him, placed it on the floor by the side of his chair. 'I could have denied the whole thing, but the medallion . . .' Taking a white handkerchief from his top pocket, he mopped and dabbed at his forehead. 'Your mother was so pleased when I gave it to her, but I never knew she wore it on a chain; that must have been after . . .'

He looked quickly at Clara, then away again. 'Oh, God, I'm telling it badly. I've rehearsed how to put it into words all the way down on the train, but however I tell it, it doesn't do me much credit. When the letter came and I heard about her being with that fairground woman . . . She was so . . . so . . .' His voice dropped to a whisper. 'You're the image of her. Knocked me back a bit when I first saw you. Yet at the same time you're uncommonly like my eldest daughter. Same set of the chin and wide spacing of the eyes . . . Unbelievable.'

'Not really, as she's my half-sister.' Clara reminded him.

'Oh, my God! Yes, you're right.' He stared at a point somewhere just above Clara's head. 'That makes it all the more . . . Oh, all this has knocked me for six, I can tell you.'

'Tell me how you met my mother.'

Clara could hear voices and footsteps in the narrow passageway outside the dressing room. Soon the theatre would be coming to life as the cast assembled for the afternoon performance, and once Daisy, the lead dancer, came in setting the kettle screaming again for the cup of tea she swore kept her going through four changes of costume, it would be too late.

There was a little bubble of hysteria in her throat as she waited for the next halting sentence. This had to be one of the most important moments of her life, she reminded herself, and if he didn't hurry up he would walk away without having told her anything. She clenched her hands tightly to stop their sudden trembling. Because he *was* going to walk away – there was nothing more certain.

'I was in London in 1906,' he said at last. 'Newly out of the Army, and just kicking my heels really until the deal on the farm came through. My parents were setting me up. Farming's been in my family for generations. Farming and the Army. In Norfolk.' He shook his head as if regretting a slip of the tongue.

'I've never been to Norfolk,' Clara reassured him, sensing that reassurance was necessary. She spoke quickly, trying to hurry him on. 'So you met my mother in London?'

'She was seventeen years old,' he said. 'A dancer in some crummy show. Living in a two-roomed flat. Out Chelsea way with two other girls.'

In a minute he'll take out his handkerchief and mop his brow again, Clara thought.

He took the handkerchief from his pocket and touched it to his brow. 'She was different from the rest. She came from a different background. A better *class*. What I mean is she wasn't some tuppenny-'apenny dancer clawing her way to the top of her profession by going with any man who asked her. She was shy ... ' He gave a derisory glance round the shabby room. 'That is as shy as anyone in this kind of job can be shy.'

'A virgin,' Clara said, saying the word deliberately to shock.

'I was the first,' he said stiffly. 'Yes, indeed. Both her parents were dead, and the grandmother she lived with in Cornwall cut her off with a shilling when she came to London. She'd had dancing lessons from the age of five, but only for deportment and the like. Certainly not with a view . . . a view to doing what she did.'

'So the grandmother, my great-grandmother, never tried to bring my mother back?'

'She died soon after, but she never forgave your mother for running away. The money went to some distant unheard-of relative in Canada. But your mother told me she didn't mind that. She was a born dancer. Dancing was all she ever wanted to do.'

'Was she good?'

A sudden flash of animation changed his face completely. 'Good? She was wonderful! When she danced across the stage it was like watching a piece of swansdown floating in space. She had the lightness of a bubble. And she could sing, too. She was destined for great things . . . great things.' He sighed heavily. 'She didn't like going out much with the other girls after the show. Money was tight, but *they* used to go to clubs with men who would pay just for the privilege of being seen out with a chorus girl. So I would visit your mother in that awful cluttered room.'

'And make love to her?'

He looked up, startled by Clara's forthright interruption. 'We were in love! Deeply in love. All right then, I admit it. I *was* engaged to be married – to a girl I'd known all my life, but we never . . . that is, my fiancée wasn't the type. Not till after the wedding.' His discomfiture was painful to watch. 'But what I felt for your mother, I've never experienced since.' The glasses went on again. 'She was the most beautiful girl I've ever seen in my life. Her hair was just like yours, but maybe a shade darker, and I never thought to see eyes that green again. I tell you, it almost bowled me over when I came in.'

'And when you found out she was pregnant?'

'I told her we'd work something out.' He stared down at his shoes. 'I had to go back to Norfolk the very day after she

249

told me. Time to forget soldiering and learn to be a farmer. Family commitments, y'know. Old man cracking up and what have you.'

'And your wedding to plan.'

He didn't deny it. 'I told her I'd come down again. Gave her forty pounds. That was a lot of money to me then.'

'To get rid of the baby?'

'It was common practice!' He was sweating profusely now. 'And I *did* come down, just for the day, but she'd gone. Sloped off on her own without saying where she was going.' He looked round, anywhere but at Clara, his eyes shifting uneasily from side to side. 'I assumed she'd done what all the others did, and that she never wanted to see me again. I couldn't blame her, for God's sake! What was I supposed to do? I was married by then!'

Behind him the door banged back almost to the plaster. Daisy came in, shedding her coat as she made for her dressing table. 'Get the kettle on, darling! Late again!'

Catching sight of the stranger sitting in her chair, she clapped a hand to her mouth. 'Whoops! Sorry. I didn't know you had company.' She tore off her hat, hurling it with a practised flip of the wrist onto a peg on the wall. 'Hope your friend isn't the modest type, darling, but I've got to get changed.' She eyed Clara's silk robe. 'And you'd better look sharp if you don't want to miss curtain-up.'

'He's going.' Clara walked swiftly to the door and held it wide. 'He has a train to catch.' Averting her head as the captain scrabbled on the floor for his briefcase, she met his eyes as he passed through the door.

'Goodbye,' she said clearly. 'We won't meet again. Don't worry. We will never meet again.' When he hesitated, she said, 'Just go away. I don't exist for you, and you certainly don't exist for me. Sorry you've been bothered.' Her voice was thin and high. 'Please go. You found your way in, so you can find your way out.'

Slamming the door shut, she leaned against it, closing her eyes against the emotion flooding through her.

Daisy's blue eyes were wide and startled in the perfect oval of her vivacious little face. 'What the hell? Who was that?

Been trying to take advantage of you, has he?' She sat down at her dressing table, reaching for a stick of pancake make-up. 'A bit old, wasn't he? For a minute I thought you were going to spit in his eye.'

'He was nobody,' Clara said, unhooking her long white dress from its rail behind the corner curtain. 'Just *nobody*. That's who he was. NOBODY!'

'Well, for someone so anonymous he's been pretty generous.' Bending down to pick up the cup and saucer from the floor, Daisy held out a cheque. 'Slipped this underneath, the crafty so-and-so.' Her eyes nearly popped from their sockets as she read the amount aloud. 'Five hundred smackers!' Her tinny voice petered out in a squeak. 'Five hundred of 'em, darling! He must have been a *generous* nobody, sweetie.'

'Give that to me!' Clara snatched the slip of paper from Daisy's hand. 'How dare he! How flamin' dare he!'

Leaving Daisy with lipsticked mouth agape, she blazed out of the door, almost knocking over an astonished Bart on his way to console or even to share Clara's joy, whichever was appropriate.

'Clara, love!' His words were wasted as she tore along the narrow passageway, down the three steps, past the stage-door keeper's little cubicle and out into the back entrance of the theatre.

'She's gone berserk, Mr Boland,' Daisy told him. 'Running out into the street like that. Running away from a handout like that.' Her red hair seemed to stand on end with the force of her amazement. 'Five hundred pounds! And if my guess is right she's after him to tell him what to do with it. Oh God, and he looked such a nice fella. Who is he, for Pete's sake?'

Outside in the busy street, heedless of the stares of passers-by, Clara stood at the edge of the pavement in her flimsy dressing gown, caring nothing that it had fallen open at the front to show lace-trimmed camiknickers. Which way had he gone? Had he managed already to hail a cruising taxi, or was he walking in the direction of the nearest tube station, congratulating himself on a difficult job well done?

Dismissing her from his mind, as he'd dismissed her mother from his thinking years ago?

Suddenly she saw him across the street, a square thickset man, striding along, the leather briefcase swinging from his hand. The traffic was heavy, taxis, cars, a motorbike and sidecar, all streaming away from the lights in the direction of the West End, but holding no dangers for Clara. In that moment she would have braved a wall of fire to get to him.

A car pulled up with a squeal of brakes as like a demented woman she ran to the other side of the road. Dodging round a nanny in full uniform pushing a high Silver Cross pram, she ran on, the dressing gown billowing behind her like a sail in the wind.

'I think you dropped this?'

When she caught up with him, positioning herself firmly in front of him rather than touch his arm, he stared at her as if he couldn't believe the evidence of his own eyes. In her headlong dash, Clara's hair had loosened itself from the neat bun she wore it in during the day to tumble down her back. From the deep lace of her satin camiknickers, her high firm breasts threatened to be revealed completely. If she didn't cover herself, he thought illogically, she would surely be arrested. Or *he* would, which would be far worse.

'This!' she repeated, thrusting the cheque at him. 'Is this what you reckon is enough to ease your rotten conscience and buy my silence?'

'My child!' He looked for a moment as if he would explode. Eyes bulging, flushing a deep beetroot red, the captain stepped back a pace. 'This is hardly . . . ' Words failed him. 'People are staring!'

But Clara was past caring. All her natural reserve, all her normal serenity had vanished. She was the child of the streets again, flamed with uncontrollable temper. 'You paid my mother off with forty pounds!' she shouted. 'You've upped your price a bit now, haven't you?' With a dramatic gesture she tore the cheque into tiny pieces, scattering them on the pavement. 'You didn't come to see *me*! You came because you were too scared to do anything else. Just as you

252

ran away from my mother when you knew she was having me.' She gave him a push with the flat of her hand. 'You *killed* my mother because you feared she might interfere with your rotten life. She died all alone, even more scared than you are now. I hate you! Do you know that? I hate you!'

'Clara!' When Bart came beside her, putting his arm round her and folding the dressing gown closely about her, she tried to push him away, but he held her fast. She was too distraught to hear what he said to the captain as he spoke in a quiet voice filled with disgust. 'Have no fear, Captain Foley. You won't be troubled again.'

'Come with me, sweetheart.' Bart's voice breathed gentleness. 'It's five minutes to curtain-up. Come on, darling. It's all over now.'

With obvious, almost laughable relief the captain stumbled away, walking at first with head bowed, then, as the distance lengthened between them, striding along with head erect as in the days of his soldiering. A man going home after a difficult job completed and done with.

'He gave me money,' Clara whispered. 'Oh, Bart, he wanted to make sure I never bothered him again.' A great swelling of tears rose in her throat, as the dam of her emotions threatened to break down completely. 'I should never have asked you to find him, Bart, and yet . . . and yet . . . ' She allowed herself to be led back across the street and down the alleyway leading to the stage door of the theatre. 'I know about my mother now.' Her voice was rough. 'An' what I know is terrible. She must have been so unhappy. So terrified.'

'I know . . . I know . . . ' Leading her back along the narrow corridor, Bart opened the door of her dressing room and almost carried her inside. 'Three minutes' he told her, taking her long white dress and dropping it over her head, with an astonished Daisy watching in spellbound fascination. 'Make up now. The minimum.' He handed Clara a stick of greasepaint. 'Come on, love. You're going on. You have to, you know that, don't you?'

For a second his eyes closed in relief as he saw Clara begin to apply her make-up with professional speed, all sign of tears dabbed away by the rose-rachael powder, the trembling of her mouth stilled by the swiftly applied crimson lipstick.

The orchestra was well into the overture before Clara joined the boys and girls of the chorus in the wings. Daisy, bursting with pride at being 'in the know', winked at her friend, a raven-haired dancer dressed in a swathe of grey chiffon.

'A bloke,' she mouthed. 'Came in the dressing room and upset her.'

The friend raised eyebrows plucked to a thin line. 'A bloke?' she whispered. '*Clara* with a bloke who wasn't her husband? Good for her! Serve that horrible husband right if his wife gave him a bit of the old tit-for-tat.'

Almost without volition she moved in to stand close to Clara just as, sensing a drama, the other dancers did the same. It was a spontaneous demonstration of affection, of unstinted loyalty for the girl who was one of them, and yet was not. Clara felt it and, raising her head, smiled.

'I'm all right,' she whispered, and without knowing why she shouldn't be all right, they touched her, tweaked at her dress and smiled. With a rusty groan, the curtain rose and Daisy danced onto the stage.

Standing by the quick-change box in the shadowed wings, Bart watched the chorus go through their opening routine, then held his breath as Clara walked to centre stage.

Her first appearance was brief, a deliberate whetting of the appetite for what was to come, but he heard a sigh ripple through the audience as the glorious voice soared clear and true, without a tremor.

His strong face softened with love as Bart listened. It was impossible to believe that hardly five minutes before she had been running down the street like a wild thing, hair streaming, to confront a man who had thought he could buy her off. Bart shook his head. How little the gallant captain knew of the girl who just happened to be his daughter.

Clara was pure gold, he told himself, verging uncharacteristically on the sentimental. But then, hadn't he known it from the moment he first set eyes on her? Hadn't he loved her from that moment? He hadn't needed to be told that she was trapped in a loveless marriage, and it wasn't fair, it wasn't right that she went on wasting her life married to a man who didn't know how to cherish her. Clara had been born to be happy, born to be loved. And somehow, when he told her of his love, he would make her see that in life people sometimes made mistakes, married the wrong one – as he had done. But that didn't mean that for the rest of her life she had to abide by that mistake.

He was watching her, not hearing her voice now, just watching her face with its changing expressions as she sang. They could be happy. Oh, dear God, how happy they could be together. 'I'm not really ambitious,' she'd confessed. Bart's lips curved upwards as he remembered.

And yet she had it in her to be greater than them all.

The matinée was over and Bart was actually standing with hand raised to knock on Clara's dressing-room door when he heard the stage-door keeper calling his name.

'Mr Boland! Mr Boland!' The shrewd eyes behind steel-rimmed spectacles were clouded with a terrible anxiety. Nodding at the closed door, he spoke in an urgent whisper. 'Mr Maynard. The flying chap. They're calling from the 'orspital. There's been an accident. They're 'olding on, sir.'

Putting a finger to his lips, Bart ran quickly down the narrow passageway to the small glassed-in cubicle by the back entrance of the theatre.

Already a couple of well-dressed dandies hovered by the wide-open door, smoking cigarettes, hoping for a brief chat with their girlfriends before the evening performance. Daisy, clad in a grey satin wrap, leaned against the grimy wall, in flirtatious conversation with a paunchy man who looked like a stockbroker. It was so ordinary a scene, so normal, and yet when Bart stepped out of the cubicle two minutes later he had changed from a man filled with optimism and love into a man who knew that dreams could fade from one minute to the next.

Life wasn't like that. Solutions didn't present themselves, not all neat and tidy on cue. Not unless scripted for a play, and a bad play at that. As he walked back down the ill-lit corridor a door swung open behind him, letting out a burst of laughter. Taking a deep breath, he stopped for a second time outside Clara's door, knocked and went in.

At midnight he was sitting beside Clara on a hard bench down the corridor from the casualty department in a hospital on the near outskirts of Croydon. They had been sitting there for almost five hours, stony-faced and silent. As if they were growing from the hard wooden seat. Directly opposite to them, on another long bench, a middle-aged couple sat close together, staring down at their knees. When a young doctor came striding towards them, white coat flying, they got up as if welded together, eyes wide and pleading in frightened faces.

'Mr and Mrs Smith?' The doctor's voice was very low, very deferential. 'Come with me, please. Mr Graham would like to see you both.'

Shivering, Clara spoke to Bart without looking at him. 'She's dead, isn't she? That's where they're going. To be told that she's dead.'

'We don't know, love. The doctor said she was very young.'

'Seventeen,' Clara prompted.

There was nothing else to say, so they sat there, listening to the subdued bustle coming from behind the big double doors of casualty, hardly noticing when a man was led in holding a bloodied towel to his head.

When the middle-aged couple came back, walking slowly, leaning on each other for support, Bart saw Clara's eyes dilate with fear. He could only guess at the courage it took for her to get up and walk towards them, hands outstretched.

'Your daughter . . . ?' Her voice failed her and she could only stand there, totally unaware of the incongruous figure she presented with her pale gold hair streaming down her back, in the long white dress and velvet cloak she'd been wearing when Bart had rushed her from the theatre.

'Aye, she's dead all right.' It was the man who spoke, in a

northern accent which Clara recognized and warmed to at once.

'I'm sorry.' Clara's green eyes filled with tears. 'I can't tell you just how sorry I am.' She laid a hand on the man's arm, only to have it shrugged off with a fierce swiping motion that brought the warm colour to her face.

'He *mesmerized* her,' the man said. 'Yon husband of yours. She'd never met anyone like him afore. Taking her up in a plane no bigger'n a flea, and hedge-hopping.' He drew himself up to his full height of five feet two. 'What was he doing, gallivanting about with a young lass like a single man while his wife . . . ' the moustache that seemed to be too big for his face quivered with emotion ' . . . while his wife disported herself on the stage painted like a tart?'

For the first time since Bart had walked into her dressing room to break the news of the accident, Clara realized she was still wearing her stage make-up. Realized how she must appear to the man staring at her with hate-filled eyes.

'You're not our sort,' he told her. '*Theatricals*.' He almost spat out the word. 'And *fliers*. Living apart.' He shrugged off his wife's restraining hand. 'Let her hear it, mother. Let her hear what a good girl our Brenda was afore she met him with his smarmy ways and his flash car.' His voice broke on the edge of tears. 'If we'd stopped in Lancashire where we belong, none of this would have happened. But I had to come where the work was, hadn't I, and he 'appened along and made out he was Charles Lindbergh. Taking her up in a two-seater, showing off flying low over fields till he hit some telephone wires. And now our Brenda's lying there dead, while he gets away with it.'

To Clara's horror, the little man, frantic with grief, staggered over to the far wall, beating both fists against it, while his wife stood as if carved from marble, watching him impassively, dry-eyed and comfortless with shock.

'They say as 'ow his back's broken and he'll be lucky if he walks again, but he's *alive*, isn't he? *He's* alive, and she's dead. Oh, God . . . She was the light of my life, an' she's dead . . . '

'Let me take you both home.' Bart came to him, leading

him away from the wall, but not before Clara saw the clenched knuckles were covered in blood. 'The trams have stopped running now. Tell me where you live and I'll take you home.'

He glanced quickly at Clara. 'You'll be all right, dear, till I come back?'

'Yes . . . yes, of course.' Clara sat down again on the long hard bench, a feeling of helplessness swamping her so that she felt physically drained and very, very sick.

The little man had reminded her of her father, the clogger. Already the memory of her real father was fading. She shivered, wrapped her arms round herself and swayed backwards and forwards, feeling the habitual guilt take her, whirling her away into an empty, vacant despair.

What was she doing here, in the middle of the night, sitting dressed in a white silk gown, with rouged cheeks and a mouth bright with lipstick? Where were the values she'd been taught from childhood? The simple truths which dictated that a woman stayed with her man, cleaving only to him for as long as they both shall live?

Slumped in her seat, she asked herself over and over again would it have happened if she'd done the right thing? The yardstick she'd tried to live by said that a woman's place was with her man. But then the men she'd known had worked in the mills or the pits, no more than a stone's throw from their houses. The husbands *she'd* known came home in the middle of the day for their dinner, to a wife whose job it was to look after them to the exclusion of all else. You couldn't compare. Surely you couldn't compare?

She started at the sound of a nurse's voice. 'You can come with me now, dear. Your husband is back from the theatre, but he won't be fully round for a long time. When you've seen him, I suggest you go home and get some sleep.'

She was a tiny girl with a mop of red hair on which her starched cap sat uneasily. She had been trained not to wonder, certainly not to pry, but where was the man who had brought the patient's wife into the hospital, the man who had sat the hours away, his face all crumpled with compassion? And what relationship was the young girl who had died to the handsome husband lying in the ward with his back broken and all his ribs smashed in? There was a story somewhere, she was sure of that.

Clumsy with fatigue, Clara stumbled after her, down the long echoing corridor, up a flight of stairs and down yet another identical corridor to a ward as long as a tunnel lined with beds in which sleeping men lay, wrapped like parcels inside mitred sheets and tightly tucked-in white cotton bedspreads.

'In here, Mrs Maynard.' Opening a screen just wide enough to let her through, the nurse smiled her professional smile. 'Just a few minutes, dear. The surgeon will have a word with you afterwards. All right?'

The long ward was so quiet that Clara could hear the scratch of the night sister's pen as she wrote up her records at the table drawn up to the coke-burning stove in the middle of the ward. Not a sigh, not a snore from the men in their high beds, stunned into sleep by the hospital's regulation hot milk, and by the acceptance that they must lie comatose until five o'clock, when they would be handed a bowl of tepid water in which to wash.

John was not there. His *body* was there, sealed in its cocoon of coverings, but his face was the face of a stranger. Waxen pale, with only a fingernail cut beneath one eye to mar the perfect symmetry of his features. Slowly Clara moved to stand looking down at him, shocked by his unnatural stillness.

John had never looked like this. Always a light sleeper, she had seen him twitch and mumble by her side, as if he begrudged the hours spent lying still. Once, bending over him, she had seen his eyelids twitch as beneath them his eyes moved urgently from side to side, searching even in his dreams. And his hair . . . that fair flop of thick corn-coloured hair, which he would dash back so impatiently with the back of his hand or with a toss of his head. Someone had combed it straight back from his forehead, giving him an air of respectability he would have scorned.

'Oh, John . . . ' His torn, mangled body was hidden by the bedclothes. Clara could only guess at the horror of it, but the doctor had said – so long ago it could have been in another life – the doctor had said . . .

'Mrs Maynard?' The same nurse was beckoning from the opening in the curtained screen. 'Can you come now? Mr Reed is here.'

He spoke to her just outside the ward, a tall man with the stoop shoulders of his profession, wearing a plain dark suit that would have been just right for a clerking job in a city office. He told her that in view of his severe injuries her husband was lucky to be alive; that his broken ribs would heal; that there was some lung damage, but as far as they could be sure at that moment there was no internal bleeding. He said that her husband was a fit man, in good health, but when he came to the bad news he stared down at his shoes, speaking quickly as if what he had to say was better over and done with.

'The spine,' he muttered in a low controlled rush. 'The spinal cord is damaged, and we won't know for a little while just how much paralysis will result.' He raised his head, and even in her own distress Clara winced at the naked exhaustion in his red-rimmed eyes. 'The one thing I can tell you definitely is that he will never walk again.' His hand, laid for a fleeting moment on Clara's shoulder, was as weightless as a snowflake. 'I am so sorry, my dear.'

He left her then, walking with quick neat steps along the corridor and down the stairs, out to his car in the concrete forecourt, to drive home to the wife and the bed he hadn't seen for three days and two nights.

Leaving Clara to make her own way back to the bench outside casualty, to sit and wait for Bart.

Drawing a small grain of comfort from the knowing that he would come striding towards her with his long loping gait, and that when he came nothing would seem quite as terrible as it did at that moment.

Eighteen

'I'd be better off dead! You know you'd be better off without me, so why don't you agree with me? Go on. Say it! One of these days you will, so why not now?'

It was a year since John Maynard had been carried up the stairs to the flat, legs dangling floppily as though they'd been filleted.

'Why me?' His still active brain screamed aloud inside his head. 'What's left now for *me*?'

Day after long day he lay, staring up at the ceiling, allowing Clara or a nurse to shave and wash him. The fresh colour faded from his cheeks and his once smiling mouth set itself in a permanent downward curve beneath pinched nostrils. Robbed of his vitality, his energetic restlessness, he nurtured sarcasm like a growing thing, a spiky cactus plant. And vented his smouldering rage mainly on Clara.

She was tired almost to the point of collapse, driven to distraction by his continual carping, physically weakened by the poison of his overwhelming selfpity.

'Do you ever wonder what happened to Joe West?' he asked her one warm June night when, after a matinée and an evening performance of the successful new show, Clara dismissed the nurse to set about the thankless task of trying to make him comfortable for sleep.

'Joe?' Hearing his name for the first time in over a year, Clara looked up quickly from adjusting a bedside lamp, then turned her face away. She was silent for a long moment, knowing she was being got at, but much too tired to speak anything but the absolute truth. 'I often wonder what happened to him.' On her face was a look of utter weariness.

'But Joe could always look after himself. "Like a bad penny," he used to say. "Always turning up when least expected." '

'What would you do if he *did* turn up?' John was out to needle her. Clara could tell that by the way he pushed himself up on his elbows unaided. 'Tell me. What would you say to him?'

'Has he been here?' Clara was not prepared to show any emotion. If Joe had really been here John would tell her. In his own good time. But her tired mind was playing tricks on her. She could imagine Joe running up the stairs wearing the camelhair coat swathed round him like a dressing gown. Joe on top of the world again, smiling his curly smile. The bad penny turning up yet once again.

'Did I *say* he'd been here?' John's eyes met hers, hard and unflinching. 'Did I so much as *hint* he'd been here? Correct me if I'm mistaken.'

'You said . . . you intimated you knew something.' Clara moved quietly to sit down on the side of the bed. 'Joe *will* call in one day. When he's decided the time is right. When he's made his own way again.' She smiled. 'Time means nothing to Joe. He disappears, sometimes for years. That's always been his way. Then he's back.'

'Sober as a judge?'

'Possibly.' Clara nodded. 'Oh, you remember Joe. He could take a thing or leave it.'

'As he took and left you?'

Clara frowned and stared down at the carpet. 'Yes. As he took me and left me. A long time ago.'

'And now you've forgiven him?' John's voice was a sneer. 'You believe in forgiveness, don't you?' The amber eyes were sick with contempt. 'Just as you've forgiven me for killing that girl, and half killing myself. Just as you force yourself to look after me. You're a bloody martyr, do you know that?' His voice rose to a wail of despair. 'Brenda was a good kid . . . and now she's dead, and I'm finished!' Tears of selfpity oozed from his eyes to run down his cheeks. 'You always wanted a faithful husband, didn't you? Well, now you've got one. You've got one so bloody faithful that if the Queen of Sheba walked in here stark naked and got into bed with me,

I couldn't oblige.'

As if at the flick of a switch, his mood changed. To Clara's astonishment he reached out and gripped her wrist, pulling her down beside him. With his other hand he twined his fingers in her hair, jerking her face level with his own.

'You'd be *glad* if Joe West came back, wouldn't you? He'd be another shoulder to cry on, wouldn't he? Well? Wouldn't he?'

Her hair felt as if it was being torn out by the roots. The pain was sharp and stinging, but she didn't cry out, although she had to close her eyes to shut out the sight of the once handsome face now twisted with spite. So she lay quite still, knowing that if she tried to get away he would only jerk her back again. She had suspected for a long time that, in spite of his obstinate refusal to submit to any form of massage or physiotherapy, the muscles in his arms were like bands of steel.

'Yes, I'd be glad to see Joe again.' The agonizing pain in her scalp was bringing tears to her eyes, but she blinked them away. 'Because then I'd know that he'd survived once more. Joe is a survivor. Always has been and always will be.'

She sighed so deeply that he felt her breasts move against him. In her weariness she was so beautiful that just for a moment the sarcastic retort died on his lips. In another moment, but for the way he was, he would have taken her, releasing the pent-up frustration in his useless body. For a second he imagined . . . then groaned as his inadequacy stayed what would have been his instinctive reaction. From his waist down he was dead. He was a floppy flaccid nothing . . . No sensation, no feeling, no desire tightening his loins.

'Kiss me!' Grinding his mouth into hers, he forced her lips apart. Something . . . surely *something* of his manhood remained? Biting, panting, he fought to feel desire, then, with all the strength left in him, he pushed her violently away from him, covering his eyes with his arms as she rolled from the bed to sprawl face down on the carpet.

'Get out!' All the frustration festering inside him was in

that tortured cry. 'Get out of my sight! If I was a real man I wouldn't want you in my bed. Leave me alone! Just bloody well leave me alone!'

Trembling and sick, Clara got to her feet. Pity and revulsion fighting for precedence in her expression as she looked down at him, lying still with his arms covering his face, a child hiding away from a situation he was too unhappy to face.

It was far too late now for her to try to adapt to him, always hoping that eventually he would turn to her. The John she had married, with his laughter and his overworked sense of fun, had died when his plane crashed. She had stopped loving him long before that terrible afternoon, but if she'd had any hope that his dependence on her would bring them closer, that hope had faded from the day she had him brought home.

There was nothing more she could say. All her attempts to help or to comfort had been viciously rejected. A half life was no good to John Maynard. If he couldn't walk, or run, or swim, or drive his car, or fly, then he didn't want to live. As he told her. Day after day after day . . .

In her own bedroom, which had once been Dora's room, Clara went straight to the tiny mantelpiece and leaned her forehead against it. There was no hysteria, no drama in her thinking as she wondered how long they could go on like this? Feet on the ground, unflappable Clara, as Bart always called her, she tried hard to face up to a future totally without hope.

She moved her forehead against the back of her hands. It was all so impossible because John had turned his back on hope. He resented her stage work and yet, without the money for the rent of the flat and his medical attention, what would they do? Clara shivered, although the air was sticky with humidity. Where were the friends who had laughed at his antics, encouraging him to be more and more outrageous? Matty and Daisy, and Bart of course, were his only regular visitors, but John was so rude to them Clara wondered that they came at all.

And his flying buddies? Where were they now? Was it that

they could never forgive him for taking up a plane without authority that afternoon, narrowly missing the hangars as he showed off to his girlfriend by flying so low? Shuddering, Clara imagined the young girl screaming with excitement as the tiny plane skimmed over the treetops. And her frozen look of terror as the engine stalled and they nose-dived into the ploughed field not a mile from the airport. Was that the reason not one of them had climbed the stairs to the flat to visit the man who had once been the joker in their pack?

There was really only Bart. Her one true friend. At least twice a week he would come and sit in a chair by John's bed, talking without getting any response, sometimes carrying on sitting there when John closed his eyes and turned his face to the window in insulting dismissal. At the very thought of Bart, Clara felt herself relax. Twice recently Bart had insisted on taking her out for an afternoon drive, a time of pale sunshine, white clouds drifting against a blue sky, carpets of blossom, and tea at Henley in an inn overlooking the river. A time of lavender-scented peace. Holding on to that peace now, she made ready for bed, so weary that her movements were slow and lethargic. She was drifting off to sleep when John called from his room, his voice loud and demanding.

'Clara! Clara! Come here! I want you!'

He was lying exactly as she had left him, but with his arms lowered. So still that for a moment Clara imagined her tired mind had been playing tricks; the voice she had heard, a figment of her imagination.

Surely he was asleep? Tiptoeing to the bed, holding her breath . . . Oh, God, let him be asleep. Please let him be asleep. She put out her hand, only to draw it back quickly as he turned his head on the pillow to smile at her, a strangely triumphant smile, which left his light brown eyes narrowed and cruel.

'Oh, by the way,' he said. 'I almost forgot to tell you. Your little playmate of yesteryear, your precious bad penny, won't be turning up this time.' He spoke with studied precision. 'Because he's dead. Has been dead for quite some time. Sozzled with the demon drink in a Sally Army dosshouse. That's how your lover died.' He closed his eyes, waving her away with a languid hand.

'Crying for you, my informant told me. Wanting you to hold his hand as he breathed his last. Now, did you ever hear a more touching story than that?'

She was near to breaking point, but she didn't break. She went to the theatre the next day and with practised skill concealed her pallor with a flush of rouge, crayoned out her pink swollen eyelids with green shadow and curved her bruised mouth with scarlet lipstick.

John was using her for his whipping boy, she whispered to her reflection. He was a prisoner in that upstairs room, day after day, night after long night. *She* could escape. Every day except Sunday she could walk out onto the stage and feel the warmth and the love – yes, the love – reaching out to her. She could stretch out her hands to gather it close, and it would sustain her if she just stayed quiet and allowed it to do so. She lowered her head so that the light above her dressing table made a halo of her hair.

'There is no power but of God,' she whispered. 'He will not desert me now.'

Silently, from her own side of the cluttered dressing room, Daisy watched her. Prayers, she muttered underneath her breath. What good would prayers do Clara now? Daisy had dispensed with praying a long, long time ago, believing only in the here-and-now, and making the best of things if need be.

'Five minutes, darling,' she said aloud, trying not to let her sympathy show, for hadn't Clara made it clear right from the beginning that sympathy in any form was unacceptable?

But for God's sake, she wondered as they walked together down the narrow passageway and into the wings, why didn't Clara stick that husband of hers in a home. Or smother him with a pillow. Him with his film-star looks and wandering hands. And him a vicar's son too. A fat lot of good praying had done him, the rotten bastard.

'Here we go, Daisy!' Dancing out into the spotlight, she beamed at the audience, an ethereal creature in a froth of silver tulle, red hair like a nimbus round her face. 'Packed in

266

like ruddy sardines tonight,' she told herself, swaying and twirling as the music soared.

'Another packed house, Harry.'

Bart stood by the stage-door keeper's little cubicle. 'Would you have guessed we'd do so well?'

'I never make guesses, Mr Boland, not in this game.' Harry's shrewd eyes twinkled behind the steel-rimmed spectacles. Who did Mr Boland think he was kidding? Making conversation and hanging about like some stage-door Johnnie? When all the time it was obvious what he was waiting for.

When the girls began to troop out from their dressing rooms, he moved back into his cubby hole, to perch on his stool and call goodnight to each girl as she passed by. High heels tapping, chattering and laughing like magpies, they came, hurrying by in a cloud of scent, short skirts swinging round silk-clad legs.

She was always the last, the little one with the voice of an angel, and she never failed to say goodnight to Harry. Even knew the name of each of his grandchildren and that his wife suffered badly from chronic bronchitis.

But tonight Harry was being tactful. One look at Mr Boland's face had told him the man was near to cracking. Turning away to peer at his ledger, Harry tried to make himself invisible.

Bart had seen her coming towards him, as light of step as all the other girls, but to him it was a jauntiness that spoke to him of her weariness, a shouting to the world that she could manage very well, thank you very much. That somehow she would always manage. Hadn't she said so, many times before?

'I'm going to take you home.' Bart stood directly in her way. 'Yes, I know it's a fine night and that you like to walk.' He winced as he saw the bruised look round her eyes, and his eyes turned away from the tiny blood blisters on her bottom lip, even as his mind screamed aloud at their implication.

Suddenly he could take no more. The long year of biding

his time, of seeing her grow thinner and paler, culminated in a moment of decision. Taking her arm, he walked her outside, up the short slope to the busy road where the late-night traffic wended its way out to the suburbs. Hailing a taxi, he got in beside her, giving the driver his own address.

'Bart,' she said, smiling at him and shaking her head. 'What is this? Do you realize what you just said?'

He nodded, his expression serious and intent. 'I said I was taking you home, but what I meant was to *my* home. It's time we talked.' His voice was a little husky. 'It's time we had a long, long talk.'

Clara twisted round on the black leather seat to look directly at him. 'But I can't go to your place, Bart. I can't go to *any* place. They'll be waiting for me. The nurse and ... and John. They'll be worried if I don't turn up.' She laid a hand on his arm. 'Tell the driver you've made a mistake, Bart. Please.' She looked out of the window and smothered a little exclamation of dismay. 'Bart! We're going in completely the wrong direction. Tell him now!'

Bart folded his arms, keeping his face averted. 'Tonight is Friday, when the nurse stays all night. You told me so. Tuesdays and Thursdays she goes home, but Friday she stays. That's the drill, isn't it?'

She started to speak, but he held up a hand. 'In my flat is a telephone. When we get there you can use that telephone and tell the nurse that you will be late home. That she is not to expect you for at least another two hours; that she can convey that message to John if he is still awake, and that when you do get back you will try not to disturb her. All right?'

'No, it is not all right!' Leaning forward, Clara stretched out a hand to tap on the glass dividing them from the driver, only to have it caught in a relentless grip.

'We're almost there,' Bart told her firmly. 'And you're going to do as I say. Otherwise I won't be responsible.'

His face was very close to hers, so close she could see deep clefts running down his cheeks. His eyes burned into hers and she found she couldn't look away. Found she didn't want to look away.

'I've never heard of anything . . . ' she whispered, and moved away from him to fiddle with the collar of her evening coat.

It was as though he had suddenly changed into a man she didn't know. This grim-faced stranger sitting beside her wasn't the Bart she had known for so long. The friend always there by her side when she needed him, the quiet-spoken elegant man ready to listen, to advise and to comfort, when she allowed herself to be comforted.

'Here we are,' he said. When they got out of the taxi he pushed a note at the driver, waving away the change. 'Just one flight,' he said as they walked into the large foyer of a newly built block of flats. 'The lift hasn't been working too well lately, so we won't take a chance.'

Afterwards, Clara was to ask herself why she had gone with him so quietly. It was very late, she was very tired and somehow the fight had gone out of her. The horror of the night before was still with her, and Bart spelled peace. Even in his present mood of domination she sensed he only wanted to help her. And oh, dear, dear God, she needed help from somewhere. Hatred was a terrifying thing, and when John had called her from sleep and told her about Joe, she had seen the hatred in his eyes. He hated her because she could still walk, because she came in from the world outside, and he hated her because she had brought him home from the hospital when she could see that left there he would have turned his face to the wall and died.

The long corridor was carpeted, silent, anonymous, with closed doors either side. A lonely place for a man to come home to each night. In that strangely passive mood she stood by Bart's side as he took out his key and opened a door at the far end of the corridor.

'The telephone is there,' he told her, pointing to a shelf in the square tiny hall. 'I'll go and mix you a drink. Through there . . . ' He opened a door leading into a sitting room, switching on the lights.

And it was easier than she had thought it would be. John was asleep, the nurse told her, then actually thanked Clara for letting her know she would be late. 'Enjoy yourself, Mrs Maynard,' she said unexpectedly. And that was that.

'What is that?' Clara looked suspiciously at the drink in a tall glass borne in a kind of triumph by Bart from the kitchen leading off the sitting room. 'It's a funny colour.'

'I call it Tiger's Blood.' Smiling, Bart handed it over to her, then came to sit beside her on the large sofa flanked by bookshelves on one side and a dining table set in the large window on the other. 'Milk, honey and sherry, the best pick-me-up I know. Guaranteed to keep you awake for long enough for me to talk to you. Come on, drink it down, there's a good girl.'

To her shame Clara felt her eyes fill with tears. Kindness is too much, she told herself. All the other I can take – sarcasm, cruelty, the physical strain of looking after a helpless invalid. Work, too. Singing night after night to packed audiences, all that too. But kindness, compassion? No, I can't take that.

Gently Bart took the glass from her before drawing her close into his arms. He hadn't meant to touch her, had steeled himself not to touch her, but the sight of those silent tears slowly rolling down her cheeks had unnerved him.

'Let it come, sweetheart,' he whispered. 'Try and cry it all away. I'm here, my darling. I've always been here. You must have known.' His fingers tangled in the scented softness of her long hair, loosening it from its pins so that it ran over his hand, so clean and sweet-smelling he closed his eyes, pressed his mouth against it, drinking in its beauty. 'My little love . . . ' His voice was a sigh. 'Do you know what it's been doing to me, watching you, day by day?'

She raised her head, saw the love in his eyes, recognized it had been there for a long, long time and, in that heart-stopping moment, accepted it.

'Bart?' Slowly, wonderingly, her fingers traced the contours of his dear familiar face. 'Love me, please.' Her green eyes were slumberous and yet filled with passion. 'I *need* to be loved. I don't think I can go on without love any longer. So please make love to me.'

He couldn't believe what she'd just said. It was so unexpected, so completely mind-shattering, he could only hold her from him, shaking his head.

'You mean you . . . ?' His voice was husky and deep as he gazed into her lovely face.

'I mean that I love you too,' she whispered. 'I've loved you for a long time, Bart. I've been loving you and watching you, and now . . . well, there's nothing we can do about it, is there?' Her head drooped. 'I'm only human, you see. And I have such a need of you and of loving, sometimes I think I will die of it.'

Lifting her up into his arms, he carried her through into the bedroom and, as if she were a child, slowly undressed her. And their loving was so gentle, so tender in its total caring, it seemed as if they were taken to a higher place where nothing mattered but their love and their anguished need for each other.

Afterwards they slept, and when they awakened became one again, moving tenderly, murmuring words of love, mouth against mouth, heart to heart, giving and taking, taking and giving.

Still in a bemused state of adoration, Bart reminded her that she must go. Half expecting her to be immediately swamped with the guilt which he knew was a part of her. Steeling himself against the recrimination he was sure would possess her when, dressed and back in the sitting room, they faced each other in the shaded light from the lamp on the low coffee table.

'I never knew that loving could be like that,' she told him. 'To think I could have lived the rest of my life never knowing love could be like that.' She was actually smiling as she pinned up her hair. 'Oh, I feel marvellous, Bart. Don't you feel marvellous too?'

'But we have to talk.' He pulled her down to sit beside him on the sofa again, and leaning against him she pointed at the drink on the low table.

'And I didn't even need the Tiger's Blood, did I?' she teased. 'You'd better drink it, Bart. You look more in need of it than me.'

'You must leave him,' Bart said. 'You must leave him and come to me. We can see that he's well cared for, but you must divorce him. He gave you grounds long before he had

271

the accident. You can't go on like this. I won't let you go on. He's killing you, my darling.'

'Joe is dead,' she said almost dreamily. 'He told me last night that Joe had died all alone, asking for me. A long time ago.' She reached for her purse. 'I have no love for John, but I had loyalty, and when he told me that, there didn't seem any need any longer for loyalty. Do you see?' Holding up a small mirror, she applied a touch of coral lipstick to her mouth. 'But I can't leave him, it wouldn't be right. I *married* him. For better for worse, and that's a vow I can never break.' She snapped the fastening of her purse close. 'I made it in God's name, you see.'

'Oh, God . . . ' Bart stared at her helplessly. 'I believe in God, too, but I break His rules because I'm human, because no one can live according to the Scriptures. Not unless they're a saint!'

'And I'm not a saint,' Clara agreed. 'I've just been unfaithful to my husband, so I'm a long, long way from being a saint.' She stood up. 'Will you ring for a taxi, Bart? Have you seen the time?'

He insisted on going with her in the taxi, sitting close to her, holding tightly to her hand, bemused and baffled, but knowing that the time for talking, for making her see reason was not now. She loved him, that was enough, and somehow they would be together.

He waited until he'd seen her open the big front door of the house in Conduit Street. He waited until he saw the hall light switched off. Then he tapped on the glass and told the driver to take him back to Maida Vale.

The nurse was in the kitchen boiling a kettle for a cup of tea when Clara opened the door. Over her uniform she was wearing an old navy blue cardigan which showed the peg marks at the sides. Her starched cap was standing stiffly on the dresser next to a bowl of fruit. She had that look about her of slight abandon which people seem to get in the middle of the night, and Clara was glad it was she and not Nurse Edwardson who always looked as if she was back on the wards and expecting matron to come round at any minute.

'Have your cup of tea, then go home,' Clara said, smiling at her. 'I don't feel like sleeping. I'm too . . . ' She tried to think what she was, then added, 'too strung up.'

'Are you sure, Mrs Maynard?' Nurse Bates said insincerely, as if she was objecting. She could be home in seven minutes if she pedalled fast enough and, with a bit of luck, if the kids in the flat next door kept quiet, she could sleep till noon. And if she slept till noon, she'd be nice and fresh for when she went dancing that night. Maybe this would be the night the young man she'd been going out with for six months would propose. 'Well, if you're sure, Mrs Maynard,' she said again, turning the gas out beneath the kettle. 'Your husband settled nicely for me.' She unhooked her navy raincoat from the peg behind the door and stuffed the white cap into its pocket. 'When I told him you were likely to be very late, he said how glad he was that you were thinking of yourself for a change and that he hoped you'd stay out all night if you were enjoying yourself.'

Clara couldn't help looking quickly over her shoulder towards the bedroom. John had said *that*? She smiled. 'Have a nice weekend, nurse. And thank you for all you do. I'm very grateful.'

There was something different about her, Nurse Bates muttered to herself as she ran down the stairs. All lit up and excited, as if she was still on stage with the spotlight shining on her and the women in the audience unpinning their flowers to throw them at her feet, the way they'd done when Nurse Bates's boyfriend had taken her to see *Lovin' You*. As if she'd come straight from the arms of a lover, Nurse Bates thought, then tossed her head at the very idea. Mrs Maynard wasn't like that . . . A pity really.

The rusty bicycle was still there where she'd left it, hidden behind some basement railings. Not worth pinching, Nurse Bates supposed, as she wheeled it back up the stone steps and out to the kerb.

Mr Maynard's life had gone wrong, but that didn't mean he had the right to be so nasty and mean-minded. Funny

273

what adversity did to people, made some into saints and others into devils. Just think about the way he'd carried on! Catching her by the wrist and pulling her down on the bed beside him, knocking her cap off and nibbling her ear, pretending he was about to ravish her. Good job she knew he wasn't capable and that it was all meant to be a joke.

'Your beauty inflames me!' he'd groaned, holding her down with arms as strong as wire ropes. Yes, a good job she'd found out right at the beginning that Mr Maynard was fond of a joke. Just as long as the joke wasn't on him.

Head down, Nurse Bates pedalled on, the Maynards forgotten before she'd turned the corner.

Clara looked in on her husband before she went to her own room.

John was lying quietly for a change, his face smooth and his arms stretched out before him on the turned-down spread. He seemed very remote to her somehow, lying there with all the ebullience drained out of him. The sleeping draught Nurse Bates had given him must have done its work. He looked as though he could be in a coma.

Still in her dreamlike state, Clara pulled the high table closer to the bed, bringing his glass of water within easy reach. She would leave the standard lamp on in the sitting room as it was now and the door slightly open, so that if he awoke he wouldn't be completely in the dark.

For herself, all she wanted was the feel and taste of the dark on her closed eyelids so that she could relive the past hours over again. She was happy, happier than she'd been for a long time. Bart's name ran like a hymn through her veins.

Over and over again she relived each moment. The way his eyes had adored her, the way he'd knelt down by the side of the bed when she was pulling on her stockings, burying his head in her lap so that the sight of the incipient bald patch on the top of his head had filled her with a tenderness so great she had felt tears fill her eyes.

He was . . . oh, he was the love she had thought would never be hers. He was gentle, and yet in his gentleness lay his

274

strength. He would never hurt her, not mentally or physically, she knew that. Not like John, or yet like Joe. For a brief moment she grieved for Joe, then let him slip away into the shadows.

She was tired, so filled with a languorous exhaustion, that the bed when she lay in it seemed to drop away beneath her. There was no past, no future in her thinking, merely the present filled with Bart's love and concern for her, and the knowledge that he loved her. When she slept a small smile curved her lips. With her long pale gold hair covering her face like a silken curtain, the years fell away and she looked like a child again, secure in her bed in the house in the little northern cobbled street, with the sound of her father's hammer lulling her into sleep.

Raised on his elbows, John listened to the small sounds of her preparing for bed. He didn't need to be told what had happened to her, because through half-closed eyes he had watched her almost float away from him and into her own room. He had known what was going to happen as soon as the nurse came with the message that his wife would be late.

What kind of a fool did that Bart Boland think he was? John had seen the way he looked at Clara when he came to visit, standing almost to attention by the side of the bed, pretending that he cared whether the thing in the bed that had once been a man lived or died.

Bart Boland was just the kind of man John detested. Upright and honourable, straight as a bloody die. Reminding John of his father, and irritating him beyond endurance because he did not want to be reminded. Remembering reluctantly his father despairing of him, locking him up in his room to swot for university entrance, when all he had wanted to do was to fly. And his mother, trying to hide her disappointment because her only son had been born with cloth ears and a voice that slid up and down the scales without hitting the right note once. He remembered his own bitter disappointment at the war ending too soon, before he'd had a chance to have a proper go at the bloody Hun.

He coughed, holding his hand over his mouth to smother

the sound. It rattled deep inside his chest and he pushed himself upright to cough again, experimentally with his head beneath the blankets like a tent. His lungs were shot. They hadn't told him, but he knew. His cracked ribs had healed, but why had they taken him into hospital three times to tap the fluid from his lungs? Was he to die drowned in his own mucus, choked by his own phlegm?

Fully awake, because after he had pinned Nurse Bates down on the bed she had forgotten to give him his sleeping draught, John thought of the day ahead. And decided he didn't want it. He even murmured a prayer to his own particular god, a mythical being who, when beckoned down, came at once, occupied naturally with John's exclusive affairs.

Bart and Clara – they would be discreet, of course. Rehearsals, an extra show, a special matinée – the alibis were all there, ready to be used. And she would come straight from his arms, as John would swear she had done half an hour ago, and stand by his bed, not touching him. He stared at the diffused light coming from the sitting room. Did she realize that by not touching him, as she always did, she had given herself away?

And because she didn't want to hurt him, Clara would be extra solicitous, extra diligent in her caring. Her bloody guilt would see to that. She would be torn apart by that guilt which was as much a part of her as her own breathing. She would jump when the telephone rang, rush for the post when it came, because her beloved Bart was often away. She would avoid mentioning his name, only to blush when someone else did so. She would become an expert liar. She would walk over to the window when she was supposed to be doing things for him, to stand there gazing out at nothing. Dreaming of him, the tall one with the long legs that could cover the distance from here to the sitting room in four strides.

Legs, proper legs with muscles and nerve ends that responded to a simple message from his brain. Jerking off the covers with a fierce swiping motion, John looked down at the lifeless, useless inanimate objects lying there, matchstick thin now, encased in the bottom half of his striped pyjamas.

And that was all he had, for the leftover life he had to live. For weeks, months, even perhaps years, if he managed to keep breathing for that long.

'Oh, God! If you are there in your heaven, listen to me!'

Clara would say – Clara had said – that, if only he would accept, blessings untold would be added unto him. But were any of the things that Clara believed in of substance and reality?

Reality was here. It was here in this sickroom, with the long curtains closed against the night. With the commode standing by the bed and the indignity of having to use it. With the bed sores on his backside and with the phlegm that choked his throat till he spat it out in the enamelled bowl always left within his reach.

It was there now, shrouded decently and newly rinsed out with Lysol by that bird-brained nurse, and beside it a glass of water with a bead-trimmed cover. And hidden by the fluted folds, the bottle of disinfectant, carelessly left there when he'd frightened young Florence Nightingale half out of her wits. He could smell its antiseptic odour coming from the obnoxious chamberpot nestling inside the commode's boxed-in lid.

Oh, little Nurse Bates, who had told him she'd hated working on hospital wards because they were all mitred corners and no fun. Scatty little Nurse Bates who liked to jolly him along, and who had panicked like a schoolgirl when he'd made a grab for her. Little Nurse Bates, with her cap hanging by one pin from her unruly hair, with her black stockings spiralled round her legs.

Naughty little Nurse Bates, leaving a bottle of Lysol around for her patient to drink if he felt suicidal . . .

John could reach it easily. The bottle was cold to his touch, grooved and dark. Unscrewing the cap he sniffed at the contents. Not unpleasant really, kind of clean and tangy, reminding him of his mother's house after the cleaning lady had been.

How much would it hurt if he drank it? Would it burn his

throat, or would it slip down like whisky?

'Man that is born of a woman hath but a short time to live, and is full of misery. He cometh up, and is cut down, like a flower; he fleeth as it were a shadow, and never continueth in one stay.'

And if to continueth was an abomination? What then? John lifted the bottle to his lips. What then?

As he finished draining the bottle, throwing his head back to catch the last drops, tearing agony caught him unawares. His eyes rolled back, his hands clawed at his throat, the top half of his body jerked in wild spasms of unbelievable pain. Then, at last, was still.

Clara slept until the sunlight of a fresh spring morning gilded the flowered curtains with a haze of brightness. Opening her eyes slowly, she smiled and slid back into her dreams, to wake a full hour later with a suddenness that startled her.

'I'm coming!' Throwing the clothes back and swinging her legs over the side of the bed, she picked up the tiny round clock from her bedside table and shook it, unable to believe the evidence of her own eyes. How could it be half past nine when normally on a Saturday she was up before eight to see to John before she got his breakfast?

'I'm coming!' she called out again, pulling her dressing gown round her, lifting the heavy weight of her hair away from the nape of her neck and slipping her feet into a pair of feathered mules. 'We've both slept late, we must have . . . '

The words froze on her lips as she walked into the bedroom. There was a vice holding her from making a sound, and yet deep in the core of her a whirlwind of feeling was taking possession, swamping her with horror.

He was lying on his back, both hands extended and crooked into claws. His eyes were wide open, rolled back in their sockets, but the worst horror of all was his mouth. Rigor mortis had drawn back his lips, setting them into a terrible smile.

278

Always a joker, it seemed as if his own death was the last most macabre joke of all.

Stumbling away from the bed, a hand to her mouth, Clara's foot caught the empty bottle of disinfectant, sending it rolling across the carpet. Whimpering now, she watched it go, eyes wide as the full implication of what he had done hit her like a body blow.

Retching and moaning, she ran into the bathroom to kneel down by the toilet bowl. Holding on to its ice-cold rim, she vomited until her throat was raw. Was it *her* making that terrible noise? She didn't know. Her long hair fell forward, ends trailing in the pan, until, shaking and whimpering, she forced herself to go into the sitting room and unhook the telephone.

When the police came she was able to answer their questions in a tight controlled voice. Yes, her husband had been asleep when she last saw him. No, she hadn't seen the bottle of Lysol on the bedside table, and no, he couldn't possibly have fetched it himself from the shelf in the kitchen

When the doctor came she repeated what she'd just said. When they came with a stretcher to take John away she went back into her own room to sit on her bed, clasping her hands between her knees, trying to shut her ears to the sounds coming from the other room.

'My dear . . . ' The doctor came to sit beside her. 'You mustn't be here alone.' His kindly face was creased with anxiety. 'This is no time for you to be alone. Let me telephone one of your friends – and then get into bed and I'll give you something to help you.' He held her wrist and checked her pulse. 'The next few days aren't going to be easy for you, my dear.'

She gave him Daisy's number, then did as she was told, getting back into bed and pulling the blankets closely round her chin. Her teeth were chattering so much that the sunlight, lying sweetly now across her bed, was a mockery. When the doctor pushed her sleeve back and she felt the prick of an injection she stared at him, her green eyes wide and pleading.

279

'He was asleep when I came in,' she whimpered. 'He was . . . he was . . . ' And all the time a little voice inside her was telling her it wasn't so.

'She will sleep for another hour,' the doctor told Daisy when he let her in. 'She is blaming herself, but you must talk to her. I'll call in again this evening.' He walked towards the door. 'A bad business, a bad business all round, but I'm not surprised. He had never accepted. In a case like his acceptance is all.'

After he had gone away shaking his head, Daisy couldn't restrain herself from tiptoeing through into the big bedroom at the back of the house. Where it had all happened. She was quite surprised to see that the bed had been smoothed over and the pillows plumped up. Just as if anyone would ever think of sleeping in it again. She had asked the doctor straight out what 'method' Mr Maynard had used to do away with himself and when he'd told her in his reluctantly professional voice that it seemed as if the deceased had drunk poison, a small frisson of excitement had tightened her own bowels.

She looked round the room, so obviously a sickroom, with books piled on a table in a corner and a bowl of grapes rotting gently in a dish, and shivered with deliciously morbid fear. She half expected to see a dark brown bottle labelled 'Poison' standing empty. She picked up the glass of water and sniffed at it suspiciously. Had he drunk it from a glass, or had he downed it straight from the bottle?

She had never pretended to like Clara's husband, so she wasn't going to indulge in the hypocrisy of grief, but all the same . . . A remembrance of a play she had once been in at drama school before she decided to stick to dancing flashed into her mind. A Roman-orgy kind of play, with men in togas and women with their hair bound in silver ribbons expressing undiluted horror as a centurion raised a goblet to his lips and drank. It had taken him an uncommonly long time to die, she recalled, staggering about and groaning, to lie twitching, clutching his stomach before what must have been a merciful death overtook him.

When the telephone rang, she jumped, as startled as if

she'd been suddenly shot in the back, then hurried with her dancer's light step into the sitting room.

'It was Mr Boland,' she told Clara, now hovering in the doorway, ashen pale, holding on to the back of the sofa for support. 'You should be asleep. The doctor said you would sleep for at least an hour.' She took Clara by the arm to lead her back to bed. 'Mr Boland is coming round straightaway. He sounded shattered when I told him what had happened,' she confided.

'No!' Clara prised at the fingers holding her arm. 'I won't see him! Don't let him in! He mustn't come! I don't want . . . I can't . . . '

Shock, Daisy told herself, helping Clara back into bed and tucking her in. The drug was taking effect again. Clara's eyes were closing, forcing themselves open, then closing once again.

'He'll put Maureen in your spot this afternoon and evening. He'll be coming to tell you it's all right. You know what Mr Boland's like.' Daisy pushed Clara's left arm underneath the blankets. 'Just you sleep, darling. That's right. Just you sleep.'

She would never sleep again, Clara told herself as Daisy closed the door behind her. There would never be a sleeping draught strong enough to shut out the memory of that terrible face with agony mirrored in the staring eyes.

'The wages of sin is death . . . '

Her sin. *Her* sin . . . Muzzily she forced herself up onto her elbows. She had sinned, and so now she must pay. She had been taught that, and taught it well. Whilst her husband was lying paralysed, she had committed adultery. She had come from Bart, and she had stood by John's bed, and she had recoiled from touching him.

And John had known.

'The wages of sin is death!'

A lay preacher in the pulpit of the chapel at the top of the street. A working man in a striped union shirt without a collar. An unlessoned man, speaking with the wide vowels of his Lancashire heritage. A man of sincerity, raising arms

281

high above his head. Bellowing his beliefs so that the congregation shrank back in their hard pews, afraid of the wrath that would surely come.

The Lake of Fire . . . Oh God, if this was it, then she was drowning in it, sinking screaming into its fiery depths . . .

In spite of her anguish the drug was having its way, and when Bart came to her she was asleep. Smoothing the hair back from her pale face, he sent Daisy away, to continue his vigil alone.

When at last she opened her eyes, he pulled her straight up into his arms, holding her tightly, whispering, soothing, feeling for the right words, knowing they could be the most important words he would ever speak. Hating the man who had played this last terrible trick on her.

'If you let him, he will destroy you from the grave,' he told her, holding her even closer. 'He was determined to destroy you for the rest of the leftover life he had to live.' His grip was like steel. 'That is a fact we have to accept and tolerate together. Even though at the moment it seems intolerable.' In his quiet voice he continued, 'You are only human, *I* am only human, and because of that we make mistakes. We are weak. We sin . . . ' Tenderly he smoothed her hair away from her face. 'How can you begin to forgive others when you cannot forgive yourself?'

Clara moved to look into his face. One minute she was seeing him, the next her eyelids closed as the drug took effect again. But one thing her half-awake mind was telling her, and that was that this man was security; he was stability, he was wisdom and, oh, how she *needed* all those things.

'I love you,' she whispered. 'And I know that loving you is happiness.'

'And not wicked?' There was a hint of a smile on his lips. 'Not a certain leap into the fires of hell?'

For a long time he held her, feeling his shirt front wet with her tears, then she pushed him away, ready, he knew, to get on with the sad and terrible things that had still to be done before John Maynard could be laid to rest.

She would do them, he knew, but not alone. For he, Bart Boland, would see that she was never alone again.

Epilogue

On 30 May 1932, Their Majesties King George and Queen Mary attended a variety performance at the London Palladium.

Up in the royal box, Queen Mary, a regal figure in her bead-encrusted gown, a diamond tiara sparkling in her white hair, sat ramrod straight. By her side King George fingered his nautical beard as if impatient for the show to begin.

Behind the stage in the darkened wings, the huge cast moved into their allotted positions, a miracle of organized chaos. Star dressing rooms were shared, with good humour prevailing on the whole, although tension crackled like electricity and nerves taut as bow strings threatened to snap. But with swift professionalism they were brought under control.

The entire proceeds were in aid of the Variety Artists' Benevolent Fund, so the fashionable audience had paid with unstinting generosity for their tickets.

In the third row of the orchestra stalls Bart Boland sat proudly between the son and the daughter he was only recently getting to know. The girl's vivid blue eyes shone with excitement, but the boy stared down at his programme in an agony of adolescent embarrassment. But as the curtain rose at last and the sixteen Palladium Girls danced onstage, he perked up visibly, sitting forward in his seat. Legs and bosoms. Bart hid a tolerant smile behind his hand. A wickedly fascinating combination to a boy of fifteen playing truant from his public school for this one special day.

There was a star-studded cast that warm May evening.

Billy Danvers, cheeky one minute and philosophical the next. Cicely Courtneidge, singing and dancing with boisterous energy, followed by Flanagan and Allen crooning songs that set feet tapping.

Bart watched them all with his critical eye, recognizing the brilliant timing of each brief act to fit the tight schedule. When Jack Buchanan glided on, suave and elegant in his white tie and tails, his voice a sophisticated whisper carrying over the footlights and up to the back of the gods, Bart saw his daughter lean forward, her young face rapt. There was a lump in his throat as he thought of the years of her childhood when he had hardly known her, and when her hand tightened on the red plush armrest he covered it with his own.

Will Fyffe, Jasper Maskeleyne, the magician . . . one artiste after another up to the intermission, with the Palladium orchestra playing selections from Noel Coward's *Bitter Sweet*.

'I'll see you again . . . ' The haunting music flooded the ramshackle Victorian finery of the auditorium, until, with the royal party back in their box, the curtain rose again.

G S Melvin, Naughton and Gold, Jack Hylton's Band. Violins, trumpets, clarinets, saxophones, blending with three pianos into tunes that had set feet dancing all over London.

Bart found he was clenching his hands together to stop them trembling, so that when the curtain rose for the last item before the grand finale he felt he had lived a whole life since coming to the theatre. Like his father before him, he had put on shows; he had lost and made fortunes, but on not one of his first nights had he felt like this.

Waiting in the wings, Clara was sure her bones had turned to jelly. At the rehearsal her voice had soared, but she knew the acoustics of an empty theatre could lie. As she walked into the shattering brilliance of the single spotlight, the audience was a sea of dim shapes, with white faces all upturned towards her. The stage was so big, so vast, the boards scarred and shabby beneath her feet. And she could sense the regal presence of her King and Queen. It was the loneliest moment of her life.

Until the music began.

'Look for the silver lining . . . ' Like a bird in flight her voice rose, each note true, every word clear as the ring of crystal. 'When e'er a cloud appears in the blue . . . '

The first song she had ever sung for Bart, the very first one, standing on the stage of the Palace Theatre in her home town. The song Joe had chosen for her.

'Remember somewhere the sun is shining . . . ' She could feel the audience responding to her. She could absorb their adulation and give it back to them in her smoky-toned voice, filling them with optimism and hope.

She knew she must not look up at the royal box, but she could sense the Queen leaning forward slightly, a faint smile of approval on her face.

'So always look for the silver lining . . . ' Clara walked slowly up to the footlights, holding out her arms. 'And try to find the sunny side of life . . . '

The applause was a roar of pent-up emotion. Holding it to her, Clara walked quickly into the wings, leaving the stage for the stars of yesterday in their grand finale: Vesta Victoria, Harry Champion, Fred Russell and Marie Kendall. Old-timers every one of them, leading the reassembled company in a rousing chorus of 'God Save the King'.

A wave of patriotism swept the theatre. The King bowed his head, and his Queen raised a white-gloved hand in gracious acceptance.

The tenth Royal Variety Performance was over. Soon the great theatre with its red plush and its gold-painted pillars would be empty and silent. The audience would stream out into the night to waiting cars and taxi cabs.

And Clara Boland would go home with the man she loved.

In the past four years Bart had taught her that sorrow and joy, the good and the bad, could be the same, sometimes even indivisible. His quiet strength had given her peace and freed her from the torment of guilt.

Now, secure in her husband's love, Clara had found a deep and lasting serenity. The clogger's child was happy at last.

GEMINI GIRLS

Marie Joseph

It was a small Lancashire town on the eve of the General Strike. A town where the gap between the rich and the poor was about to erupt into a bloody field of battle.

Libby and Carrie Peel, the beautiful, spirited twins, were among the privileged. Tom Silver, the determined union leader, was not. And yet it was he who had won their hearts – and threatened to turn them against the comfortable world into which they had been born – and against each other as well.

MARIE JOSEPH

Marie Joseph is one of Britain's top-selling authors and her books are available from Arrow. You can buy them from your local bookshop or newsagent, or you can order them direct through the post. Just tick the titles you require and complete the form below.